# ESCAPE FROM KOLYMA

# ESCAPE FROM KOLYMA

## ABORIGIN
### IS A BEAR REGION

CHESTER LITVIN, PHD

# ESCAPE FROM KOLYMA
# ABORIGIN IS A BEAR REGION

Copyright © 2019 Chester Litvin, PhD.

All rights reserved. No part of this book may be used or reproduced by any means, graphic, electronic, or mechanical, including photocopying, recording, taping or by any information storage retrieval system without the written permission of the author except in the case of brief quotations embodied in critical articles and reviews.

This is a work of fiction. All of the characters, names, incidents, organizations, and dialogue in this novel are either the products of the author's imagination or are used fictitiously.

iUniverse books may be ordered through booksellers or by contacting:

iUniverse
1663 Liberty Drive
Bloomington, IN 47403
www.iuniverse.com
1-800-Authors (1-800-288-4677)

Because of the dynamic nature of the Internet, any web addresses or links contained in this book may have changed since publication and may no longer be valid. The views expressed in this work are solely those of the author and do not necessarily reflect the views of the publisher, and the publisher hereby disclaims any responsibility for them.

Any people depicted in stock imagery provided by Getty Images are models, and such images are being used for illustrative purposes only. Certain stock imagery © Getty Images.

ISBN: 978-1-5320-6544-6 (sc)
ISBN: 978-1-5320-6543-9 (e)

Library of Congress Control Number: 2018915240

Print information available on the last page.

iUniverse rev. date: 01/21/2019

In memory of my late mother, Polina
Gimelfarb, and my father,
Max Litvinov

# CONTENTS

PROLOGUE . . . . . . . . . . . . . . . . . . . . . . . . . . . . . xiii

INTRODUCTION . . . . . . . . . . . . . . . . . . . . . . . . . . xv

    Disease of Virus of Radicalization . . . . . . . . . . . . . xviii
    The Differences in Reaction to Viruses . . . . . . . . . xxii
    Family and Pseudocollective . . . . . . . . . . . . . . . . . xxiii

CHAPTER 1 . . . . . . . . . . . . . . . . . . . . . . . . . . . . . . . 1

    Way to Freedom . . . . . . . . . . . . . . . . . . . . . . . . . . . . 2
    Nazis in Malantia . . . . . . . . . . . . . . . . . . . . . . . . . . . 3
    Stepan Luchko, Survivor . . . . . . . . . . . . . . . . . . . . . . 4
    Rivka's Life in Greben . . . . . . . . . . . . . . . . . . . . . . . . 5
    Uncle Ben's Thankfulness . . . . . . . . . . . . . . . . . . . . . 7
    Dachas . . . . . . . . . . . . . . . . . . . . . . . . . . . . . . . . . . . 8
    The Borderline of Byelogoria . . . . . . . . . . . . . . . . . . 14
    Byelogoria's Battle with Doctrine . . . . . . . . . . . . . . . 15
    Isaac's Hatred of the State . . . . . . . . . . . . . . . . . . . . . 16
    The Ubiquity of Hypocrisy . . . . . . . . . . . . . . . . . . . . 18
    The Infestation of the Killing Field . . . . . . . . . . . . . . 19
    Bondarenko . . . . . . . . . . . . . . . . . . . . . . . . . . . . . . . 20
    The Enemy of the State . . . . . . . . . . . . . . . . . . . . . . 21
    Commissar Bondarenko: Fertile Ground for
    Perdition . . . . . . . . . . . . . . . . . . . . . . . . . . . . . . . . . . 23

Bogdan's Lack of Sophistication ................. 24
Luchko's Family ................................. 25
The Stupidity of the Killing Field in the
Village of Pine Trees ........................... 28
Victims in Byelogoria ........................... 29
Sara Waited for the Commissar .................. 31
Bondarenko in Power ........................... 32
The Red Terror ................................. 34
The Brainwashed Objects ....................... 37
Fate of Bogdan ................................. 39
A Tense Situation .............................. 40
The Structure of Polytheism ................... 43
The Diamonds of the Kolyma River ............. 45
Way to Freedom, Part 2: Lies in the Killing Field ... 48
The Bazaar in Baku ............................. 52
Real Dialogue .................................. 54
The Vicious Collective ......................... 57
Isaac Played Cards ............................. 64
Isaac Took Action .............................. 68
Galena ......................................... 74
Celestials of the Gorgeous City ................ 77
Aaron and Sashko's Resources .................. 84
Sofia Kaufman, Actress ......................... 90
Sofia's Life .................................... 91
Sofia's Second Marriage ........................ 92
Aaron's Struggles .............................. 94
Gulag .......................................... 97
Maniacal and Illiterate Leaders ................ 97

The Criminal Code of Honor.................104
Isaac's Negotiations.........................108
Baku, a Cosmopolitan City ..................110
Way to Freedom, Part 3......................112
The Search of the Solid Psyche ................115

# CHAPTER 2 .................................. 118

Dora, Aaron's Wife ..........................119
The Habitants' Affliction.....................121
Accusations of Rape in an Infected Country ......123
Sashko's Infidelity ...........................124
The Luck of Sashko Belay.....................125
Eric Belay..................................127
Eric and His Mentally Ill Grandmother..........127
Eric's Appearance ...........................129
Eric's Bullies................................131
Eric's Love for the Gorgeous City...............132
Eric's Skills.................................134
Eric's Kingdom..............................135
The Misfortune of Hypocrisy ..................136
Eric's Wake-Up Call .........................139
The Privileged Position ......................140
Eric Belay's Luck............................141
Eric's Beautiful City .........................142
One of the Gifts the Jews Did Not Need .........144
Common Enemies ..........................145
Rome: Way to Freedom, Part 4 ................146

Informers Can Be Anywhere................... 149

Golda ........................................ 151

Vlad ......................................... 152

Way to Freedom, Part 5: The Leader of the
Collective ................................... 154

The Killing Field's Fakes ...................... 156

Aaron's Letter................................ 158

Aaron's Secret ............................... 160

Givi the Kingpin ............................. 161

Givi's Gang................................... 162

Dr. John Nash ............................... 164

Gaming under Givi ........................... 165

Givi's Mother ................................ 167

Givi's Father.................................. 167

The Card Game: A Duel ...................... 169

Immigrant Girls............................... 171

Pimping the Young Mothers ................... 173

Uncle Cat .................................... 174

The Cautious Uncle Cat....................... 178

Givi's Egomania.............................. 181

The Children of Talented Parents .............. 185

Vlad's Naïveté ............................... 187

Misled Immigrants............................ 189

Aaron's Freedom ............................. 193

The IQ Test of Cards ......................... 197

About Byelogorians .......................... 199

Ashkenazi Jews .............................. 200

An Efficient Way to Save the Brain ............ 201

The Founder Father ........................... 203

Founding Father, the Lunatic .................. 205

The Founder's Burial ......................... 206

Way to Freedom, Part 6 ....................... 208

Byelogorians Were Special .................... 209

Trade Unions ................................ 210

Leo Tolstoy and Fyodor Dostoevsky ............ 211

The Chastised Farmers ....................... 213

Slavery at the Kolyma River ................... 217

Isaac and the Dangers of Kolyma ............... 220

Prison Informers ............................ 223

Gorgeous City in Aborigin .................... 229

The Past of the Gorgeous City. ................ 230

Abusive Children ............................ 239

The Life of Sashko Belay. ..................... 241

Learning to Survive. ......................... 244

Animal Instinct Took Over ................... 250

Low Morale in the Killing Field ............... 253

Pseudodogma Promised Fast Changes .......... 261

Greben, Malantia............................ 264

The Taboo of Wealth ........................ 266

Nowhere to Go from the Source of Primitivism
and Aboriginian Existence .................... 270

Denial of Collective Association ............... 275

Paradise Island.............................. 277

Negotiation as a Part of a Sailor's Psychology .... 280

Prince Kropotkin versus Superior Leader ....... 283

The Bets and Games ......................... 285

The Triumph of the Superior.................296
False Celestials and Terrestrials ................307
The Pseudocollective as Pathology ..............314
Pseudocollective Chaos ........................318
Primitive Vulgarisms..........................329
Infection of Degeneration .....................335
The Communalist Army ......................338
A Sailor's Psyche ............................348
Plebeian Background..........................355
The Collective Seized Paradise Island ...........356
Old Habits Remained ........................369
Hypocrisy....................................371
Conclusion ..................................371
The Curse Caused a Split .....................372
Sailors' Psychology ...........................373
A Description of the Infection..................374
The Collective Stole Identities..................377
Persecuted Uniqueness .......................378
Falsified Bible................................380

BIBLIOGRAPHY ............................ 385

# PROLOGUE

Kolyma had a network of labor prisons in Aborigin. Aborigin was not the original name of the area; the name was changed when a psychological virus affected the inhabitants. The plague-ridden land's virus was named ultimate sociopathic and stingy recidivism, or USSR. Because the virus damaged thought processes, the names of the localities changed. People's brain chemistry changed, and people lived in a pseudocollective. Contrary to the false collective, a true collective existed too. It was located in a place that had a real name. The Sailors' goal was to find the location of the true collective.

# INTRODUCTION

Professor Kryvoruchko, PhD, was a scholar who provided the translation of terms. He mentioned that Malantia and Byelogoria were part of Aborigin. Greben was a city in Malantia. Paradise Island was in the Black Sea. Aaron Kaufman liberated the Aboriginian emigrants from criminal authority. His father, Isaac Kaufman, escaped from Kolyma. Like the biblical Joseph, who was in slavery in Egypt and became a wealthy man who helped others, Isaac left slavery in Kolyma as a wealthy man, along with a beautiful woman who became his future wife. He liberated himself, his wife, and his stepdaughter.

Professor Kryvoruchko stated that Aborigin had various types of psychological infections. The professor listed the below types of brain damage, which were caused by psychological bacilli in carriers. Symptoms included entitlement and lawlessness. The list of infected included the following:

- Dumb heads: The unintelligent crowd in disease-ridden locales. They claimed that because they belonged to a special genetic structure, they could do complex tasks better than intelligent habitants. For example, a cleaning lady could manage a big factory.

- Empty heads: Diseased inhabitants of Aborigin who believed they were entitled to take everything by force.
- False celestial natives: Plague-ridden, antisocial individuals who believed that the knowledge of pseudodoctrine, the fraudulent Bible, gave them extraterrestrial cosmic power to capture the whole world.
- Terrestrials: Tainted inhabitants of a pseudocommunal setting. They accepted the power of celestials and served them. They dwelled in countries soiled by infection. They pretended to be intelligent but showed foolishness when they followed doctrine.

Professor Kryvoruchko wanted to find the source of the infection. He distinguished between Superior Leader and Founding Father as sources of the infection. The Founder, a stargazer, assumed that his dream land, Aborigin, did not need any sophistication and could flourish with primitivism and ignorance. He was the one who created the virus that radicalized the land. Founding Father, a dreamer, was the originator of the pseudocollective state. Superior Leader designed the slavery camps in Kolyma, and a crematory for many prisoners was located on the northern border, by the Arctic Ocean. The network of labor camps, in actuality, were extermination camps.

Superior Leader moved terrain infected by the ideological virus back to Golden Horde times. Superior Leader was a dictator and tyrant and changed Aborigin to his liking. In the swindling doctrine of the pseudocollective, thoughts were always abnormal and muddy. Even in a madhouse, the psyche wanted something resembling normal life, but in the pseudocollective, a normal life was not possible. The structure of the fraudulent collective looked like the psyche of a disoriented psychotic without any instances of enlightenment. The craziness of the setting was a paradox and antimony.

Professor Kryvoruchko explained that those not infected by the psychological virus were called Sailors. Those courageous individuals successfully crossed oceans of negativity and entitlement. The professor, Aaron, and Isaac were Sailors. They resisted the pseudocollective psychological structure of Aborigin, whose name was an abbreviation for "A Bear Region." Professor Kryvoruchko declared that the fragments in a Sailor's psyche were characterized by different periods of his life or images of significant people in his psyche. Dialogue was a way of thinking. The Sailor's dialogue happened between fragments that had the same goal: to find truth. Sailors identified their fragments and dialogues as self-talks. By using dialogues, Sailors' psyches were united in a true collective. The essence of the psychological structure of Sailors was distinguished and unique. The true collective was in the design of a Sailor's soul. It was a place where the Sailors discovered their individuality. Sailors were separating the real from the fictitious. In their vicinity, distinctiveness was respected, and reality testing was the main basis of their thoughts. They represented the true collective. A Sailor moved away from the source of primitivism and Aboriginian existence. By encouraging internal dialogues between his fragments, a Sailor had a cohesive, solid, and interconnected psyche.

## Disease of Virus of Radicalization

Professor Kryvoruchko believed the external pseudocollective society was a product of psychological disease. The illness's parasitic venom created an epidemic in different parts of the world. The infection damaged its surroundings. The disease changed minds and created a marketplace of suffering and terror. The diseased became obsessed with feelings of entitlement and did not feel ashamed of stealing from others and using violence. As a result, they became deadly. In its most severe form, the illness did not have an antidote. It infected a lot of territories and had four derivatives with the same name. The first name was the structure that the ideological parasite built. The second name marked the place where the virus was captured as a parasite. The third held contention of the indoctrination philosophy. The fourth was a toxin of radicalization, the outcome of the butchery doctrine. The ideologists persuaded crowds to follow imprudent ideology as if it were an undeniable truth.

Professor Kryvoruchko labeled the disease as ultimate sociopathic and stingy recidivism. It infested psyches with sociopathic and stingy fragments that created a marketplace of horror. The bug could appear in different colors, such as red for the pseudocollective and black for Nazis. There were a few historians who wanted to whitewash the repression of Nazis toward the world. They mentioned that Nazis who killed many people were good to the pregnant women. Nazis paid them for several years to be with their babies. It was like a soulless killer who buried the dead in his yard while grooming apple trees in the same yard, and he was a conscious gardener. Mass killers who were good to babies still were killers. The Nazis were mass killers, and nothing could change that.

According to Professor Kryvoruchko, the infection produced sociopaths without real emotions. Any guilt of having taken advantage of others was removed. The infected had moved millions of prisoners as slaves to national projects to immortalize their name. They did not make any sacrifices of their own. They wanted to build projects equal to the Egyptian pyramids. The difference was that the Egyptian pyramids were standing—for now—but the national projects in Aborigin not exist. The slaves died for nothing. Most of the ideologists were recidivists who often repeated their criminal behavior. Their conduct included robbery, torture, and rape. All of them banded together under a parasitic doctrine. They allowed crime without any penance for the major atrocities toward the habitants of various ethnicities and, especially, those who resisted primitivism and had a higher-than-average level of intelligence and nobility.

*Wikipedia* explained the terms in more detail. Ultimate sociopaths were characterized by diminished empathy and remorse. They displayed enduring antisocial behavior and were uninhibited by their audacious doctrine. Many forensic psychologists, psychiatrists, and criminologists used the terms *sociopath* and *psychopath* interchangeably. Sociopaths tended to be nervous and easily agitated. They were volatile and prone to emotional outbursts, including fits of rage. They were likely to be uneducated, live on the fringes of society, and be unable to hold down a steady job or stay in one place for long. It was difficult, but not impossible, for sociopaths to form attachments. They were stingy, miserly, and closed to all reason. They promptly took from others but were reluctant to pay others back or part with their own money and goods. According to *Wikipedia*, *stingy* meant "unwilling to share, give, or spend." Recidivism was the tendency to relapse into a previous condition or mode of behavior, especially criminal behavior.

The unification of sociopaths was characterized by invading the space of others and creating a lot of misery around them. Affected by disease, the plague-ridden did not understand that taking from others was not right. The attitude captured many psyches by infecting them and then spreading to others. It created a structure of involuntary submission and punishment for resistance. It restricted and prevented any individuality from flourishing. It was a marketplace of surrealistic dreams with different tinkles. The psychological sickness kept habitants in a surrealistic horror. The area of Aborigin was establishing pseudocollective craziness and communal horror. The disease quickly expanded to widespread zones, infecting Aboriginians and many others.

Aborigin continued to disintegrate. The pseudocollective was built on a dysfunctional construct. The meaning of *collective* was captured by a bunch of primitives who never had any original ideas. They tortured the world with their demand to abandon any complicity and make everything primitive. If they did not understand something, it was not supposed to be. Only primitive ideas existed, and then everyone would be equal in a row of imbeciles.

In a communal setting, everything was pseudo and presumed.

The pseudocollective had a territory diseased by the black and red bugs. It became a place where the life of the individual cost nothing. There, all plurals could be answered by a singular noun. The infected could kill legitimate owners and take merchandise by force. Examples of cruelty were found in the millions of victims in Kolyma and other death camps.

On the terrain populated by Aboriginians, the illness completely destroyed Western-oriented civilization. The nation came back to its Eastern roots. It was back to the time of the Golden Horde. The sickness created the pseudocollective and pseudocommunal.

Prolet-Aryans and presumed Aryans were in regions dirtied by the deadly malady. Those infected by populist ideas believed they were genetically superior and did not need special skills to perform complex tasks. They believed they were great and could do everything better than others.

The terror was in countries tainted by the red or black bugs. The infected, brainwashed populists violently attacked the uninfected to achieve their political goals. They wanted the hegemony of Prolet-Aryans and presumed Aryans. Their violence toward the uninfected resulted in a death camp on the Kolyma River and gas chambers in the middle of Europe.

Aborigin was intermediate terrain between West and East. For two hundred years, it had been an inseparable part of the Golden Horde, though it denied influence from the Golden Horde and insisted on belonging to the West. Aboriginians were the main builders of the pseudocollective. They claimed they and Malantians had the same history, but Malantians denied it. Aboriginians wanted to be Western but presented the Eastern-type structure of totalitarian interactions and military superiority. Malantians too wanted to be Western, but first of all, they wanted to be free from the Aboriginians.

# The Differences in Reaction to Viruses

One infected by the black bug declared himself as a ruler of the world, and others were subordinates. Those infected by the red virus created the diseased doctrine of communal living, which was based on asceticism. Many habitants lived in little rooms and shared one communal toilet and kitchen. Each room had its own water and electricity meter and also a doorbell outside.

In summary, there were two main similarities between the black and red bugs. The nation sickened by the black bug created the terror of Nazis. It violently staffed concentration camps in the middle of Europe, where perceived enemies of the regime were gassed. The gas chambers were more visible. The results of infection by the red virus were extermination camps built by the false collective in the Arctic, North Siberia, and other rural areas of Aborigin.

The red virus had brought time back to the Golden Horde and the Mongol-led army of Tatars. Aboriginians had been riding as equals with Mongols for two hundred years. Infected by the red virus, Aboriginians recreated the Golden Horde in the modern time. They continued living in an external pseudocollective similar to the structure of the Golden Horde. They always proclaimed they were the strongest military power in the world.

Interesting was a comparison between the Golden Horde and the Khazar Khanate. The complete opposite of Golden Horde militarism was the spirituality of the Khazar Khanate, whose territory was part of Aborigin. Those habitants lived with spiritual identities. The

Khazars were powerful Turkic habitants of the Jewish religion, inhabitants of Malantia. There was controversy over the mystical relationship between the Khazars and the Ashkenazim, the European Jews.

## Family and Pseudocollective

*P*rofessor Kryvoruchko was a part of the family that resisted infection by the psychological bug. He was a Sailor who explored the vastness of the human psyche. He understood that there were many psychological germs. He stated that dictators were happy with the disease. They proclaimed that infection by psychological illnesses was needed and desirable. Dictators endorsed untested primitivism, which was a product of the malady. They promoted it as an elixir for everything they dreamed about. Dictators called it an omnipotent and perfect doctrine. In the name of doctrine, they killed sophistication and individuality. They created an atmosphere that allowed dictatorships to exist. The infection created an epidemic that took away uniqueness and distinctiveness. It destroyed originality. Decency and nobility were replaced with cunning and guile. Germs that had existed long ago in the time of the Golden Horde were reactivated in an altered form. Bugs were differentiated by color. They were red, black, and more. The professor analyzed the red bug, USSR. The professor saw a terrible disease that was destroying distinctiveness. He described some frightening observations. The red bug was deadly. Habitants infected by the disease had awakened violence and low-lying instincts. Illness enforced the notion that a pseudocollective structure superseded any uniqueness. The epidemic glorified primitivism. It imposed an assumed-collective and assumed-communal state. The infected collectivists took others' wealth without any guilt.

The virus of communalism killed distinctiveness and uniqueness. It declared an exclusivity of putative collective thinking. It facilitated the resurgence of goon mentality under the name of the assumed collective. The affliction created in its surroundings a putative feeling of entitlement and superiority. It created primitive thinking that suppressed any humanity. Behind every assumed collective was a dictator.

# CHAPTER 1

# The Sailor's Spirit

Professor Stepan Kryvoruchko uncovered information that members of his family were in Kolyma. He was related to Aaron Kaufman and his father, Isaac, who'd escaped from Kolyma. Aborigin did not mention Kolyma anywhere, as if it did not exist and as if millions had not vanished. For many years, the whole country was a prison closed by an iron curtain, and escape was impossible. Attempted escapees were hunted and killed, and their families disappeared. It was not possible to escape, and habitants were suffocating.

After the death of Supreme Leader, passage opened. Professor Kryvoruchko and Aaron Kaufman left Aborigin. By escaping the country, they were escaping Kolyma. They moved to North America, the land of opportunity. Professor Kryvoruchko and Aaron Kaufman left the putative collective, the cursed land. They took a chance when the iron curtain around Aborigin was destroyed. They left at the right time, when the country was in stagnation. They traveled away from subjugation. They became Sailors who saved their own and other habitants' lives.

For Sailors, it was important to save lives. Because Professor Kryvoruchko sailed from oppression to freedom, he represented a Sailor's spirit. He had the courage to sail from the presumptive collective to a foreign land free from cruelty. He was not frightened of the unfamiliar surroundings. He had a lucky passage. Because he left his hometown, goons called him a traitor. He did not fight for change in his birthplace. He did not care. He realized he was not a Don Quixote. He could not fight with windmills. It was too hard to change anything. He did not feel any debt to the germ-infested terrain. Once in a safe place, he was able to learn his family's past. He found out there were many Sailors in his family. They all were individualists who resisted collectivist thinking.

## Way to Freedom

For a long time, Professor Kryvoruchko did not know that in his family was a courageous man named Isaac Kaufman, a Sailor. Professor Kryvoruchko discovered that he was part of a decent clan. Isaac Kaufman was an escapee from a prison on the Kolyma River. He escaped with his girlfriend, Glasha. They took with them a little bag of high-quality diamonds. In place of horror, he found a beautiful wife and his wealth. He lived and died in Baku, Azerbaijan.

Professor Kryvoruchko and Aaron Kaufman were currently living in the USA. In their new homeland, they were happy. Some natives suspected they'd come to the new homeland with the goal to infiltrate and sabotage. They did not argue with them. Once out of the pseudocollective, Professor Kryvoruchko went to school and became a professor. Aaron Kaufman created several businesses and employed many immigrants from Aborigin. They demonstrated that their objective was only to be happy and share happiness with others.

## Nazis in Malantia

During World War II, Jews suffered from antagonism in the vicinity of Malantia, part of Aborigin, and were victims of many hostilities. The prejudiced Malantians inferred that something was vicious and evil in the Jewish character. They put all Jews into a genetically undesirable category. It was an idiotic concept to create a big monster. Jews, through their history, experienced the entrance of many other genetic inflows. The Jewish appearance continued through their mothers. Their fathers could be from various genetic pools. Malantia's xenophobia was relayed on an insane basis. The first idiotic postulate was that Jews were genetically greedy and were using their special genes to patronize the rest of society. During the Nazis' time, people felt justified in reporting their Jewish neighbors to the local police, who, as a result, sent victims to extermination camps. Malantia's Nazis showed an extraordinary hatred of Jews. Many Malantians were guards in concentration camps and got away with a lot of murders.

The pseudodoctrine created by the disease was not able to protect their citizens, including their women, children, and elderly. Those selected to die included Rivka; her baby daughter; and her father-in-law, Hershel Kryvoruchko. They were destroyed by Malantian Nazis. They were savagely murdered. There were places where thousands of Jews, selected by the infected, were slaughtered. Those Jews, picked by gruesome executors, met a heartbreaking fate. Both collectivists and Nazis finished off many of them. It seemed that a black cloud enclosed that particular part of the world. After the Nazis' defeat, the dark cloud did not move away from Malantia.

## Stepan Luchko, Survivor

Stepan Luchko was kept safe. In Aborigin, which was polluted by germs, longevity was a mystery. Among the population, sometimes inconsistencies happened. For some reason, the lives of some were spared many times. It was a possibility that Stepan Luchko would live a long life. His destiny was to save Professor Kryvoruchko's life. The unexplained contingency happened frequently. As a teenager, Stepan Luchko was skiing and crossing a lake one day, when he fell through the ice into the freezing water. He'd fallen into a hole covered with snow. On his feet were heavy skis. He immediately sank. Stepan Luchko needed to find a way out. The ice was everywhere. He was wet and confused. It was dark. By luck, Stepan's hand found the hole in the ice above. He was able to pull himself up to the surface. The temperature was low. He ran on the ice to the edge of the lake, carrying his skis. He was afraid of punishment for losing them, as they belonged to his school.

On land, the snow was high, and he trudged through it in

his socks, carrying his skis. To his luck, he saw smoke from a chimney. He knocked on the door of the house, and an old man and woman opened it. They gave him dry clothes and hot tea. He then went home and changed his clothing. He did not tell anyone about being close to death. After that experience, he believed that he was enchanted and that nothing bad could befall him. Throughout his life, he did not argue with anyone, and he never had any enemies. Stepan Luchko faced death and survived many times. He became numb inside. He was unmoved by the ugliness of his surroundings.

Stepan Luchko ended up as a spy and a war hero. His daughter was the mother of the professor, but he did not know about it. The professor met Luchko in Canada. The professor already had served in the Israeli army and was married. At the time, Stepan Luchko was an undercover spy for Aborigin. When he found out that Professor Kryvoruchko was his grandson, he saved the professor from the corrupt agents of Aborigin. Otherwise, if Stepan Luchko had not interfered, the professor would have been dead for sure.

## Rivka's Life in Greben

When the orphaned Rivka arrived in Greben, her mother was dead, and her father was in prison. She was a niece of Uncle Ben, who was a big man in the flea market, the famous Greben Bazaar. He knew that Rivka's beloved mama had perished. Her daddy was in a penitentiary, and she needed a caretaker. Uncle Ben was a widower. He was childless and was glad to welcome his niece Rivka into his household. Uncle Ben sold construction materials.

In Greben, he was one of the wealthiest uninfected blackmarketers. He was friendly with another widower, Hershel Kryvoruchko, who had a son named Alex. Alex was the same age as Rivka. The widowers trusted each other, and their friendship continued until Ben's death.

Hershel Kryvoruchko was generally frank and was uninfected. It was always a good feeling to be around him. Hershel Kryvoruchko was homely and openhearted. He was far away from any trickery. To cover his private activities, he worked at a factory as a tailor. To make a decent living and make more money, he sewed suits at his home. Ben Kaufman used suits tailored by Hershel to bribe officials needed for his cover, or, in other words, his roofs. They needed protection from the dog tails, racketeers, and authorities. His roofs also protected him from ideologists and other officials in power. Hershel was a good tailor, and all the officials loved his products. Ben paid him handsomely. Both were happy with each other. Their friendship had started many years ago, when Hershel sold a suit at the flea market to an undercover policeman. The transaction was illegal, as the government did not allow any private enterprises. The law of presumptive collectives was merciless to all private producers. Hershel Kryvoruchko was one of them. The collective protected factory merchandise by severe punishment without any remorse for the private producers.

The police arrested Hershel for the illegal activity. During that time, his wife was alive, and she was a best friend of Ben's wife. Ben got involved and resolved the problem. The art of bribery required some skill, and Ben had a gift. He paid off a policeman. Hershel was not sent to Siberia. If Ben Kaufman had not interfered, Hershel would have ended his life in prison. He would have been one of the dejected and deplorable. If not for Ben's intervention, he probably would have been dead. Hershel understood that. Being honest and weak, he was not prison material. He would not have adapted to life in prison. He was thankful to Ben and wanted to be helpful. He was happy with the work he did for Ben. Because of Ben's help, he was able to afford a dignified life for his family. He also was proud that Ben's dacha and car were registered in his name. Ben became a Sailor because he saved Hershel's life. He was able to bring Hershel to a safe place in a dangerous whirlpool. Hershel too was a Sailor because after his wife died, as single father, he led his son safely to a comfortable life.

## Uncle Ben's Thankfulness

It brought Uncle Ben pleasure to have his niece Rivka around. It was nice to have a kindred spirit close to him. He was thankful. His wife had died and not left any children. He'd loved his wife with all his heart. He'd taken care of her. He'd washed and fed her, but his effort had not been enough. She'd died during the delivery of their baby. The baby had died too.

Uncle Ben made a lot of money and had the status of the big man at the flea market. He'd mastered the art of laundering money. He was proud he was able to challenge and beat the diseased system. Those in power, through contagious illness, had forced the uninfected to become insignificant. To be somebody and survive, Uncle Ben bribed the police. In a slave society, he was living a life of the rich and notable. In Aborigin, the birthplace of morons tainted by thought-twisting disease, that was rare.

# Dachas

*I*n city apartments, habitants had one bathroom for ten families. They did not even have a bathtub. Nevertheless, some wanted to live well. In the city, they lived in a communal setting for cover. It was a necessity because in doing so, they showed that they were close to the working class. The dachas were heaven for many miserable habitants. The dachas were private places away from informers. In Greben, habitants dreamed of dachas. The few who were rich were afraid to be questioned about their income, which mainly was illegal. They needed their dachas for a sense of stability. They knew how to get money. Their positions allowed them to receive bribes or pick up some undetectable earnings. In the village, they could have everything they wanted. They would buy summer cottages under the names of their poor relatives or friends with simple jobs. The condition was that those habitants, whom they trusted, were not involved in any risky transactions.

The shadow economy bowled around. The habitants who lacked business skills found ways to make a living. For little money, they sold their names to be registered owners of the dachas. They kept the money of someone rich in their homes. Many properties and cars also were covered by their names. Business habitants felt safer when the police did not have evidence to arrest or blackmail them.

Ben Kaufman sold everything, most of the time stolen building materials. He was careful and knew with whom to deal. The secret that kept him alive was that he had the talent of being able to bribe everyone. He did not give money, but he was always ready to offer liquor. He bribed with alcohol stolen by the workers from a liquor factory. The workers stole pure alcohol and took it out through security in enema containers hidden under their clothes. Ben did not drink alcohol. He bought it because it was the best item to bribe the powerful. Bribing with alcohol was not as insulting as bribing with money and was an accepted means for everyone to show gratitude. It looked like a gesture of friendship. The scheme was working for him. In the city, having a private flat to live in was a big privilege. Instead of a communal setting, Ben had his own kitchen, his own toilet, three bedrooms, and no snitches on his back. He had a private flat in the city and a chalet in the village.

There was plenty of room in his apartment, where he lived with his dog. Miki was a five-year-old Labrador retriever. Miki was a friendly dog. He accepted Rivka as a friend and allowed her to walk him twice a day. Miki was glad for the opportunity to have Rivka with him. Besides walking with Miki, Rivka went to the same school as Alexander Kryvoruchko, the son of the hardworking tailor Hershel.

Ben and Hershel had shared business associations. Hershel was the fictitious owner of Ben's hideaways. Ben trusted Hershel and helped him financially. Ben and Hershel were family-oriented. They both were widowers. Ben's wife had died during the delivery of their child, and Hershel's wife had died in an influenza outbreak. Hershel raised a son, Alexander, who was a student. He wanted to be an accountant. Rivka was the light of Ben's life. Ben had a good piano of German origin, and Rivka took music lessons. She played the piano with inspiration. Rivka wanted to be a music teacher. Ben could not believe he had a family.

The rules of the presumptive collective were based on a criminal concept that made habitants poor and insignificant. They were supposed to be happy with empty promises. Ben Kaufman was able to organize a normal life.

He had a nice house on the Dnyapro River, near Greben, which had rooms for everyone and small holdings attached. Ben was attached to his dog, Miki, and often walked in his company. Ben also planted strawberries, gooseberries, and black and red currants and offered them to his guests. On the site grew cherry trees. In the evenings, under the cherry trees, Ben, Hershel, Alexander, and Rivka played cards. The light breeze from the Dnyapro River caressed their faces. It wasn't good to live alone, but in the past, Ben had lived alone. He remembered the day his wife had died; he'd been sad but could not stay home. He'd gone to the bazaar, which was his whole life. At the bazaar, he had friends and activities he loved. While selling to others, he would get high on adrenaline and feel accomplished.

The bazaar, a flea market, was a place where habitants could find their calling. Ben was a store manager publicly, but in reality, he was a big shot in the underground construction business. Construction was supposed to be controlled by the government, but the construction of dachas was not. The most important part of being a rich man was to have a dacha. Habitants also repaired the bowers. The dachas were a symbol of success and stability and were out of government control. The desire to have a dacha came from a previous time when all rich habitants spent the summertime close to the water. They had retreats on the banks of the biggest river in Malantia, the Dnyapro River. For Ben, achieving the good life was the basis of his existence. He would never come to terms with life in a communal setting. He would do anything to get out of those conditions. The flea market gave him that opportunity. The flea market was a perfect model for habitants involved in common activities. Everyone in the flea market structure benefitted from it.

Unlike the bazaar, the collective was a structure that

imposed doctrine on the population. To promote Superior Leader, the habitants were supposed endure hardship. Diseased dogma motivated the population to support imperial ambitions of worldwide hegemony. Unfortunately, many habitants in that world wanted to sacrifice their quality of life and even gave up their lives altogether for their doctrine. Habitants who surrendered their lives to doctrine were brainwashed idiots. The flea market motivated habitants to benefit from transactions and be more prosperous. The flea market structure was not glorious and might not have been heroic, but it resisted doctrine. Ben was spending his life creating wealth instead of spending his life imposing stupid doctrine on the habitants.

In many areas of life, the bazaar defeated the draconian dogma. The flea market motivated habitants to benefit from transactions and be more prosperous. The flea market was opposed to thoughts of worldwide hegemony. In the killing field, the black market was flourishing. Black-marketers learned quickly how to launder their money to avoid informers and denunciations. The rich habitants were also afraid to keep money and jewelry at home. They hid their treasures in the kitchens and bathrooms of trusted habitants' homes. Ben was less scared than others were. He understood that documentation was the most important thing in the killing field. He always had fake invoices. He created a world constructed by double invoices. If the police were to stop his truck, he always had the correct amount of transported materials. In his second invoice, the number of transported materials was much lower. He would sell the difference. He shared his income with the manufacturer's representative, who received a regular salary as well as revenue under the table. He was not afraid. He dealt with different habitants. His philosophy was that money was essential for everyone, and he acted according to that view.

Money was necessary for the factory's general manager, the shoemaker, the storekeeper, and the bookkeeper. He knew that a position in a factory meant nothing. Sometimes the boss in a factory was a simple storekeeper who had the power to do all transactions and shared money with the superintendent. In many instances, a simple bookkeeper was the decision-maker, while the manager was just an empty space or letterhead. That was all part of the gerrymander known as the black market. Ben was well oriented in that setting and felt like a fish in familiar waters. The commissars never caught him because he paid them off.

In the meantime, Alexander and Rivka completed school. They got married. Rivka went to a music academy to become a music teacher. Alexander did not want to be a tailor like his father. Alexander went to an industrial university to become an accountant. In the middle of his studies, he changed his mind. He studied accounting but became a soldier. Alexander was one of the naive who helped his motherland. He followed the special appeal of the government to reinforce the military. Alexander attended military school. He became a professional soldier and lived in barracks. He was an officer who took an oath to defend doctrine. If he was captured, he was supposed to kill himself. With Rivka, he had two children: a boy and, later, a girl. He and his son lived long lives, but his wife and daughter died. His dead father, Hershel, like many others, had tried to adapt to the norms. He'd wanted to have a normal life. Ben's life was an oasis in the barren desert of collectivism. In a place dirtied beyond description by venom, the uninfected wanted to have normal lives.

Ben peacefully passed away just before the Second World War started. He was lucky he did not know a lot of horrors, mainly what happened to his beloved. In

Aborigin, which was adulterated by the thought-altering toxin, it was lucky to die at the right time and from natural causes. It was timely for Ben to die before the Nazis came to Malantia. Ben never saw slaughtering villains wagging axes and butchering habitants. He did not know that the Nazis were in Malantia and were killing civilians. He did not know that being a Jew was a death sentence.

The deadly psychological poison had several modifications. Malantia was a fertile field for killing. Malantian Nazis killed Jews and Gypsies. The morons and goons of different branches killed the uninfected and talented. The abominable structure was not able to protect women, children, or the elderly from awful men. The targets were savagely murdered. There were many places where hundreds of thousands of Jewish habitants were slaughtered. It seemed that a dark cloud covered that part of the world.

In Malantia, it did not take long for some beloved neighbors to become Nazis. Contrary to the ideology of equality, they hated their neighbors and waited for the right moment to destroy them. That time came, and the compatriots did what they wanted to do for a long time. They killed many habitants. They were executors of their fellows in beloved Malantia. Rivka, her little daughter, and old Hershel were killed with an ice crowbar by a local Nazi. In the moment of her death, Rivka was stripped of her clothes. She covered her little daughter with her body. She saw the death of Hershel and his fractured scalp. Her daughter lived a couple minutes more than she did.

The deadly epidemic that came to the world created many graveyards. The hate created villains, killers, and victims. That time was deadly. The world was a big cemetery. Life was a big marketplace filled with surreal dreams. Too many habitants in the world chased incongruent fantasies.

Many became bacilli carriers of a variety of sicknesses. The different psychological diseases that handicapped the terrain left its habitants wandering through irrational dreams. After the black bug was defeated, the dark cloud stayed. The big meat grinder was not overpowered. The tragedies did not stop. The infected had limited understanding about themselves and the problems of the habitants surrounding them. Only a few had an awareness of feelings and actions at that time. They developed genuine relationships with themselves and the world around them. They eventually found existential goals and did not want to push toward the abyss. They all became Sailors. One had to go a long way to get a Sailor's spirit and move away from the abyss.

One survivor of the massacre was Rivka's son.

## The Borderline of Byelogoria

*A* village of pine trees was located in Byelogoria, in the southwestern part of Aborigin. It was on the border of Poland. The village was in a forest, and the habitants were peasants. The scenery was breathtaking. The houses, gardens, horses, and habitants all looked like parts of a beautiful painting. However, the revolution that had created infected communal realities infiltrated that village on the edge of nowhere. Byelogoria was surrounded by powerful neighbors. In the villages, hidden from view by the forest, lived mystical descendants of many ancient tribes. The infectious doctrine did not leave that gorgeous place alone. Ideology brought commissars to the villages. They confiscated the possessions of the wealthy. The previous order of the universe was broken, and a new one of hatred and fear had taken its place.

## Byelogoria's Battle with Doctrine

*I*n Byelogoria, Isaac lived in a big house with two horses, one cow, chickens, and a big garden full of fruits and vegetables. In the past, the local habitants had been able to adjust and coexist with other metropolitans. Those habitants had been hard workers, smartly chosen their associates, and avoided confrontation. A new time had come to that vile corner of Byelogoria, gulled by doctrine. It was a rural place, one of many, far away from metropolitan influences. The strict communal setting imposed its grip on the established old lifestyle. Isaac and his wife, Fay, had four children: Rudi, Aaron, Sara, and Rivka. His older son, Rudi, was a lawyer. Rudi had a wife and lived in a big city. His older daughter, Sara, was married to a blacksmith's son and lived in the village. Aaron and Rivka were teenagers and students in school. The activists knew that Isaac had a lot of money and was a big shot in the marketplace. They knew he bought and sold gold. The diamond business, however, was a big secret. Isaac and Fay used to constantly have their house searched by the government. The commissars searched their house many times but found nothing.

Isaac Kaufman was a smuggler of diamonds, but he concealed his dealings as part of the shadow economy. As a cover, he had a repair stand in the market, where he fixed watches and jewelry. He also sold and bought gold. His backstreet activity was smuggling diamonds. At that time, gold was cheap. Gulps stole many artifacts from the estates of the rich. They did so in the name of revolution, and such robbery was not considered a crime. After commissars confiscated gold from the rich, they would sell it to Isaac. Because he gave the highest price on the market, he had a lot of customers who wanted to sell. Every commissar was after the gold. It was called appropriation of unjustly distributed funds. The wealthy habitants were considered to have gained unjustly. Criminally oriented commissars did not have an obligation to respect somebody else's property. Hundreds of them, in leather jackets, showed different papers that, in the name of revolution, allowed them to take everyone's possessions. Overall disregard of others' property was a clear sign of disrespect for individual life. Beyond the border of Byelogoria, gold was expensive.

Isaac used the situation in Byelogoria, where gold was cheap. Without any prosecution, the mob robbed prosperous habitants because the wealthy were portrayed as an evil class. The wealthy were declared enemies of the nation and called exploiters. Some rich habitants sold gold for a pittance because they needed to buy food, and their possessions had been confiscated by the police or stolen. At that time, everyone wanted diamonds, which were expensive, because they were easy to hide. The police had information that said Isaac was hiding gold and diamonds.

## Isaac's Hatred of the State

*I*saac hated when men unlawfully captured positions of power. He vowed to himself that he would give them none of his possessions. In fact, he wanted to acquire more goods. The local police were after Isaac, but he was careful, and he did not hesitate to bribe authorities. His game was dangerous, but he was afloat because like everywhere else, in the killing field, authorities liked kickbacks.

Isaac saw an opportunity to sell and buy gold and establish himself as a businessman. He often illegally crossed the border of Poland to exchange gold for diamonds. He was careful, and he went to the border without any gold. When approached by frontier guards, he had nothing on him. He then waited in the bushes for his delivery. One of his relatives, Bogdan, delivered the gold to him on a horse-drawn carriage, and only near the border would Isaac take over. From there, he'd move on foot with a bag, with the gold carefully hidden. His backpack was heavy, but Isaac was a strong man. The smuggling took place at nighttime. One of Isaac's helpers would create a distraction. For example, he would start a little fire, and the border soldiers would busy themselves with it. Meanwhile, Isaac would move through the swamp toward the border crossing. On the Polish side, he gave Polish soldiers pieces of gold and went to the city where he knew a jeweler. They spoke in Yiddish. They'd known each other for many years, and the prices were already settled ahead of time. Isaac traded gold for diamonds, ate a little food, and went back home. The way back was much easier because he was not carrying a heavy backpack anymore. The diamonds did not weigh much. Isaac knew every little place in the border area and did not expect any surprises. His helper waited for him on the other side.

Isaac trusted Bogdan to bring home the diamonds. They went home by different roads as a precaution because the local police were after Isaac. If the police stopped him and searched him, they would not find anything incriminating on him. In case he was stopped, he also always had vodka and other tasty offers ready for the policemen. Despite their strong animosity for the rich, police officers became weak when they saw vodka, and they always let him go. Isaac knew exactly what he was doing and designed a system to reach his goal. His family always had money, and for as long as he was alive, he would always have plenty.

## The Ubiquity of Hypocrisy

Hypocrisy was everywhere, and Isaac used it to his advantage. He knew how to bribe authorities, and he did it well. Officials repeated slogans of honesty but then waited for bribes. Brokers were around to help with bribery if people did not know how to do it themselves. Some individuals had a talent for bribing officials. They did it skillfully. When asked how they did it, their answer was simple: they just were showing respect to authority. The secret was that the supplicant would explain his request and then quietly put the number on a piece of paper. If the superior disagreed, he would put down his own number or just motion with his head. No words were spoken, but a deal was done. At the end, they burned the paper with the numbers because no one wanted to leave evidence behind.

Isaac knew that even from the time of Mongols, habitants had brought many gifts to authority. The worst position was being a scientist or engineer because it was difficult to be bribed. To get papers signed for anything, officials always bribed. Even to buy tasty food, someone required connections. Best of all was an exchange of favors. Habitants requested favors and received favors in return.

A gift to an official was a sign of respect to the position he held. From ancient times, many habitants had looked for advantageous ways to make a living by receiving bribes. Isaac himself was an expert at bribing officials.

Isaac was careful because the killing field butchered private enterprise. Its disease had wiped out the old bureaucracy too. The old ways of doing business had not been fast, but they'd been productive and gotten the job done. The new establishment did not have any education, experience, or knowledge. Some were infected by dogma, and others only had a desire to get rich. They acquired what they wanted by using intimidation and brutal force. They had audacity, leather jackets, and guns. Contrary to previous rulers, they were cruel. Because they wore the leather jackets and leather pants, they felt empowered. They waved their carbines in front of habitants. They yelled and did everything possible to show their supremacy.

## The Infestation of the Killing Field

*I*saac understood that communalist regions gave undeserved qualities to the character of poorly educated habitants. With the populists' slogans, the rulers gave the false and unproven expectation that they could solve problems of inequality. In reality, they just created a lot of problems. The main task of the new superior leader was to take money from the well-to-do population. With his brutality, he took away feelings of guilt. The commissars worked as gangsters with guns when they stole somebody else's property. The important task was to figure out what to do with the property. That task created a lot of problems. Uneducated habitants knew how to steal but did not know how to use the stolen holdings.

In Isaac's perception, the greediness was enormous. The epidemic destroyed law and order. The police were brutal and needed baksheesh. Even Isaac bribed local authorities, but he was not able to bribe everyone.

One day militia from the regional center came to Isaac's house. They took him and his wife to the local jail. Isaac's older daughter, Sara; her husband, Bogdan; and many other villagers were in jail already. The police separated males from females. They put many habitants of the same sex in one room. Detainees could not sit down. In the little space left over, they placed two pails as toilets. After a few days of standing, the prisoners' legs were swollen, and the pain was unbearable. The terrible smell of human waste and unwashed bodies filled the room. That torture was called the sauna. The police wanted to find where habitants hid their possessions. There were no courts, judges, or lawyers involved.

## Bondarenko

One of the most vicious torturers was the chief of the local police, Bondarenko, who was infected by dogma. Bondarenko felt that villagers who hid their possessions were enemies. The commissar, who was a dogmatic, decided who could be detained and who could go. The villagers, after a few days of torture, would give up everything the police were looking for. Bondarenko believed that villagers were not entitled to have any possessions and that whatever they had belonged to the collective bursa. He believed that individual possessions should not exist. He felt that everything should belong to the government.

Bondarenko never had studied any criminology. Against any common sense, he was placed in a job where he oversaw lives. Without any knowledge of social or economic areas, he felt entitled to make decisions for others. Instead of a feeling of guilt, he experienced feelings of entitlement. Lunatic Bondarenko believed that all injustice was caused by individual possessions. He believed in the concept of poisonous dogma, as in the Bible. For him, without any material attachments, new habitants were created, and new relationships were built. He dreamed about new ideal relationships between parents and children.

Commissars put a lot of habitants in one room and kept them standing up, which was a way to give them a chance to surrender their wealth without shooting them. The militia had a sort of competition. One who got detainees to surrender faster was more valuable. Bondarenko honestly felt he was not torturing habitants but helping to rehabilitate them.

## The Enemy of the State

Professor Kryvoruchko analyzed the actions of Superior Leader, who was a monster, and figured out that terror was cosmopolitan. The regime was cruel to every ethnicity without any exceptions. They carried out their deeds smoothly and quickly. The collective detained many habitants and labeled them enemies of the state and helpers of the enemies of state. It arrested a variety of wealthy and professional habitants and used them as slaves. The collective was a big slave driver. As part of the regime, Bondarenko used simple technology to enslave villagers. If someone reported to him that a villager had money, it was enough evidence for the regional militia to detain the person.

Bondarenko sent his dogs to search Isaac's house. The police could not find Isaac's money. They were frustrated. Isaac and his other relatives were arrested. Bondarenko did not have any prejudice against Jews, nor did he have any xenophobia toward minorities. He simply followed doctrine that described and distorted values. It plagiarized part of the Bible, which stated that villagers should love each other. In the regime's doctrine, the word *love* existed only toward Prolet-Aryans. It spread hatred to the other classes. Bondarenko believed that doctrine of loving one another was limited to villagers who were members of the working class, who were his informers. Bondarenko hated other villagers, who were presumed to be exploiters or their cronies, including white-collar workers, administrators, scientists, businessmen, and well-to-do farmers. They were all supposed to be hated and destroyed.

Commissar Bondarenko, suffering from mental deterioration, acted the same way the Nazis had in the time of the führer. He believed that he was special and that his destiny was to rule the world. Commissar Bondarenko was infected by psychological germs. To spread them, he picked Bogdan, who was the only non-Jew among his relatives. Not without careful calculation, Bondarenko chose a victim to infect with the virus. His reason was that Bogdan was from a blacksmith family. In Bondarenko's opinion, Bogdan was from the same class he was. In their conversation, Bondarenko manipulated with slogans and patriotic stories. He reiterated that most Prolet-Aryans brought to the communal revolution all of their strength and all of their possessions. They were building a new world, but there were a few who resisted. Bondarenko believed the land was for everyone, but some wanted more for themselves than for others.

## Commissar Bondarenko: Fertile Ground for Perdition

*B*eing infected, Commissar Bondarenko was fertile ground for perdition. He was a bacilli carrier. He was sure the rich were depriving poor habitants of having equal opportunities and expressing their talents. He felt that success for many was not available. Infected Bondarenko displayed the symptoms of narcissism and delusions of grandeur. He felt he was right. He assumed he had a great destiny and was an older brother to all other ethnicities. Because he had a working-class background, he believed he could rule the world. The venom polluted his innocent soul with impressive ambitions. Bondarenko believed that in the past, he'd been deprived of future advancements through unequal distribution of goods, and he deserved more. The imbecile wanted to be a professor. The infection created many unrealistic expectations.

Infected simpletons, such as Bondarenko, had many victims. The evil Bondarenko wanted villagers to report on others and even implicate themselves. He did not care about a presumption of innocence. He worshipped fears. He was a guardian of hatred and imbalance, the main features of the regime. Bogdan was one of many who listened to rusticity. He acted as patsy. It was out of his character. He was not afraid of standing up day and night in his jail cell. The only places to sit down were on the toilets, which were pails covered with plywood. Those spots were taken by the elderly. They allowed the detained to relieve themselves, and then the elderly sat down on them. In one moment, Bogdan honestly felt it was wrong to be rich among poor habitants. According to the doctrine, all habitants should be oppressed and equally miserable. It seemed that some habitants, such as his father-in-law, always lived better than others. He understood that by being around Isaac, he benefited, but in his confused state, he felt Isaac was not on the right side. In that moment, Bogdan felt that the right thing was to use all his energy to help others who did not have any inspirations and talents to be successful. He had disturbing thoughts that it was wrong to have ambitions to achieve self-success. Bogdan was a villager and not educated. He acted like an idiot. He couldn't sleep. He gave in to the psychological effects of the insane creed. He could have sustained and tolerated any pain, but he was not ready for psychological torture. As was the case with many of his compatriots, he became a victim of manipulative rhetoric.

## Bogdan's Lack of Sophistication

*U*nsophisticated Bogdan overlooked the fact that the infected Bondarenko was torturing villagers. He displayed the illness of brutality. He felt entitled to torture others. At that time, many things were not lawful. In Bogdan's programmed brain were thoughts that his father-in-law,

Isaac, did something bad against villagers. His father-in-law always had food and money and acted with self-confidence. Bogdan worried not about the legality of Isaac's business but about the status of being affluent. He identified himself with the disadvantaged, and he thought about higher fairness. Brainwashed by foolish chatter, Bogdan became overly concerned with the fact that for some reason, there were villagers who were not affluent and could not enjoy life. In his mind, his father-in-law was committing a crime.

Bogdan was sleep deprived, naive, and easily infected by psychological poison. As one of the infected, he felt it was not right to be rich, because other habitants were poor and despondent. It was a mystery how he so quickly became affected by the inflammatory rhetoric. He was a physically strong man, but he lost his head. He divulged to the police the secret place in Isaac's attic where Isaac hid his gold.

Physical torture did not affect Bogdan. Physical suffering was not a reason to betray his father-in-law. Bogdan also was not prejudiced against Jews. Bogdan did not believe in such discrimination and hatred. He just was radicalized to the point that he became an informer. He also did not avoid the revelation about his part in smuggling and implicated himself as Isaac's accomplice in all evil deeds. The goal of the infection had been achieved. He became a complete imbecile like everyone else.

## Luchko's Family

*B*ogdan Luchko was a handsome man. He was Malantian, but he lived in Byelogoria. His father had come to Byelogoria because of job opportunities and because a village was looking for a blacksmith. Bogdan had grown up among Byelogorians and Jews. He came from a family of three children.

Sara, Isaac's daughter, had fallen madly in love with Bogdan Luchko, who'd been an attractive uniformed equestrian. He'd served in the cavalry and looked gorgeous on his horse in his military uniform. After his military service, Bogdan had come back to the village and worked with his father, Maxim, as a blacksmith. Bogdan was a strong man. The torture did not have any effect on him physically, but it was psychologically damaging. The brainwashing caused him to feel rejected and to be an outcast. He experienced great emotional suffering and guilt. His psyche felt apart.

Isaac Kaufman and Maxim Luchko knew each other but lived separate lives. In a small village, habitants lived poles apart. Maxim was busy with horseshoes and many others blacksmith chores. When he was too busy to repair the horse carriages, Isaac was busy repairing watches. He sold and bought jewelry. Isaac asked Maxim many times not to yell obscenities close to his shop. When he was drunk, Maxim scared away Isaac's customers. Maxim laughed and said Isaac should not take him seriously because he was a goy, or gentile. Maxim meant that one should not expect too much from a goy. When sober, Maxim was an amiable man and did not wish to offend anyone.

Bogdan did not drink and did not like to work with horses. He was not a regular farm boy. He felt that blacksmith work was primitive. He loved watches and jewelry. He'd known that Sara was Isaac's daughter, even though she lived on the opposite side of the village, behind the synagogue. He, a blond Malantian boy, had fallen in love with a Jewish girl. He knew her older brother, Rudi, whom he'd had a wild fight with as a child. Rudi, along with a bunch of other boys, had run after Sara when she went to see him. Bogdan rode stallions and looked like a real horseman. Sara was a romantic and had fallen in love with him. Against the families' advice, the two had gotten married and had two children. Bogdan worked as a blacksmith with his father. Later, he had become friends with Rudi.

Blacksmith work was a cover for Bogdan because he helped Isaac with smuggling. He was the one who provided a variety of distractions. He also took merchandise to the border to be smuggled. He brought a horse carriage for Isaac to ride home on the way back. Isaac protected Bogdan and never allowed him to cross the border. Isaac believed he could handle any crisis better than someone else could. In the little village, different destinies came together, and dissimilar fates became connected.

Isaac figured out that in the killing field, being innovative meant following the unclear rules of the communal setting. The revolutionary was supposed to sacrifice his or her life for collective success. The villagers were brainwashed and encouraged to see the opposite of reality. They excitedly saw the illusion of a bright, fake future in front of them. According to Bondarenko, the counterrevolutionary force consisted of villagers with a narrow vision. He declared that uninfected villagers were not smart because they refused to see the benefits of unproven doctrine. It was true that uninfected villagers did not want to ruin their lives for stupid dogma. In Bondarenko's way of thinking, no one could do something for him- or herself without having feelings of guilt. He gave fiery speeches and talked about unacceptable individual behaviors that were against collective dogma. Bondarenko talked about irresponsible, antisocial loners who went against the general trend. A big mass of his informers checked on all the habitants who were displeased and reported them to him.

Everyone who openly diverted from Bondarenko's doctrine was severely punished. In general, the structure of pollution was also part of the criminal code. Instead of a commissar, the criminals had a kingpin as the head of their structure, which was built on manipulation and confrontation. Commissars were instigators and took possessions from habitants. Acting belligerently and justifying robbery, they diseased decent villagers with infected dogma. It was a crime to look after the well-being of one's family and have a life without sacrifices. When villagers attempted to have self-profit, the commissars eliminated them.

## The Stupidity of the Killing Field in the Village of Pine Trees

The Village of Pine Trees was an example of implanting the doctrine of the red terror in villagers' minds. It removed the chance for resistance. Business-oriented habitants were easy targets. They were neither aggressive nor violent. Ideologists victimized them and were not afraid the victims would avenge themselves. The chief policeman, Commissar Bondarenko, was an egomaniac. When he took Isaac Kaufman and his wife, Fay, back to their house, he found all their hidden gold and money. The policemen took all of the family's possessions. Unfortunately, Bondarenko's behavior was not an exception; there were many others like him. They felt they were special. Together with thieves and alcoholics, they were the basis of the infection. There was enormous stress for victims.

Tragedy struck quickly. Before the policemen took Fay away, she had a heart attack and died. Paradoxically, her fate was not as miserable as others'. She did not go to jail and was ultimately saved from suffering. Isaac was taken to a bigger jail in the city of Bobruisk and then to a prison in Siberia. The pseudocelestials thought of themselves as rulers. In reality, they were narcissistic fools with lower-than-average intelligence. Most of them had little education or intellectual ability. They came from various provincial cities and villages. They had big goals in life but later ended up as slaves in a variety of labor camps, just like their victims. The sickness was worse than thievery or alcohol dependence.

## Victims in Byelogoria

Back in Byelogoria, Isaac Kaufman was resisting indoctrination. In simple analysis, he was a victim of doctrine. To resist depersonalization and poverty, he risked his life by being a smuggler of gold and diamonds. He was arrested and stripped of all his possessions. The monster needed more victims. Isaac was sent to northern Siberia. He was an enemy of people. Though Isaac was a smuggler, he was sent to prison not because he broke the law but because he was a rich man. No one cared about him handling contraband; his crime was being rich. As a wealthy person, he did not have any protection by law or justice. The biggest hypocrisy in the world was Aborigin, the killing field. The infected talked about fairness and equality while feeling entitled to take from others by force. The doctrine emphasized wealth redistribution, as some had many things, and others did not.

The other victims were Bogdan and Sara. They had a good household, which was rare in Aborigin's diseased locality. Without any second thought, they would have given up their lives for the sake of their children. Professor Kryvoruchko emphasized that Bogdan was separated from the generator of indoctrination, and he went back to being a father and husband. He was healed of the infection. The family were normal villagers without any of the rotten narcissism that was a side effect of the perdition. Sara was a loving woman, the wife of a man who was brainwashed by an insignificant manipulator.

Under the influence of disease, Bogdan acted out of character. He became a zombie. The family could not understand him. The brainwashing changed Bogdan into an imbecilic blockhead. Bogdan was deceived by the bane. He became a blind puppet with unfounded vanity and weak common sense. He was converted into a lackey of the regime and became easily victimized. As a slave, he was used as cannon fodder. In the killing field, the witch hunt for slaves began, including those the regime called helpers of the enemies of the state. Professor Kryvoruchko mentioned that leaders figured out how to use slave labor to decrease their expenses. Uneducated management blamed everyone and provided as many slaves as demanded. That devastation of dogma was associated with the biggest slavery practice in human history. Ideologists did not care about managers and used them too as whipping boys and scapegoats.

## Sara Waited for the Commissar

One night, Sara waited for the commissar near the precinct. It was late when he left his office. She approached him and asked what would happen to her father and her husband. Bondarenko informed her that her father was an enemy of the state. He added that in a time when imperialists wanted to suffocate young communalists, her father had capitalistic inclinations, and the best outcome for her father's fate was a few years in a slave labor camp. He was lying. Bondarenko also told Sara that Bogdan had implicated himself too. He said that because her husband had helped the investigation, he probably would spend only a few months in jail. Sara knew that with new power, everything quickly changed. A couple months in jail could become a death sentence. She understood that the commissar was a terrible manipulator and liar. She knew that commissars often complained about overcrowded jails. They arrested more and more men, but they did not release any of the inmates. Sara knew they shot them. She had just lost her mother and father, and she did not want to lose her husband, the father of her two children. She needed to act quickly.

Sara was a quick thinker. She used a form of manipulation: seduction. She opened the buttons on her blouse to show her big breasts. She cried and told the commissar that she was depressed and wanted to talk to somebody. Bondarenko really believed he was able to help her with his ideological bullshit. The commissar himself was brainwashed. He believed that a housekeeper could be in government and make important decisions, and he could be a healer. He thought highly of himself. He was obnoxious and believed in dogmatic blather. He thought communal ideology could make villagers happy.

## Bondarenko in Power

*B*ondarenko acted like Napoleon. He believed he could manipulate Sara so that a rehabilitated Bogdan could be a better husband and a rehabilitated Isaac could be a better father. Without any guilt, he sent villages to slavery. He was not prejudiced against Jews. He actually felt the doctrine liberated Jews and made them equal. He brought Sara to his modest apartment not far from the village jail. She continued to cry. Even though she was from the enemy class, the commissar wanted to accommodate her somehow. He started his manipulation.

Bondarenko was a manipulative baboon. He placed on his table a modest dinner that consisted of vodka, black bread, boiled potatoes, and pickles. He spoke the usual propaganda nonsense and offered vodka to Sara. She did not refuse but drank little. When Bondarenko talked, Sara proposed they drink for different party leaders, and Bondarenko, being dedicated to doctrine, drank to the bottom of the glass. Sara poured him more. Soon Bondarenko's head fell onto the table, and he was sound asleep. Sara helped him to his bed and took the shoes off his feet. She checked the pockets of Bondarenko's jacket and found the keys to the precinct and jail, which were behind the commissar's office. She'd found what she was looking for: she had the keys and wanted to use them. It was a crazy idea, but she hoped it might work. Sara did not have any feelings of guilt for her actions. In fact, she experienced feelings of contempt. She was sure her husband must escape from jail. When she left Bondarenko's apartment, the commissar was still sleeping.

Sara skillfully fooled the egomaniac and did the unimaginable. Driven by love, she acted recklessly. She was a strong young woman who came from strong and adventurous villages. She knew what she had to do. She went to rescue her husband, the father of her children. The police office and jail had only one policeman on guard, who locked himself inside. He was asleep on the couch in the office. No one was guarding the jail. Sara opened the door and came in. She knew the jail because only a couple days ago, she'd been incarcerated with her other relatives. First, she opened the door of the closest cell. She was lucky and immediately found Bogdan, who was alone. She told him to follow her. Then they ran to Bogdan's father. She left keys in the door.

In the killing field, there were not enough men. In the Patriotic War, a lot of males were killed. The females sought out the males. They even paid them for sex. Sara risked her life to save her husband. She wanted her children to have a father. Propaganda talked about women who gave their lives not for their families but for the sake of doctrine. No one spoke about a woman's love for her man. Sara wanted to protect Bogdan. Her risky actions were for the sake of her household. Sara would have given her life for her man.

Commissar Bondorenko did not value her heroic deed. He thought only about himself and his ego. He was a nutcase. He found the keys in the morning, but he did not alert the authorities. He did not send a telegram to police headquarters about the jailbreak. He was not sure what the reaction would be. They might dismiss him as head of the precinct.

# The Red Terror

*I*saac observed that during the red terror, many orphans were in prison. The streets were replenished with unwanted children. The youngsters were a problem. They were not welcome in the killing field. The streets were crowded with a big quantity of stray broods. They were everywhere, and they did not have any social support. They kept their lives afloat through street crime. They attacked and stole from habitants. They fought to control their territory. They hit people with brass knuckles and did a lot of damage with sharp screwdrivers. Homeless children, befouled by the area's sickness of pomposity, survived only by criminality.

The red terror was a product of the dark forces that continued the torture and repression that produced more homeless children. The police did not suppress lawlessness and were useless because the victims of the attacks, well-dressed women, were from an enemy class. Thieves were socially similar to pseudocelestials. Normally, children were supposed to be blessings from God, but in the killing field, they were messengers from hell. The stray children found work on streetcars. There were schools for waifs. Running streetcars were the proudest achievement of areas infected by psychological disease. As a declaration of technical advancement, every city was supposed to have streetcars. They were packed with travelers. Adults taught the strays how to steal watches and pick pockets. The instructions included means of distracting attention and handling their stolen merchandise. They attacked old ladies with big leather purses, snatching the leather straps and running away. Some ladies did not give up their possessions and resisted the snatchers. The snatchers worked in pairs. One young mugger ran next to a woman with a purse. After he knocked her down with his brass knuckles, she could not hold on to the purse anymore. The other mugger took her possessions. The youngsters were the horror of the killing field. They emptied the pockets of pedestrians and victimized dwellers. The biggest achievement of communalists was a military with more than a million soldiers. In the future, the stray children would become heartless members of the military. In underground bunkers, they would torture, torment, and kill. Their goal was to rule the whole biosphere. Most of the world did not recognize right away the danger of the epidemic. The whole societal structure was mortally infected.

During the red terror, stray children, infected by sickness, wanted to copy the adults. To get money, they gathered in packs and attacked children and adults. The children also raped and killed. They acted like scoundrels and were the horror of big cities. The street children played orlyanka and other such games of chance. One of the many popular games required dexterity with a pocketknife. Orlyanka was more popular. The historical roots of orlyanka were interesting. Per *Wikipedia*, orlyanka was "an old gambling game widespread in many countries. The meaning of the game is as follows: toss a coin of any value, and the one who guesses on what side she falls, wins it." Gambling in Aborigin originated in ancient times as an essential sign of commodity and money relations. It did not stop there. The disorderly children gambled after a hard day of stealing and harassing. The communal state had orphanages, but they were worse than torture chambers, and children ran away from them. There were other ways in which collective thinking took care of homeless children. They were incarcerated. In prison, like rogue rats, they attacked, stabbed, bit, and defecated on other prisoners. Many were secretly shot by policemen.

Isaac realized that the ideologists in the killing field knew how to force habitants to act stupidly. After strong brainwashing, the habitants became bacilli carriers of a sickened psychological structure. The side effect of their influence was a different hierarchy of thoughts; reasoning became incomprehensible. The brainwashed habitants followed doctrine that was a stupid imposter of irrational thought. It was similar to the Bible, but instead of Christ, it praised Superior Leader. It closed the way to God and destroyed temples. Spirituality lost importance, and political correctness took its place. In every area, creativity had to be subservient to doctrine. If an idea sounded stupid but was politically correct, the infected supported it. Without any proof, the lackeys of doctrine would declare it valid. The fragment representing political correctness took over the entire brain and requested immolation.

Isaac appreciated that in a business setting, there was always a place for God, and in business, many temples flourished. Contrarily, with fake doctrine, habitants lost their flexibility of thought to the power of insane suggestion. The brainwashed developed a fragment that screened all information according to political precision. The brainwashed structure of one infected other brains. It continuously inseminated other brains with pervasive information. The indoctrinated were supposed have inexplicable guilt if they simply were eating well, had a place to sleep, and were looking out for their health. The doctrine declared that business-oriented habitants were the bourgeoisie. It claimed they had evil prejudices and ultimately connected them with antirevolutionaries. The ideologists claimed that aristocrats hated the bourgeoisie, which was not completely correct. When an aristocrat spoke with contempt about business-oriented individuals, it was different.

Aristocrats were wealthy habitants with refined manners who disliked the new rich and their clumsy interactions. The goons, on the other hand, did not have any right to criticize the business-oriented. In every country, the bourgeoisie were the middle class. If a nation wanted to prosper, it needed to improve its middle class. Goons were not able to replace the bourgeoisie. Along with the upper class, the disease killed the middle class. As a result, homeless children were everywhere. They were the bitches of the new society, spreading trouble, mockery, and filth. The idealists babbled about fairness and equality. Those words broke the defense of tough men to follow infected dogma. Women were different. To survive, women learned to be brevier because they knew their own strength. At worst, they could improve their security with sex. Some, desperate and weak, were without work and food. They abandoned their children. In a time of turbulence, children were a problem for their parents because the responsibility of having children was too much to handle. Parents, ruined by disease, did not want to know what happened to their children.

## The Brainwashed Objects

Isaac sensed that the objects of brainwashing were under tremendous stress. Because the ideas were weak, the propagandists put a lot of pressure on the subject and did not take no for an answer. They forced habitants to declare allegiance to the killing doctrine. To prove their nonsense, they provided untested suggestions based on their own fantasies. For commissars, convincing others became a goal and a way to prove their own strength. The function of the illness was to infect as many habitants as possible. The infected felt better about themselves when they infected others. Seeing the results of their actions was a big benefit for them. It appeared they felt better when around others who were just as stupid as they were.

Isaac reported that the land was fouled by a curse. It had the inescapable signs of a repressive regime. It denied that business-oriented habitants had talent that could be considered equivalent to the gifts of art, music, and engineering. The regime declared that business-oriented people were thieves. The social hierarchy was built on subordination, just like in the criminal system. Kingpins controlled all sections of that construction. One of the pervasive suggestions was that hardworking, uneducated people could easily replace the educated. The facts did not prove that hypothesis. Facts showed there would be a dead end in implementing their plans, but ideologists did not care about evidence.

The indoctrinated region showed an inability to achieve anything useful. It was deceived by the glorification and cover-up of poor results. There were habitants who talked about the benefits of the communal structure. They denied the undeniable. Without business orientation, it was difficult to manage a successful business. It was difficult to determine priorities and decide what needed immediate attention. Without business-orientated habitants, a big layer of bureaucrats was created. They spent long hours formulating plans and doing a lot of paperwork but were not able to accomplish anything. Their work was not productive and was, in fact, destructive. The communal setting was afraid of innovation. If, God forbid, something went wrong, they were not able to fix it. The top of the bureaucracy was corrupt. It functioned based on nepotism, cronyism, and favoritism. The side effect of perdition of sanity was confused thinking.

Isaac realized that the plague-ridden terrain was inseminating the brainwashed habitants with a utopic political structure. When the brainwashing grew weaker, the programming became more pervasive. It provided many ridiculous suggestions. Poison had damaged the whole structure of brainwashed habitants. The hierarchy of thoughts was erroneously reprogrammed. First, it affected the side of the brain that cataloged information. As a result, the infected continued to repeat the same nonsense and misinterpreted the past. In a brain damaged by ruination, the exactness of dogmatic blabbering became more important than anything else. Every area of a brainwashed mind was subservient to the mutual. It was driven by dogma. If something supported the political schemata, it accepted any new modifications as valid. The fragment representing political correctness controlled the entire brain. The conditioned zombie completely lost flexibility. The brainwashing spread and controlled all information. The damaged brain persuaded all the other habitants to copy it. The contagious damnation injured all other minds in its surroundings.

## Fate of Bogdan

As soon as empty-headed Bogdan got away from the place of indoctrination, he eventually understood what he had done. He started crying. He already knew that his mother-in-law, Fay, was dead and that Isaac had been sent to Bobruisk. From jail, he and his wife ran to his father's house. The old man, Maxim, understood the extraordinary significance of the moment. The old blacksmith saw that his son was crying and understood that with the help of his wife, his son had escaped from jail. The old man helped them but not before saying a few words. He said, "What a terrible thing you have done! Yes, I did not like what Isaac was doing. But everything he did, he did by risking his own life. He never took anything from others. The police had no right to torture, humiliate, and detain villagers for being rich. By taking wealth from others by force, they could not make life more just. They could have helped the deprived with different tactics. They could have helped the poor to acquire better skills in order to be more successful."

Bogdan continued crying. He listened and understood the extent of his deeds. Eventually, he recognized that nothing could be changed. Bogdan also looked upon his wife. She did not say anything, but he knew she was with him. She stood by her man.

## A Tense Situation

*T*he situation was tense. Bogdan realized what he had done by betraying his father-in-law and felt remorseful. He understood that it was not the time to talk because they had to leave his father's home as soon as possible before Bondarenko found them. There was no time for apologies. He also knew that Sara stayed by him despite the fact that because of his stupidity, Sara's mother was dead, and her father was in jail. He also knew that he would never forgive himself for being brainwashed. He was sorry for all the terrible things he had done.

The red terror was simple: it enslaved citizens' insights and spread its influence to other countries through military intimidation. A big military displayed nationalistic pride. Collectivist thinking was militarized and made the killing field into a huge barrack. The infection stirred the sleepy lives in the Village of Pine Trees. Some habitants were temporarily radicalized by doctrine, whereas others were not changed for a longer period of time. The radicalization of villagers was performed through adulteration by poisonous ideas. It was similar to radicalization by religious extremists. Because the climate was criminal, Bondarenko acted as a bandit and liar. He did not respect any rules, internal or external. He did not like fairness. Infected terrain did not act as other big industrial powers did. The diseased acted as if they were entitled to get everything for free.

There were villagers in the killing field who hid themselves from the authorities. It was not easy. Bogdan and Sara understood that they would be like them. They knew they might be on the run for a long time. They took with them only their children. They could not be responsible for Sara's brother and sister. Sara needed to decide what to do with Aaron and Rivka. Since the police had closed off Isaac's house, Isaac's children stayed with Sara, but she could not take them on the run. Isaac's children were too little, and they did not have any reason to run away. She decided that Sara's little brother, Aaron, and her little sister, Rivka, would stay in the Village of Pine Trees for a short time. Bogdan's father, Maxim, agreed to take care of them. Later, he would send Aaron to his older brother, Rudi, in a gorgeous city, while Rivka would go to Greben, the capital of Malantia, where her uncle Ben lived.

Bogdan's father agreed to take them by horse-drawn carriage to the Bobruisk train station. Bogdan was sure his blacksmith profession and the knowledge of watch repair he had learned from Isaac would help him to provide for his family everywhere. Bogdan and Sara packed their and their children's belongings. They decided to go south to the Caucasus Mountains. They'd heard about the city of Baku on the Caspian Sea. Maxim bought train tickets for them, and they headed southeast to Baku, the capital of Azerbaijan, where the Azeris, Turkish-speaking people, lived. The new language was not an issue. For the family, the most important thing was to be together and safe. Maxim wished them luck. He secretly crossed himself.

Bondarenko felt that a belief in God was a dangerous uniting force. His main goal was to separate habitants from everything decent. He was part of the red terror that moved cattle cars with slaves in all directions. He called God an opiate for the villagers. He promoted complete isolation. He fabricated myths of many enormous giants that plotted against infected land. Bondarenko declared that most farmers did not believe in doctrine because they were religious fanatics. He invented fictitious horror stories of being persecuted by internal and external forces. He placed blame on everyone for everything imaginable. As result, life in villages came down to the primitive relationship of master and slave. The population of the villages became downtrodden, acting as morons. Villagers were watched by informers and intimidated by the police.

In the meantime, the leaders became deeply paranoid. Policemen incarcerated anyone who had the guts to speak his or her opinion that the killing field had a problem. The population needed a Moses to liberate them, but he somehow was late. Without belief in God, the land was struck by lawlessness and mayhem. The red terror destroyed businesses, as only business orientation and the acquisition of business skills could resist the evil notions of theft and violence. To flourish, a business-oriented life required justice, freedom, and human rights. It did not participate in stealing wealth by force or disrespecting others for money. The violent people were soldiers and fighters. In fact, real business mainly created wealth based on respect for innovations and the law. It relied on a unified psyche and the resistance of splitting by psychological sickness.

## The Structure of Polytheism

The infected built a structure of polytheism that was associated with slavery. In that structure, the masses could not understand what was going on in their surroundings. The basis for polytheism was a belief in many gods. Ideologists labeled their leaders, who were basically baboons, as heroes devoted to ideology. The citizens were brain-dead, beaten by ambivalence and confusion.

The biggest functions of Aborigin were infecting the military force and creating droves of slaves. Supreme Leader also built many demons. The atmosphere of fear and uncertainty split minds, which was helpful to the regression created by unqualified managers. The ordinary habitants lost their ability to analyze reality. They accepted a regime that was a gathering of imbeciles. The days were driven by stultification from poorly educated rulers who lacked sophistication and wanted to achieve something primitive. Slavery was dragged out from the past. The red terror was a step back toward primitivism. It was not a step forward toward the advancement of society. As with all primitive organizations, the pseudocollective relied on the military. All their relations with neighboring countries were built on confrontation and military domination.

Communalism disorganized minds by presenting the puppets of the regime as fighters of demons. It preached polytheism by allowing different supreme leaders to act as gods. Contrary to the pseudocommunalists' dogma, monotheism believed in one God, and it united habitants with humanistic ideas. For infected rulers, it was dangerous. They unleashed a wind of persecution and incarcerated many who believed in God. The propagandists' rhetoric replaced the meaning of God. Leaders also understood that only idiots could believe in their fairy tales, so they unleashed the red terror on the whole population. The masses were demoralized and broken. The stump orators used manipulation and confrontation. They were against a monotheistic structure wherein habitants believed only in one God associated with love. God's love had humanistic inspirations. God promoted a desire for justice.

For divine reason, God did not make everyone equal, and some habitants had more talent than others. The world was ready for competition. Ideologists were attempting to prove that the scriptures were wrong. The notion of the fake doctrine was based on vigilant resistance to the creation. The ideologists forcefully promoted their view. They went backward in history and quickly recreated an inquisition. They implemented the same attitude for punishment. Agitators, infected by psychological illness, were liars. They covered up lawlessness and rampages with inflammatory phraseology. Habitants were encouraged to sacrifice their lives for crooked doctrine. Ideologists proclaimed that they were doing positive work and cleaning the world of the socially undesirable. They were sneaky and shamelessly misled the masses. A belief in God was not acceptable. It did not match the doctrine of "fairness". They fought unfairness, meaning they punished habitants who had any talents.

Commissar Bondarenko was as big as Napoleon in the Village of Pine Trees. He was a nut and followed stupid principles. He felt he had knowledge of the incontrovertible truths of life. He was primitive and believed that everything in life was entirely black and white. He had power in his hands. He decided who lived or died. He knew that for his brutality, he would not experience any penance or punishment. He was free to do whatever he wanted. He also was a manipulative goat and sadist. He did not discharge Bogdan from jail and told him that the town activists would decide Bogdan's fate.

## The Diamonds of the Kolyma River

Professor Kryvoruchko stated that Kolyma was a place of suffering. The pseudocollective was active in the development of the northern territories and was looking for placers of diamonds. Life was harsh. It was difficult to survive working in the diamond quarries. In wintertime, the temperature dropped below fifty degrees centigrade. Prisoners had little food and were starving. One night, a sleeping bear came close to the prisoners. The prisoners attacked it with ice picks. They killed the bear, jumped on it, and tore the bear to pieces. They ate raw pieces of its meat with fresh blood. The hungry prisoners ate the symbol of Aborigin, the bear.

Because of Isaac's ability to take risks, he had special relationships with prisoners and guards. Being a wise man, he had a high status with a lot of privileges. He stole diamonds and hid them in his clothes. It was a rule that the guards shot anyone caught taking stones out of the quarry. Not many had the courage to take diamonds. Isaac took a tremendous risk, but he was an experienced smuggler. He knew how to hide diamonds. Because of his status, the guards did not search him as thoroughly as they did others. Everyone wanted to do favors for him. He showed everyone that he remembered any favors. He rewarded and repaid all of them lavishly. He skillfully used his knowledge of diamonds and his intuition to find them. He also used the stolen rocks to bribe and get favors. He did not think much about his ability to be a giver, but others knew and valued his giving. By giving gifts, he was able to get others on his side. He did not think twice about how to get gifts. They just came to him naturally. He won them by playing cards.

Most importantly, Isaac did not keep those gifts for himself. Isaac's eyes were looking for something more important. He looked toward the possibility of getting his freedom. He knew that his plan was risky. He would be burned badly if something went wrong. He shared his plan only with his noblewoman, Glasha, whom he'd saved from prostitution. She was his confidante.

In Kolyma, Isaac could survive for a while. Around him, habitants died like flies on sticky paper. He was not sure how much more time he had; in a moment, everything could change. He planned an escape. He had someone to trust. Glasha was a perfect companion. She was honest and was his fiduciary. She had a daughter, who was waiting for her help. To go ahead with their plan, Isaac and Glasha pretended a lot. They were like small rabbits among predators. The difference was that Isaac was a skilled player. He created workarounds for many treacherous traps, even more than he needed. His strategy was working. The rabbit was able to confuse the pursuers.

Isaac had inherited his IQ. It was not possible to drink it away or lose it. He was a good cards player and a skillful designer of cunning schemes. Eventually, he came up with a clear plan for escape. His plan required preparation. To avoid any surprises, he took care of every detail. He made an effort to foresee every possible outcome. The doctor would attest that Isaac and Glasha were dead. Isaac and Glasha would be in cadaver bags taken out of the camp. Isaac had already bribed the driver of the truck, who would take them to a ferry. A calligrapher was working on producing fake papers for him and Glasha. They had special tailor-made bags for adamants, which they could attach to their bodies. Isaac dried some bread he'd won by playing cards and stashed it in a hidden place. He also stashed clothes he'd won. A carpenter made two dummies resembling human bodies. Isaac would put in them his and Glasha's clothes and then bury in the mass grave. Between other remains would be their clothes, tagged with their names. In the event of exhumation, the wood would rot the prisoners' clothes would prove their death. In case something went wrong, Isaac bribed the camp ruler, a powerful colonel, in advance, even if he did not know for what purpose he got the gifts.

The truck driver drove them to the ferryboat. They got

onto the boat using false papers. Isaac was counting every detail. He was constantly improving his plan.

Isaac was genetically business-oriented. In the past, he'd done all his projects well. He was a good card and chess player. He also had completed elementary Jewish school, in which children were taught to read the Torah and other books in Hebrew. He read books in different languages, including the communalists' language, Yiddish, and Hebrew. He was, by his nature, a game player and had a sharp mind. Now he was facing the biggest game of his life.

Thus, he helped a noblewoman by blood and upbringing to survive. Later, he would help Glasha's daughter and his own children have a better life. He did not know yet that in the future, he would marry Glasha and live with her for many happy years. He was born to be a winner and Sailor.

## Way to Freedom, Part 2: Lies in the Killing Field

*I*saac and Glasha ended up at a train station. They had millions in diamonds, but they did not have any real money. In the daytime, Glasha hid the diamonds on her body. Isaac helped passengers with heavy trunks, baggage, and suitcases. He was physically strong and carried a lot of serious loads. He never asked for money but accepted everything given to him. With his earned money, he bought a heavy belt and a white apron to look like a hauler. All baggage carriers wore white aprons for visibility. He would work all day, and at the end of the day, he would go to the public bath, which was close to the train station. Isaac or Glasha alternately kept the stones. Isaac would go to the bath first, and then Glasha would go. They looked clean to avoid any suspicion. They would eat the cheapest food they could find or just a piece of bread. With the rest of the money, they would buy two tickets on the train to go as far south as possible. They traveled at night and slept on the train. They avoided talking. If somebody asked them something, they would answer. They said they were on their way to visit their children. Railroad controllers did not look at the correctness of passengers' papers but merely made sure the passengers had them. Isaac was not afraid to show his papers to them. Isaac and Glasha knew they were not on the list of those who were wanted. On the train, they were an ordinary couple. They tried to relax. In the would-be collective, everything was fake. To survive, everyone had to lie. One who could not lie died. Glasha easily talked to everyone. In advance, they had prepared answers to every question. They did not stir any interest. They even had an old suitcase in which they'd placed their cheap clothes.

Isaac and Glasha looked as primitive as possible. They came from the north and knew many heartbreaking stories of men and women pulled out from families because they were smarter and uninfected. The best minds were in Kolyma, including businessmen, scientists and specialists in genetics, psychologists, and educators. They were badly dressed and, in the cold water, digging for diamonds and gold. At the cost of their lives, they kept ailing pseudocommunalists protected from contagion and extinction. For a hamlet of morons filthy with the toxins of desperation, the price of losing the best minds was high. As a result, the hamlet was ruled by imbeciles.

Primitivism flourished. Many uninfected families were talented, and the would-be collective was breaking them apart. Top scientists, entertainers, and the ordinary uninfected by disease were sent to the north. They were the casualties who lost their lives to find gems. Because only the diamonds were real, slaves looked for them and died in harsh weather. The strongest might stay alive for a year, but they would raise a lot of money for the Prolet-Aryan cause. The gems, the fruits of lost lives, possessed a beauty that had been revered by countless admirers for many centuries. They were produced by slaves who did not have any rights and were already dead meat.

The diamonds and gold were sold to the West and kept the thought-altering bug in power. Celestials and terrestrials were infected. The diamond trade allowed celestials who preached doctrine to brainwash terrestrials they had advanced. Celestials enjoyed private movie theaters in their summer cottages. They watched Hollywood movies and enjoyed many privileges. No one knew how many diamonds were sold to the West and the Middle East to support lavish lifestyles and the hierarchy of slavery. The diamonds sponsored the stupid projects of deadhead rulers. The jewels of Kolyma paid for the many wars of liberation in banana republics. They bought collaboration in politics and sport.

Isaac and Glasha had a treasury and kept it a secret. In several weeks, they ended up in Bazar, in the city of Baku, the capital of Azerbaijan. There, habitants did not know well the indoctrinate ideology, and ideologists did not like them. The celestials called them donkeys. The smart man, Isaac, was surviving. He took charge and helped Glasha. They were wandering souls. They got to the southern border of the would-be collective. Contrary to the ideologists, Isaac and Glasha loved the city and wanted to stay there. Bazar smelled of Middle Eastern spices and juicy fruits. The would-be collective created a negative stigma around Bazar in Baku. According to ideologists, it attracted self-centered people who had low inspiration and were concerned only with their own lives. In reality, Bazar was a magnificent place where the uninfected learned sophisticated ways to resist the control of the would-be collective. They pretended to be stupid and too dim to learn doctrine and avoided punishment from indoctrinate celestials. In Bazar, the uninfected Azeris used their hands and spoke loudly in the Turkish language. They used donkeys everywhere.

Isaac felt at home because he knew how Bazar was structured. He right away found a few uninfected who spoke Yiddish. He started gathering information. Everyone who talked to him saw just a middle-aged man in wrinkled clothes; he did not create any suspicion. No one in Bazar looked at his papers. He got situated quickly. He knew how to repair watches and got a job right away. For him, the bazaar was a marvelous place. There he could buy everything, including juicy fruits, cheeses, smoked fish, and meat. The old aristocrats sold vintage porcelain, crystal, and silver. There were Persian rugs, silk, different clothes, linens, and watches. Bazar was a settlement in the killing field. It was an oasis of the old time. It had a sovereign rhythm and a different ideology. Despite informers and bullies, Bazar was far away from indoctrinate ideology. Many business-oriented individuals had found refuge in Bazar. They lived by different norms that were not affected by doctrines.

## The Bazaar in Baku

The bazaar could not have been imagined without Armenians who were business-oriented, sociable, and uninfected. They were able to do things that were difficult or impossible for others to do. They were friendly and did not ask many questions. They were family-oriented and masters of barbecue. They invited Isaac and Glasha to a barbecue of sturgeon. When Isaac made money, through his Armenian friend, he got clean papers for himself and Glasha. The authentic papers used his and Glasha's real first names but different last names and birthplaces.

Isaac told the Armenian a fictitious story. He said he needed the new papers to avoid paying alimony to his demanding wife. Isaac's story was not a complete fabrication because Kolyma was worse than any demanding wife. In his story, Glasha had had an opportunity to get away from a jealous and abusive husband. Armenians were trustful and companionate. They understood what love really meant and were happy to help.

As soon as Isaac received genuine papers, his thoughts were about his children. Glasha also had a daughter in an orphanage in one of the cities of the would-be collective. She wanted to see her, so they changed their image. Their behavior and attitude had transformed because of their time spent in prison as slaves. For many in prison, their old lives ended. They started new lives as prisoners. As a result, they forgot their past when they were free. Isaac and Glasha were affected by life in prison, where their daily lives were a hair's breadth from death. In Bazar, they adjusted their behavior and looked different. They did not appear like the new generation of rulers in leather jackets and chrome boots. The women wore chintzy scarves. Isaac had three-piece suits, and Glasha had clothes of dim colors. He bought Glasha new shoes and a new fur coat. Isaac purchased a fashionable coat and a men's fedora. They had a nice look, mannered and classic. Isaac was perceived as a respectable man. In reality, it was true. He was a millionaire.

In his possession was a bag filled with the highest-quality diamonds. Isaac understood that in time, he would sell some of his treasure. He was looking forward to meeting a buyer for his treasure. He and Glasha were congenial actors. Isaac and Glasha completely changed their appearance. They were different from those who were in prison and had stamps on them. It was hard for them to portray the ones whose behavior they'd forgotten. They also had a goal. Isaac and Glasha played the roles of individuals who never had been in prison. They did their best. Isaac needed a rich buyer.

The would-be collective was a big monster that extended its tentacles all over the world. It had grand imperial ambitions and did not care about individuals. In the big would-be collective, Baku was only one cosmopolitan city where escapees could rebuild their lives. One day Isaac was working in the bazaar, when he saw his son-in-law, Bogdan, who was buying fruit. Isaac was a fugitive and never had dreamed he'd see his family. He did not believe his eyes. He had increased heart palpitations and felt a shortness of breath. If Bogdan was there, then his daughter Sara and other children were in Baku as well. Isaac was cautious. Bogdan had betrayed him once. His son-in-law, whom he'd trusted, had told the commissars about his hidden gold and caused his arrest and transport to Kolyma.

Isaac followed his son-in-law and found out the place where he lived. After Bogdan went into the house, Isaac waited. He could trust his daughter, so he was waiting for her. In a little while, his daughter came out. Isaac moved closer to his daughter. She saw her father, but she couldn't believe her eyes and could not say anything. She felt a choking sensation in her throat. "Papa, how did you get here?" she whispered.

When he saw that his daughter was on the verge of crying, Isaac asked her, "Where can we talk?" In the pseudocollective, the uninfected did not have a lot of meetings, but that meeting was exceptionally unusual. It was a meeting that unified wandering souls. Such a thing happened rarely, but when it took place, it changed lives. For Isaac, the meeting gave him a new meaning of life. Escapees from the iron arms of the poison of the ideological virus had met in Baku.

## Real Dialogue

*T*he dialogue happened after a genuine meeting. Sara said that not far away was Upland English Park, which was on a hill. There they could talk freely because at that time of the day, there were not many habitants at the park. She said she needed to pick up her children from school, and then she would come to the park.

Isaac's heart pumped strongly in anticipation of something fantastic. It was a miracle that he was near his daughter. He almost fell to the ground. He couldn't believe he could see his daughter and grandchildren again.

Sara went into her house, and soon she came out. In her hand was a bag containing pies and milk. Isaac and Sara took the funicular to the park on the top of the hill. In the park, they hugged. Sara was crying. She stated that until then, she had not understood what had happened with Bogdan. What he had done was unexplainable and cruel. She said he'd not been thinking clearly or considered the consequences of his actions. He had not done it to save his life. He'd been brainwashed. Now he was stricken by guilt. Sara said that Commissar Bondarenko had brainwashed Bogdan to betray his father-in-law. Nevertheless, Bogdan had had a hard time too. Like his father-in-law, he'd been in jail but had been able to escape. They'd become runaways. Sara also mentioned that she and Bogdan were fugitives and lived under different names. She also informed her father about his younger children, Aaron and Rivka, and assured him they were well. Isaac told her about his situation and said he was in town with Glasha, his common-law wife. They talked in Yiddish so the patrons of the park would not understand them.

The ideal dialogue between father and daughter was not affected by language. The prerequisite for dialogue was a genuine meeting. The father and daughter did not just meet physically; it was a meeting of their souls. In many lives, dialogues did not happen often. When they happened, they healed the mind and gave the participants strength to continue with their destinies. Between Isaac and Sara was a real meeting with genuine dialogue.

Isaac did not want revenge or display any aggression or desire to punish others for his suffering. He was overwhelmed with a feeling of joy. Sara reassured Isaac that he was safe. She invited Isaac and Glasha to dinner. She explained that the family lived in a hostel with fifteen neighbors. She told Bogdan about their meeting. He was shaky and numb. He cried for forgiveness.

The pseudocelestial rulers of the false collective were known for their confrontations, irreconcilability, and vigilance. The illness of the homeland created an atmosphere of suspicion, confusion, and despair. The native land was a big prison. It was not a place for forgiveness, and everyone was guilty of something. The false structure was built on the view that the poor were victimized. It emphasized that the world owned them. It cried for vengeance. Isaac did not want vengeance.

When Isaac and Glasha came to dinner, they saw a big dark corridor with many doors in a communal setting. Every door led to overcrowded rooms. One of the doors led to his daughter's room. When Isaac and Glasha entered the room, Bogdan came down on his knees and asked for forgiveness. Few could learn from their mistakes if they were not die-hard radicals. Bogdan had been brainwashed by a powerful commissar. He was honest and naive. He'd listened to the flammable slogans of the red propagandist. As soon as he'd gotten away from the producer of radicalization, he'd understood his mistake. He was crying. He knew he'd been wrong in implicating his father-in-law. He was broken with feelings of guilt.

Isaac recognized that Bogdan was the true love of his daughter. He was a loving father of his children. During their meeting, Isaac only saw the happy face of his daughter. His bitterness washed away, and his anger left. He forgave his son-in-law. They ate as a family. Isaac understood that life was short, and the family was more important than anything else. He stopped blaming his son-in-law. As a result of all the terrible vicissitudes of his life, Isaac became sager. Isaac and Glasha were fugitives from a big prison camp. Fortunately for him, Isaac had taken a little bag with the best diamonds from the Kolyma River. He hugged his family.

Isaac was able to understand that his son-in-law had been brainwashed. Forgiveness made him a wiser man. He agreed that an indoctrinated young man was weak but not guilty. The system of so-called fairness that allowed goons to humiliate, rob, and kill was responsible. Isaac and Glasha had been saved because God Almighty worked in mysterious ways. Good things began to happen. Isaac and Glasha had escaped from Kolyma. Sara and Bogdan had escaped too. The runaways from injustice had accidentally met in Baku. The meeting of father and daughter was dramatic. Isaac, Glasha, Sara, and Bogdan talked about the terrible fates of the business-oriented and uninfected. Idiotic doctrine increasingly justified atrocities.

## The Vicious Collective

When Isaac met his daughter, he was emotional. Glasha saw that he was overwhelmed and was silent. Her thoughts were with her daughter who was in an orphanage in Byelogoria. Now that she had escaped the labor camp, all her thoughts were about her daughter. She grieved the horrible fates of her husband and mother, who'd belonged to the aristocracy. Both had been killed by the false collective state. She shared her thoughts only with Isaac, the man she trusted. They'd met in Kolyma, where many were like animals and would kill others for a piece of bread. She'd found her man. The false collective was vicious to him. It did not want him to have a good life. He decided to change the trend of misery for his family. Isaac was a gambler, and he carefully planned his bets.

The fortuitous meeting with his family uplifted him. Now Isaac had a strong desire to help Glasha. He was ready. She was now a big part of his life. He came up with a plan for how to help her. For his games, Isaac liked to use a systematic approach. First, he wanted to find an Azeri who could help him find a wealthy diamond lover in order to sell his product.

He needed money. He decided to sell his first diamond. He was fortunate that he had the means to reverse their terrible fate. If he was not careful, his desire to have a good life for his family might bring problems. It could jeopardize his freedom. For now, the situation was stable. According to their new documents, Isaac and Glasha were Azeris, native Azerbaijanis. They needed to learn the Turkish language, the native language of Azeris. Isaac mainly spoke Yiddish and Aborigin, the main language of the communalists. Glasha spoke Aborigin and German, which was close to Yiddish, so they understood each other. Sara and Bogdan already spoke some Turkish. The neighbors called Sara, in the Turkish language, Saria Khanum.

At that point, Isaac decided to sell one of the diamonds. He knew that only someone who understood diamonds could appreciate their quality. Isaac looked forward to having rich customers because he had diamonds of high quality. He respected hardworking habitants and those uninfected by emotional illness, but he asked for good money for his product, so he also understood that only a rich person could satisfy his demand. To be a diamond lover and collector, someone needed to be on another economic level.

Isaac thought about his son-in-law. Bogdan knew someone who was connected to diamond lovers. Isaac was business-oriented, and he believed those who stumbled were capable of learning from their mistakes. In business, many made mistakes and lost everything. Then they learned from their mistakes and got rich again. Isaac believed that his son-in-law deserved a second chance. Isaac was not disappointed. His son-in-law had changed. He understood that he'd been influenced by the dull indoctrinate ideology of grandiosity. He'd become immune to brainwashing. Isaac decided to accept Bogdan's help.

The official propaganda of the false collective was quick to blame. It repeated the lie that because of enemies, the poor pseudocollective was suffering. The propagandists stated that sacrifices were needed for a rich future. They insisted that before becoming rich, it was normal to be in distress. Everything was a lie. Only morons could believe in fairy tales. Without luck, the poor would not get rich. In spite of that demagogy, inside the collective, the rich and uninfected continued to exist. They kept their status regardless of the red bug's infection. They existed in the government of the false collective. There were a few sanctuaries of rich habitants surrounded by morons. In terrain made unclean by the individuality-destroying infection, there were habitants looking forward to investing in diamonds. In a time of uncertainty about the future, the wealthy understood that the brilliant could easily hide. No one had trust in communalist money. Only diamonds could provide help to survive the troubles. But to be rich was dangerous. In the domain of morons, those dirty with thought-altering disease believed everyone should be poor. The uninfected with means lived in a separate cycle. Bogdan had a connection. He worked as a jeweler for

Ahmed, a business-oriented Azeri who had an unregistered little shop for jobbing jewelry. Ahmed was connected to the rich. He was short, slim, and fast. He did not waste any time. He was quick and knew many habitants.

Ahmed made his living by faking jewelry to look as if it were old and done by famous masters. He had in his possession markers of old masters and could fill them with the different products. He had good gold markers and attracted customers who loved old jewelry. Ahmed was not a poor man, but he was not a purchaser for Isaac's diamonds. For Isaac, it did not matter who the buyer was. Ahmed had a different quality. He knew a few rich connoisseurs. In terrain made unclean by the individuality-destroying infection, his connections were valuable. It was not easy to come within reach of rich uninfected habitants. It was challenging and almost unmanageable to get close to them.

Through Ahmed, Isaac gained passage to a circle of diamond lovers. The rich had different relations in business. They trusted their associates and did not expect any betrayals. They also paid for protection. It was a necessity to have go-betweens. Among the rich, *trust* was a big word. The rich, as was the case with many others, had difficulty in recognizing and avoiding informers. To be safe, the uninfected did not let newcomers get closer. They knew each other from childhood. When the rich habitants saw someone dubious, they kept themselves far away. They were cautious of finks and snitches. They lived in secluded communities. They enjoyed their trusted neighbors and felt safe. They bought dachas in close proximity.

The world of diamonds was different because morons did not understand it. Not even all of the business-oriented found beauty in diamonds. Few appreciated them and got excited. As connoisseurs of diamonds, they were far from the slogans of the false collective. They were in a world where special colors, shapes, and weight resided. Counterfeit diamonds and quality diamonds had different customers. The doctrine of the false collective rejected comfort and promoted an ascetic style of living. That did not work for the rich, who could not kill the desire to live better. The rich customers wanted a sure thing. They did not want any counterfeits and trusted the go-between.

Bogdan introduced Isaac to his boss, Ahmed. Bogdan told Ahmed that his friend wanted to sell a diamond. Isaac retrieved one of the adamants from a hidden place. Because he'd learned to trust Glasha with his life, only she knew the location of the gems. Ahmed recognized that Isaac would not sell it cheap. In front of him was a man who knew his goods and was looking for a serious buyer. Ahmed knew that in the transaction, he could have a good commission. Challenged to increase value and avoid suspicion, he wanted to sell diamond as a complete product. He would choose a gold ring, and Bogdan could work on the jewelry. He decided to frame the diamond and mount it in a gold ring.

Ahmed calculated the commission he could get. He also knew that he would get commissions from both sides. He was looking forward to making a sale. He negotiated his cut in the commission. The diamond was big and clean. It had a halo around and a long crest in the middle of its back. It had exceptionally bright color. Those kinds of nuggets were called *yakutat*.

A connection existed between uninfected habitants. Ahmed already knew to whom he could sell the diamond. He had in mind a talented and famous doctor, Ali. Isaac knew the market and how much the asking price was for that kind of diamond. All his life, he'd bought and sold diamonds. He knew the price of his rock was high and asked modestly. He needed money quickly. He decided he would use the money to save Glasha's daughter. With the money left over, he would buy a better living space for his daughter Sara and her family. He did not feel any regret about selling his treasure. For him, money was not a problem. He always had money. He believed he would always have it in the future. With his diamonds, he was rich. He was sure that without diamonds, he would be rich anyway. He would use the different opportunities that life offered. He would be wealthy no matter where he lived.

Dr. Ali Zeitiev was an intelligent diamond lover, a business-oriented person, and a rich man. Those kinds of characters could survive only in Baku. In the past, deals between businesses-oriented parties had been pleasant. Baku was a dream city for business. Dr. Ali worked with a cardiograph, interpreted cardiograms, and could diagnose different maladies and find treatment with the specific placement of electrodes. As a young man, he'd lived in Holland and studied cardiology. He knew the work of Dutch doctor and physiologist Willem Einthoven, who'd lived from May 21, 1860, to September 29, 1927. In 1903, Dr. Einthoven had invented the first practical cardiograph: the electrocardiogram, or ECG or EKG. In 1924, he'd received the Nobel Prize for Medicine.

Dr. Ali went further in using the electrocardiogram. He used it to find locations to administer electroshocks. He put electrodes on different parts of the body to locate the weak spots. He had tremendous success. There was a rumor that he even reanimated the dead. Dr. Einthoven had done his work for free. Dr. Ali cured many, but he did not work for free. He was not a saint, just a gifted doctor.

He was paid handsomely for his discovery. Otherwise, the patient had to go to a regular hospital. Somehow, Ahmed was a distant relative of Dr. Ali.

Ahmed trusted Isaac, whom his employee Bogdan recommended. He respected the proposed condition for selling the diamond. Isaac would discuss the price directly with the buyer. Isaac's request was reasonable. Ahmed was sure he would receive his commissions. Ahmed told the good doctor about the gem and negotiated the commission. Dr. Ali was an intelligent and voracious man. He understood that not all habitants were infected by psychological germs. When the doctor met Isaac, he somehow knew that Isaac was real and that his diamond was real. He did not care how the diamond had come into Isaac's possession. He simply knew he could have faith in that man. It was an intuitive connection. He could not explain it. He recognized that the man in front of him had a unique psychological structure and was not capable of deception.

Business-oriented habitants were uninfected by psychological illness and did business without quarreling. When Dr. Ali saw the diamond, his heart palpitated, and he fell in love with the beautiful jewel. He trusted that the diamond was uncontaminated and not sought by police and that the transaction was clean. He also understood that the price was reasonable. After little mediation, he paid the asking price. Both were satisfied with their deal. Dr. Ali also mentioned that if Isaac had more diamonds, he should come to him and not to others. With appreciation, Isaac paid commission to Ahmed. He understood that he'd gotten in touch with a serious connoisseur who was well connected in society and understood diamonds. Dr. Ali was pleased with his purchase. He mentioned that he played cards with his friends every week at his house and said Isaac was welcome to join them. It was an unexpected development and required an adjustment in Isaac's plans.

## Isaac Played Cards

Isaac had played cards with thieves and bandits in places of sickness and dirt. The new partners at the table were clean, educated, wealthy, and uninfected by psychological disease. He knew he must watch what he said in order to avoid language that came from prison. He also wanted to make contacts for the future, as the uninfected could be useful. Being with the affluent was more difficult. They had thin skin. The most important task in dealing with them was not to offend them.

Isaac helped Glasha's daughter. He used the best of his abilities. The smart and capable had a responsibility to take care of children. The game of liberation was not easy. When Isaac was playing cards at Dr. Ali's house, he met several of Dr. Ali's friends. One was a Russian who worked for the health department. Isaac focused on the Russian, who lost a significant amount of money to Isaac. To start negotiations, Isaac returned the money and then asked for a favor. He mentioned that the daughter of his distant relative was in the Byelogorian orphanage, which was under the supervision of state security. He asked the Russian if the girl, based on concerns for her health, could be released from the orphanage to distant relatives. His new acquaintance stated that he never had done anything similar. He proposed that the request should be sent to

Byelogoria from the health department of the whole false collective. He mentioned that his boss had a big roof in the health department of the false collective, meaning his boss had someone above him whom he paid for protection. The Russian promised to talk to his boss.

Isaac was not naive. He knew how the minds of blabbers in government offices worked. He predicted what he should do. To liberate Glasha's daughter, he needed to pay. In the false collective, chains of payoffs were everywhere. Officials paid higher-level bosses for protection. Positions were given not for professional quality but through bribery and friendships. Behind the inflammatory speeches of the ideologists emphasizing the importance of sacrificing life for a beautiful future, there was a primitive desire to have less stress and live comfortably. The higher positions offered an opportunity to have less stress and a better life. It was no secret that bribery was the main key to having a good life. Corruption existed on every level. Everyone wanted a sweetener. Isaac used all available passages for his game. The largest trump card under his sleeve was the habitants who could do jobs. He planned to use them for different playoffs. He was a mastermind in a successful effort to liberate Galena, Glasha's daughter. Isaac could rely on habitants who had not lost their individuality, but in Baku, he was not sure who the right players for his game were.

The effort to liberate Galena was a validation of Isaac's abilities to do his job well. He created a plan that required knowledge of gambling. His plan gave a young girl a new destiny. She would have children and grandchildren. Otherwise, she would die from malnutrition or violent assault. His skills were needed immediately. Isaac created developments that cleared the way for Professor

Kryvoruchko's future arrival. The game was a life-or-death game for Galena and facilitated the future coming of the professor. In the meantime, he was stuck in a brainwashed country. He was moving to a new project to save lives. He became a Sailor.

The brutal world had many underground connections among the business-oriented. In Azerbaijan, officials were not as afraid as they were in other places. The new acquaintance's bosses always encouraged him to find a new way to make money. The Russian was a go-between. Through his contacts, he provided protection for many rich. As a result of meeting with Isaac, the new acquaintance performed a complicated calculation of how much to ask Isaac for to produce the needed paper. His calculations included bribery of all bureaucrats. Producing the paper involved a chain of officials. The Russian also asked Dr. Ali for references regarding Isaac's ability to pay. The good doctor confirmed that Isaac was legitimate. Isaac agreed with all conditions. He paid the asked money, and the requested paper was produced and signed by high officials. Isaac was not thinking about the price because for him, it was not important. He was simply happy that with his money, he could free Glasha's daughter. He was a gambler and was anxious to see if his plan would work.

In Baku were many ethnicities. They were fast and slow, walked speedily and sluggishly, and ate hastily and gently, but all of them thought rapidly. They did well. Because of peculiar geographic and ethnographic properties, Azerbaijan was under close observation by neighbors. Baku was an international city located close to Iran and Turkey. The natives, the Azeris, were one of the Turkish groups. Because of the gaze of neighbors, the false collective was not as rampant there as in other areas.

Azeris were sensitive and peaceful. They were uninfected by the psychological illness, but they were touchy. If they became agitated, they remained disturbed for a long time. In their relations with the Jews, Azeris showed constant comfort and tolerance. Azeri was one of few Muslim ethnicities that did not have anti-Semitic prejudices. That did not mean xenophobia could not somehow take over them. The relationship between Azeris and Armenians suddenly changed, and it became volatile. They became worst enemies. Armenians did not live in Azerbaijan. The Armenian refugees were in different countries. Azerbaijan and Armenia were in a state of war for many years, and no one could see the end of the hostilities.

In the meantime, brainwashing in the country of morons moved to a more advanced level. It was creating men who acted in completely imbecilic ways. In that situation, knowledge of genotype selection was not accepted. The science of genetics was forbidden. Intelligence disappeared. Everything was in the name of the indoctrination. The cream of the crop of society were lost. Aborigin was the headquarters of thoughtless, shortsighted, imbecilic cretins. The transfer back was impossible. Being imbecilic was without return. The agitators created a new unknown and untested theory that focused on being members of a communal heaven. Theory was a mirage. Parvenus were not fit for any research. The heads of state in power were complete idiots. The virus was changing genetics. It proved that being an imbecile could be a hereditary illness. Imbeciles were bred as imbecilic. It was a big test proving that the discoveries of genetics were valid. Idiots, even with power, remained idiots. The shortsighted were breeding the same imprudent offspring. Every scientific test could prove that the fictitious parvenus were not fit to rule civilized society. They denied any past traditions of honesty, dignity, and honor, which were the characteristics of nobility. Instead, they established conditions to prevent the ruling of the intelligent and educated. High-level positions were up for grabs by imbeciles. The hordes of dropouts, vulgar habitants, pretenders, parvenus, and jackanapes were taking positions of power.

The theory of genetic equality challenged a big territory and brainwashed an area far beyond Aborigin. Every part of the theory was wrong, but the false collective did not allow any doubt. In the communalists' dogma, the new dogmatic structure would easily bring a miracle. In reality, the danger of untested jolting was harmful. The disastrous ideas, instead of moving the nation forward, left Aborigin behind. Millions were killed, were misplaced, or vanished, and the area lost its most productive members of society. As result, the field moved back to medieval times. Stupidity became the winner.

## Isaac Took Action

*I*saac sent a message to his older son to come to Baku. When Rudi arrived, Isaac was happy to see him. He was glad that his younger son, Aaron, was doing well. Rudi mentioned that Aaron was also capable of making money. Isaac tried to give Rudi money, but his son refused. Rudi's face was categorical. He had not forgotten that his successful life in a marvelous city had begun with Isaac's money. Rudi, like his father, was a money-making machine and did not need any help. He loved being rich, and the thought of being poor made him sick. He loved money. He always had money. He was confident that in the future, he would have it too. He wanted to give back certain cash to his father, but he knew his father would never accept his money. Rudi stated right away that he had plenty for supporting his family and did not need any.

Rudi was not antimoron but was anticommunalist. Because of morons, he made his money. His biggest horror was life in a communal apartment, and he would do everything to avoid it. Rudi had a fashionable apartment in the center of a beautiful city. He was not involved. He was on guard for his family. Glasha was a newcomer in his family. She was dear to her father, and he accepted her right away. He did not always act in the same way. When he had the choice to protect his brother, he was a deserter. He was ashamed but acted as a coward. He got side of his daughter. In the situation of liberating Glasha's daughter, he was honestly helping his father. Rudi, without any questions, was committed. He used his knowledge to do the task assigned to him. He would pretend to be a government employee, and the paper from the center would help.

Galena was in an orphanage for children of enemies of the state. Their parents were either sentenced to death or incarcerated in prison. Her father had been shot, and her mother was in prison. She was a little girl stuck among unruly children. She came from the nobility and was a gentle girl. The bigger girls picked on her. She folded her clothes before she went to bed, and her shoes were clean, but in the morning, she would see that instead of her regular clothes, she had ragged ones. Somebody was replacing her clothes. It was senseless to complain to the counselors. She knew that if she fought for her rights, she would be transferred to the prison. She would be charged as a young enemy of the state who was not able to follow the rules of communal living. Instead of putting on the torn dress and dirty shoes, she sewed the torn dress and then washed it. She cleaned the shoes. She did not dream that someone had an interest in her life. She did not imagine that working for her liberation were a group of serious, rich, uninfected people. Those habitants did not like to lose or abandon their tasks. If she'd known all the facts, she would have known their work was effective.

Isaac was man of action and was able to design his game. He designed the task of delivery of the paper. His son Rudi, a lawyer, was tasked with taking Galena from the orphanage. Isaac was supposed to give the diamonds to Rudi, who could wisely invest them, but he changed his mind. He thought the diamonds would be more beneficial in his possession. In time, many unexpected things could happen. With diamonds, he would be better equipped to help his children. In a country of imbeciles, they might get into a predicament, and he might need the diamonds to get them out.

As for the plan for Glasha's daughter, Rudi had a fake ID that identified him as a government employee. Isaac had ordered the ID through his Armenian friends. He was a master of telling different stories. He told them that Glasha's daughter was in the custody of Glasha's husband. He characterized him as a monster who was using his daughter to blackmail his estranged wife. Rudi, in pretending he was a government official, had official papers from the capital of Aborigin that asked for the release of Glasha's daughter. The paper was real, and all the stamps were genuine. Rudi pretended he was an inspector in charge of child custody.

Rudi knew how to play a government official. As a lawyer, he met a lot of them. He knew that the custody papers would stay in the orphanage, but his ID would not. He would just show it to the officials. He needed to bribe the officials in the orphanage. He would do it in case someone had doubts about him. He was supposed to bring the girl to Bogdan's father. Rudi was able to do any task successfully.

The girl would not meet her mother soon. Isaac, as an escapee from Kolyma, could not do anything risky. He understood that bringing the girl to Azerbaijan would be too dicey. Stepan Luchko, Bogdan's brother, helped Rudi to get Glasha's daughter out of the orphanage. He was a strange choice, but Isaac accepted him. Stepan Luchko was a conformist. He never disputed anything around him. He lived in his own world. It did not shake him that the dogma was not based on facts. He was self-controlled and followed orders. He admired his brother, Bogdan, and would do anything his brother asked. Bogdan told him that a girl was in trouble and needed help. Stepan did not expect that in the future, Galena would become his wife. Because Bogdan asked, he did not think twice about the risks involved and agreed. He was not a gambler. He did not know anything about the laws of genotype selection. He was just following orders. He was scared but did his task.

Rudi presented Stepan as the brother of Galena and said he needed to reunite with his sister. Stepan never had seen Galena before, and Rudi organized everything. Rudi bribed everyone he needed to. He understood that poor workers wanted him to bribe them. He did all the technical parts, including showing the powerful letter from the high chancellery headquarters of Aborigin.

Rudi and Stepan visited Galena. The caregivers in

orphanages acted like guards in a prison and abused the little children. They would not listen to complaints of abuse by the children. They themselves often hit the little children. Who cared about the children of enemies of the state? They were from a hostile class. No one cared that one daughter of an exploiter and enemy of the state stole a dress from another daughter of an enemy of the state. The caregivers were simple village women. They needed to feed their own children. They did not care about anyone besides their own families. They chose to believe that the children whose parents were enemies of the state deserved harsh treatment. For counselors, it was easier to think in that manner. They stole food from the orphans. They, the deplorables, assumed that now was the time to fix historical unjustness. They abused the little children because their parents were from a different class.

In Isaac's plan, the emotional part was up to Stepan. To the staff of the orphanage, he pretended to be Galena's brother. Stepan told the officials that his sister had been very young when she became an orphan, so she did not remember him. He stated that he'd been adopted into a new family loyal to the regime, and they wanted to educate his little sister in a new way so that she would be a proud member of the communalist society. Stepan also told Galena that he was her brother. He mentioned that as little boy, he'd been adapted into a different family. Stepan told her that she did not remember him because she'd been too little when he was adapted. To prove his legend, he told several stories that Glasha had told them. The task was not easy, but Rudi and Stepan managed.

Isaac, who was a master of the game, designed all the movements. They carried out his plan to save the girl from the orphanage just in time. The caregivers in orphanages were criminals. Galena's tolerance was on the verge. It was unfortunate that such a nice girl had ended up in that terrible place. Galena was good-natured and talented at any work. She also was a quick learner. After liberation, though aristocratic by blood, she was doing peasants' work. Stepan Luchko was impressed by all her abilities and fell in love with her. He later would marry her. He lived happily because he felt lucky to be in the company of his beautiful wife. He did not have any conflict with doctrine and never questioned it. He was able to live a long life, and for many years, he was a believer in the idiotic doctrine. He was surviving in an infected society where habitants did not achieve what they wanted. He had a tremendous ability to blend into any surroundings, and that was the main reason for his durability. His lips were glued together. He was a hero of the collective.

Per Isaac's plan, after her release from the orphanage, Galena had to go away from the eyes of officials. Galena would move to Malantia. She would live on a collective farm with Stepan's aunt, his father's sister. The farm was a safe place, and the habitants on the farm did not ask for any birth certificates and other papers. When Rudi and Stepan brought Galena to the new place, they had money, clothes, and presents for everyone in the house. Galena was welcomed into the peasant family. After the horror in the orphanage, her new life was like a dream. Eventually, she was told the truth that her mother was alive. She was the happiest girl in the whole collective. Only one thing was disturbing: Galena could not see her mother right away. It was too risky. Glasha and Isaac were fugitives, and seeing them was not safe. Galena could not be seen with escapees. She required a clean history to continue her life as a regular member of the collective. Nevertheless, in few years, she was able to see her mother.

# Galena

Galena flourished like a gorgeous flower. She became good at peasants' work. Stepan's aunt was proud of her; an aristocratic girl was able to learn a farmer's work. She was no different from other girls in the village. They blossomed on clean air and organic food. It was obvious Galena was happy. Stepan's aunt was a good teacher, and Galena was a good student. She learned how to cook tasty food, clean a house, milk a cow, decorate a home, and perform many different important skills. She could beautifully embellish the farmer's home with flowers and plants. In time, Galena went to school and became a teacher. Stepan also became a teacher. He was not blind to her beauty and recognized that Galena was a precious diamond. He proposed to her. They were married and taught in a village school in Malantia. As a teacher, Galena continued to have cows and goats in her backyard. Nevertheless, her noble origin was coming out. She had aristocratic blood. She kept her house in more sophisticated ways than the peasants did. It was easy for her to gain the qualities of an unpretentious foundation and live as a farmer. It was more difficult to transfer a simpleton to a refined routine than for an upper-class person to get situated.

The ideology of collective thinking declared that the collective reversed historical injustice. It was not possible to transfer simpletons to sophistication. Aborigin became a country of morons who justified their viciousness and lawlessness by declaring that the future was on their side. The leaders took away from their minions any guilt for savagery. Justifying their viciousness, they asserted that the mistake happened when something important came up.

They said that everyone who did wrong to the innocent was acquitted in the face of history. They were criminals covering for ferociousness.

Stepan Luchko was a survivor. As a small baby, he'd fallen into an open well left unattended by workers. Before the water had filled up the well, someone had saved him. Stepan's life had been spared. Another time, as a baby, he'd had chills and a fever. A local healer had given him an infusion of herbs, and the illness had stopped. Now he survived the ideological war. He was not involved. Mainly, he kept his mouth shut. He did not ask questions. He also did not disagree with anything. He had the right background to be a proud member of the collective. He'd grown up in the family of a blacksmith and was used to hard work. He belonged to the correct origin. Nevertheless, he did not embrace the propaganda trap of feeling superior to others. He did not use any speculations of collective thinking. He did not declare himself a ruler of the world. He did not show any grandiosity. He lived quietly in Malantia in his aunt's village. He did not react much to any wrongness. His blindness to social injustice and his numbness to casualties were characteristics that created the direction of his life. He moved from Byelogoria to Malantia because he felt comfortable there. He was not a Kaufman, with their business orientation. He was not a Jew. He was Malantian but never had any anti-Semitic anger. He did not feel that Jews were stealing something from him. He did not care about others. As a child, he'd seen death, and in later life, he did not care about politics. He was one of the few characters living happily in mud. Stepan made the crucial decision to be blind and deaf to injustice. He was selfish and did not have any problems. He refused to think about complicated moral issues. He limited his thoughts to primitive ones. He had only one desire: to be happy. He dreamed of life in different countries, and nothing bothered him. He was a teacher of geography. He was good at his profession. In his later life, he ended up in Canada. He spied for the collective's secret police.

Stepan Luchko was a good member of collectivist thinking. He was a conformist. He was one of the Aboriginians who agreed with the regime. Nevertheless, together with Rudi Kaufman, he was able to save a class enemy, Galena, and he later married her. He was disconnected from political babbling. He acted like a traumatized bird, and he had a guardian angel. He was a survivor. Stepan Luchko did not declare his own political views. He learned to believe what the leaders told him. He did not have any negative feelings toward others. Stepan also did not hate his father, though his father was unnecessarily strict with him. He found justification for his father's strictness. At a young age, Stepan Luchko left his father's house. He did not feel his father was his enemy and pushed him away. He knew that if he stayed home, he would be a blacksmith. He understood that his father wanted more for him and pushed him out of Byelogoria. After helping Galena, he moved to Malantia, and later, he was able to complete college. With his Malantian last name, it was easier for him than in Byelogoria to get into college. In Malantia, he was one of them. College acceptance was based on quotas for different ethnicities. He had the right background. He became a teacher of geography and was happy to dream about distant countries. Many things happened to him that were significant and shaped his psyche. Stepan Luchko was a survivor. On top of that, he was a lucky man. He was able to marry a beautiful woman.

During World War II, as a soldier, Stepan Luchko was

captured but was saved. In later life, he had a dangerous job as a spy for the collective in a Western country. Challenging experiences occurred all throughout his life, but nothing bad happened to him. Many times, he was supposed to vanish. Stepan Luchko likely had a guardian angel who was watching out for him when everyone thought he was dead. As a young man, Stepan had been playing somebody else's game. Stepan was a good follower and met his future wife. He was able to save Professor Kryvoruchko, who, in his honor, was named Stepan. By saving the professor, who was targeted for assassination by an operative of the communalists' secret police, Stepan Luchko acted as a Sailor. When he heard about the plan to assassinate the professor, he went to the Canadian authorities. He told them everything about himself and saved the professor. He was pardoned and continued to live in the West.

## Celestials of the Gorgeous City

Life in the city was complicated. Many youngsters wanted to be powerful, and many wanted to be famous. In a habitation soiled by contagion, the youngsters were no different from those in other places. Rudi's daughter Sofia decided to become an actress. She read books about theater and had many daydreams of being on the stage. Her mother had constant delusions about being an aristocrat. She supported Sofia's dreams. Rudi did not care but accepted his daughter's wish as a new challenge. He was a practical man. In the past, he'd done a favor for the head of a repair crew in one of the theaters. That man, in turn, was friends with the head of a repair crew in a theatrical school. In that domain adulterated by the venom of corruption, no one could keep a good job without connections. A job in any academic setting was privileged. It opened up a great opportunity to make money. The entry requirements for many institutions were too high. Many citizens of Aborigin paid bribes to get their children a free education. The biggest source of pride for parents was in bragging that their children had gotten their education without bribes.

Rudi did not believe those fairy tales. He knew that free cheese was only in a mousetrap. He recognized that the head of the repair crew had some kind of connection. How would he have kept his job otherwise? Rudi's contact had done many free jobs for his bosses and had close relationships with them. Many masters of theatrical art needed repairs done in their dachas. The repair person was bribing all of them with his work. The repairman was the one who set the price of accepting the new student to theatrical school. Rudi's contact would tell his price to the bosses. The most essential qualities were that Rudi was important and had a good reputation. He could return favors. The price, whatever it was, had been settled. Sofia got a paid tutor, a member of the theatrical staff, who prepared her for her entrance exam. Many children from insignificant parents who were naive required a lot of attempts to pass the entrance exam in theatrical school. Most did not pass. Eventually, they realized they could not reach their desired goals. Another way to enter was through sexual favors. Attractive enrollees could use their sexuality. They also got in. With her tutor's help, Sofia, who was a good student and had good grades in high school, was accepted to the theatrical school.

For morons polluted by the toxins of grandiosity, a position at the theatrical school opened up different opportunities. It was easy to benefit from being in the collective as a member with a respected position. Many workers declared that if they'd been unable to take advantage of their positions, they would not have wanted those positions. Some teachers took advantage of their students. During Sofia's first year in school, an attractive instructor of fencing gave her his attention. He requested a sexual favor to pass his course. Fencing was a major subject in acting school. The instructor, like everyone else in the region of morons dirty with germs of exploitation, used the advantage of his position to get benefits. Without his position, he would have been a zero. In his position, until that time, not one of his students had refused his advances. Sofia, who fought her chubbiness, eventually became cute, tall, and slim. She was fashionably dressed. The teacher placed his hand on her and controlled all her movements. In every lesson, he criticized her. After every class, he would tell her to give up and accept his appeals. He claimed she would feel much better if she did. Other female students who passed through the same treatment recommended she stop resisting. First of all, he was good looking. Second, by failing the class, she would be expelled from school. In a theatrical school, instructors taught the students to forget their own selves. They instructed them to play their roles and get completely out of their own bodies. Teachers lured young students into their embraces. They hugged students. They stroked their hair. It was foreplay. It also was an invitation to visit them in their dwellings. Besides sex, the teachers expected students to bring gifts. Because of their positions, they felt they were entitled to everything.

Instructors said that actors were supposed to sacrifice their own bodies and study how to act out convincing sexual interactions. Instructors said they were preparing students to experience sexual interaction. Sofia was smart enough not to listen to that brainwashing. She complained to Rudi, who resolved the problem quickly. He made a visit to the man who was protecting him, an agent in the secret police, whom he regularly paid. The next day, the fencing instructor received in his mail an invitation to come to the secret police office, where he was given a lecture concerning sexual harassment. The fencing instructor shook with fear. With a tearful voice, he asked for forgiveness. He also got a command to apologize to Sofia. He knew he needed to follow the order from the secret police. He apologized to Sofia. With a little help from Sofia's father, justice was served. She received the highest possible grade for the class. When the instructor asked why Sofia had not told him that she had high connections, Sofia just smiled.

In school, there was a rumor that she was untouchable. In the future, she did not have any problems, and she safely finished school without any trouble. Her teachers told others who desired free sex that she was untouchable. She achieved all her dreams. She had a father who never had an official position but was able to make things happen. With the help of her father, instead of allocation to the provincial theater, she gained a position in one of the highest theatrical art settings. Sofia was on top of the world. She also had a man she loved. The collective used art products to promote insane doctrine. Teachers had the freedom to bully and teach compliance. Because of her resourceful father, Sofia got everything she wanted without too many sacrifices. Contrary to other students who walked through the bedrooms of many teachers in order to graduate, she did not have any problems. She lived with her parents. In the dormitory, students had many parties involving alcohol and invited their teachers. The dexterous competed for their teachers' attention. Passing through a teacher's bedroom was a guarantee of credit for classes. Later, when those students worked in theater and played lead characters, they regularly visited the producers' bedrooms. Their lives were completely aligned with irrational doctrine. The jerks in the upper echelon always asked regular Aboriginians to sacrifice their lives. In a neighborhood of morons polluted by the zymotic, starving actors quoted the senseless slogans like parrots.

The collective was skilled at manipulating the naive. In theater, many female stage actors were used as mistresses by the party leaders. The leaders, who were regular visitors to theaters, promised their mistresses better positions. In a population of morons soiled by disease, the artists were poor and without any financial support. If one saw a man without shoes and wearing old galoshes without socks on the street, one knew he was an artist. The artists starved if they refused to paint the chubby thrushes and the steelworkers in boilers' suits. Only a few of them could sell their work. Forbidden also were naked bodies in paintings. Nudity was called exploitation of the human body and of models. Because art was supposed to be ideological, working models could not be nude. If models accepted an assignment to pose nude, they were ostracized and called backward and irresponsible. As a result, there were a lot of paintings of women who covered the private places on their bodies with paddles and other nonsense. The luckiest artists were able to emigrate and become wealthy in the decaying West. Otherwise, they were destined to paint workers in uniform and athletes with sports equipment.

In the tightly controlled populace, artists were contracted by government officials. Without those contracts, they starved.

Art in the cities of morons dirtied by the illness of arrogance was losing its luster. Before collectivists and communalists, the culture had been bright. Populist doctrine killed innovations. The slogan was that Aboriginians did not need any sophistication. No one expected them to understand anything original. Life had a populist flavor. Populism was everywhere. Those slogans were handy for the uneducated and infected. To be published, writers and poets bragged about their past as soldiers of the Red Army. They highlighted their working-class backgrounds. The working class was pleased that their leaders magnified them and made them as smart as any wise man and as noble as any aristocrat. They did not understand that clever manipulators had tricked them into believing that without education and skills, they could replace the old professionals. The poets and writers glorified simple folks and simplicity as a whole. In ordinary folks, they stirred up unreasonable expectations. Only a few artists did not work for the collective. They preferred to die from starvation and sicknesses rather than grovel to the regime.

The bucolic art was filthy with the toxins of haughtiness. Polluted actors sold their souls to the pseudocollective. Tainted writers created fictitious stories about the superiority of Prolet-Aryans and the excellence of frozen dullards and stooges from the working class. They became lickspittles, sycophants, and courtiers. Ultimately, they did not have a choice. Otherwise, they were destroyed and eliminated. Poets sang praises and dithyrambs to the primitive folks. Even the intellectuals did not understand what kind of danger they put themselves in. They became enablers who, with the laudatory hymns, blinded and deceived the masses. They were not servants of a poetic muse but lackeys of the authorities. To survive, they became flatterers and yes-men. Nevertheless, the horrible day came. Leaders became paranoid. The corrupt lost their pedestal and became persecuted. Poets and writers ended up in prisons as enemies of the nation.

In a nation of morons tainted by the sickness of dregs, the desire to become important was an obsession and created many swindlers. Contrary to the notorious, the famous had many benefits from their positions, which included the opportunity to have many sexual interactions. The infected did not have any religious breaks. Infidelity was not a transgression. There were ménages à trois. For ordinary adventurists, it was common to speak with unacquainted women on the street and have sex immediately. If men had the guts to speak to female strangers on the street, they got lucky. Many women bragged that they were popular, and men followed them everywhere. The young males on the streets were hunters looking for easy prey. The young writers and poets were distinguished by their clothes and mannerisms.

Living in a fantastic city, Sofia promoted her husband and put him on a pedestal. Sashko, her husband, played guitar and memorized the songs of other songwriters, which he, without any shame, claimed as his own. Many popular youngsters played guitar. Songs were not protected because they were not ideological enough. They never were approved by censors and never published. Their songs, which they presented as their own, were plagiarized. Nevertheless, many girls had their first sexual experiences with those liars.

Sofia was proud of Sashko. In different actors'

gatherings, she asked him to play guitar and mentioned that he was a bard. Sashko quickly learned how to pretend he was someone important and became good at it. Sofia would say that her husband had bad luck, and his problem was that envious songwriters did not recognize him as a genius.

## Aaron and Sashko's Resources

Aaron became more mature. He grew in size and had several romances with different women and even fathered a child with one. Sashko continued to be in love with Sofia, Aaron's niece. Sashko was not only a friend but also a business partner. He drove Aaron's car and shot photos of peasants and their children on Aaron's equipment. In return, the friends took samovars, fireplace clocks, mantel clocks, icons, and other antiques. They also sold thin pieces of mica, the isinglass stone, which was used to cover the little windows in kerosene stoves. It was popular in communal settings. Through a little isinglass window, the user of the stove could see the burning wick and regulate the intensity of the fire. Isinglass was resistant to high temperatures and gave a clear view of the wick.

Aaron's mind constantly checked his environment. He was looking for his own place in the world and wanted to be wealthy. He always was able to find areas where he could make money. He thought big. As a business-oriented person, he did not find any task problematic. For him, something obvious that others did not think about could bring benefits. Aaron and Sashko quickly learned how to simplify things that sounded challenging. They established relationships with the isinglass factory and had plenty of isinglass to sell.

The suppliers of isinglass developed production of cubic zirconia diamonds. At the isinglass factory, they had unreported production. The material was not to be mixed up with zircon, which became a zirconium silicate. They developed a completely new product. They generated cubic zirconia from zirconium dioxide. The newly synthesized material was hard, optically flawless, and usually colorless but could exist in a variety of different colors. It was erroneously called cubic zirconia. Because of its low cost, durability, and close visual likeness to diamond, synthetic cubic zirconia remained the most gemological and economically important competitor for diamonds. Aaron and Sashko were trusted companions and had an unlimited supply of cubic zirconia. For friends, selling cubic zirconia became a simple task.

Aaron and Sashko delivered what they promised. For the business-oriented, contacts were important. They knew who did what and how they could benefit. The suppliers had an astonishing product, but they were afraid to sell it. Chemists were not able to sell their product. For them, selling was an enormous task. They were afraid they would put at risk other illegal productions going on at the isinglass factory. They could not do anything to jeopardize their activities on the black market. By dealing with Aaron and Sashko, they knew they had reliable friends who would do the job. Even under duress, friends would not report on them.

The friends also rented a photo studio where they kept isinglass stone, cubic zirconia diamonds, and photography of farmers. The photos on the fancy frameworks were produced by artists working at home. The friends developed a new line of jewelry produced by homeworker jewelers. They shared their profits with peddlers. They sold by using the wholesale method and asking for less money for more merchandise bought. They mainly sold their goods to intermediate contacts in the province. They tried hard. In the production of cubic zirconia, they were ahead of everyone. Their next step was selling artificial caviar they financed to produce from cheap fish.

The friends knew what they were supposed to do to avoid suspicious eyes. They were cautious and did not buy anything that would bring attention to their illegal activities. Nevertheless, in the killing field of morons fouled by an illness of disdain, their activities could not last long. Aaron, Sashko, and all the chemists ended up in strict security prisons, and their new invention was lifeless for many years. After the friends' imprisonment, the artificial caviar and cubic zirconia ideas died. If the friends had had that invention in a capitalistic society, they probably would have become millionaires.

In the meantime, the friends had fancy cars and ate in nice restaurants. They rented a summer cottage on the seashore. They took steps to hide their richness. Aaron covered his wealth. He drove his car under somebody else's name. He paid someone who had a primitive job and did not have any connection to the black market. Every luxury thing in his possession he bought under somebody else's name. He paid someone to give his ID to him in order to make purchases. It was a common way to avoid police scrutiny and extortion. Aaron and Sashko were pioneers in many things and displayed a level of creativity above the other merchants'. They were not crowned but could have been called the kings of the black market.

In the collective, families hid their earnings. To be on the safe side, Aaron and Sashko rented summer chalets instead of buying them. In their world, the owners of dachas bought bower anchors or dwellings under the names of distant relatives or friends. It was a chain of purchases using other names. For Aaron and Sashko, being rich was good. They were young. The best part for them was to be safe while still knowing how to have fun. They paid cash to property owners, who in turn paid someone else to cover their housing activities. Homeowners registered their houses in the names of relatives who were members of the working class. If the black-marketers did not speak against the government, they were relatively safe. In vocational resorts were many extravagant business-oriented dandies who covered up their wealth. The men had long hair and frilly manners. The women wore flared pants and smoked long cigarettes.

The business of isinglass flourished. In the communal setting, habitants cooked in their rooms on kerosene stoves. The isinglass used in kerosene stoves was valuable on the black market. The workers hid isinglass in their clothes when they passed the clock houses. Isinglass was a popular and necessary item. Kerosene stoves were used in the sleeping quarters in communal settings. To avoid informants, the communal apartments built their own structures. Their lives resembled spy movies.

Aboriginians cooked their food in their sleeping quarters on the kerosene stoves. It was the best way to avoid unwanted eyes. If unwanted visitors showed up, they could not see anything, only sniff. The peasants too loved kerosene stoves. Unmovable, big wooden stoves, which were in nearly every house, required a lot of effort to use, but the portable stoves were easy to operate, and kerosene was cheap and widely available. The friends also paid the security guards to be less vigilant in the clock houses. The friends' empire got bigger. They were looking for a new place to produce false diamonds. In the collective, life resembled a minefield. Only diamonds brought stability to their holders in that turbulent time. Their owners had a chance to enjoy real beauty instead of empty blabbering and cockeyed doctrine.

Many Aboriginians could not afford real diamonds and purchased fakes. Aaron and Sashko provided stability for many. In the eyes of the terrestrials, they were the diamonds. Aaron always warned the buyer that the diamonds were false. For him, it was important to have a good reputation and inform those who could not distinguish the false from the real. Aaron was business-oriented, but he was not a fraudster. In his dealings, he was called a felon. In some ways, that was true. In lands soiled by the illness of the mindless, all private enterprises were forbidden. In reality, he never did anything dishonest to his clients, which might have been one of the reasons no one reported him to the state police. Another reason was that he had a guardian angel who led him through the minefield without being busted. He was just lucky—but his luck changed.

The low morality affected the lives of the friends. In hypocritical structures, morality was unstable and often broken. Aaron and Sashko rented a chalet on the seashore for their women and children. Many times, they slept in villages far away from their families, where they had a lot of business. They had affairs. When they went to Arcadian land with their photography business, there were many women. Aaron spoke easily to all of them and brought different gifts for every one. He never stayed with one mistress; he always was looking for someone else. On the contrary, Sashko felt tense and was not comfortable with women. He continued to be driven by Sofia's feelings toward him and did not cheat on her. In time, a redhead got his attention. He started to see her regularly. He did not lose interest in Sofia but was taken by the moment. Sofia had been Sashko's first real sexual experience. Now he was with another woman. He felt like a macho man. His moral values did not stop him from infidelity, and he became reckless. Sofia's mother right away perceived that Sashko was not the same as before.

Sashko was in danger, though he did not realize it. In the collective, it was easy to get even with someone. One could report others to the police. Some women were jealous and angry. Some were mad and vengeful. They did not forgive betrayal.

One hot summer day, Sashko and Aaron sent their women and children to a hamlet on the seashore. They enjoyed being with their mistresses. The summer was hot, and the friends kept beer on ice. The friends and their women were walking around naked, when all of a sudden, the door opened, and Sofia walked in. She saw the party and immediately left. Sashko put on his pants and ran after her. He could not catch up.

In Aborigin, the secret police were threatening. On an impulse, Sofia did not go to the regular police and instead went to the secret police's headquarters. Sofia specifically went there because she guessed that Sashko and Aaron had a contact in the regular police. In their interactions with the world, the friends were careful of what they said. They did not expect to be objects of interest for the secret police. She reported to a security officer that the friends used photo equipment to produce antigovernment posters. It was a complete fabrication. Sofia's vendetta was so intense that she reported nonexistent political activities.

Sofia supplied the secret police with the address of

a laboratory where the friends kept the stolen isinglass, cubic zirconia, and many photographs and handmade frames for photos. The security officers also found blank waybills with nonexistent company names. Every waybill falsified some government entity. Because everything in a communal context belonged to the government, the citizens were not supposed to have businesses. To make unregistered businesses look legal, habitants created nonexistent government companies that worked under fabricated names. The friends produced false waybills with photography montages. The secret police found all of Sashko and Aaron's dealings. As evidence of political activities, they found photo-development laboratories. Because the friends did not have any protection from political accusations, they were in deep trouble. As a result, the friends were arrested.

## Sofia Kaufman, Actress

Sofia Kaufman became a prominent actress. She did not become a Sailor. She worked for a theater in a gorgeous city. Many years ago, she'd married and had a son with Aaron's friend Sashko Belay. The son became a famous actor too. He and his father had never met. Eric Belay never knew his natural father. He had a stepfather, who was a director in one of the theaters in his city. Eric became an actor in the same theater. He, his mother, and his stepfather lived in a big apartment that Aaron's brother, Rudi, had left to them. They had a lot of art, antiques, and precious items Rudi had collected. A long time ago, before she'd become famous,

Eric's mother had divorced her husband, Sashko. He was an enthusiastic guitar player and adventurous. He was saved but did not save anyone. He did not become a Sailor.

Sofia Kaufman had a wealthy lifestyle, but she was brainwashed by doctrine and dreamed of having a special life. Sofia was infected. In her past, Sofia Kaufman, in a jealous rage, had reported to the secret police that her husband, Sashko, and her uncle Aaron were selling false diamonds. She'd put them in jail not because they did something illegal but because of her husband's infidelity. She had a good record with the secret police, and they called her when they needed her. As a young girl, she'd dreamed about mixing with the simple habitants, even though she lived as an aristocrat. Sofia had a desire to be part of the working class. She idealized the simple habitants. Her first love had been Sashko Belay, the son of an alcoholic woman who worked in a leather factory. Many ideologists preached the need for simplicity. Because society was primitive, the guardians of the malady of madness put all habitants in simple workers' coveralls. It was one way to please their leaders. Supreme leaders were uneducated and mentally unfit. They were afraid of habitants with strong imaginations. In a society like that, having a bright mind was considered heresy and treason.

## Sofia's Life

Sofia fulfilled her mother's dream of glory and wealth. Her father was able to give her a good life. With the help of her late father, she achieved her dream and became an actress.

She was happy and played many different roles. Out of her many different stage performances, her best role was the role of a princess. Her mother was ill and, in her delusion, spoke to invisible habitants. Those habitants were all aristocrats. Sofia fulfilled her mother's dream to be famous.

As a young girl, she'd dreamed of meeting a poor boy and making him happy. Children often dreamed of saving habitants. Her first husband, Sashko, was pitiable. Unfortunately, the poor boy grew up and right away showed his ingratitude to his wife. He misbehaved and had mistresses. He did not fulfill Sofia's expectations. She was mad. She informed the police of his illegal activities. Sashko was arrested and sent to prison. Her romance with simplicity fell apart. Her fragile fragment did not survive, and she got under the surviving fragments.

When the war with the Nazis started, she was able to leave the city with a theater where she was working. Eventually, she understood the real meaning of being rich. During the war, she lived well. When habitants were starving, she was selling different valuables from her father's collection. After the war, she married the director of the medium-sized theater. She lived a bohemian life around actors and movie producers. Her second husband made her a star in his theater. He was business-oriented, and Sofia could buy more expensive things and kept her lifestyle.

## Sofia's Second Marriage

Sofia was married the first time to a terrestrial. She experienced a deep sexual attraction to her first husband,

Sashko. Her second husband was from a pseudocelestial environment. He was older and a kind man. They lived together happily. She danced the Argentinian tango in performances. She was famous and acted on the stages of several theaters. Her son also was a famous movie actor. On the stage, he portrayed politically advanced members of youth organizations. In reality, their wealth came from their inheritance from Rudi Kaufman, a business-oriented man. He had known how to keep his wealth away from scavengers.

With her second husband, Sofia experienced emotional closeness. She had a prosperous existence. Despite her dreams of playing a princess, as an actress, she portrayed milkmaids and workers at pig farms. She also portrayed many other workers who were advanced because of radical doctrine and employed in various metal factories.

Sofia Kaufman was a Jewish woman, but she did not have any connection to Jewish culture. She was a typical pseudocelestial. Her father had spoiled her with goodies the collective could provide. She was not limited in her ambitions. She'd successfully fought her chubbiness and become slim. She was able to reach possible highs onstage and in dance. She was one of many who did not have any problem with her ethnicity. She changed her last name from Kaufman to Belay, the last name of her first husband. She did not have any feelings of inadequacy. The complex of inferiority missed her. As a young woman, she married a man who was handsome but from a poor family. She gave birth to a child of mixed heritage. Her son, Eric, looked like his father and was handsome. He did not know much about the details of the split between his parents. He simply knew that his mother had divorced his father and did not have any contact with him. Eric was happy with his status. He became a popular film actor, but he did not become a Sailor.

## Aaron's Struggles

Aaron's brother, Rudi, unfortunately, did not help his brother. Some strong men were weak in front of women. They were henpecked. Sofia threatened to kill herself if Rudi helped his brother and his son-in-law through his contacts. In addition, his delusional wife could not comprehend how a peasant like Sashko had cheated on her lovely daughter. She also threatened to leave her husband if he helped his brother. Rudi could not withstand the pressure. He gave up on his brother. Aaron and Sashko were sentenced to ten years each in a high-security prison. The friends were sent to Turkmenistan to build the Main Turkmen Canal.

Small numbers of business-oriented and uninfected habitants survived. One of the dreamers in the gorgeous city was Rudi Kaufman. He believed he had a guardian angel who helped him to survive. He wanted to re-create in his home the time of Leo Tolstoy. During the heyday of the collective, the city was not the same as in the time of Tolstoy, when the city had many ballroom parties and graciously mannered inhabitants. There were no longer heroic people in the gorgeous city. There were savages living in communal apartments. In stores were big lines for food. A once fantastic, gorgeous city had become a place where Aboriginians lived in the company of bedbugs and cockroaches. It was a war zone where primitive predators declared war on sophistication. It was a caricature of the past. The houses in the city looked the same but now housed Aboriginians who were worse than any animals. In his book *Notes from the Underground*, Fyodor Dostoyevsky gave a description of people like the Aboriginians. It seemed he'd predicted many things. The quest for power for the habitants was an endless drive. Countless tales of greed, strife, and triumph stemmed from the common ambition. The collective had a primitive structure, and Dostoyevsky had graphically displayed it.

Rudi did not make an attempt to save his brother. In truth, he could have at least tried to help somehow. He had a moment of weakness and chickened out in front of his woman. He had a reputation as a lawyer who knew all the trickeries of law. The justice system in the collective was based on a quota to produce slaves needed for Kolyma and other such places. In the collective, everyone was presumed to be guilty. The law was nonsense; nevertheless, Rudi was capable of helping. His skill was that he knew complex trickeries and got many cases dismissed. He was famous, but he had not studied much of the collective's useless laws; instead, he spent his time learning about the judges. To a judge with a young wife, he brought perfume, and to a judge with a more mature wife, he brought kitchenware. To anglers, he brought fishing gear, and to hunters, he brought hunting gear. He did not offer money up front, but judges often borrowed from him and forgot to pay him back. As a result, in the courtroom, his clients received lenient treatment. Because of his reputation, his services were costly. Nevertheless, he helped many of his clients avoid labor camps and stay alive. Contrarily, other lawyers who relied on knowledge of law got their clients sent to Kolyma.

Rudi felt terrible that he did not prevent his brother's

certain death. His excuse was that Aaron's case was in the hands of the secret police, so he could not help him. In reality, he did not even try to help his brother. For Rudi, his wife and daughter were his entire life. He silently observed the punishment of his brother and son-in-law. After his death, he left all his riches to his family. His family had everything. During the war, he never left his blockaded city because he was afraid his possessions would be pillaged. He was shot by a stray bullet, but all his possessions survived. His corpse had a terrible, savage fate: starving compatriots cut the pseudoaristocrat into pieces and ate him. They could not waste the fresh corpse. Cannibalism was a way of surviving.

The gorgeous cities in collectivist lands brought decay in every area. Predators were everywhere. To survive, writers and poets glorified presumed collective thinking. They sold their souls to the devil. Teachers took advantage of students and covered up their vulgar intentions by citing crazy doctrine. Some artists and actors were poor terrestrials. They did not have any connections. To endure, they needed to be lackeys and snitches. They desired to impress the core ideologists. Musicians paid to publish their work. They named their creations with slogans from barmy doctrine. The youths registered as pioneers in ideological lands were required to snitch on their parents.

In the collective, no one was immune from being thrown in jail for any reason. Aaron, who was careful and perfected the art of laundering money, was caught. He was convicted as a saboteur and a swindler of the national economy. Aaron was just an innovative person, and he had nothing to do with the shaming. It was not his fault the state did not accept any novelty. Innovators faced terrible punishments. The secret police also charged him with political offenses. Later in his life, in the West, Aaron became a billionaire, but in the presumed collective, he was destined for prison. It was true that his morality was not the strictest, but that was not a reason for his downfall.

## Gulag

The presumed collective state needed slaves. The big communal state focused on big projects. It was involved in those projects to glorify its leader. The slave camps were the meanest discovery of all. They were created to accommodate the biggest pomposity in the world's history. Millions of prisoners fulfilled the dreams of sick minds. Aaron and Sashko were shipped in boxcars to Turkmenistan. They and thousands more dug sand with picks and shovels and carried it away in wheelbarrows. No one counted how many prisoners died from hunger and inhumane conditions. The collective was not able to nourish so many. It decided to outright eradicate them. With the purpose of covering mismanagement of the farms and factories, the collective started absurd undertakings to take attention away from famine and the shortage of necessities.

## Maniacal and Illiterate Leaders

The new projects were a disaster. They were the killing field. The leaders were shortsighted. They started absurd projects, including cultivation of virgin soil in the desert. The projects were monuments to the cretinism of primitive minds. Imperial ambitions and colonial pomposity found a way into the Turkmen's desert. Collective mismanagement destroyed the most prosperous agriculture, and millions died from hunger. The communal leaders were stocked with the system that was not working. The collective state tried to cover the malfunction of the communal setting by starting gargantuan projects. They did it in a primitive way by using slave labor. They arrested millions and sent them to slave camps to become slave labor. They created a quota for how many should be arrested and sent to die. Later, excavations discovered that the sites of the colossal projects were covered with the bones of dead prisoners. No one claimed retribution for that nonsense. The colonialist ambitions of the collective state were high. The projects were built on notions of *maybe* and *perhaps* and had illiterate and imprecise calculations and analysis. Not one of them was completed. The gigantic projects eventually evaporated. They became history's biggest cemetery.

The canal was a large-scale irrigation project in the communal state. Its development was designed for the Amu Darya, the main river in Turkmenistan. The channel was intended to transport water for irrigation of the desert from the Amu Darya River to the Caspian Sea. The channel was going to transport water through sands and desert to the ancient ways of the Amu Darya riverbed. An enormous weir was built, which was combined with a hydroelectric power plant. The hypothetical purpose of the canal was to increase cotton growth, bringing glory to the collective in the Karakum desert location.

Loggerheads in the collective planned to open navigation from the Volga River to the Amu Darya. Their ambitious plan never came to fruition. The length of the canal was planned to be more than 1,200 kilometers. Every kilometer of the canal required thousands of working slaves. The secret police provided the requested amount of slaves. The uninfected were arrested on denunciations and shipped to work. The court system was a joke, and the homeland quickly replaced dead slaves. The Turkmen Canal was supposed to get irrigation to dry soil, but instead of water, it ran on the blood of slaves. The enormous project in the killing field, tainted by ruination, was not completed. If it had been completed, it would have caused a great ecological catastrophe.

The slave camp was always accepting new victims, including many Prolet-Aryans who were, on false accusations, declared to be criminals. The Prolet-Aryans were reeducated to follow the code of honor for criminals. The unlawful concept of honor survived troubling times. Surprisingly, the criminal concept of honor was fairer than the code of honor for communalists, which was adulterated by perdition. Life in prison was not by the book of law either. The slave camp was ruled by rogue thieves who were labeled as socially close to the Prolet-Aryans. They never had political desires. Their minds were set only on stealing. Lawlessness was everywhere. Only the criminal code of honor kept some order. It did not use any contracts or receipts because everything was based on the honorable word. If someone gave his word, he did what he promised; otherwise, his reputation would be damaged, and he would receive punishment. There were repercussions from the criminal authorities when someone did not honor a promise, such as a criminal meeting and then resolution with punishment according to severity.

The collective did not let anyone know that the native

land needed slaves to build the Turkmen Canal. No one dreamed of being free from the slave camp. The prisoners never had a chance to get out of prison and tell about their slavery. Aaron and Sashko had to push barrows without wheels filled with sand under the scorching sun. Teddy boys got the worst treatment. They were brought to hell. Sometimes they helped an overthrown past politician carry his wheelbarrow because he was too weak. If he fell down, the taskmaster would hit him with a whip, and he would die from the drubbing. The workday was long, and the conditions were horrible. They did not have enough food. The water was warm and dirty, but they drank it anyway. The barracks had political prisoners on one side and thieves who'd dedicated their lives to crime on the other. They were rogue thieves and were able to pass the initiation to receive the status of rogues. They had their own concept of how to relate to other thieves and other prisoners. They looked on others like on the sick with Fiddle Dee. Some of the prisoners once had been big shots but now were eating watery soup with thieves. Political prisoners had many different fractions, and they did not get along. They also were confused and helpless. Some of them believed they were casualties of mistakes that would someday be corrected. They honestly believed that truth would prevail, and they would receive their freedom. If they were able to survive, which was almost impossible, they eventually understood that there were no mistakes. Everything was planned.

Beside rogue thieves were kerns, such as Aaron and Sashko. Kerns were embezzlers in the frenzy economy. They were behavioral delinquents who did not have money to bribe. In prison, they were helpless. They were uninitiated and disempowered. Therefore, rogues played cards with the lives of kerns. When rogue thieves played cards, those unfamiliar with the game could not even come close to the card table. The kerns were gaming chips. As the lowest of slaves, they were not humans but small change for gambling. Everything in their possession, including food and their lives, was a bet for the rogue thieves. The unfortunate kerns did not have any clothes or food. On their first day in prison, everything was taken from them. Many couldn't give much, but they could be raped, injured, spit on, bitten, and urinated on.

Rogues could not cheat in card games. After the game, the winner would tell the loser the name of an uninitiated kern to be killed, raped, or mistreated in whatever way the victor wanted. By the code of honor or rogue ethics, the loser had to comply. Paying the card game's debt was the highest honorable concept of the code of honor for rogues. In rogue ethics, everything was punished by death, and dishonest playing in the card games was punishable as well.

The rogue thieves had different ranks in the criminal hierarchy. They were forbidden to fight any rogues. They resolved their grievances through higher ranks. Thieves could not steal from other thieves, but they could steal from kerns and political prisoners. The criminal code of honor was a rule for prison, and everyone in prison followed it. Among thieves, playing cards was a great means of entertainment. Rogue thieves spent many hours playing cards. A good player had high honor.

The leaders of the collective had the same system for entertainment, but instead of cards, they played chess. Communalist ideologists loved chess, and good players were honored. In both prison and the outside world, cheating was not possible and was punishable. In prison, an individual life did not have value. There were not many choices to survive. The loser of a card game always had to fulfill any of the winner's wishes.

One prisoner who was a friend told Aaron that Sashko had been named for rape because of his good looks. Aaron trusted the man, whom he helped to carry a barrow. He understood that the man had put his life in danger by telling him that information. Telling secrets of the rogue thieves was a punishable offense. Aaron thanked the political prisoner but did not have anything to give him in return. The good man did not expect anything. The information was his payback because the friends had helped him before.

Aaron had to make a decision. The time when Aaron had depended on Sashko as a child had passed a long time ago. For many years, Aaron had been the one who made decisions, and Sashko had learned to depend on Aaron's directions. One possible solution was to send Sashko to the guards and have him sign up with them to be an informer. The guards would keep Sashko in isolation for a couple days, but eventually, he would come back. Even if he was placed in a different barrack, he would not be safe. That solution was only temporarily. In prison, rogues often initiated the good-looking men into the position of whores. Among the whores were informants, losers in cards, and handsome newcomers chosen from the kerns. Groups of thieves raped the unfortunate kerns in bathrooms or showers, which was their initiation into being whores. They ate from bowls on which women's names were scratched. They were supposed to satisfy the sexual demands of thieves. Nobody cared about whores. They were the lowest level of the slave hierarchy. In the collective, anyone could be sent to die in gigantic projects as a whore. Few terrestrials were luckier. They were arrested and immediately executed.

Lot was falsely arrested and sent into slavery. The methods used in the homeland for imprisonment were trickery, deception, and cheating. Individuals without any protection soon became servants of rogues or quickly raped as an initiation to be whores.

For the friends, time was slipping away; they needed to work quickly. One solution the friends seriously discussed was killing the winner of the critical game. The first problem was that they had not killed anyone before and did not know how it was done. The second problem was that murder would break the concept of honor, and Aaron and Sashko might be tortured and then killed.

There was another solution, but it was shaky and might make their situation even worse: Aaron could challenge the winner in a game. He never had told anyone of his knowledge of card games, but he often observed games from a distance. His sharp eyes saw that the winners were cheating. He decided to take on the tremendous risk. He told Sashko to wait close to the card table and prepare to yell on his signal. Aaron went to the table and told a winner that he was prepared to play on any winner's wish. Normally, the card game was only for thieves, but the winner did not anticipate any problems from a kern and was agreeable. It was up to a rogue thief to take the challenge or refuse. He knew his own strength. A rogue could disregard the challenge from a kern, but the refusal would leave a mark on his reputation.

## The Criminal Code of Honor

*I*nside the slave camp were the strict rules of the criminal code of honor. The card games brought out a lot of emotions. A card game was a serious deed, and a cheating player's life would be in danger. Because of the changing luck in any card game, chances could rapidly change. Aaron was in a danger of becoming a sexual victim, a killer on the order of the winner, or a slave of the winner.

When the game started, Aaron saw that the winner stole a card. He blinked. Sashko started to yell and pointed to the game table. In every barrack was a taskmaster chosen by rogues. He reacted to the yelling, and Sashko aimed him at the card table. In the meantime, Aaron took the winner's hand and shook it. The man's hidden card fell onto the floor.

The barrack was quiet. One could hear his own breathing. The game stopped. Because the deprecated winner had broken the concept of honor, the situation changed. It was clear that after that incident, the loser, who was supposed to rape Sashko, would not dare to do it. Further, the prior winnings in the card game were questioned. In the barracks, many proud rogue thieves were offended by those who broke the code of honor. The culpable was marked for death. The cheater ran to the guards. The guards kept the cheater for a few days in the guardhouse and then brought him to another barrack. On the same day he returned, he was killed. The concept of honor was fulfilled.

With repressions, the Superior Leader showed that he did not care about norms of civilized society. The state was filled with Aboriginians who were candidates to be slaves.

Everywhere were massive areas of land where executed terrestrials were dropped. Superior Leader created his own honor code for the population. He became a king by being sneaky and cruel. In his life, he changed his last name many times. Depending on the circumstances, he could be Armenian, Jewish, terrestrial, Aboriginian, or celestial. He did not show any attachment to his original name. In his life, he adopted the name Superior, which meant "Greater." His choice of name revealed his search for stability. He used his power under the name of the collective. He was free to do everything he wanted. Anyone who criticized him or had the audacity to doubt the power of doctrine became a slave in the schizoid's projects. Anyone who had doubts of his wisdom or broke his honor code was eradicated.

In Baku, Aaron's father knew of his son's troubles. His older son, Rudi, had informed him in a letter that his younger son, Aaron, and son-in-law, Sashko, had been arrested, convicted, and sent to prison in Turkmenistan. When Isaac received the sad news, he understood that his son being in a slave camp was equal to his receiving a death sentence. Rudi did not mention that his son-in-law and brother had been arrested because of his daughter's denunciation. Rudi did not do anything to help because of pressure from his wife and threats by his daughter to kill herself. In the letter to his father, he said that his brother and son-in-law had been arrested by the secret police and that he did not have any connections over there. Rudi was not completely truthful, because he did indeed have a man in the secret police. He might have been able to save Aaron and Sashko considering the corruption in the collective state and the fact that the arrest had not received much attention from the political elite.

For the friends, being in the slave prison was the same as being already dead. A responsible parent, Isaac would not give up. He would take care of his son. Most escapees from prison would not have thought about putting themselves in danger, but Isaac was different. His son was in a deadly predicament, and he did not care about his own safety. He would do everything possible to save his son. A father's love was not in making a big scene but in being ready to do something dangerous in order to save his son.

Isaac did not think for long. In that situation, time was enemy number one. He simply took a ferryboat from Baku to Turkmenistan. The ferryboat was big and had many cars as cargo. Merchants sold them for good prices in Turkmenistan.

He arrived in the capital of Turkmenistan. After being in Baku, a city with parks, promenades, and a Mediterranean lifestyle, coming to that city was like going to a village. It was poor, dusty, provincial, and ordinary. Isaac found the headquarters of the slave prisons. He stayed in front and intuitively waited for something. Consciously, he did not know what he was waiting for, but in about one hour, he saw a familiar face: the head of security in Kolyma River. The man was heavier and moved slower than before, but Isaac recognized him anyway. Isaac decided to approach the officer even though he had a high rank in the police and could have arrested Isaac as an escapee from prison. Isaac knew he was risking his life, but he also understood that the life of his son was more important. He had in his possession two diamonds from Kolyma River secretly hidden on his body. His legal wife, Glasha, had sewn a little bag for the diamonds and attached it to his clothes. The diamonds were the best in all of his collection, cleaner and larger than the others. They were graded by color and size. Isaac knew that some officials would have taken his adamants and done nothing and, even more, arrested him too. He did not care. He had vigorously dedicated himself to helping his son at any cost, even his own freedom. For anyone who was so determined, the chance would come.

Isaac saw the familiar face of the officer, crossed the street, and called to the officer, using his first name, the same way he'd done when he'd secretly brought him the diamonds of Kolyma River. In the past, they'd drunk vodka and called each other by their first names. The officer stopped. He waited for the stranger to come closer. He right away recognized his informer and supplier of diamonds. He looked at him with disbelief. "You are alive! I thought about your death for a long time."

Isaac answered, "Please allow me to say something. I have all my legal papers. I am asking for help." The officer understood that Isaac had come for something important. He said he was busy at the moment but could meet Isaac in the evening in the restaurant on the main street. Isaac understood that if the officer had been single-minded, he would have made a show of catching an escapee and arresting him. The officer let him go.

Isaac came to the meeting an hour before the appointed time. He knew the power of a favorable atmosphere in negotiations. In the collective, political bosses had many resorts where they would invite important visitors. Those places had fantastic kitchens, good liquor, healing water, and high-quality live performance artists. Isaac had been to many restaurants in Baku and knew what to order. He recognized that success in negotiation depended on a good atmosphere. He ordered the best: French cognac, beluga caviar, oysters, sturgeon shish kebabs, and other delicious food. The officer was pleased when he saw all the goodies.

He drank French cognac, ate mouthwatering fare, and listened. Isaac negotiated with the officer for the lives of Aaron and Sashko. The atmosphere for negotiation was right. The table in the restaurant was near the window and faced the sea with a fantastic view. An orchestra played slow Middle Eastern tunes. The pleasant smells of barbecued meat and smoked sturgeon filled the air.

The collective was built on bribes. As a system, it had a confederation. It provided bribes for other countries in many forms, including building electric and atomic power stations and a big dam and giving many presents, such as jets and military equipment. The effort led to an increase in supporters, which led to more entrapment for degenerates. The population read in the papers about those gifts and felt proud. Contrary to big outside politics, inside the region, rulers, infected by the illness of distrust, pacified their areas with unheard-of cruelty and cheap liquor. They used brutal force to turn individuals into marionettes. They used alcohol to confuse.

Being with the officer, Isaac was terrified. For strength, he had a father's love for his son. For him, it was the biggest benefit of all toward saving his son. He overcame his fears. In a crisis, he needed to be strong. Isaac did not have sizable gifts to offer. He had something small but valuable.

## Isaac's Negotiations

*I*saac was negotiating with a serious person an important issue: the life of his son. For Isaac, the benefit was the freedom of Aaron and Sashko. To negotiate, Isaac provided benefits to the other side. He was ready to pay. He knew he was speaking to an expert in gems when he described one of the diamonds. The eyes of the officer grew large when Isaac mentioned the diamonds. The officer said he needed to know if the two prisoners were connected to the celestials from the ruling elite. Isaac denied it. The officer said, "Give me their names, and I will consider how to help you."

The next day, Isaac met the officer in the same restaurant with the same delicatessen. The officer said he had good news: he'd found the prison Aaron and Sashko were being held in. He said they'd been sentenced as political prisoners, but he could help anyway.

Isaac shook his head. "No, no. I guarantee with my life that it is a mistake; they are apolitical." He swore by putting his index finger to his teeth. By the criminal code, he swore with his life. That meant if he lied, he volunteered to be a whore. The officer had been given the highest guarantee in criminal ethics, and he was not a stranger to the criminal code. The officer continued. He said he had a plan, but it would cost another diamond. Isaac had other diamonds and was willing to trade another for the freedom of his family. Thankfully, it worked. The diamonds from Kolyma River saved lives. The officer mentioned that new regulations had just come out. Because of the infectious disease and the prevention of epidemics, a doctor could sign a terminally ill prisoner a release from prison. He added that he had a trusted doctor in a prison who would be able to do it.

Isaac paid the officer, and in two weeks, Aaron and Sashko were free from the prison with papers of release because of sickness. Isaac knew that any negotiations should benefit both sides. He had the freedom of Aaron and Sashko, and the officer had his gems. The negotiation was fair for both. However, as a result, Isaac got even more than he'd expected. The story of the diamonds never ended; it was just another point in the favor of negotiations.

Sofia had not forgiven Sashko. They were never together again. In the meantime, Isaac sold another diamond that was of lower quality and bought two houses: one for Sara's family and one for himself and Glasha. He lived next door to his daughter. They often had barbecues with sturgeon and shish kebabs. The story of the Kolyma River diamonds continued for a long time. Fair negotiation reaped its harvest. The officer in Turkmenistan gave Isaac a letter to his brother, who had a high rank in Baku's police force. Through his connections, Isaac helped many to gain freedom, but he did not forget his interests. He made a lot of money by being the go-between for folks in trouble. In Baku, he was a respectable man. As an investment, he occasionally bought more diamonds. He did not ask about their origins.

## Baku, a Cosmopolitan City

*B*aku was itself a hidden diamond in Aborigin. The residents came from many different ethnicities. Isaac was a socialite and played many card games with his rich friends of various ethnicities. He knew that connections were important. He could help to gain freedom for numerous falsely accused. He helped many in trouble. Isaac made money by helping many in despair. He was not a hero. He was an opportunist. He was one of many. In Baku, the society of the rich and wealthy existed in reality. Rich habitants knew how to make money. For Isaac, it was desirable to be one of them. The uninfected were not powerful, but they organized society based on prosperous and honest relations. They helped each other and enjoyed their friendships. Isaac and Glasha appreciated life among those uninfected by the indoctrinating blabber. They trusted their neighbors. They could entrust them with merchandise without any collateral. The society of the rich resembled the dream of futurists. The affluent had different dealings, and their interactions were without dirty tricks, confrontations, and manipulations. They had status and did not do anything to jeopardize it.

Isaac's house was close to Ahmed's and Dr. Ali's houses, as well as those of many other well-off neighbors. Isaac was between the gem lovers. He multiplied his stock of diamonds. He bought and sold them. In the evenings, they usually went to see Dr. Ali and other neighbors. They ate pilaf, shish kebabs, lulu kebabs, stuffed cabbage, sturgeon, caviar, and more. After the nutritious meal, they played cards. Isaac and Glasha were happy. They could trust others and not be afraid of informers and con artists.

For Aaron and Sashko, their days in the slave prison seemed to be an awful dream. By analyzing their lives, Professor Kryvoruchko assumed that guardian angels existed. The experience unified their psyches and made them solid. The friends survived because they, like Isaac, had a guardian angel. Being in the slave camp was equal to a death sentence. On top of that were various complications of being humiliated and tortured. Professor Kryvoruchko looked at one episode after other and put them in sequence, creating a chain of inconceivable events that, without a guardian angel, was impossible to comprehend. He mentioned that the Kaufman family probably had their own guardian angel who'd saved their lives. The guardian angel saved lives. Kerns in slave prison did not live long.

It was also a big disadvantage to have good looks. Sashko was good looking, which created problems. He was blond, with blue eyes. The rogues planned to use him as a sexual slave. The guardian angel saved him when Sashko was in a jam. Sashko did not have any protection. He was nobody. In the criminal structure, he was an insect. All kerns in prison were unsafe. It seemed nothing could help him, but he had his friend, and Aaron had a guardian angel. A card game could be mortal. If a player cheated, he died, and his winnings were not considered valid. Aaron had proven that the winner of Sashko's fate was a cheater. He'd done so in front of many. That move had saved his friend.

Aaron extended his friend's life, but that was not all. One couldn't forget the guardian angel. In a different situation, Sashko would not have lived much longer. In prison, both friends were supposed to die from inhuman conditions, but Aaron had a guardian angel.

## Way to Freedom, Part 3

The project in Turkmenistan was one of the deadliest parts of the slave prisons. It was the meanest innovation of the collective. The slave camp was utilized in a chain of many crazy projects that used slave labor. Outside, the mistrust and sickness were splitting minds. For the nation, it would take a long time to recuperate from the infection and gain a solid psyche. One of the most demented failures of the collective was the Turkmen Canal. It was supposed to irrigate the sands of central Asia. However, it was not properly designed and not correctly calculated. It was a stupid venture founded on slave labor. A hundred thousand slaves died in order to implement the delusional idea. They carried sand on wooden stretchers under the searing sun without protective clothes, food, or water. Aborigin needed slaves. The ideologists brainwashed habitants with the idea of fake enemies. They created fictitious enemies whom they called saboteurs, traitors, and spies to send them to slavery and to replace the dead. The community was overrun with snitches, finks, and informers. Aboriginians were afraid of everything. To survive, they repeated devilish doctrine as prayer. It did not help.

In slave prisons, the rogues had a lot of power. They trusted each other. The doctrine of criminals was based on the concept that a tribal leader had ultimate power. In criminal doctrine, the kingpin was a leader with the responsibility to adjudicate if the rogue criminals broke the tribal rules. The kerns pushed the barrows. They were objects and insects. They did not have any rights. The guards, the rogue criminals, and their kingpins were celestials. They ruled the prison. That thinking was a collective doctrine. In criminal life, card playing was both enjoyable and a display of intellectual capacities. A good card player was considered a champion and had a lot of privileges. The criminal structure had special rules for playing cards. Cheating in cards was the biggest offense. The matter of paying a card debt was unquestionable. A default on the debt was a punishable offense. The rogues did not have money, so they played with the lives of kerns and whatever was left of their human dignity.

In his mission to liberate his son, Isaac definitely had the help of a guardian angel. Fortunately, Isaac was on the move as soon as he found out about his son's misfortune. A strong-minded Isaac met an authority who was ready to play his game. Isaac knew something about the art of negation. He knew that the atmosphere around the table was important. He was a player, and as his bet, he put on the table the biggest jackpot he had. He provided amazing benefits that the other party could not refuse. The deal was sealed. Aaron and Sashko were free. In his future dealings, Isaac successfully used various negotiation techniques and became a reputable man.

As a result of his negotiation in Tajikistan, Isaac benefited and got richer. He also helped a few others become wealthy. He lived around the rich, and the rich had a different attitude. The diabolic doctrine promised too much and was not able to deliver. The confused Aboriginians did not see any solution. They felt the doctrine was a better answer than complete terror and mayhem. The Aboriginians, instead of taking wealth by force, could have learned negotiation skills and become rich like Isaac. Instead of killing, stealing, torturing, and raping, they could have found a way to help the terrestrials move closer to the celestials. Isaac's life was an example that the doctrine was wrong. He was an individual with a solid psyche. He was able to make a difference for himself and others. He refused to be an object. With the help of a guardian angel, he was not thrown into the muzzle of a killing machine. The solution, which required taking wealth from others by force, was a stupid outcome of the deadly infection by the red bug. That force did not fix inequality. Aboriginians did not acquire business skills. They did not become richer. Contrarily, the lives of the rich were the opposite. The rich were creative, trustful, and respectable. They enjoyed negotiations. Their air did not smell of dogmatic rot.

## THE SEARCH OF THE SOLID PSYCHE

Many were killed in the Great Patriotic War. It was a dark time, but the guardian angels continued to be around the Kaufmans. During the invasion, when the Nazis were close to Baku, Sara's and Ahmed's sons volunteered for the military. At the time, the boys were only sixteen years old. A couple hours after enlisting, not yet trained and without ammunition, the volunteer soldiers were sent into battle. Under fire, the schoolchildren without guns ran on the Nazis' positions. They were supposed to pick up any weapons from the dead. In half an hour, Sara's boy had shots in many places and was declared dead. If not for his friend, he would have stayed dead. The collective used young boys as cannon fodder. It did not care if they lived or died. They hoped that from a thousand, a few might get through and hold a piece of land covered with corpses. It was a bad strategy, but the collective used it everywhere and survived the war. The Nazis did not have enough bullets to kill or enough gasoline to move their troops. They lost. The black virus was exterminated.

Ahmed's son carried his friend for fifteen miles to Sara's house. He was exhausted. However, he did not think about leaving his friend behind, which would have been dastardly. He'd made a promise. Before the boys had gone to the battlefield, Sara called them and warned that they should look out for each other. She'd stated that if one of them got wounded and the other did not bring him to safety, she would kill herself in front of the coward. She'd sworn to God, and the boys believed her treat. She had the reputation of being a tough woman.

Sara proved she had her own voice. She bought fruits

wholesale and then resold them retail at the bazaar. Every one of her suppliers knew she paid a fair price. She had a little store at the bazaar. With the help of Isaac, she bribed officials. She had a permanent place and a permit. For individual suppliers, it was not advantageous to pay for places and permits. They sold their products to Sara. Ahmed's son helped her in the storage room, and she paid him generously. He knew she always did what she promised. When Ahmed's son brought the boy, Sara and Isaac took the boy to the hospital. However, the hospital did not take him because doctors had declared him dead. Isaac brought the boy to Dr. Ali, who stopped his other activities and attended to Isaac's grandson. Dr. Ali used his new invention and, with the help of a guardian angel, resuscitated the youngster. The boy lived a good, long life and had many offspring. It was a miracle. Sara's son, along with the rest of his family, ended up in Israel. His children were soldiers in the Israeli army. They were fighters for good.

During the Second World War, the citizens of Azerbaijan, including Isaac, Dr. Ali, Ahmed, and many of his neighbors, donated a lot of their diamonds to build tanks. When the Nazis were close to Baku, almost all the men were mobilized. They were Azeri, Armenian, Jewish, and Aboriginian. Many died, but the Nazis were repulsed. Baku was saved.

After they buried the dead, a peaceful life came back to Baku. It was a multiethnic city. It had Mediterranean impurities. The air smelled of Eastern spices. Even in befouled terrain, a fantastic city flourished. The business-oriented were able to prosper and have luxurious lives. Isaac and Glasha spent warm evenings on the porch of their house. In their backyard, several citrus trees cast shadows. Near their terrace was a barbecue area where

Isaac made juicy shish kebabs. Ahmed and his son were neighbors and welcome guests at their gatherings. When Isaac traveled with diamonds, Ahmed's son, who was well built, guarded him. He knew a few policemen, and in case of problems, he was able to call them. The neighbors were happy. For saving Sara's son, Ahmed's son was rewarded many times. Like his father, he became a jeweler. He continued to be friends with Sara's son. Isaac and Glasha lived long lives and were buried in Baku. They had large memorial sculptures on their graves. They saved lives, and they were Sailors.

# CHAPTER 2

Aaron Kaufman had the misfortune of living in Aborigin, an area soiled by ruination. He lived in a situation that would have been impossible for others to imagine. For Aaron and the others around him, the purging and devastation continued for a long time. The atrocities took the lives of millions, including many of his relatives. The habitants continued suffering from the consequences of the horrible atrocities imposed on them. Despite all his struggles, Aaron was able to survive. He was the husband of Dora Kaufman and had two children; each was married. He'd always respected and admired his father, Isaac, who was a business-oriented man. Aaron, without any extensive command of the French and English languages, which were used in the West, became a multimillionaire. He had the gene of business orientation, which was a real diamond in his possession. Many scientists believed that business orientation was hereditary. It was difficult to learn. Many business-oriented individuals lacked a formal education. A few of the business-oriented survived infection by the toxin of nutcases. They avoided lives in the shackles of collective thinking. They declared that the business-oriented had not said their last words. They were capable of saying a whole lot more.

## Dora, Aaron's Wife

Dora was born in Udmurtia, where her mother was a housekeeper for the rich. Her father died when she was only three years old. All her life, she hated being poor. She did not like the city where she was born, which was noted only for being the home of the brilliant composer Pyotr Ilyich Tchaikovsky. Otherwise, it was just a regular province. The city had a tramline. As a young girl, Dora was a tomboy and commuted by jumping in and out of the tram. She was not scared of anything.

Aaron impressed her. He acted rich, and everything he touched was a success. When she married Aaron, she knew he was in prison. She also knew that in the past, he'd had a girlfriend and a son. He was also older, but she did not care. In her life, Aaron was only a tool to achieve her dreams. She wanted to marry a rich man, and Aaron was a right candidate. Dora knew that during Aaron's time in prison, his girlfriend had married a military man. With Aaron's son, she'd left to her husband's place of service. Aaron was not able to find her and his son. Information about military persons and their families was not available. Dora believed that the past was not repeated, and she put all her bets on her husband. Her children were grown. She was content even though she did not have grandchildren yet. She thought it most important that her children were married, and she believed that everything else would happen in time.

She felt happy. Her husband was generous and treated her like a princess. He was able to make her a happy woman.

The venomous supporters of the intoxicated land should have listened to the wives of the businessmen. Instead of killing, they should have left the habitants alone, and the nation would have prospered. Before killing them, the leaders should have listened to the wives of the victims. Dora believed that Aaron had made her dreams come true. Near him, she always was rich and secure.

Before emigrating from an unsafe country, Aaron was arrested again. Dora's maid left her and took Dora's mink coat. Fortunately, Aaron had powerful connections left to him by his father. The times had changed, but the old guards in the state, tainted by blight, still had a lot of power. In modern times, the old guard was corrupt in the same deep-rooted way. Aaron got out of jail, and Dora reunited with her mink cost and again had an obedient housecleaning lady. Aaron was able to make her happy.

Contrarily, the perdition resulted in millions of unhappy people. Aaron and his business-oriented friends at least knew how to make their wives happy. Dora Kaufman was Aaron Kaufman's love. She was an average woman polluted by venom and unhappy. However, after marriage, she was able to enjoy delicious food, travel abroad, and live in spacious dwellings. She was a pragmatic woman and did not care about idiotic doctrines. Dora did not talk much about her husband's family. She only knew that all his relatives were prosperous. They dwelled in the darkness of the shadow economy. Their biggest crime was being wealthy. In the opinion of those infected by ruination, it was a crime to be prosperous. The obscenity robbed families of their possessions. It raped and murdered them only because they were affluent. Aaron's father was rich. He could make money. He was in prison, but he escaped. The dark shadow was over the heads of everyone. Aaron's father, Isaac, was a fighter. He was not conquered by the forces of darkness.

The collective selected Aaron, who was able to live, while others were not. Millions moved to obscurity. That selection eliminated the most active part of society. It left the less capable and less intelligent in charge. Managers were from the weakest part of the insecure society. Only the silent masses, crippled by fear, were able to tolerate the torture for long. Contrary to Aaron, the rulers in power were thickheaded, ignorant, and illiterate schemers. They had only one goal: to manipulate and confront others. Because of their venom, many ended up in the blackness. Different habitants were affected by abnormals. They were rich and poor, smart and stupid, educated and illiterate. The real function of the diseased rule was moving habitants from the light to the shadows. They used different methods, including ideological purges. They exposed class enemies and started unnecessary conflicts. They worked silly machinations by inciting one part of the population against another. They purged religious and spiritual leaders, artists, scientists, and dissidents. They used all the necessary tricks to deprive habitants of the light.

## The Habitants' Affliction

Aaron's son, Sam, as a young man, was not a Sailor. His problems were from debauched luck. He loved Aboriginian culture, songs, and stories, but he had a typical Jewish face and a Jewish last name. Because of his ethnicity, he was kept from expressing those feelings. He was not proud to be a Jew and did not feel secure or like a real Aborigin. He was not tall and did not have blue eyes. He felt guilty that he was short and had a long nose and brown eyes and hair. He was miserable. He wanted to be like the native Aboriginians but did not know what to do about his problem. He dreamed about doing a heroic feat. Feeling unlucky, he got himself into a terrible predicament. He, at one point in his life, made a wrong move. Because Sam did not like himself, he made a poor choice. He got into trouble with one of his girlfriends. He did not meet her expectations for romantic love. Sam wanted sex but did not want to marry. In the communal state, romantic love and sexual lust were a dangerous alliance. When a girl decided to marry a sexual partner, it was often difficult to get out of the situation. The girl would report rape to the police without any fear that she would be liable for wrong accusations. The girl usually said she'd been forced into sex. The victims of those predicaments were mostly young men. A common method of punishment already had existed for many years, but not everything was so simple. There were different ways to deal with those accusations.

Sam's girlfriend reported him to the police. Sam did not ask his father for help. The easiest way out of trouble was to pay bribes to the police, but then he would have needed to ask his father for help. Sam was a proud person. He paid his debts himself. He believed he'd be able to get out of his predicament, even though his father could have made it easier. He did it in a different way, paying not with money but with his integrity.

As one of the infected, Sam was polluted by doctrine. He was a believer and became an informer for the secret police. He did not have any shame in doing it. He reported on dissidents and emigrants. He kept his secret to himself. By order of the secret police, he left for the West and continued to report on fellow emigrants outside of the collective's butchery. He got married before leaving Aborigin, but his wife did not know anything about his past. His parents and sister also did not know anything about his activities.

## Accusations of Rape in an Infected Country

Sam was not happy with himself and did not like himself for a long time. He came from a stable house. Psychological brainwashing split his psyche. As was the case with many kids from rich Jewish houses, he studied to be a medical doctor. His father was jailed a few times, but their home was full of goodies. During his life, Sam did not have a shortage of anything. He came from a home where habitants knew how to deal with predicaments. He looked at the incident of his girlfriend's accusation as a test of his abilities. He wanted to understand what would happen next and waited. Becoming an informer changed his whole life. It was hard to imagine, but Sam gained something from that incident. A crazy secret police agent who was a paranoid killer planned the assassination of a professor. Together, Sam and Stepan Luchko were able to get the killer arrested. Sam became a real Sailor. It was not easy, but he overcame many of his barriers. He got to know Professor Kryvoruchko and found out they were somehow related.

Professor Kryvoruchko and Sam did not know much

about their relatives. For a long time, they did not know about each other. The Kaufman clan had many colorful characters. They lived in the world of negotiation. When looking at that family, it was hard to deny that negotiation skills were hereditary. They also were able to defend their lives and the lives of others.

## Sashko's Infidelity

Eric's father, Sashko Belay, married a wealthy woman. She was from a different world. As a child, Sashko grew up in a little borough in a communal setting with one toilet and one kitchen for several families. Because of his handsome looks, he ended up living in private quarters with his wife, an actress. He was accepted by many artists. With his friend Aaron, he was active in business. Sashko Belay was a terrestrial Aboriginian, but he produced Eric. He came to the Kaufman family because he saw an opportunity to have a good life. Sashko Belay did not possess any business skills. In his work under Aaron Kaufman's guidance, he made some money. He did not have any illusions about himself. He did not know how to protect his money. His mother was a worker in a leather factory. He was used to the smell of leather. It did not bother him. He was able to learn a shoemaker's trade. Sashko Belay was not a Kaufman. He did not know much about many complicated things, but he had tremendous luck in staying alive. He survived in a slave prison created by the red monster. He also survived the Patriotic War.

As soon as he and Aaron separated, Sashko was by himself. He knew he was unmindful and oblivious regarding business matters. Frightened by his suffering in prison, he kept as low profile as possible. He had an insignificant life. He was one of many whose psyches were crushed by the disastrous virus. He ended up as the sperm donor of a movie star. According to doctrine, Sashko Belay was supposed to be a ruler of the infected land, but in reality, he was a worthless person. During the blockade of the gorgeous city, Sashko Belay left it. He did an appalling thing: during the war, he switched sides. For him, there was only one way to stay alive. He left the starving city and went to the other side. He ended up on the side occupied by Nazis. The border was on the brink of the city. He bribed a starving border policeman, who let him pass through. He left the red scourge for the black scourge.

## The Luck of Sashko Belay

Sashko Belay was fortunate to survive the savage war. Supreme Leader, infected by the red disease, wanted him dead. The policeman was more humane and let him leave. In the surrounding city, more than a million died of hunger. Rather than endure senseless death, he saved himself. That fact did not please the mad leader. The city was left without any food or supplies. The Nazis waited until everyone died. As a result, more than a million died. They died from the stupidity of the authorities, who wanted victory at any cost. It was a Pyrrhic victory. The losses certainly outweighed the gains.

Because of the mismanagement and carelessness of the authorities, more than twenty million died only on the collective's side. Sashko was a stayer. Sashko's papers, which Isaac Kaufman had bought for him, mentioned that he had an infectious disease. The papers worked for him. Sashko was decommissioned on both sides. Upon arriving on the Nazi side, Sashko showed his papers proving he'd been released from the slave prison for health reasons. The policemen on the Nazi side knew the horrors of the slave prisons and knew that habitants did not get out easily. They were afraid of the infection. The Nazis did not take him to serve as a soldier. Because his last name sounded Malantian, Sashko ended up in Malantia. He was not involved in war crimes. For both sides, he was just a disabled man.

Sashko Belay did not forget the time when he was rich and lived among the wealthy. By lucky chance, he lived around the rich. He experienced for a while the life of rich folks. As soon as he left them, he returned to the same social status he'd known as a child. Sashko Belay was a sock. He was lucky to be alive.

After his second marriage, he had a happy family life. Some were born to be shoemakers, and he was one of them. Sashko never again saw his older son, Eric, who became a movie star. He had two children with his Malantian wife. Sashko Belay was a simple man and floated through life on different currents. However, his children had their own voices. In the postcollective time, they wanted to achieve historical justice for Malantia. He was close to one of his sons, Sashko Jr., who became a leader of one of the nationalistic movements. His son got involved in the Malantian nationalistic movement known as Sector Five. He fought the influence of collectivism and proclaimed that Malantia should be for Malantians. He was a fighter for an independent Malantia. Sashko's son was ready to give his life for his beloved homeland and later was killed by a stray bullet in a skirmish with another nationalistic group. Sashko Belay lived through his son's death. He died in his bed at an old age, surrounded by his grandchildren and great-grandchildren.

## Eric Belay

*U*nlike his father, Eric was born in a rich house with a lot of antiques and paintings by famous Aboriginian artists, as well as a priceless painting by a famous classical landscape artist of Jewish descent who'd died in 1900. Eric became famous and lived life in the limelight. He lived among famous and creative habitants. He had more than enough fame for himself. He lived in the gorgeous city built on the 101 islands. The islands were connected by many bridges. Some of the bridges had buildings on them. Habitants walked around those constructions and did not know they were walking on bridges. Being the son of Sashko Belay, Eric inherited the looks of his father and resembled a hero of Aborigin's epics. Eric wrote poetry about the mystical place where he was born. It was a fantastic city and had the most gorgeous girls in the whole universe.

## Eric and His Mentally Ill Grandmother

*E*ric was influenced by his grandmother. She talked to invisible habitants. She told a story that her mother was a dressmaker in the royal house and had an affair with a king. She told Eric in secret that she was related to the czar. After hearing those stories, he too was confused and lived in dreams. He did not like to be around his relatives. He was not close to his stepfather, who was a director of one of the theaters. He suspected the real love of his stepfather was not Eric's mother but a big black German shepherd. His mother lived her own life and had many daydreams too. His stepfather loved to walk with his dog and often took the dog to their summer cottage. He was famous, and the neighbors recognized him. In contrast, Eric was a loner and liked to walk. In the gorgeous city, water was everywhere. He liked water and often sat on the embankment of the legendary river.

A lot of habitants, infested by the psychological ailment, had secrets. Eric looked like a traditional Slavic hero but had one secret: from his early childhood, his mother had colored his hair a blondish color. He looked unquestionably Slavic. It was an obscure area, and he took advantage of his appearance. The movie and stage performances of that time and place were about brave and fantastic-looking Slavic boys and girls. The government's ideologists entirely controlled the entertainment industry. To please the government, movie characters were intended to increase the productivity of the government-owned factories and farms. Ideologists also showed typical Slavic actors as a metal workers. For the viewers, the quality of the story was not essential, but handsome actors were important. Eric's mother did everything to make Eric look exactly like an actor described by ideologists. She prepared him to be a man of popularity and admiration. In terrain soiled by perdition, Eric was in demand.

## Eric's Appearance

For a different reason, bullies attacked Eric. It was difficult to be good looking and not dirtied by irredeemable germs. Actually, he was lucky in that area too. As a student in school, he did not make many friends. He was good looking, and bullies who were jealous of his looks often beat him up. He was even afraid to go to the restroom. He did not know the reason for the attacks. Once, he overheard a conversation of two boys who planned to beat him up. From the conversation, he understood that in the school was a group of children of single mothers who'd been impregnated by Nazis. During the war, in the surrounded city, many died from hunger. The many displaced came to dwell in empty apartments. Afraid of persecution, the bad women ended up in the city of the dead. Because they slept with enemy soldiers and were afraid of imprisonment, they ran away from their villages. According to indoctrinated norms, the women were supposed to be in jail for any connection to the enemy. They were hiding in the city. By bribing officials, they had no problem in falsifying their records. They faked their names to be the relatives of the dead. There were many vacant apartments to settle in. Without any difficulty, those impregnated by Nazis found available dwellings. Later, their offspring organized a resistance group. The Nazis had lost the war, but Nazi ideology flourished. Bullies were after Eric because they thought he was a Malantian. They felt that Malantians betrayed Nazi ideology to have their own.

Underground, Nazi ideology was flourishing. According to that ideology, Aborigin was supposed to be an older brother to other ethnicities. The belief created inequality. It seemed as if the other ethnicities were defective. It sounded as if something were wrong with them. It appeared their older brother was striating them and providing a clear direction. The official national policy gave undeserved honor to Aboriginians. The Black Hundred and Remembrance nationalist movements flourished. They summoned habitants who were willing to glorify Aboriginians. They put down everyone who was different from them and hated with deepness in their hearts. They participated in actions to hurt others. Additional movements were not as visible but existed. The surviving offspring of the Nazis wanted to reclaim their superiority. To be great, they put others down. They bullied Malantians, Armenians, and Jews.

In the infected region, being Jewish was somehow shameful and not safe. Many Jews hid their identities. If a habitant identified himself as Jewish, someone assumed he was joking and immediately asked if he was serious.

Eric's good looks created a lot of jealousy. He never mentioned to anyone that he had a Jewish mother. Bullies beat him up because the assailants thought he was Malantian. No one had any suspicion that he was a half-breed. In school, Eric learned that it was best for him to pretend he adhered to the dominant nation. Students despised each other because of ethnic features. They detested others for no reason at all. To Eric, they all were nasty jackals. Among the students was a boy with a Jewish last name. Somehow, he was not scared and had independence. It seemed he was not afraid of anyone. Eric, who was looking for support, decided to talk to him and revealed that he was half Jewish. The boy listened to him. He said he never had thought Eric had Jewish blood; on account of his blond hair and blue eyes, he'd thought Eric was half German. The Jewish boy reassured Eric that he'd been correct to open up to him. Eric found out that in the school, there was a group of boys with indigenous Slavic last names but Jewish blood. As it turned out, several of them were savage bullies. Because of incorrect assumptions, they previously had beaten Eric up.

## Eric's Bullies

*F*ierce boys mainly beat Eric because they thought he was a German. After they learned the truth, all of them were on his side. His new friends beat up some of his past assailants who were part of the Nazi gang. Eric was safe, but when he saw his past assailants savagely trampled, he did not feel good. The Jewish boys did not have mercy, and some of them were more aggressively hateful than the Nazis. They believed the violence of Nazis needed to be punished with maximum strength. He observed that his previous Malantian supporters, who hated the Jews, were beaten up too. By luck, Eric's life changed in a minute. He understood how important it was to be among the right habitants. He felt free and not scared anymore. He was able to eventually join the right crowd.

Eric made the right choice. All his future life, he kept close ties with the boys who had Aboriginian last names but Jewish mothers. Many of them became important. They were going up in their careers and helped Eric to climb as well. In the cultural area in which Eric became successful, some gained high positions and supported him, and he helped them become his protégés. He too had an indigenous last name, and his face was in accordance with high standards. On his identification document that listed his ethnicity, he had the correct ethnicity. Those factors were his assets. He knew that many of the land's most talented, because of their wrong ethnicities, were put down. In movies, Eric played the handsome boy with Aboriginian features and patriotic thoughts.

A lot of Jews were bulwarks of Aboriginian culture because of their mastery of language, but no one would accept them as equal or significant. In Aborigin, Jews carried identification documents that described them as Jews. It made them filthy by a curse of ignorance. The Jews were whipping boys for many who hated the Jewish ethnicity. It was ironic that as soon as Jews left the bewitched country, in the eyes of foreigners, they became Aboriginians. Eric was lucky not to have a Jewish last name.

## Eric's Love for the Gorgeous City

The gorgeous city was full of secret places and mysterious attractions. Eric discovered places described by great writers. When he got older, he was able to talk to girls on the street and had company. He would enter with girls through the entry doors of communal apartments. To promote the communal lifestyle, the hallway doors of those houses infected by misfortune were always open. He hugged his companions in the stairwells. He even made love on windowsills. A lot of times, he never saw his companions again. He often went to the movies and sat close to single girls. During the movie, his hands would go to hug the girl, and sometimes the girl would kiss him. He was engrossed in the adventures the mysterious city presented to its travelers. Everything was going well, and later, Eric started having parties in his home. His mother, stepfather, and dog went to a chalet in the village, and the whole house was his. Being often alone, he brought girls over. Many girls fell for his looks. He had a sweet tooth and changed girlfriends daily. He was a Casanova. He was lucky that none of his girls took advantage of the rich boy. He was part of the city in the same way its monument of Peter the Great was. In that fantastic city, no one wanted to think about stinky communal apartments and corrupt police. Eric's best talk was about the many monuments and palaces. He knew the city up and down and could impress with his knowledge.

The police were corrupt. The widespread corruption ruined many lives. Eric, if he had been accused of rape, would have faced a stressful situation in his life. If he'd had a problem to resolve, his mother would have lost a diamond ring from one of her fingers or maybe even two. Many girls worked together with the police and put out false reports that rich boys had forced themselves on them. The corrupt police did not listen to the rich boys or their guardians and demanded money. Many accused men who had their own places in big cities gave up their belongings to the police. Rape was shameful and against the criminal code. In jail, rapists performed the roles of the girls and sexually satisfied the criminals. Because of the aristocratic etiquette he used, Eric never had any misunderstandings, and girls admired him. No girl even thought to report him.

He loved the killing field befouled by perdition. He pretended a lot, and he enjoyed himself. He avoided all the obstacles. The boys of his age were often drunk, but he did not drink alcohol. He was happy without it. His addiction was women, and it did not give him any problems. Eric was lucky and enjoyed a beautiful city and beautiful girls. He was a womanizer, and he knew how to handle his women.

Eric was a celestial. Around Eric was a lot of promiscuity. It was common to talk on the street to strangers. Men made rounds on the beach and approached single women. Eric was not an outsider. He was comfortable on the beach. He would see a girl sitting next to the water and approach her. It was customary to talk to single women. It was called checking them out. The custom did not require any sophisticated punch lines. It could be an introduction of oneself. Eric simply told the girl that he liked to look at the water. For him, what he said was not as important as how the girl answered. One day he spoke to a girl who was older than he was. He was eighteen. She was twenty-two. She told him she was divorced, worked in a hospital, and lived close by in her parents' house. It seemed she had a lot of experience with men. Eric's boyish looks were working. He knew it and talked to the girl more surely. The day was hot but not boring.

## Eric's Skills

Eric was a real Belay but not a Sailor. He did not save anyone. He had a lot of sexual interactions. Sex was a way to relieve stress. One of his partners, Lora, was a nurse and wanted sex. In her job, she ran around a lot. The hospital had too many patients. The beds were everywhere. In some rooms, there were ten to fifteen habitants. The infirmary was overcrowded, and everyone asked for something. Lora worked hard. She did not have anyone to support her. Besides her old folks, there were not any significant persons in her life. She enjoyed sex. She liked Eric, who was not pushy and allowed things to go slowly. She appreciated his patience. Other boys would be all over her. She did not like it. She felt that she was in control. Lora kept Eric's penis in her hand and moved it around until it became strong and large, and then she put it inside her. She enjoyed every second of sex. Despite his young age, Eric knew how to please a woman. Eric already had been around a few girls. He knew that lovemaking required being nice, and the rest would be in his favor. In a killing field populated with rough and inconsiderate adolescents, his behavior was fresh and attractive to girls.

## Eric's Kingdom

The city and everything in Eric's life were perfect, and he was in heaven. One hot summer day, he was riding his bicycle and saw a blonde girl riding in front of him. Eric loved blondes. He got closer to her and said, "Hi." It was a crucial moment. She looked at him with a screening look. If he passed her screening, he might have a chance. Eric put his chest up.

She answered, "Hi, but I do not know you."

Eric responded, "I just want to welcome a fellow bicyclist. Have you done it for a long time?" The conversation started, and Eric understood that he'd passed her screening. For a girl, meeting with a polite and good-looking boy was an escape from the communal apartments. It was a boring life with electrical meters, separate bells for everyone, and one kitchen and one bathroom for all tenants. She was happy she had met someone nice. She was riding her bike on her lunch break. She was older and told him she worked as a group leader for a children's camp. She was tired of children's noise. Broods yelled and screamed without reason. Between boys, fights were common. The girls too called names and pulled each other's hair. The bicycle girl encouraged them to follow the rules and regulations. She wore a red tie, demonstrating to unruly children that red was a color of sacrifice. The children were taught that a red tie represented the blood of revolutionaries. The ideologists hoped that with the memory of victims of the revolution, children would behave. Stress at work was high. The girl used sex as a way to reduce stress.

Soon Eric and the girl were hiding in bushes not far from the freeway. He was fast, and he understood exactly what she looked for. They didn't talk. Eric took out his penis for a blowjob. She did it, and his penis was hard. Then he got on top of her. After climaxing, the girl lay down with a look of satisfaction on her face. The red tie suited the blonde girl. Her tie enhanced the charm of her hair. Eric was on top of the world. He felt he had done a good job. He deserved to wear a red tie too; he was a good Boy Scout.

## The Misfortune of Hypocrisy

Eric was a happy lover, but his thoughts were about the hypocrisy in his surroundings. It looked as if everyone were acting. Habitants talked a lot about love, but no one spoke about sex. It was not an appropriate topic. Many ideologists were womanizers and seduced women. They lied about their sex lives. They were not lovers at all. They just brainwashed their women into submission. Eric was different. He would spot women on the street and follow them. He was able to wait. He could verbalize all his actions. He did it seriously and talked about sex without any shame. He openly said to the girl what he desired. He undressed the girl if there were no objections.

In the atmosphere of lying, boys did not speak to girls about sex. No one asked for verbal consent. Boys mainly pushed unprepared girls if they resisted. The boy's main understanding was that girls were supposed to resist. The boys acted tough. It was ritualistic behavior. Compared to other boys, Eric had an advantage. He was not pushy. He never wanted to be a victor. He wanted sexual partnership. Before he started any intimacy, he waited for consent from the girl. He was a negotiator with soft manners. He whispered something into a girl's ear and quietly asked for her consent. He was able to arrange sexual encounters without pushing. He never had a girl get angry with him. If she was against sex with him or looked suspicious, he would stop and walk away before she could get him in trouble. Because he had a good attitude, he enjoyed consent. His biggest advantage was that he was a smooth lover.

With Eric, sex never was dirty. Eric had enjoyable sex and always used protection. His favorite position was from the back. Eric combed the streets to find voluptuous partners. He had a big raincoat to cover the girls. He turned his girls to face the wall in hallways, and if someone passed by, his girls would cover up with his coat. Eric loved blonde women, though hair color did not enhance his sexual feelings. Maybe Eric was following the stigma of hypersexuality attached to blondes. He had sex everywhere. In many different cultures, it was bad manners for men to approach strangers on the street with the goal of finding a sexual partner. Eric was a womanizer but treated his women with respect. Even though he was an adolescent, he acted like a man.

Eric would walk the streets and look at the beautiful girls. Eric's role model was Casanova, who had been passionate about women and had many devoted lovers. He kept a good appearance. He was a smooth talker. His best stage role was the story of Don Juan, who was an excellent lover too. He invited girls to his fashionable apartment. He was well dressed, and women loved him. Eric was honest and did not lie to girls. He spent a lot of time and energy on attracting women. He created techniques for how to approach women. Like his father, he was an excellent guitar player, and he knew a lot of good chansons. Basically, he was an entertainer with a love of sex. As an actor, he played factory workers, but it was not his choice. He wanted to be able to play the roles of heroic lovers.

In Aborigin, there was a lot of policing of sex because in the communal setting, lovers were in individual relationships. Eric was lucky and was never accused of breaking the moral code of collective existence. In the theater where he worked, some women had different positions of authority. The crucial test for him was pleasing the older women who were guardians of morality. However, he was sure that if anything unforeseen happened, his mother and stepfather would save him. In the meantime, he continued to love his homeland and avoided political thoughts. He did not allow any doubts about the correctness of the land-sickening rules.

Interestingly, he felt comfortable in the land stained by the toxins of madness. Being Sashko's son, he was good looking. He had a handsome Aboriginian face. He acted in many movies glorifying the simple man. Eric did not care that the notions of morals and love were disappearing. In the theater were many ideological judges. He avoided them. Agitators called for following the morality code that was supposed to be a building block of communalism. Eric stayed away from agitators who continuously repeated imbecilic doctrine. He intuitively understood that the empty space of law was filled with the criminal code. Aborigin was ruled by tribal concepts. Doctrine was based on perceived unquestionable fidelity to the leader as head of the family. The leader could punish his family at his own discretion. They believed one should not have to worry about anything. The leader took responsibility for morality. Ahead of ordinary habitants, the few antisocial were crowned as supreme leaders. In reality, they were godfathers and criminal kingpins.

## Eric's Wake-Up Call

For the first time in his life, Eric told a woman he did not want sex. The new young actress who played small roles but had gorgeous looks got his attention. She had big blue eyes and brown hair. When she moved, her hips swayed. One day he saw her walking on the street and stopped his car next to her. He saw that she already had a few drinks in her. Eric offered to drive her. She sat in the front seat next to him. When the car moved, he felt her hand on his knee. He drove to his home, and the woman came to his room. She asked for more vodka. Eric drank with her, and then he wanted to kiss her. She said he should wait and, before kissing her, admit he was a Jew. If he admitted it, she would sleep with him because he was an honest Jew. She said that despite his Slavic looks, she felt he was a Jew. She claimed the Jews were everywhere and were devils who beguiled Aboriginians. She said that to control their blameless reputations, Jews duped and flustered innocent Aboriginians with alcohol. She said Jews were impudent and shrewd, but she could see through them. According to her, all Jews were liars, and she felt he was one of them.

Eric said he was tired and wanted to rest. The woman was feeling comfortable and did not leave. He persuaded her to go by telling her he was required to be in the theater early in the morning. He took the woman to her home and immediately left. It was a disaster.

He found he was going nowhere in his life. He decided to have a stable relationship and stop his womanizing. He felt he was mature enough to marry a Jewish woman and have Jewish children. Eric's children would have his name and ethnicity on their identification documents, but they would have a Jewish mother. It was the best combination for Jews to keep them hidden from damnation.

## The Privileged Position

Eric was Aborigin's hero but with Jewish intelligence. He was an accomplished member of the Kaufman clan. He understood that his looks were his best asset. He needed to negotiate his asset in the best terms. He knew his effect and behaved carefully. He avoided big gatherings and did not have many friends. He was a loner. Contrary to actors from Hollywood, Eric did not want anyone to know his secrets. In the West, to bring attention to themselves, actors made up stories about their passions. They craved attention and provided proof that they were always desirable and successful. Eric felt differently. He broke the moral code of communalism. He did it secretively. In his life, Eric was a pseudocelestial and showed pseudofidelity to the ideological doctrine. In theater, he proudly played villagers, handsome boys who worked as harvesters, toolmakers, and builders.

Eric's real life was far away from ideology. Eric was fortunate to have escaped the ideological illness. The toxicity of disease had not decomposed his mind. In his resistance, he knew his limit. He was immune because he crawled like a worm. He was able to demonstrate to the power holders that he was not against the doctrine. Eric was lucky because nothing indicated that he was connected to Jewish culture.

Though he was generally safe, he still looked for protection. In the homeland, only Jews helped other Jews. Eric did not care about Jews. He was focused on his life. He never left or questioned the habit of collective thinking. For his dedication to the collective, he ended up receiving the Title of Merit, the highest honor for actors in Aborigin.

## Eric Belay's Luck

*E*ric focused on pleasure. No one knew he did not have any patriotic thoughts. Otherwise, he would have been criticized and perhaps reported to moral experts who represented the ideological authorities. Eric was careful and was able to avoid the spotlight. He was a lone wolf but an efficient lover. Eric invited women to join him in pleasure. They were free to leave, but they did not. If they did, they would be sorry for the rest of their lives that they had not taken the opportunity. Women wanted to be with him.

## Eric's Beautiful City

*E*ric was born in a city on the shore. He enjoyed the beautiful city, where water was everywhere. From childhood, Eric was surrounded by castles, mansions, chateaus, and palaces. It was difficult to avoid the magnificence of the city built by Peter the Great. The quality of the city included splendor, opulence, pomp, and pageantry. When Eric walked on the streets, the water reflected the palaces and the clouds. It was difficult to understand where the reflection ended and reality began.

Despite the fact that Eric was raised in that beautiful city, his artistic work was in a different direction. In his homeland, actors were responsible for increasing productivity on factories and milk farms. Eric was one of the few who was able to reach the peak in the field. Actors projected lies by saying they had good lives and were rich and capable of spending money on their girlfriends, habits, and comforts. Even in movies, they played farmers; they represented the fantasy of a lifestyle full of pleasure and adventures. It was a big deception. The majority of actors were poor. In the minds of terrestrials, they were rich and famous and had whatever was possible to be happy and enjoy life. The terrestrials did not care that actors' womanizing was against the cryptographic doctrine. Eric did not care about doctrine. His secret was that all the comfort in his life came from his grandfather Rudi Kaufman, who'd left his offspring an elitist apartment packed with antiques, a country mansion, and his connections.

Eric was secretive about his ancestry because he knew that since ancient times, cursed habitants had used Jews as scapegoats. Terrestrials were mistrustful of them, and celestials were skeptical. The Jews were always treated as inferior and savage. First, they were accused of using the blood of Christians in their rituals. The indigenous population did not accept Jews as equals. They were perceived as cowardly, sneaky, unmanly, cravenly, and weak. According to their stereotype, they supposedly looked like monsters. They were not mainstream compared to the characteristics of the regular Aboriginians. They did not show depth and openheartedness. Jews looked bad. They looked greedy and ugly. Young Jewish boys united in gangs to defend themselves from harassment and whipping. They attacked instigators of hate. They were forced to do it. To be safe, they had to be crafty and find out whom to join and whom to attack. It was their adaptation to the infection.

Eric knew from childhood that authorities in Aborigin never did what they preached. He kept his mouth shut and did not expose controversy. The city's authorities were miserable worms. They did not care that dregs on the streets spoke badly about Jews and other minorities. No one cared. They did not hear and did not react. The basis of the epidemic was a bug, a parasite global in scale. It made zombies of the infected. Acting as imbeciles, when they saw a crime, they looked away. No one wanted to stop crime.

Their behavior also could have been a survival instinct. Nevertheless, they allowed bullies to run amok. In that atmosphere, Eric kept his mouth shut. He became famous and had numerous fans. Women proudly talked about meetings with him. Until he married, he focused on trailing women and having sex. Eventually, he got married, had children, and kept happy memories.

## One of the Gifts the Jews Did Not Need

Aaron, the uncle of Eric, thought of the audacity of the ideologists. As a gift, they had assigned to Jews a piece of land in the Far East, on the border with China. According to nasty and venomous laws, everyone needed to register his or her ethnicity to attached land. Jews received a piece of land allocated to them. The assigned land was a joke. It did not have any of the Jews' historical roots. It seemed it was God's forgotten land. It was a land for the displaced. On the border of China, Jews were alien. Everything was against them. The land was populated with mosquitoes and other bugs. Nevertheless, the formality was honored.

Because of that piece of land, Jews had a legitimate ethnicity written on their IDs. They were assigned to land that had a primarily Chinese population. Because of the piece of land in the Far East, Jews got on their IDs the famous paragraph five that identified them as Jews with a home place on the border of China. It was another tool of oppression. It meant they did not have opportunity in Aborigin. It limited their chances of getting a good job in Aborigin or getting accepted to university. It caused many attacks from Aboriginians, who said their place was in the Far East. They accused Jews of taking jobs that did not belong to them.

## Common Enemies

Aaron Kaufman felt disgusted that the epidemic had created an image of the wealthy as a common enemy. The lie frightened the population and united them against a supposed monster. The ideologists insisted the epidemic also made internal adversaries. The newspapers mentioned that many in the population did not comply with dogma. They called them rats who hated the collective and who were collaborators with the West. Ideologists encouraged the population to snitch. Everyone needed to show progress that he or she had been transformed by doctrine. Jews were always required to provide evidence that they'd been rehabilitated and accepted doctrine. It was not easy to be a Jew in the homeland. The acceptance of doctrine was an indicator that habitants were rehabilitated. The collective justified all atrocities. The persecution of Jews was done in the name of indoctrinated ideology. Because Jews were considered Western, they were not part of the indigenous population. In the eyes of the inhabitants, they were outsiders and were enlisted by Zionists, who were enemies of communalists. To stay alive, the Jews needed to provide additional proof that they were indoctrinated. Aborigin was ruled by idiotic doctrine that claimed Jews were part of Western society and were servants of the external colossi, who stubbornly resisted the power of doctrine.

## Rome: Way to Freedom, Part 4

Aaron Kaufman ended up in Rome as an immigrant. Before moving to Rome, Aaron also spent one week in Vienna, Austria. Life there was pleasant and honeyed. Aaron felt relaxed. At last, he did not see the angry faces of his former compatriots. He did not notice any darkness or lines in stores to buy deficient items. There were a lot of bright colors. Habitants had intriguing clothes. The city was in lively tones. Habitants smiled. Aaron and his family spent all their money in Vienna by visiting the opera and eating in restaurants.

Aaron next arrived in Rome. The family was placed in a little motel next to the train station. Aaron did not have any money left. Nevertheless, in his possession, he had Cuban cigars, Bulgarian cigarettes, and Matrioshka and Stolichnaya vodka. Close to his hotel, he put an Italian newspaper on the ground next to his shoes. He placed on it all the items he wanted to sell. Passersby right away began to ask him how much his goods cost. He answered in broken English and used gesticulation: "As much as your conscience tells you." Aaron did not reject anyone with a proposed price. All of a sudden, a police officer saw him selling and smiled. He wanted to buy a cigar. Aaron gave him a Cuban cigar and did not take his money. Aaron needed money. The price was not important. It did not matter how low or ridiculous the offer was. As a result, in a half hour, he had the needed money. It was enough for his family to find a restaurant with the sweet name of Trattoria.

For the first time in their lives, they ordered Neapolitan pizza and a bottle of Burgundy. They enjoyed the food and drink tremendously. After the meal, they took a walk around the fabulous city. They visited the Piazza di Spagna and sat on the famous stairs. They enjoyed the monuments on the Trevi Fountain. They were speechless before the greatness of the Coliseum. Rome had an air of freedom. Aaron was overwhelmed by everything he saw. He was not intimidated. He felt good in Rome. He felt the air of that business-oriented city. Most remarkable was the number of bars where passersby could drink coffee. Habitants would drink a little bit of strong coffee and have a sip of brandy. He found out from other immigrants that Rome had a big bazaar called Americano. In Rome, habitants bought and sold everywhere.

In Italy, Aaron was happy. He loved what he was doing. He felt like a rich man again. Immigrants bought and sold. Aaron bought souvenirs from immigrants. All day long, Aaron sold linen sheets, perfume with a romantic scent, and other products of trade, among them painted toys called Khokhloma. The communal state did not allow taking money out from Aborigin. The immigrants knew in advance what goods were marketable, so the affluent immigrants took with them moneymaking merchandise. They sold different items that covered their expenses. Aaron wanted to have enough funds to rent a villa on the Mediterranean coast and enjoy Roman holidays. He made money from selling merchandise. He also received monetary assistance from the immigration authorities. Aaron said he never had been poor because he refused to be poor. He always acted like a rich man.

For Aaron, Italy was a relaxing place. He knew how to survive. In the early morning, Aaron's family took their possessions to a bus going to the Americano market. It was a big place where a few hundred habitants sold everything from the newest electronic equipment to pans and old galoshes. A man named Luigio approached Aaron. The aged Italian male sold photo equipment. He asked if he could have Matrioshka that had a lot of dolls inside. In broken Aboriginian, he explained that for one Matrioshka for his grandson, he would provide for Aaron a place to sell souvenirs. Aaron already knew that for the right to sell something, he was supposed to pay a market cashier. He did not have money and was happy to give the man a Matrioshka. Aaron discovered that Luigio spoke reasonable Aboriginian. He asked Luigio if he wanted to buy photo cameras and spear guns. When his family had left their birthplace, each member had been allowed to take one movie camera and one spear gun. As a result, Aaron had six spear guns and six professional cameras. Luigio was happy to buy them and gave Aaron a large amount of money. Aaron did not know if the price was right, but he consented. Later on, Aaron found out that Luigio was an honest man and had given him a fair price.

In the past, Luigio had been part of an Italian regiment fighting on the German side. After losing the war, the Italian man had been a prisoner of war. In prison, he'd seen many atrocities but survived. He'd learned Aboriginian. He remembered the harsh Aborigin winters and terrible conditions. Eventually, Aaron became good friends with the Italian man. Luigio was straightforward, but he also had a secret. Italians, like habitants of the territory of Aborigin, were affected by the epidemic. They had their past too.

## Informers Can Be Anywhere

*I*n Aaron's family, Sam was one with a secret. Sam was a spy. Among the Italians were different habitants. Luigio had not suddenly appeared at the Americano. Before his departure from his homeland, Sam's mentor from the secret police had given him Luigio's telephone number. Sam had called Luigio the night before. One characteristic of the epidemic was the presence of informers in all parts of the population. Sam emigrated from the epidemic with his wife, who was ethnically Aboriginian. He was a dreamer. He was fond of everything in Aborigin. He loved the songs, books, beautiful views of churches with golden domes, picturesque campsites, and other lovely scenery. He loved girls with brown hair and blue eyes. He married one. He felt that Italy was breathtaking, but he still loved his homeland more. He was ashamed of his father's business orientation. He wanted to look like the rosy-cheeked boys from propaganda movies. His secret was that he was a spy brainwashed by the epidemic. When given an invitation to be an agent, Sam had accepted the opportunity with great enthusiasm. He felt it was a privilege to be an informer.

As a student, Sam was bullied by his classmates. He did not care. He felt his peers acted like morons. He felt they did not deserve to live in a heroic nation where many great revolutionaries resided. He believed in the propaganda stories about the brutality of the White Army and the heroism of the Red Army. Sam remembered clearly the first day he came to the building of the secret police. He was taken to the secret police headquarters by the regular police. They questioned him about one particular accusation: a girl had complained that he had forced her to have intercourse. It was not true. In reality, the girl wanted to marry him, so she used accusation, a common tool of procuring marriage in the rotten field. Marriage could resolve accusation.

At the same time, the secret police looked for informers to report on refuseniks, who were denied exit visas from the killing field. In the secret police, Sam was supposed to inform on future expatriates to Western countries. Sam knew that if he married the girl who accused him, the charges would be dropped. He could have asked for help from his father too, but he did not think about it. He felt he had a great opportunity to be helpful to his homeland. Most amusing was that his homeland had not done anything to him. He was smart from birth and got himself into a university without his father's help. Aaron was in jail when Sam passed his exams in medical school. Sam was a good student, and his father did not need to bribe his teachers. He was self-sufficient. He did not ask his father for any assistance. He always was in a position to help others. As a medical doctor, he consulted many habitants without any payment.

Sam did not have any plans to leave the homeland. He left to help his mentor in the secret police, who sent him on a special assignment. Not many immigrants were proud to be informers. Sam was proud to be a snitch. Lately, he had a special assignment: he'd been directed to protect a son of his mentor, who was a sailor and had jumped his ship in Montreal. Sam was supposed to be around his mentor's son. He was apportioned to help. He also had an assignment to report to his mentor about the immigrants who surrounded the mentor's son, as well as everything else about the mentor's son. His mentor ordered him to leave Aborigin for Montreal, Canada.

Sam decided to emigrate with his relatives. Sam influenced his sister's family and his parents to immigrate to Canada. He felt responsible for the decision to leave the homeland and helped his relatives as much as he could. Before leaving the homeland, he married an Aboriginian girl and was happy. She spoke several European languages, including English and French. Those languages were spoken in Montreal. Besides the languages, which were a big advantage for him, he liked his wife, who had blue eyes and blond hair. She was the daughter of the dean at the medical school where he'd studied to become a physician. His wife, a medical doctor as well, did not have any idea about Sam's double life. She did not know anything about Sam's secrets. Unfortunately, the son of Sam's mentor was killed. Nevertheless, Sam, together with Stepan Luchko, was able to save the life of Professor Kryvoruchko.

# Golda

Golda, Aaron's daughter, was a shy girl. In the diseased field were many introverted girls. She was always reading books. She completed university as a biology major and worked with animals. All her life, she did not like her big nose. Habitants mocked her and grimaced at her appearance. She cried a lot. Eventually, she decided to get a nose job, but she was unlucky. Her plastic surgeon was an alcoholic and cut too much off. He made her nose too small. Then she was self-conscious about her short nose. Golda had long legs, but she did not have much success with boys. Her girlfriend introduced her to one Aboriginian man.

# Vlad

Aaron's son-in-law, Vlad, dreamed of leaving the infected field and was looking for a Jewish wife. At the time, Jewish wives gave Aboriginian men the opportunity to leave the killing field. Contrary to Jews, the native Aboriginians did not have any opportunity for escape. Immigration was not available for them. Only Jews, Armenians, Greeks, and Germans were approved. Many males looked to marry someone who was able to emigrate.

Vlad was a good-looking Aboriginian male. His nickname was Pretty Boy. He wanted to be rich. On his own, he could not make it. He was not business-oriented and came from a working-class family. His parents were factory workers. He understood that having a business and making money were illegal in the killing field. Despite the draconian law, Vlad wanted to have money and a good position. He dreamed about an opportunity to receive bribes, but it was not possible. He was a factory worker. He found out that Golda had a rich father. He did not care about the size of her nose.

Eventually, Vlad ended up in Italy and then in Canada. Vlad would never, not even for a minute, regret that he married Golda. In Montreal, he became a VIP in his father-in-law's company. Golda was a good wife who helped him everywhere. She also had another nose job and became an attractive woman. She worked in a hospital as the head of a medical laboratory. If she'd stayed in Aborigin, Golda would have been one of the freaks, who usually ended up being unmarried women. Because of sudden opportunity, she was able to marry a good-looking man. When she ended up in Italy, she bought clothes that made her look like a model. All her life, she'd been afraid to offend others' sensibilities with her nose. In Italy, the headquarters of big noses, she was free.

When Vlad met Golda, he understood that she was a winning lottery ticket in his life. In his genes, he was a pigeon and a goof, but he dreamed about business. Without Golda, at the best, he would be the junior loader in some metal shop. He went to Golda's home and saw tapestries and antiques as well as precious art on the walls. He saw Aaron and understood that in that family, he could not lose. He married Golda and emigrated with her family. He was thankful to have the opportunity and was attached to his new family.

Vlad knew that in Aborigin, he did not have a future. He could not get any position. Vlad saw that payoffs, swindling, and cheating were everywhere and brought a lot of money. Getting bribes was a matter of pride for many habitants. In Aborigin, any infected clerk wanted bribes. Ass-kissing was one form of bribery. Hypocritically, kickbacks were ostracized and forbidden on moral grounds. In reality, everything was rotten, and authority could not be trusted. Only the criminals could help to straighten things out when swindling occurred. They were tough guys and respected. In his homeland, Vlad did not have the stomach to be around them. In Italy, criminals were in power as well. Among immigrants, being a rogue was a symbol of status. They appeared to be dashing guys. They were perceived as authorities. Vlad got confused. He changed his attitude about honest business. He became anxious to be accepted by criminals.

# Way to Freedom, Part 5: The Leader of the Collective

*I*n Italy, Aaron thought a lot about leaders. Aaron enjoyed selling and buying. For him, it was hard to understand the hatred of leaders in Aborigin. Their killing rage was absurd. One interpretation was that the supreme leaders, including the Founder and the Superior, were traumatized individuals. They might have been running away from memories of abuse. They treated Aboriginians as objects. They started bloody wars to prove their masculinity. They were monsters of modern times—bloody dictators. They made a lot of ways but could not escape their past. If it was true that they had been victims of pedophiles and molested as children, that tragedy did not vindicate them. It did nothing to justify their killing rage, cruelty, and slaughtering of innocents.

Aaron witnessed the hypocrisy of leaders. They played games. In harder times, they looked for help. They were not tough and did even appear to be human. In the new climate, habitants were allowed to go freely to churches, mosques, and synagogues. Many movies addressed the goodwill of different ethnicities. They declared that all ethnicities were equal. They kept quiet about the higher wisdom of the older brothers, the Aboriginians. Together with other countries, they defeated the Nazis' regime. The attitude changed right away since they did not need any help from anyone anymore. They showed their real faces.

Aaron observed their victorious gaucheness and disrespect for everyone and everything. It was impossible to trust anyone in a grisly region that placed habitants in labor camps where they were tortured and killed.

Aaron also remembered his arrests and his life in prison. Buying and selling for profit was considered a crime. It was severely punished. Aaron was arrested twice for different offenses of buying and selling. There were many restrictions. Any business dealings were a crime. Aaron was not an angel and wanted a good living. He often broke the draconian laws. His first offense was the production of fake gold frames and false diamonds. Those false items were in demand in the killing field.

Aaron never cheated his customers. With the help of his business partners, he was able to generate the production of cubic zirconia diamonds, which had a base of zirconium dioxide. Synthetic cubic zirconia was the most gemological and economically important competitor for diamonds. Aaron never presented the cubic zirconia as real diamonds. He always informed the buyers of what they were purchasing. He did his part honestly. He let his customers know they were receiving false diamonds. That did not matter. In the eyes of nefarious lawmakers, any business was a criminal enterprise. In the killing field, habitants were simply numbers. A large number of them were imprisoned. Part of the population went through slavery. Many already had been in prison several times. The rest of the population were just waiting for their turn.

Aaron felt that life in Aborigin was not normal. It was like the delusion of someone crazy. Selling fake diamonds was more beneficial than selling real ones. Aaron's father, Isaac, was from the old school and did not sell false items. Contrary to his father, who had the honor of selling real things, Aaron sold a lot of fake items. He sold photos to farmers. He retouched them and then mounted them on frames that looked like golden ones. The business was good. Aaron sold a lot of photos. Farmers would not buy anything they did not like. They did not care how much it cost. They also knew there was a good chance they could soon be sent in cattle cars to Siberia. They wanted good memories. They wanted to look firm and brave in their photos. Aaron also sold false diamonds to habitants who did not have the opportunity to buy real ones. The habitants pretended the false diamonds were real. In the killing field, nothing was real. The realm was built on false and fabricated assumptions. Aaron was arrested because his niece Sofia informed the secret police about him. On her denunciation, he was imprisoned for producing fakes.

## The Killing Field's Fakes

Aaron was sure the dogma was a fake and created many other fakes. The concept of brainwashing was built on fairy tales. Children and shortsighted adults could be easily deceived. Aaron understood that the killing field was a fake and bore many other fakes. The concept was not tangible and therefore could not be proven with calculations of reliability and validity. The brainwashed did not have any opportunities to understand what was real or false. The ideology was built on fabled ideas. Aaron figured out that the brainwashing was successful because the ideas had a romantic sound. Aaron observed that the ideas were discredited as soon as habitants tried to implement them.

The doctrine was also fragile and built on utopian thinking that was not workable. It used a sledgehammer to put unproven ideas into practice. As a result, a nice dream became an ugly reality. The epidemic did everything possible to sabotage and destroy its original notion. Art, literature, movies, architecture, and theater were staged to mask the ugliness. Long-legged beauties with long hair in braids danced on stages decorated by green lawns to lure the naive. They looked for someone to blame for disasters. They sang about beautiful feelings about a life that was stunted by enemies. As with any fantasy, the songs were heartbreaking. Ideologists could have their fantasy, but it was wrong to push their fabrications onto others and blame innocents.

Aaron saw that in the brainwashed homeland, the spirit was a false creature. It was the opposite of the authentic spirit of emigrants. It was completely different. The courageous spirit of the emigrant was to smuggle something out from the killing field. Aaron brought to Italy a few cubic zirconia diamonds hidden in his luggage. Transferring cubic zirconia was not a crime, but it was difficult to explain where he'd gotten them. In the meantime, Aaron rented a villa because he'd taken a lot of rubles with him. Before leaving the area, the emigrants hid their rubles in rubber pipes. Using rubber pipe had been the idea of corrupt customs officials, who took bribes depending on the length and width of the rubber pipes. Outside of the infected territory, the emigrants brought the rubles to exchange places and converted them to dollars. The Western banks did not take them, but some exchange places took them. They resold them cheaply to tourists who'd traveled great distances to see the moronic killing field.

Aboriginian police considered money laundering less dangerous than antigovernment publications. The secret police looked more for antigovernment manuscripts, gold, art, icons, sculptures, bronze, and precious metal and stones. Money was easier to smuggle. The new immigrants proudly shared how many meters of rubber piping they'd been able to take out of the killing field. Aaron took a lot of rubber pipes stuffed with rubles and exchanged them for dollars. He risked a lot when he took rubles out from his homeland, but he took the risk. He never had been and never would be poor. He did not want to be poor like everyone else. He was a son of his father. Even in the killing field, the Kaufmans never were poor. Aaron was not used to resting. After ending up in Italy, he wanted his time in Italy to be a Roman holiday for him and his family.

## Aaron's Letter

One of Aaron's friends had given him a letter to give to an Italian man named Luka, whom Aaron's friend had befriended during the war. He'd told Aaron that Luka was trustworthy and sincere. Aaron called Luka, and they met. Luka invited him to his home, and Aaron gave Luka and his wife presents, including vodka and sturgeon caviar. With the delicatessen, they came to a house in the suburbs of Rome. Italians did not like to shave, but for some important occasions, they received close shaves. Luka was clean shaven and not tall but elegant and well dressed. He lived with his wife and two children in a comfortable apartment. Luka spoke some Aboriginian and translated to his family what Aaron and his wife said. Luka mentioned that he had roots in Aborigin. In the time of Napoleon, some wounded Aboriginian soldiers were left in Italy. They married Italian women and had children. Luka mentioned that he was related to one of those soldiers. He also hinted that he had connections to the Italian Mafia. He could help with any legal problems. In Italy, that connection meant freedom to do many things. Most importantly, it could protect immigrants from assault and robbery.

Aaron realized that many Italians and a few non-Italians were associated with the Mafia. By talking to Luka, Aaron understood that Luka was a valid addition to his gallery of friends. He could be helpful. Aaron knew, Luka was an entrepreneur. He had several shops that sold photo cameras, but he also had some connections. Aaron did not look for help. He thought it was good to have someone like Luka around.

Aaron was strong in the area of business. He already was in a position to choose with whom to conduct business. Luka made a proposal that Aaron could not refuse. He would buy photo equipment from new immigrants and bring it to Luka to be resold for a profit. Luka said that in Venice, he had a photo shop. There had not been any emigrants from the killing field, so no one knew about emigrants' photo cameras, which were much cheaper than European cameras. They had good quality regardless. The photo cameras were taken out from Aborigin legally. The immigrants gave them to property owners as a deposit for rent. After selling them, immigrants bought pieces of fashionable clothes and ate delicious Italian food. Aaron accepted Luka's proposition. He knew many who wanted to sell him photo equipment. He gave them attractive proposals. He never took anything on commission, as other buyers did. He paid right away in cash. He easily supplied Luka and Luigio with a variety of photo equipment.

Aaron waited for a visa to Canada for a long time. He used his Italian connections to make a lot of money. He also had some protection. There were many compatriots who wanted to take money from him. Aaron was protected against them.

## Aaron's Secret

Aaron had a secret. It was indecent for an immigrant not to have a secret. He was an excellent card player. He had a good time in Italy, and he had money. He did not want money from the games. In the evenings, he invited his neighbors to play cards, but his talent was a secret. During his incarceration, his skill at playing cards had saved him and his friend Sashko. He did not want immigrants to know he had spent time in prison. He also did not want immigrants to know about his skills. He played with ordinary players who did not know his past. For several reasons, he let himself lose card games. First, he wanted to have friends. Second, he was afraid his neighbors would not play with him again. For him, small losses were not comparable to the pleasure he got from being at the card table. He also provided wine and food for players. Time went quickly. Aaron followed his own rules and did not want to win. In the meantime, he had a hobby and wanted to enjoy it. Back in the homeland, all his family had the same interests and were good card players. Through the hobby, they received connections with the powerful. Because of his leisurely journey, Aaron got in trouble.

Aaron stayed away from rogues and altercations between them. He was careful, but a bad thing happened. He once intentionally lost a little cash in a card game. The fellow was an ordinary player and was far below his level.

It was late at night. It happened that Aaron did not have cash on him. He went to another room. As he looked for cash, he saw a false cubic zirconia diamond. The sum of the loss was insignificant, so he grabbed the cubic zirconia and asked his partner if the young fellow was willing to take it instead of the lost money. The fellow was speechless. He took the cubic zirconia. He ran away quickly before Aaron could change his mind.

In a couple weeks, a few rough fellows visited him. They were boxers and worked for a man named Givi, a Georgian man who was an excellent card player. He had transformed a billiard room into a card club. He rented the place from an Italian, the owner of a poolroom located close to Rome's Fiumicino Airport. The boxers forcefully invited Aaron to go with them.

## GIVI THE KINGPIN

$G$ivi was a scammer. Many habitants wanted friendship and fairness, but Givi chose different ways to relate. He wanted to dominate. To achieve his goal, he became a manipulator and cheater. The best example of obsession and domination was Superior Leader, head of the dirty locality named Aborigin. Givi was the biggest con artist. Givi did not have as many opportunities to kill and torture as Superior Leader, but he was a dangerous individual. Givi had a good teacher in his family; Givi's mother was a manipulator from the highest leagues. Surprisingly, despite being a nasty character, Givi also was a mama's boy and lived with his mother. Givi's father was a criminal kingpin and taught his son tricks in cards. His whole life, Givi cheated in cards and in life too. Immigrants loved gambling. They got on his hook. In collective thinking, gambling was a protest of the primitive lifestyle. In Italy, some immigrants continued to gamble.

Immigrants thought that in Givi's gambling house, they would win, but they lost everything. As soon as they felt the excitement of winning, Givi and his friends would empty their pockets. The eager immigrants continued gambling even when they were losing. They played on credit and owed it to Givi. They were not able to repay their debts and ultimately became his slaves.

The immigrants were the objects of skillful manipulations. Givi duped them into becoming slaves. They became prisoners of the local kingpin after they left the plague-crippled, prison-like territory of Aborigin. Instead of enjoying their freedom, they suffered again. Givi and his henchmen skillfully used the temptations of the new land. Habitants saw plenty of enticing displays of goods, alluring restaurants, and an atmosphere of luxury that was irresistible. The immigrant girls were tricked and forced to do favors. They were forced to be prostitutes. Other immigrants were tricked by different swindles and also became victims.

## Givi's Gang

When Givi and his gang visited someone, it meant trouble. They were snakes who targeted the exiled to swindle them. The cons knew that immigrants were given some money by immigration officials. They had financial assistance if they did not have any money. Their interactions with Italian authorities were sketchy, and they were afraid. They brought their experience over from the communal state. They believed rumors. Immigrants also got money from selling their goods. If they complained about stolen goods, then the immigration service knew they had some funds. As a result, the immigrants would lose their allowance from the immigration officials. Most importantly, it could affect the status of the refugees. Immigrants believed those rumors. Whether they were true or not, no one knew.

Immigrants understood that the authorities in Aborigin played their power games like cheaters. In Italy, immigrants perceived the authorities as deceitful. They thought the authorities were treacherous and wanted to catch them. The chronic illness affected immigrants' thought processes. It tricked the population into becoming mistrustful. It was ridiculous, but immigrants saw the criminal authorities as a force to help them receive justice. Sometimes it worked. Outside of the killing field, they continued to be confused and relied on criminals.

The infected criminals played with victims a game of domination and confrontation. Outside of the killing field, immigrants wanted to try their good fortune in the games. They played to test their luck and often looked for a safe place with no cheating. The criminal code required that criminals play an honest game. The playing houses were supposed to be under the honest supervision of criminal authorities. In the immigrants' minds, the criminal kingpins and godfathers were supposed to protect them. It did not work out. Some of the kingpins were among the biggest cheaters.

# Dr. John Nash

Dr. John Nash (1928–2015) was a brilliant mathematician who came up with the concept of game theory. According to Nash, it was impossible to win any game after being brainwashed. In his theory, the game could only be a real success when players had similarity and understanding for each other. He calculated the comparability of different systems and came close to understanding the basis of human behavior. In the killing field, games, such as chess, cards, and dominoes, were important activities. A game was a reflection of the external world. Habitants played with similar individuals whom they trusted. The sophisticated habitants played complicated card games that resembled bridge. The simple-minded played blackjack and other simple games. Habitants also played chess, checkers, Bahamas, and billiards.

In game theory, negotiation and manipulation were the two opposing means of human interaction. Manipulation was a game in which a conscience-free and unashamed attitude won out. It had many different roots. Because they were cheated, the habitants could not properly evaluate chances. Some could not accept defeat and cheated themselves to increase their chances of winning. In summary, manipulation was a dishonest game in which a player did not care about his opponent or about the rules of the game. For the manipulator, interaction with others was a con. The manipulator did not follow any rules and used everything in his possession to crush his opponent. In the short term, he might win, but in the long term, he lost. When he got in the game, he did not think respectfully about his challenger. That was his mistake. Eventually, he was caught and punished.

Professor Nash implied that human reality could be a negotiation game. Life was considered a game, and in many situations, habitants could calculate the probability of success. Many researchers felt that competitive feelings were part of human genes. Professor Kryvoruchko summed up that in negotiation, people recognized the wishes of their opponents. They stepped into others' shoes to understand them better. In those interactions, success was more feasible. When the opponent was similar, the player understood him better. Business-oriented people successfully participated in business interactions. They followed the rules of the game and understood their opponents. With those qualities, they successfully negotiated many deals. The honest game excluded cons. Mutual respect was the main engine of the game. In an honest game, a good gamer could direct luck to his side.

## Gaming under Givi

*U*nder Givi's guidance, the losing game was unquestionable. Deception was well covered. It did not look like fraud. The immigrants were misled by skillful con men. By criminal code, if the deviation from the rules was discovered, the game was declared illegitimate. In Givi's stall, that did not happen. The immigrants trusted Givi. They blamed themselves for being easy prey. Every game had the possibility of having cheaters, and among the immigrants were charlatans too. There were two types of tricksters: those without authority and those with authority. The immigrants quickly identified swindlers without authority. They cautioned others to stay away from those individuals. They could not speak the same way to cheaters with authority. First, it was not safe. Second, those cheaters were shrewd. It was difficult to find the necessary evidence to implicate them. Without proof, accusations were senseless. Someone had to be brave to condemn a criminal authority. An accuser needed to have a lot of proof and strong backing to reinforce such a claim.

Givi, a major manipulator, was smart. In the immigrants' community, Givi appeared impressive. He was a fashionable dresser and always had the best suits and fancy ties. He used greed and intimidation to play with immigrants' lives. As a child, he was a mama's boy. He had a strong affection for his mother, who herself was a strong manipulator. She gained control over her son. She constantly repeated that he was special. His mother told him that only she understood his talents. She paid all his expenses. She did not allow him to get into any risky enterprises. She had a reason for doing so: by keeping her son so close, she controlled Givi's father, who was a kingpin in the criminal world. He was not legally married to Givi's mother. He was often in jail. After some time spent in prison, he always came back to her. By criminal law, as a kingpin, Givi's father could not be married. Instead of having many women, he had only one: Givi's mother.

Givi knew how his mother adeptly handled his father. When she saw that her man followed young and pliant housekeepers with his eyes, she would say something with a covered meaning. She would loudly praise her son for being noble and not chasing the young housekeepers, as his father had done. Givi learned the art of manipulation from his mother. Everything suggested he was a mama's boy.

## Givi's Mother

Givi's mother knew many different means of skillful manipulation. If she did not like something, she would tell Givi's father to stop acting that way. She called him a poor role model for his son. She would use guilt against Givi's father. She told him about behavior she did not like and said their son would grow up to be like him, a thief and a convict. Her manipulations worked. Around his woman, the kingpin was a regular henpecked man. Nevertheless, Givi admired his father and copied all his habits. More than anything, he wanted to be a kingpin like his father. He was a good student in school, but his mother let him skip school too often. She said that school was for the poor and that Givi was fortunate to be rich. When he became a young adult, he told his mother he wanted to be a kingpin.

## Givi's Father

Givi's mother asked Givi's father to help their son. His answer was that a kingpin should spend time in jail. Givi's mother said he did not love their son and simply wanted to torture him. By inflicting feelings of guilt, she could always manipulate Givi's father. Eventually, because of her manipulations, he gave up. Givi was crowned as a kingpin without the required imprisonment. As required by the title, he already played many games. He became a skillful card player. He broke the criminal code and became a con artist. He designed many rip-offs. He was influenced by his mother. He did not feel any guilt or shame. He felt he could do whatever he pleased. He derived pleasure from abusing the weak.

The tricks to cheat in cards shown to Givi by his father were for protection from swindlers. Many good card players knew how to cheat. They did not use their knowledge, because as soon as they used it, they became cheaters. Givi promised his father he'd use his knowledge only as a last resort. In the criminal world, the punishment for cheating in cards was severe. In many instances, it meant death for the cheater. Under his father's authority, he felt secure in using tricks in games. He knew that no one would dare to accuse him of cheating. When he played cards, no one could doubt that the son of a kingpin who also was a kingpin himself was not following the criminal code of honor.

Givi used every opportunity to practice the tricks he'd learned from his father. Indubitably, he was good at cards. Eventually, he felt that he'd perfected his con and that no one could catch him.

After the death of his father, Givi's authority was shaken, and other kingpins wanted him out. His mother was afraid for his life. She was the driving force for Givi to leave Georgia. He left with his mother and his brother, a young ballet dancer in a corps de ballet. In Italy, he lived not far from the game house he operated for immigrants.

Later, in a German city, Givi opened a bar with a restaurant and rooms for billiards and cards. He was gunned down and killed by a hitman. The assassination was not solved, and the reason was never discovered. After his death, his mother was depressed. Her younger son lived in America and had his own life, whereas Givi always had been with her. He had not had a wife or any children. The most significant person in his life had been his mother. Only near his mother could he be a little child. With others, he was a conniving monster. He cheated, lied, and deceived and was a representation of communal brainwashing. Still, to his mother, he was a little boy.

## The Card Game: A Duel

It sometimes happened that because of a game, one of the players ended up dead. The games in the place next to Fiumicino Airport in Rome continued day and night. Immigrants took chances. Despite tough regulations in the killing field that forbid playing for money, gaming flourished. In Italy, the players were immigrants who'd escaped deceptive dogma, and they were addicted to the games. They played billiards and cards for money. Givi did not play much, but he directed his bodyguards, who were also his bouncers. Some players were able to smuggle through customs old icons, silver, gold, old paintings, antiques, and money. Bouncers hammered the debts out of losers.

The immigrants who had funds spent time playing cards. They wanted to increase their fortunes through the game. Givi's card room was like a little casino. He was a kingpin crowned in Georgian Republic and supposedly observed the rules of the criminal world. The first rule was not to cheat in cards. A cheater ended up dead. If immigrants had problems, they did not go to the Italian police but instead asked Givi for help. The players were sure that in Givi's bar, the games were honest, and scammers would not take their money. Givi, by using his status, guaranteed the winner would receive his money. For his guarantees, he took commissions. Givi too played with some high-class players and had many spectators who watched his games. He felt like a star. Among immigrants, he was an example of wealth and happiness. He was a talented card player, but he transferred his technical skills to other areas and activities that were not good.

Givi was a significant figure among immigrants. Someone strong could be a liberator and protector but also a bully. He had a part in many different enterprises and always charged commission. He rented rooms in hotels where he used young women as prostitutes. He had his own ways of enrolling them.

When immigrants left tainted territories, they shared their victories over the customs authorities. Few brought valuable items with them. Givi had informers among the immigrants. They would look for girls who'd gotten something valuable out of Aborigin. First, they were beautiful. They had gorgeous faces and figures and magic voices. To Givi, they offered the best possibility to make money. Italians went crazy when they saw those girls. Unlike chubby Italian whores with short legs and big asses, those girls were princesses. Some of the girls were easy objects of manipulation. Givi's bouncers knew how to trick princesses into becoming prostitutes. They had a blueprint for deception. Givi's brain focused on deception. He was great at the card table, but he was ugly in all other activities. The safest thing for girls was not to get in front of him.

## Immigrant Girls

*I*n Italy, the girls were blinded and shocked by the abundance of merchandise. The girls, adulterated by the psychological curse of a dogmatic existence, had never seen anything like it before. As per the Bible, in the Garden of Eden, life was thriving, but regardless, Eve was tempted by the snake. The girls saw plenteous cosmetics and lots of restaurants and bars. They'd come to a land of lavishness from a land of scarcity where elegant and modern clothes could only be found on the black market. They wanted everything, but their husbands and boyfriends could not give them much. The bouncers, pretending to be rich bachelors, would approach them. They would date the girls, and the girls would forget their husbands and boyfriends.

The girls' husbands and boyfriends protested, warning their women of the consequences, and at the end bouncers beating them. To avoid more beatings, they hid. The girls did not listen. They saw the power and were proud of their new friends. When the girls trusted their new friends, they would show them the items they'd brought through customs. In many instances, those items did not have much value, but Givi's bouncers would pretend they were relics. They made it seem as if the items were valuable. The lures of innocent girls by con artists were even uglier. The con artists knew how strong temptations were and based their cons on them.

The bouncers played the poor girls like fiddles. Evil always looked for the naive. The deception continued. The bouncers would begin a game of false expectations. They brought to the girls an immigrant pretending to be an American or Spanish aristocrat and a connoisseur of art.

He would put a high price on their items and offer to buy them. The poor girls felt rich and were excited.

Givi's bouncers pretended they cared about the girls and advised them not to sell quickly or cheaply and to take time because serious merchandise required special buyers. Soon they told them that they'd located a buyer who was willing to pay double the price and that the girls should keep the price high. They met another person pretending to be a buyer. That time, to impress the girls, the bouncer organized a meeting in a fancy hotel. The false buyer would look over the items and find them real. He continued to bargain. On the advice of the bouncers, the girl kept the price high. Eventually, the false buyer would give up. He agreed to the price, but to be sure, he wanted to show the items to his partner. He asked the girls to leave the items for one day. The naive girls agreed because they did not notice any deception. The trap was set. The girls were hooked. Their innocence was grasped by cruelty. The naive were like butterflies. They thought the world selflessly enjoyed their splendor. Later, they learned their beauty could help some vicious bouncers make big money. The bouncers became their pimps.

There were many ways the shrewd pimps tricked naive girls. The scenarios were simple. After a day of waiting, the girls did not get their money or their items. The answer was that the buyer had asked for more time. After a week, the girls would cry and beg the bouncers to give them back their treasures, even for half price. The verdict was that before the girls got their treasures back, they had to perform favors. They were supposed to show respect for the men by sleeping with them. Soon the men rented rooms in hotels and sent patrons. With a day of work, the girls would cover a month's worth of all the pimps' expenses. In the gangsters' mind, the girls were born with something to sell, and they used it.

Italians were the biggest lovers of female flesh and had many different publications with erotic and pornographic content. On the road, big women would burn balefires to tell customers they were waiting. They were heavy like horses, but they had one good quality: they were cheap. In contrast, for the same price, the immigrant girls were miniature statuettes with blue eyes, brown hair, and romantic names, such as Natalya. For lecherous Italian men, those girls were rare delights that they otherwise could not have afforded.

## Pimping the Young Mothers

Aaron knew that usually, the recruiting pimps used young mothers with small children. The girls' husbands and boyfriends were not a problem. Among the immigrants, there were a few who were not happy with the setup. The pimps considered them bad seeds. The pimps beat them up and chased them from the street if they saw them. The victims were scared to protest. They were terrified that if they went to the authorities, their immigration status would be damaged. As a result, they could not see their children or sleep at home.

Aaron knew one victim who was beaten several times by pimps. The young man said that all of a sudden, his wife turned against him and became a prostitute. When his wife went to the hotel where pimps and patrons were waiting, she gave their baby sleeping pills so the little child would not cry. He actively protested the mistreatment of his baby. His wife complained, and the pimps approached him. They said they would have his ass. The young man was scared and did not go home. Aaron understood that to intimidate, the pimps would go through with their threats. Aaron gave the young man food and a place to hide. The man slept on his balcony. It was terrible that immigrants who ran from abuse in their homeland were abused by their own compatriots. Fragments of vile men, especially Superior Leader, still were in some psyches. Aaron knew that inside dirty territories, mockery and outrage were a daily reality. Outside, for some, the monstrous attitudes did not change.

## Uncle Cat

Tattoos in the killing field had different meanings. Aaron, having served time in jail, understood their meanings. He met an old tattooed immigrant when he walked to the post office to get his mail. The immigrant did not have a permanent address and received his mail in the post office, where many immigrants congregated and talked. Aaron met many tattooed immigrants, but that man was special. By his tattoos, Aaron immediately knew the life of the man, because most of the tattoos had been done in prison. For prisoners, tattoos were like curriculum vitae. Aaron saw that the man was an old thief and kingpin who'd spent most of his life in prison. The psychological sickness sent many felons out to emigrate. To clean up the prisons, the infected leaders sent many criminals to Western countries. They also used the criminals to compromise immigration. However, the attempt did not work. In the USA, many criminals from Aborigin became model citizens. Meanwhile, Aaron got close to the man and talked to him in Fenny, a language often used among criminals. Aaron was polite. According to his tattoos, the man was a godfather. His tattoos were not for decoration. He was one of the grim immigrants who deserved them. Tattoos did not lose their relevance if the owner gave up his position. For impersonating kingpins by using false tattoos, the users of falsifications were killed.

Godfathers, kingpins, and *vory v zakone* were a communion of criminals with a distinct code of conduct that had initiations and rituals. Criminals did not use their own names but had soubriquets. Thieves' monikers were tattooed on their hands. The man's tattoo indicated that his name was Uncle Cat. Aaron told Uncle Cat he'd been in prison twice and told him the names of the kingpins and guards in his prisons. Uncle Cat knew all of them. At a different time, he'd been in the same prisons. He also mentioned that he was no longer active in the criminal hierarchy. He'd broken the rule that kingpins could not marry. He mentioned that he was not a kingpin anymore, despite the fact that his tattoo said differently. He mentioned that at a thieves' meeting, he voluntarily had resigned from his godfather position. He did not want to be a kingpin. Nevertheless, even after he gave away his followers to another kingpin, he continued to be an authority in the criminal world.

In the killing field, there were many tattooed kingpins who had an obligation to keep alive the norms of the criminal world. They were the dark side of the epidemic dogma. Prison life was an everyday reality for many. Outside of the prison habitant, criminals respected the criminal code. A criminal kingpin was dedicated to criminal life, but Uncle Cat said he was just an immigrant. He'd broken the code of thieves. He could not be a kingpin anymore, even though he'd been crowned as such and spent most of his life in prison. A few years before, he'd married a madam from a bordello. He was happy that he and his wife had received an offer to emigrate. Now he and his wife lived in Italy and waited for the girls from his wife's bordello to join them. They wanted to go to Australia together because there was a shortage of girls there. He wanted to start a legal business. He said he wanted a new, honest life and did not want to keep his past connection to criminals. For him, an honest life meant owning a bordello in a land where there were not enough women. He distinguished himself from others who wanted to emigrate and continue their criminal activities. Uncle Cat was an immigrant like everybody else and had his own plans. His ideas were original, but he wanted to live an honest life.

In Italy, there were several kingpins in different times, and sometimes a few kingpins existed in the same time. Uncle Cat knew a lot about criminals. He had his own opinion about Spider, Givi's sobriquet. He was not willing to answer any questions about Spider's past, but he disapproved of him. Outside of the killing field, some kingpins did not strictly follow the criminal code.

Aaron knew there were quite a few criminals among the immigrants, but not all of them were associated with Givi. Uncle Cat was an immigrant like everyone else. He hated what the criminals had done to immigrants. He believed kingpins should protect immigrants from lawlessness, not the opposite. Givi, who was a kingpin, did everything he could to squeeze every penny from the immigrants; he threatened them and ran them down. He made them feel miserable. Uncle Cat did not approve of Givi. He said that in Italy, kingpins were changing and no longer followed the criminal code for behavior. He said Givi was a cheater and a lawless man. Givi's activities were against the criminal law that honest kingpins were supposed to reinforce. He felt it was not by chance that Givi had the nickname Spider. Givi never had been in prison but brought to the immigrants his imaginative attitude toward prison relationships.

Aaron observed that during transit to Italy, there were different kingpins at different times. Before leaving Italy, the godfathers applied for the immigrant visas. They left Italy for their destinations, and then other criminal kingpins arrived. The killing field was cleaning out the prisons. Ideologists counted on criminals. They deliberately sent troublemakers out of the prisons to create nightmares for immigrants. Other immigrant kingpins from disgusting territories were in transit and did not stay long. Soon they left for different countries.

Aaron understood that the kingpins had a lot of power and usually controlled their own pieces of territory. They reported to more powerful criminal authorities and contributed to criminals' purses. Hideous with infection, they covered their operations on the black market and took a percentage from all criminal operations in their territories. They also acted as judges in disputes between different criminal groups and individuals. Kingpins were powerful figures among immigrants because many could not imagine their lives without criminal authority. They saw their lives as resembling their home, where closeness to criminal authorities could provide connections and solve many problems.

Uncle Cat said the kingpins were mainly good, but not all of them were. The present kingpin, Spider, was a recent emigrant from Georgia. Uncle Cat had mixed feelings about him. Eventually, he told Aaron that Givi had received the Spider moniker when he was crowned a kingpin. Givi got it only with the help of his father, who was a kingpin too. Uncle Cat also mentioned that Givi's crown, in his opinion, was not a valid one. Despite the code of thieves, which stated that kingpins should have a prison history, Spider had never been in prison. In Uncle Cat's opinion, Spider's reign in Italy reflected lawlessness and chaos. He attributed it to the fact that Spider did not have jail experience. Uncle Cat was from the old school, and he believed that only in prison, where prisoners lived by the criminal code, could someone earn the right to be a godfather. In contrast, Givi felt invulnerable and encouraged lawlessness by breaking the criminal code. He felt that because he contributed much to the common fund of criminals through the money he collected, he could do whatever he wanted.

## The Cautious Uncle Cat

Uncle Cat was careful about joining card games because among card players were a lot of crooks and card sharks. He said that Spider, like his father, was an excellent card player. He added that he also was cautious in his judgment because he did not believe in continued luck. He had known Spider's father. He could not prove it, but he believed that Spider was not like his father and was a cheater. He trusted Aaron and said that he had not seen Spider cheating, but he somehow always had a top card. He suspected Spider might have a special spot in his clothes to hide an extra card and replace a low card with a high one. Uncle Cat said that Spider also might know how to place the cards in a special order, because when Spider dealt cards, he shuffled them very quickly. During Spider's reign, there was much lawlessness, and Uncle Cat said he would be glad if Spider were caught as a cheater. In the criminal code, the worst offense was cheating in cards. If a kingpin got caught cheating at cards, he could be killed. Aaron listened but did not know yet if the information could help in the future. He was an observer of immigrant life and understood that immigrants were special. Among them were courageous people who gave up their freedom so others could have justice, righteousness, and the right to emigrate. There also were scoundrels who were parasites and sneered at the immigrants' naïveté.

The criminals among the immigrants were different. Few were sadists; instead, some chose crime as a protest against brainwashing. The second type became normal habitants after leaving the collective state. Uncle Cat was a second type. He chose the criminal code instead of lawlessness. He believed that real criminals should spend time in jail, which was like a school for the criminal code of ethics. He believed violence could be used against other criminals who broke the code of ethics. He was against patronizing anyone who was innocent by force. He believed criminals could find women willing to be prostitutes purely for money. He was against enslaving girls and forcing them to obey. He was involved in prostitution through his wife and treated all his girls fairly. As an immigrant, he gave up his kingpin status. He believed that Givi could not be a kingpin because he did not have jail experience. Afterward, Uncle Cat would support Aaron in neutralizing Givi. Aaron would help immigrants to be free from abuse and enjoy the pleasures of Rome. In other words, Aaron would prove to Uncle Cat that he was a real Sailor.

Aaron found in Uncle Cat a supporter and close associate. Among thieves, card playing was a test for professional fitness. Even an excellent card player could be a criminal but not a kingpin. Spider, because of his excellent card playing, was admitted to the position of kingpin. In the distinguished code for kingpins, the initiation could take place only for a thief who had a history of incarceration, but for Spider, his father omitted the rule. Aaron saw that Uncle Cat was not happy that Spider had broken the thieves' code and did not approve of him being a kingpin. Uncle Cat noticed that Spider always won at cards, and he did not believe that one man could have so much good luck. He would be glad if someone could catch Spider cheating, he said. Aaron was that man.

Uncle Cat mentioned that he was against lawlessness toward immigrants. A godfather was supposed to care for habitants and their well-being. He said Givi was a lowlife if he was a parasite toward his fellow immigrants. Because of him, the immigrants lived as if they were behind barbed wire, even though they could be free. He also added that Italians were the best hosts for refugees from the epidemic. The criminal code forbade stealing from people who gave sanctuary to the persecuted, as well as from some who escaped from prison. In fact, it required helping escapees. Uncle Cat mentioned that in his opinion, all the heinous territories were a big prison. He added that Spider acted against the thieves' code. His cronies made up stories, saying he helped immigrants and resolved conflicts. They made it look as if he serviced the wronged and always sided with victims. In reality, he was corrupt. Givi often was an independent judge between two arguing sides, and he always was on the side of whom he could gain from.

Uncle Cat suspected it was a lie that Spider had substantial connections to the Italian Mafia. Because of that hearsay, Spider took a percentage from all thefts. He was a liar. He did not have any shame in lying and preying on immigrants. He did not have any real connection to the Italian Mafia, but it was true that he'd hired an Italian lawyer to protect the thieves who robbed Italians. The pickpocketing thieves paid him for protection. The thieves stole from everyone. They worked everywhere on the streets, in marketplaces, and on buses. They stole even more from immigrants. Abominable with germs, publications put a lot of dirt on immigrants. They knew what they were doing by sending criminals, such as Givi, into immigration. Givi lived up to their expectations. He put a dark spot on the whole process of immigration. In contrast, Aaron was a bright light.

## Givi's Egomania

Givi was an egomaniac and wanted to be a legend. There was a lot of anger in Givi because he did not feel appreciated. He brought a lot of money to the common criminal fund. Everything he did was for his own exaltation, but his efforts did not gain him the benefits he expected. He wanted to be the most famous and powerful kingpin of all. He did not care how he achieved that status. He did not care about immigrants. They were mere mosquitoes on his way to glory. He abused immigrants without a twinge of conscience. In one scam, Spider's cronies pretended the immigration authorities had sent them to the immigrants who had papers to leave Italy. Most of those immigrants were rich because they'd risked their freedom to bring something valuable from the native land. They'd bribed the customs officials. Those immigrants had things they'd illegally taken through customs. The thieves, through their informers, knew when wealthy immigrants had visas to leave Italy to lands of their choice. They knew the luggage of certain immigrants held precious items. Pretending that immigration officials had sent them, they used false immigration trucks to bring the luggage of departing emigrants to the airport. As a result, the luggage never arrived at the airport, where the crooks pretending to be from immigration told the anxious departing emigrants that their items would be late. They said that their trucks were experiencing technical problems and that immigration would send the baggage later. They also told emigrants their visas could be canceled if they stayed to wait for their luggage. The emigrants were helpless. They felt they could not miss their flights out. Everyone was afraid his or her visa would be collected. Thus, they departed without any delay. After they left Italy, they would not see their luggage again. The baggage would never arrive, and they could do nothing about it. The thieves would sell the goods at the Americano market. Uncle Cat was against evil perpetrated against the helpless, and it did not matter if they were poor or rich. Those actions came from a lawless kingpin who not only broke the criminal code but also showed that he did not respect it. Uncle Cat disapproved of Givi's leadership. Aaron's conversations with Uncle Cat were

Printed in the United States
By Bookmasters

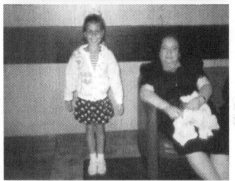

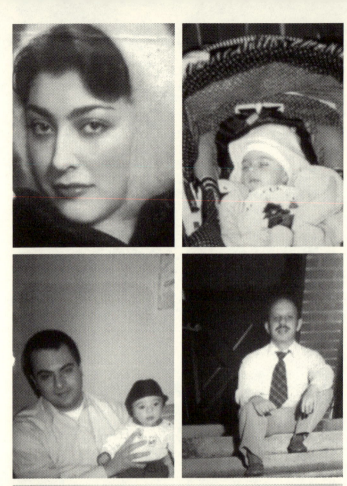

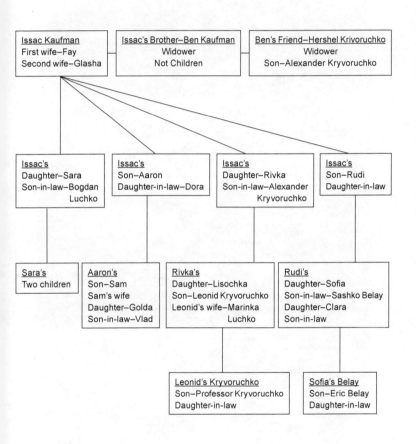

## Luchko Family

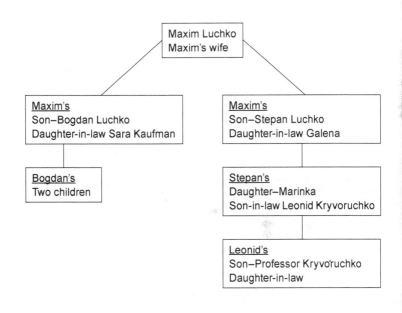

## Genealogical tree template for Professor Kryvoruchko

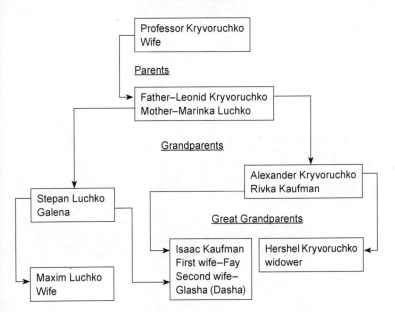

# BIBLIOGRAPHY

Bandler, Richard, and John Grinder. *The Structure of Magic I: A Book about Language and Therapy*. Palo Alto, CA: Science and Behavior Books, 1975.

Buber, Martin. *I and Thou*. 2$^{nd}$ ed. Translated by Ronald Gregor Smith. Edinburgh: T. and T. Clark, 1937.

Friedman, Maurice. *Martin Buber's Life and Work: The Early Years, 1878–1923*. New York: Dutton, 1981.

Klein, Melanie. *Envy and Gratitude: A Study of Unconscious Forces*. New York: Basic Books, 1957.

Kohut, Heinz. *The Restoration of the Self*. New York: International Universities Press, 1977.

Professor Kryvoruchko had a solid psyche. His distant relatives were his fragments.

※ ※ ※

This is my third attempt to talk about Sailors' psychology and Professor Kryvoruchko's diverse fragments. I talked about his closest relatives in the books *Life of the Sailor* and *Sailor's Psychology*.

With respect,
Chester Litvin, PhD

to their Khazarian roots. Aboriginians, once free from the virus, would rebuild the spirituality of Khazar Khanate.

Professor Kryvoruchko was a Sailor who moved away from the fraudulent doctrine to the freedom of exploring his internal world. Because he looked for facts, he asked many questions, but he did not always find acceptable answers. His identity consisted of numerous supporting fragments. He identified his fragments and had dialogues with them. By using dialogues, he unified his fragments. He had control over his own psyche. Contrary to the restraint of collectivist thinking, his fragments met through dialogue.

He was a Sailor who traveled to a land free from oppression. He had a solid psyche. He had his own perspective on everything. He did not need to follow the directions of other leaders, even the superior one. He became a whole character. He made honest assessments that were the antipodes of many doctrines. He explored the misery of collective thinking in colonies. He found some answers that were controversial. He continued looking for many routes he could explore. He presented uninfected ideas that did not lose their uniqueness. A Sailor's lifestyle was not always politically correct, but he did not get enslaved by the system. He did not fall under the communalists' spell. He represented the uninfected. He did not throw away his uniqueness.

As a Sailor, he discovered who he was and accepted himself. A solid psyche was a true diamond. Sailors represented a whole psyche. They connected fragments by using dialogues. Connections between fragments were the beginnings of diamonds in one's life. Sailors' biggest wish was to find a vaccine against the collective and prevent the epidemic from ever affecting the world again.

covered their real identities with masks. It pushed them to recite the collective's postulates. Like zombies, habitants followed all external commands. As a result, they could not understand who they really were. The collective glorified the uneducated and those infected by the psychological virus and presented them as enlightened. That was not a joke. It was the harsh reality. Many were easy marks. The collective turned them into goons.

Instead of internal dialogues, they were forced to follow external commands, external images of propaganda, and the repetition of doctrine. The danger of the infection was that its venom could poison every psyche. It eventually changed the health and the state of mind of the entire nation. Supreme Leader created the perdition. The toxin of lunacy infected the population on an epidemic scale and made habitants act like goons and imbeciles, including the fake celestials, terrestrials, and morons. The real celestials were an ancient race of armored beings who were present in galactic communities. Fake celestials, like terrestrials, lived on the earth. Everyone infected by the deadly psychological germs became a goon. Pseudocelestials and terrestrials demonstrated the possible range of sociopaths. The terror of the pseudocollective was in the killing field diseased by the red bug. It violently staffed concentration camps in the Northern Territories, where the perceived enemies of the regime were exterminated.

Many resources of Turkish and Jewish history covered the Khazars in Byelogoria and Aborigin. It was not clear if the Ashkenazi and Khazars were the same habitants. Could it be that Aboriginians had Khazarian ancestry? Professor Kryvoruchko believed that eventually, Aboriginians would abandon the notion of being Prolet-Aryans and get back enlightened by doctrine were entitled to take everything from others by force. The doctrine was a pseudo-Bible that contradicted the postulates of the real Bible. It was fraudulent and created the Aboriginian existence.

Only a Sailor could resist infection by the psychological virus, and Professor Kryvoruchko was a Sailor. That meant he had a solid psyche in which all fragments were united in a true collective. He declared that he was not able to find a true collective. He was against the external pseudocollective because it was primitive. He was searching for a true collective. He stated that the true collective existed only inside the human psyche, where the fragments—collections of different experiences—had access to one's memory, emotions, and reactions. Sailors' fragments were united through real internal meetings and genuine internal dialogues. A Sailor's psychological structure was healthy and uninfected by the psychological virus. It was the true collective. To become Sailors, people had to resist many psychological infections that signaled an emotional split.

The pseudocollective was large. It had many different regions with various ethnicities. Geographically, Byelogoria was indisputably a Slavic land. Malantia was a Slavic region too and wanted to gain independence from Aborigin. Malantians claimed to be unrelated to Aboriginians, whom they proclaimed to be the successors of the Golden Horde. They accused the Aboriginians of plagiarizing Malantian history.

Impaired by a curse, habitants were not able to identify their fragments or have dialogues among them. The infected did not know who they were or what kinds of internal excavations they could perform. The collective wanted them to act like robots. It controlled them and killing, and raping. They wanted to achieve equality by taking wealth from the uninfected. The regimes, affected by sickness, did not allow any originality. The land was a big prison. The Founder and other leaders wanted to gain more power and become the rulers of the world. They used untested populist doctrines and primitive slogans to justify their crimes. They were tireless and without any guilt in destroying those uninfected by germs. They demonstrated brutality that compared only to the savagery of the Golden Horde. The resurrection of goons was accompanied by a militaristic approach to achieving all objectives.

Remarkably, the Founding Father of the putative collective changed his attitude. He focused on an economic component. For some unknown reason, Founding Father passed away soon after. Ultimately, nothing changed in Aborigin. Goons continued acting as morons in the old capacity. A gathering of communalists filthy with illness did not allow any deviation from doctrine. Goons, to advance their positions, constantly recited the doctrine. They constantly bragged about the doctrine's advantages. Their leaders positively illustrated the doctrine more than the other infected habitants had.

## Falsified Bible

Dogma was in countries affected by the affliction. The doctrine attempted to replace the Bible and was known as a falsified Bible. Populist blabber infected the population. They were forced to worship as incontrovertible truth the insane principles of the doctrine, which claimed that those epidemic started. Even prior to activation of the ailment, the population resented the affluent and nouveau riche, who were mentally well and had business skills. Proclaimed Aryans were blind with hatred. They never were sure what was real or false. Even into the present, the discussions continued. Most proclaimed Aryans hated one group who'd used the Aryans' language as a basis for their own. Vocal Nazi ideologists, through their inflammatory speeches, infected the population with animosity toward the language appropriators. As a result, the entire proclaimed Aryan group felt offended. They proclaimed that the Jews had stolen their language and created their own, the Yiddish language.

A craving for blood was characteristic of different groups in the active face of illness. They did not care about individuals; they just needed objects to satisfy their thirst. Infected by germs, ordinary haters received permission to kill. They did their work enthusiastically. They slaughtered many uninfected individuals. They wanted to see the whole world infected by disease. The more they murdered the uninfected and immune to sickness with their indoctrinate ideology the better job they did. It was difficult to say which of the bugs was worst. All of them were similar, and the infected groups killed millions. The number of deaths had no precedent in modern history. That was why Sailors moved out of the putative collective and established themselves in the West. Because the Sailors had to leave, their departure was not tragic. Even though the familiar East was their birthplace, they could not stay. When individuals were in an oppressive setting, they had to leave as soon as possible.

Professor Kryvoruchko's analysis revealed that the collectivist and communal settings had the goals of robbing, to prove something fictitious. Their arrangements were based on the opaque presentation of evidence. The external structure affected the internal, and the pseudocollective became a psychological structure of Prolet-Aryans and presumed Aryans.

## Persecuted Uniqueness

Professor Kryvoruchko emphasized the word *uniqueness*. He analyzed the past of his family, who repelled infection. Some of his relatives were business-oriented and uninfected. They resisted the infection of putative collective thinking, which destroyed uniqueness. They were Sailors, which made them immune to the epidemic. Predisposition to infection was the main reason the illness increased; the conditions had existed before. It was not by chance that Nazis and collectivists were right on target. The infected groups were carriers of the psychological illness. Eventually, it clung to their throats and came out. When the illness was in a dormant state, the groups did not kill but just passively hated others. The function of the infection was to achieve the ideological objective of hegemony and spread throughout the whole world.

A few types of killing had a genetic component. Nazis, full of the black bug's illness, were selective killers who targeted specific racial and ethnic groups. When the red sickness was in an active state, the putative collective too were choosy: they killed uninfected people who had business skills and high IQs. Those abilities were genetic.

Biases against those qualities existed before the

incarceration, wherein prisoners were separated from the outside world and lived under the supervision of turnkeys. Ideologists called the structure by different names. They avoided the term *slavery*, which correctly described it.

## The Collective Stole Identities

*T*he difference between the pseudocollective and the Golden Horde was that the Golden Horde had a genius leader, but the assumed collective did not. Sick leaders took over the assumed collective.

In memory of the many innocent victims, one had to declare that the pseudocollective had the uglier structure. Misrepresentation was a reality in the killing field of morons dirtied by toxins of stupidity. The collective had criminal intent and used the immoral falsification of facts. Diseased ideology demanded that innocents see the distortions as reality. Their interpretation was based on misleading assumptions. The actualities were impossible to separate from hallucinations. Some tangential ideas existed only inside the minds of those infected by the plague. The plagued state substituted the fictitious for the real. Everything was wrong. They presented slaves as freedom fighters. Morons dirtied by disease achieved dictatorship positions. They spread pseudothinking and destroyed evidence of failure in every area. They required the bogus to appear to be concrete. They never used experimental paradigms and always substituted with impressions of evidence-based actualities. They used propaganda and fabrications and misrepresented facts sickness created the illusion that the psyche was an insignificant part of the larger collective. The bug was a parasite. Its biggest goal was to destroy individuality. Infected individuals acted unreasonably and gave up their identities. The sickness used indoctrination with the ideas of populism. The country became a community of morons and imbeciles. Some antisocial, distorted individuals took advantage of the exhaustion and confusion. Behind the collective always was an antisocial dictator. The Sailors attempted to understand the origin of the psychological bug and identify available remedies. They hoped their work would help to find a remedy.

The description of reality in dictionaries was clear. Reality was a state in which things were as they existed rather than as they appeared or were imagined. A broader definition of *reality* included everything that had existed, existed presently, or would exist. The leaders of the collective rejected those definitions. They pushed fraudulent ideas on hundreds of millions infected by the ailment of inanity. Philosophers, mathematicians, and many others ancient and modern thinkers, such as Aristotle, Plato, Wittgenstein, Russell, and Sigmund Freud, provided a distinction between the fictitious and the real. The imaginary could not be considered real, but in a communal setting, the imaginable was presented as real. The malady of the collective killed uniqueness in perception and thought. The pseudocommunalists' ideology called reality unrealistic and delusional, claiming it existed only in the mind of the deranged dreamer and was not tangible. Pseudocommunal thinking was an illness spread by psychological germs throughout the population. It took the form of an epidemic. The communal reality was based on sickness and denied actual reality. Life in the communal state was similar to facets built from anything a person's mind brought in, including diverse moments of life, different ideologies, and real and false memories. Fragments could include one's own behavior or the behavior of different habitants the person knew, including relatives, friends, and a variety of characters from books and movies—everything one could imagine. A person's fragments were an interpretation of external forces and made up one's individual personality. Through the process of unification of the fragments, people could prevent external structures from destroying their individuality and breaking their psyches. A unified psyche was solid, and the fragments had access to the person's memory and normally joined with others in peaceful coexistence. The goal of the uninfected was to unify their fragments by using dialogue and become Sailors. By learning business skills, people could resist the urge to take from others. The hazardous fragments, in the form of psychological germs, took people away from becoming Sailors.

Psychological illness created the collective and communal settings. Psychological germs split the psyche from human values, morality, and a comfortable way of life. Contrary to unifying with the goal of enjoying the wholeness of the psyche, the germs split the psyche. The change brought suffering. The structure of the psyche, split by sickness, became unresponsive to human values and morality. Habitants became empty-headed and acted as if they were damaged goods. Colors, movements, tastes, and everything else changed. People's thoughts and tastes became absurd; instead of spaghetti, insects became an everyday food.

The illness radicalized the psychological structure and made habitants feel unimportant. It changed people's most important existential goal: to preserve the identity by resisting radicalization and populist demagogy. The to build and defend their businesses. That approach did not move rapidly but was surer than any quick solution to eliminate social inequality. The main effect of real dialogue was an emotional lift from meeting someone special and having an exchange of ideas.

# A Description of the Infection

*P*rofessor Kryvoruchko discovered that the infection replaced noble kings with criminal kingpins who destroyed a sophisticated civilization with primitiveness and violence, luring the weak with promises of progress and a special collective mission but then leaving them in isolation and devastation. The epidemic destroyed the wonderful genes that characterized nobility, dignity, and honor. It demolished business orientation, one of the energizing forces of the human psyche. The disease infected too many for the uninfected to contain it. Weak minds were not able to resist the temptation to take wealth by force. The sickness moved erratically and created big holes inside people's psyches. The forces of splitting used confrontation and manipulation to create disorder. Various sabotaging forces split psyches. They became antagonistic and incompatible. The splitting forces created turmoil in psyches and changed habitants' existence. Eventually, minds stopped functioning, and only a desire to steal was active.

The parasitic structure of the venom was based on a desire to take from others by force. The infected had some common symptoms: their psyches were split and filled with many plague-ridden fragments. Every psyche had many was a creation of damnation and was deadly. It made the infected sick and violent. It caused a split in the population that was practically an epidemic. Zonked habitants gave up their freedom. They became zombies controlled by fools. In his analysis, Professor Kryvoruchko focused on the disease and the symptoms of sickness displayed by infected habitants. He researched the ways in which the psychological germs split psyches. When he thought about the perdition, he could not keep his feelings of anger inside. He was supposed to be among the infected. To protect himself from the infection, he used a clown mask, but he did not feel like a clown. He let off steam in a different way. He overcame disgrace. He was exposed to vile toxins but survived and had to live with his surroundings. He declared that solid, cohesive psyches were not affected by the toxins of frenzies. The owners of uninfected psyches were Sailors, and poison could not destroy them.

## Sailors' Psychology

Sailors' psychology declared that a Sailor was part of the modern generation. Stepan Kryvoruchko had a Sailor's spirit and left the cursed land for a land of opportunity. He lived in the USA, where he went to school and became a professor.

A dark cloud was over the world and never completely left. The anathema continued to live in the biosphere. Sailors' psychology proposed a way to resist psychological bugs. Instead of taking affluence by force and killing, habitants had to learn how to build solid and cohesive psyches and gain prosperity. They needed the know-how make everything around them more primitive. They made the word acceptable to the minds of morons. If they did not understand something, they weren't supposed to. Only the ideas that clicked in their limited brains could exist.

The system blindfolded habitants. It declared that there was no need for intellectual stimulation. The habitants became a horde. The vile and shrewd took over the society. They tricked habitants with vague passages and meaningless, idiotic slogans. The primitive horde, narcotized by empty, ignitable slogans, followed them. The pseudocollective's structure helped those in the horde who were antisocial. Primitive thinking was the basis for primitive slogans. The pseudocollective's decision-making was based on false premises.

When a less mature but more aggressive fragment took over the human psyche, the psyche became a false collective. To avoid the traps of the false collective, the Sailors encouraged dialogue between all of one's fragments. They chose to represent the true collective, the fragments that were wiser and better intellectually stimulated.

## The Curse Caused a Split

Professor Kryvoruchko documented an epoch during which the greatest psychological split in human history took place. He unmasked the red terror, whose indoctrination brought psyches to an embryonic level. They were not able to resist the unproven populist influences. They were unable to separate empty phraseology from a meaningful approach. Collective thinking and the communal state justified killing in the name of their doctrine. The collective

## Hypocrisy

Because of the fiction everywhere, the collective was never close to being what it pretended to be. Hypocrisy was the biggest trump card in manipulation. The shadow economy superseded the indoctrinated blabbering. In a land filthy with psychological pestilence, the infected resorted to gambling. There were no casinos, but there were many private houses where the infected played cards day and night. Gaming was part of life. In every yard, many played the land's most popular game with rectangular domino tiles. It was a smart game in which cheating was a challenge for players. Dominoes, the gaming pieces, made up a set, which was sometimes called a deck or a pack. Chess, checkers, and Bahamas were popular games too. Kids played games for small amounts of money by throwing little clasp knives or ricocheting coins off the wall. Gambling continued in the era of tyranny, replacing dance and other art. No one was immune. Aborigin was a big casino. The collective's hypocrisy didn't die; it lived on in many psyches. It was built on dreams about the treasures that could be taken from others.

## Conclusion

The collective was a dysfunctional structure. The meaning of the word *collective* was, unfortunately, captured by a bunch of primitive thinkers who could never produce anything original. They tortured the world with their demands to a dictator, he himself became a dictator. One of his many foolish actions was to give Paradise to the Byelogorians. He opened up a can of worms. Byelogorians did not have any historical roots in Paradise. They raised pigs, which was outrageous behavior to Muslims and Jews. The new supreme leader was like the protagonist from *The Prince and the Pauper* by Mark Twain. He went from being a servant to being a boss. During his rule, his policies were idiotic. Even his cronies understood that he did not belong and dismissed him. He later bragged that he was an initiator of space exploration and sent the first spacecraft to Mars. He did not mention that many in the community of scientists had been placed in extermination prisons. *Sharashkas* were jail-like communities comprised of prisoners, including the best scientific minds. The sharashkas were eventually destroyed but should have been shattered a long time ago.

The communal setting resembled an ancient, primitive structure ruled by insidious kinglets who feared being captured, tricked, and humiliated. They feared being destroyed. New Supreme Leader was no different. He always sang his own praises. His bragging was ridiculous. He endorsed primitive solutions and disappeared in inanity. As a primitive leader, he did not take into consideration many possibilities. His blunt actions did not solve anything; they only created a big split in the relationship between the new regime and the rest of the world. Supreme Leader failed in all his endeavors. He gave Paradise to Malantia. He apparently miscalculated everything. A new federation replaced Aborigin and wanted Paradise back. The new federation annexed it. Paradise always was provocative and caused a lot of confrontations.

resources. In addition, it should have had a communal economy, consensus in decision-making, a nonhierarchical structure, and ecological living. A collective state was supposed to involve the voluntary unification of the particular classes and have them be a part of the organized experience. It was intended to make habitants happy. In theory, a communal state got together and organized through dialogue, but real dialogue involved having respect for others and finding common ground in order to relate better. The main purpose of dialogue was to find mutual inspiration for growth.

Professor Kryvoruchko affirmed that in the communal colony, reality was bleak. The pseudocollective committed unimaginable deceptions on all humans. The communal propaganda created distorted justifications for their pseudodoctrine. The existing communal and collective state was repulsive. The biggest untruth was in the portrayal of the state of dismay as a realm of working-class bliss. The collective was actually a state of horror, with rotten communal apartments, foul-smelling communal hostels, and many inhumane state prison camps.

## Old Habits Remained

Professor Kryvoruchko stated that the dictators changed, but old habits remained. After Superior Leader's death, the next leader talked about the horror of the dead Superior Leader's cult of personality. He wanted a quick resolution to stop any controversy about leadership and to proclaim himself as a different type of leader. By toppling received those benefits. They thought they received the trips and land for their hard work.

Many beautiful girls enjoyed southern beaches and villas because of free vouchers for their sexual services. Some of them had regular meetings with party ideologists in special places. Men received the same for being stool pigeons and betraying friends. The infested were forced to be compliant and listen to commands and orders. Strangely, the diseased were happy with their handouts. It was pure manipulation. By declaring that they were using dialogue, leaders manipulated their helpless, plague-ridden subordinates. However, ideologists did not know what it meant to have a dialogue. They insisted they looked out for their subordinates. The ideologists were liars. They implied that the poor and infected were victims of the rich. Instead of using negotiation, they urged all the poor to unify and fight back. It was not a dialogue because dialogue was not built on dehumanizing any group. In that particular situation, in their view, the educated and rich were bad. The ideologists called for confrontation; they wanted unification with the goal of destroying and degrading the uninfected. It was an effective means of manipulation. They wanted the infected to be aggressive and merciless, stupidly follow orders, and treat others as objects. The unification took place with the goal of attacking the uninfected. It was a confrontation that had nothing to do with dialogue. Aborigin was a communal colony with a structure of slavery.

Professor Kryvoruchko conveyed that the communal philosophy and reality in Aborigin were two different things. By definition, the communal state was supposed to be an intentional community of uninfected living together and sharing common interests, property, possessions, and pseudocommunalists' leaders, including the most important among them, were all womanizers. A beautiful woman walking the streets of any city in Aborigin might see the car of a leader's associate, who might be a policeman, pull up next to her. The officer would show her a badge and ask her to follow him. In the precinct, officers would ask her where she worked and what her marital status was. They also requested that she keep their conversation a secret. They asked her if she wanted to meet one of the leaders. Most of the women did not dare to refuse. For many women, having sex with one of the leaders was an opportunity for change and a display of patriotism. As a result, sex was free for the party leaders because the nation paid for it.

Sex for bosses was well organized. When the woman came to work the next morning after being questioned by the officers, she was called to her manager's office and granted paid release from work. Right away, the woman was taken to the airport to board a plane. She was taken to the leader for sexual pleasure. A nurse checked her, and then she took a bath and was dressed in a nightgown and robe. A nurse accompanied her to the bedroom, where she provided sex for the chief. After the sexual encounter, she was delivered to her home. She promised to keep the encounter a secret from her family. The next day at work, she was called to see her manager and presented a deed to her own piece of land. Government offices, for the purpose of rewarding the ideologically strong, had villas and several garden plots. As benefits, they also gave free trips to resorts near the warm sea. The women received such rewards for sex with ideologists. With those benefits, many families built dachas on the land and planted gardens. The families did not know why their wives and daughters mistresses. Criminals did not always follow generally accepted standards, but they agreed with the general rule that the rape of a woman was shameful and a heinous crime. In its criminal base, criminal life had pleasurable purposes and pride. The more the criminals spent on women, the more self-respect they gained. There were many stories told and songs written about the generosity of criminals to women. In the criminal code of conduct, the top criminals were not allowed to marry, but they had many mistresses. Criminals treated women as objects and showed their attachment to women through material things. In their opinion, all women could be bought. In criminals' minds, the rape of a woman was taking pleasure for free. They felt that having nonconsensual sex and taking pleasure by force damaged criminal honor. According to the criminal code, the punishment for the rape of a woman was to put the rapist in the place of the woman and make him satisfy a man.

The leaders of the collective also bragged about their success in spending on women. Similar to criminals, they felt that by spending money on women, they gained more respect. The leaders of the collective wanted sex and could get it by ordering it and providing an exchange of different privileges. Because Aborigin had a militarized structure, everyone was required to follow any command with no questions asked. One taboo that no one spoke about was same-sex love. The hypocrisy of the collective was so strong that no one talked about it, as if it never existed. An evil structure reframed reality to claim ugliness as beauty.

Professor Kryvoruchko noted that the top ideologists were dirty with profanity, loved sex, and had many mistresses. Their trusted assistants drove around different cities to find gorgeous ladies for them. The were helping the homeland. Punishment awaited any who turned away from the ideologists.

Professor Kryvoruchko stated that the gays in the collective were seen as sexual deviants and were sexual slaves in prison. After the Great Patriotic War, there were not enough men for reproduction purposes, and the collective inflicted severe punishment on gays. For practicing sex inconsistent with the norms, homosexuals were incarcerated. In the history of the precollective, when a soldier's duty to the military was twenty-five years, many old soldiers protected the young and had sexual relationships with them. In the soldiers' barracks, it was normal for two beds to be pushed together for the sake of sex. For a long time in communalist history, there were many incidents of homosexual relationships. Dignitaries and the ordinary population were involved in atypical sex. According to rumors, even Superior Leader did not discourage other males from atypical interactions. In prisons and among the ordinary infected and uninfected, there were a lot of homosexuals. There were many love stories between gays in the domains of art, ballet, and theater and even between ideologists. There were stories of ménages à trois among many celebrities. The rumor was that the Superior Leader of the collective had atypical sexual relationships.

Professor Kryvoruchko stated that one thing in the criminal code was right: the rape of a woman was a violation of the norms of civilized society. Other things were wrong. The criminal concept in relation to women was disrespectful to women and made women into objects. For a criminal, his woman was more than an object; she was a matter of status and self-respect. Criminal norms were based on pride, and criminals spent money on their jail, they were separated from other prisoners and became sexual slaves. The prisons of the collective contained many sexual slaves who had an obligation to provide sexual service; otherwise, they would be dead.

Professor Kryvoruchko observed that many shortsighted patriotic habitants were fouled by diseases of barking and howling. When they drank, they cried about the so-called mother collective, but once they sobered up, they wanted to take advantage of their native land. Nevertheless, when drunk, it seemed they loved their homeland. One could love many dangerous things. Some loved venomous snakes. As soon as they trusted the snakes, they became careless and lost their fear of the snakes' dangerous bites. That was a mistake. A snake eventually would bite. Loving the collective was the same as loving a venomous snake. A snake was merciless. The lovers of the collective should have been careful not to fall into any traps. Only the shortsighted could have loved the collective, but many did not have another choice.

In prison, by request of the jailer, men raped other men for the sake of humiliation. Leaders used rape as a tool to keep habitants compliant. The criminal norms for shame had been established even before the collective. The penalty of rape by another man was used for a long time to punish those who disrespected the criminal authorities or violated criminal norms. It was also used to test devotion. Ideologists used the rumors about rape in the prisons to keep habitants in fear. No one wanted to offend the authorities and get raped in prison. The fear of prison helped authorities have as many informers as they wanted. Many infected individuals became volunteer informers. They were the most shortsighted habitants in the world. They squealed on their neighbors, and they thought they different system of justice. In the prisons of the collective, child molesters were usually killed. Rapists, homosexuals, and drug users became sexual slaves. Drug addicts were considered weird because the hamlet was ruled by alcohol users, and alcohol was cheap. The criminals had a strict rule against drugs. All who were convicted of the above crimes became sexual slaves in prison. The sexual slaves in prison were males. For many Aboriginians in the collective, it was disgusting even to think that a man could become a rapist. In the native land, there were many unattached girls; for every single man, there were more than five single women. Lots of unattached females were in the area infected by perdition, but many boys were arrested on false reports. They needed rich relatives to rescue them from jail; otherwise, they faced serious consequences.

Professor Kryvoruchko stated that by the criminal code of honor, the criminals in the colony did not abuse their women. The criminal code required them to respect women. Only peasants and bumpkins beat their women. The hardened criminals were proud and boasted how well they treated their women. By criminal norms, sex was never free, and every woman was a prostitute and supposed to be paid. Criminals bought women gifts and bragged that they could always please their women's desires. They felt that pampering their ladies was the norm. Their logic was that if men followed the criminal code, they must have many women on their side. The criminal name for the act of rape was a shaggy robbery. The name hinted at the woman's vagina, which, in the criminal mind, was not cheap. It also meant that men wanted something for free. Harsh criminal punishment applied to the rapists of women, as well as to homosexuals and child molesters. Criminals considered those acts wicked and illegal. When the accused were in never investigated accusations of rape. The collective was just trying to placate women with the declaration that they were safe. They could work in offices and factories, and then they needed to work at home and attend to children and the elderly. The position of women was bleak, but as usual, they were used for propaganda and boasting. The leaders talked about equality that never existed.

Professor Kryvoruchko pointed out that the police created a false reporting system that was profitable. The police encouraged everyone to report not only rape but also attempts of rape. Anyone could report anything. The accuser did not face any repercussions for false accusations. One could not have imagined how much money the police took from the accused and relatives of those who were reported. They asked for a lot of money in order to drop the case. They were able to give the accused an ultimatum: go to jail and become a sexual slave or pay money. There was another way to drop the case: if the police wished, the accused could become an informer. The collective always had a big pool of frightened accused individuals who could not pay bribes. They were enrolled to be informers. As a result, many of the accusations were false. That was one of the displays of the ugliness of the police state. The police created policies of horrible population control. They created a draconian regime. It seemed as if the police were guarding the habitants, but everything the police said was a lie. Underneath police action were profit and an army of enslaved informers. In that system, women were never protected.

Professor Kryvoruchko stated that in the eyes of the collective, homosexuals were sexual deviants. For practicing anomalous sex, they were incarcerated. Child molestation was rarely reported. In jails, there was a

The infected became the rulers of the pseudoland. They annihilated the most advanced part of the population. The act of obscuring one class, ethnicity, or religion was dangerous and instituted genocide and the Holocaust. It ushered in different wars and unbelievable prejudice. The virologists and brainwashed specialists were confused. The Second World War took place to defeat Nazism. The finale of the Cold War brought to an end the conquering diarrhea of idiocy, but it was ridiculous that so many were still infected and continued to repeat the nonsensical doctrine. Professor Kryvoruchko mentioned that the ideologists of the collectives looked for primitive solutions to end inequality. They acted the same as those looking for perpetual motion. They did not inspire workers to become more sophisticated. The desire for primitivism and foolish insolence continued. It was surprising that many still wanted to sacrifice their lives for idiotic ideas. They used the black-and-white us-versus-them thinking of pseudocelestials, saying, "We are the clean and beautiful, and the others are schemers and scoundrels."

Professor Kryvoruchko discovered that the collective spread the lie that in the communal setting, the women had achieved equality. It was a fabrication. The collective lied in saying that the horror stories about the terrible consequences of rape and attacks on women were in the past and that women were safe and equal. They promoted the mendacious notion that police and the state guarded women's rights. The biggest violators of women's rights were the police and its leadership. No one disagreed that rape was a horrible crime and that rapists must be in prison. In the collective, safety was not part of female equality. Alcoholic husbands beat their wives, and there were still many violent rapes. As a matter of fact, the police beginning that the collective and communal states were primitive. Time showed again and again that the doctrine was impractical and without a future. The leaders whipped a dead horse by insisting the doctrine was correct. The main idea was that in that land, anyone who could do a simple job was clever enough to build a new reality. The idea was based on the presupposition that everyone infected with the plague who had a relationship to the working class was smart. It did not matter that the ideologists spouting those hypotheses were mainly misfits and social outcasts. The simplicity of the concept attracted many followers in the same way the concept of Nazis being superhuman attracted many followers in Germany. It was tempting to sacrifice uniqueness to become part of something exceptional. They emphasized that the collective was the opposite of the individual and was protected from any mistakes. The collectivists placed all responsibility on the masses so they wouldn't be responsible for their failure. In contrast, the business-oriented uninfected took responsibility for their own actions.

Professor Kryvoruchko stated that the collective's ideology was primitive and seemed to border on stupidity. It stated that if the infected were liberated, they would flourish. In countries with many uneducated citizens, the idea that all manual workers were smart by birth simply because they belonged to the working class was appealing. It seemed no effort was required to become somebody. It was enough just to be from the right origin. The ideologists felt they'd discovered the way to create social equality. Instead of bringing the lower social class to the middle level, they decided to cut down the upper and middle classes. Unfortunately, they merely created an equal society for those infected by the virus in Aborigin.

primitive lifestyle celebrated the medieval patterns of barbarians. The collective never accepted responsibility for any of its own misdeeds. It did not want to be flexible; strictness was its main quality. The collective called it devotion to doctrine. The doctrine held priority and was more important than common sense. The collective attempted to destroy business orientation and wipe out business culture. The collective was categorical and inflexible.

Professor Kryvoruchko declared that contrarily, business and scientific orientation were based on flexibility and the ability to learn from mistakes and correct them. Sailors uncovered the false pretentions. They fought for freedom and used dialogue and negotiation in the face of manipulation and confrontation. Professor Kryvoruchko felt that the success of individuals in business and growth in scientific progress were predicted by genetic predisposition. The crucial characteristics of business orientation were independence and management of self-destiny. The collective was involved in the massacre of the business-oriented, scientifically oriented, and uninfected. The collectivists' behavior constituted genetic murder. Their doctrine encouraged population-wide contempt of the rich. It was against the uninfected who had money, and it incited disrespect for innovation. The new power glorified simplicity and rigidity.

Professor Kryvoruchko stated that pseudocelestials were manipulators. They did not think about others. They used any follies to boost their egos. The collective forbade the infected from managing their own destinies. Everything had to be done through chains of authority. The collective created stagnation. It prevented deviation from a doctrine-driven approach. It was clear from the brought fruitful land to the mountains. No one cared or gave them any credit. On Paradise Island were the graves of many nationalities. Many came to Paradise to steal and died in the process. The trouble continued. Presently, the future of Paradise was not clear. The fight for Paradise would never stop. The future of Paradise was unknown. Paradise should have belonged to those uninfected with plague, those who historically understood Paradise's past. They knew how to blossom it.

Professor Kryvoruchko stated that the disease of collectivism spread quickly and became an epidemic. He analyzed the residual effects of the malady of the collective's thinking. Because of the plague's viciousness, one infected by the illness could be named by different blasphemies and profanities with the same meaning, such as asshole, goat, buck, motherfucker, sow, and salamander. Communalists acted like vicious rats who wanted to populate the whole world. The infected in the killing field became the red rats. They did not have any nobility or honor; they were ugly creatures whose sicknesses were contagious. Along with the landscape, they also took over minds. The goons who pretended they were celestials should have had a Nuremberg trial for what they did to unbelievers in their supposed genetic superiority. Goons imitated celestials to keep up the appearance of being special. Goons were not celestials. They demolished morals, religion, family, and the human spirit. They were judged by history, but they needed to be judged by people.

Professor Kryvoruchko stated that the goons tricked the uninfected and then tortured and killed them. They were skilled at brainwashing and inventing terminology. The goons polluted the world with profanity. They called themselves Prolet-Aryans and Aryans. In reality, their

Leader destroyed all petitioners who asked him to give the land to the Jews. The Paradise cape held many secrets of those killings.

Professor Kryvoruchko stated that Paradise's Tatars were victims too. They were incarcerated and sent to Siberia. Many died from cold weather and hunger. The ideologists did not care about facts. They falsified the past. Paradise's Tatars were detained. The existence of Jews in Paradise was not mentioned anywhere. Superior Leader and Supreme Leader were not ready to give Paradise to the Jews. They gave it to others who did not have any relation to Paradise. They were liars. They forbade the disclosure of any information about Jews in Paradise. Historically, Jewish settlers had been inventors and created heaven on earth. Their lifestyles were so attractive that the Jewish religion moved from Paradise to Asia and became the main religion of Khazar Khanate on the Caspian Sea, as well as several other regions. Into the present, the truth about Jews in Paradise's history was not spread and was kept sealed. Historians hid the fact that even Catherine the Great wanted to acknowledge the contribution of Jews to Paradise and settle them there.

Professor Kryvoruchko detailed that Paradise Island still was attractive and tempting. It kept the secrets of many battles between many civilizations. Perhaps long ago, Paradise had been a world center of civilization. Many enjoyed the astonishing beauty of the land. They were appreciative users. Others were not careful with it and did damage. Paradise was a big part of the lives of the Jews who'd always lived there. The habitants had sophisticated systems of watering and gardening, carefully running wells and fountains. They created irrigation systems and brought down drinking water from the springs. They

# The Collective Seized Paradise Island

*P*rofessor Kryvoruchko stated that the colony seized Paradise Island with their tentacles. The history of Paradise was volatile. Contrary to the surrounding ugliness, its attractiveness was tempting. Paradise was a dreamland designed by God to be attractive. It was a diamond, and many wanted to steal the gem. Paradise was a jewel of the Black Sea. Throughout history, many countries had wanted to rule Paradise. It was a place where the uninfected could enjoy life. Unfortunately, the place attracted predators. There were vicious fights for the land. On one side were the armies of France, Germany, England, Turkey, Aborigin, Malantia, Byelogoria, and more. On the other side were farmers, builders of aqueducts, creators of intricate passages of spring water and irrigation systems, and many selectors of exotic plants. It was easy to appreciate the beauty of the land.

Communalists thought they owned Paradise. They enjoyed it. They slept covered by linen sheets while the breeze from the Black Sea caressed them. They drank tasty ice water, roamed the sandy beaches, and dreamed that the land belonged to them. In reality, they were only consumers. They had not done anything to make the land irresistible. By all means, Paradise should have been independent.

Professor Kryvoruchko stated that before and after the Holocaust, many prominent and uninfected habitants begged their tyrannical leader to give the land to the Jews. If he had listened, the Holocaust might not have happened, but he did not listen and refused. Superior felt safe when goons were in the colony. Goons used a primitive black-and-white vision for all problems. They trusted only numbskulls. In fact, it was a crime to be smart. It was forbidden to be an individual and an independent thinker. The jerks in the colony, devastated by and dirty with blasphemy, treated the business-oriented uninfected unfavorably. Huns were afraid of them. To destroy them, they presented them as greedy. The assemblage of morons, polluted by toxins of desperation, performed a systematic annihilation and obliteration of individuals with success in business enterprises and science. The colony did not want any independence in thinking and prevented the uninfected from having any original ideas.

## Plebeian Background

*P*rofessor Kryvoruchko discovered that the other name for the collective was a herd. Individuality was a punishable offense. A court's ruling was based mainly on whether or not a defendant was faithful to collectivist thinking. Goons who bragged about their plebeian backgrounds were pardoned. For similar offenses, those who were business-oriented were found guilty and imprisoned. Infected ideologists demanded that everyone provide examples of fidelity. To have a small chance of survival, intelligentsia presented themselves as indivisible parts of the collective. They were a flock of dummies who congregated with deputies. They unconditionally followed all directions from the top down. They remained in existence and were still resistant to change. They wanted to keep their status.

make the world more prosperous. Professor Kryvoruchko stated that communalists declared that their mission was to defend working habitants from exploiters, and to achieve that goal, they used slaves. They sent to die millions of perceived class enemies accused of having uniqueness in their thoughts. Their fatalities showed the terrible misery at the end of the regime.

Professor Kryvoruchko declared that genocide flourished and was performed through the systematic destruction of the intellectually advanced and uninfected. Those infected with damnation promoted a simple existence that included an unpretentious lifestyle and primitive clothing. Everything in the collective's behavior and mannerisms resembled rednecks. Even wearing spectacles was a cause for criticism. The wearers of glasses were perceived to be intellectuals. The assumption was that those who read a lot of books and lost some eye power were free-thinking individuals. The ideologists claimed the continued use of eyeglasses to read books pointed to a desire to be smarter than others. They accused those with eyeglasses of being detached from the populace.

Professor Kryvoruchko noted that because business orientation and science were based on innovative culture, Superior Leader was afraid of them and crushed them. Some scientists survived by being involved in the military. Only innovations that increased the strength of weapons of war bloomed. Leaders wore military-style jackets with many insignias, orders, and medals. Perhaps they, as dullards, believed medals made them important. Proclaiming to be indispensable, all leaders had undeserved military ranks. They put the whole of industry into an embryonic state but pushed militarists ahead.

Professor Kryvoruchko said the presumed collective

had infected minds. They became butchers and imbeciles who repeated failed doctrines. Nazis got the name Aryans by shortening the name Prolet-Aryans. In fact, the two were similar. The Prolet-Aryans and Aryans were savage animals infected by profanity.

Terrestrial goons wanted to be celestial goons, even though they were not. As a result, both of them created a big assemblage of imbeciles under the name of the collective and communal state. In the world, there were many salamanders. In Professor Kryvoruchko's inventory were groups of habitants who acted like monsters in a dysfunctional family. The older brothers called themselves Prolet-Aryans, and the younger brothers called themselves Aryans. The Prolet-Aryans were infected by the collective, and the Aryans were infected by the Nazis. They did not want to share the world. They got into fights with each other.

The Nazis prophesied that Aryans had a mission to impose a new order. The Nazis simply repeated doctrine that promised to achieve something elusive. It did not have any tangible values but, regardless, required mass killings. The Nazis fought the entire world and marked many for extermination in the gas chambers. One group irritated them the most, and they hated them. The Nazis despised them because they were rich and smart and used the German language but called it Yiddish. Their older brothers, the communalists, took upon themselves a mission to rule the world by using a gangster's approach in the fight of the classes. Collective thinking, which was basically mob mentality, promised fools that they would move from ocean to ocean and bring progress to the backward. It sounded funny, but no one was laughing. The goons were not able to feed their own but declared they knew how to their opponents stood. Contrarily, goons were infected. They were always confronting and manipulating. They disputed and argued. Goons did not want to find common ground in negotiations. They did not look for ways to coexist. The ideologists were goons. They did not care about their opponents. They pushed through their own lines of conduct, which rejected uniqueness and embraced the collective's lies and primitive doctrine.

Professor Kryvoruchko classified the infected population. The goons and loggerheads were goofs and die-hard opportunists. The ideologists did not care that some disagreed. They labeled opponents as class enemies and accomplices of imperialists and were always digging up dirt on their rivals' lives. The loggerheads jumped at the chance to take the lives of their opponents. Goons' interactions had nothing to do with negotiation but were instead manipulations. The infected were also morons. They were gullible and foolish. They did not know how to negotiate. Morons were polluted by different obscenities. They were frequently in quarrels and disputes.

Morons pushed their opinions on others. Their way to relate was through quarreling; many growled and threatened to report opponents to special ideological services. The infected brawled and fussed. To prove their points, they used manipulation and confrontation. Ideologists and agitators, soiled with blasphemy, murdered all discussion and had the unanimity of bullies. Meanwhile, Sailors wanted dialogue among their own fragments and negotiation with others. Sailors wanted as many discussions as possible.

Professor Kryvoruchko noted that the pseudocollective and the Nazis proclaimed their missions to rule the world. Looking back, it was clear that Prolet-Aryans and Aryans talented habitants gave in to the lies and craziness. They were laid back in the face of atrocities. A Sailor was always on an internal voyage inside of his psyche and did not have the goal of patronizing others. Refuseniks resisted the doctrine, and they were honored and revered. Unfortunately, goons were different. They were enablers and spreaders of epidemics. Even into the present, a few remained who could not accept the fact that the goons' behavior was shameful, and they gave in to collective marasmus. Of course, they had important positions in the collective. Without any qualities, they were in the limelight. It was a shame there were few willing to give up their status as bullies. They were butchers of uniqueness. Fortunately, as time passed, there were fewer and fewer supporters of madness.

In his analysis, Professor Kryvoruchko found that those who suffered from the plague did not recognize that others could be dissimilar and have diverse opinions. They treated other habitants as inanimate objects. Contrary to that attitude, dialogue and negotiation were part of the discussion of unique individuals, wherein one wanted to understand his or her opponent and come to an agreement. They were Sailors, who traveled to find a treasury of harmony. For Professor Kryvoruchko, the avoidance of confrontation was a potential benefit of healthy negotiation. The dialogue and negotiation themselves were the main benefits. A real dialogue created a meeting that could enlighten the participants' existence. Sailors presented themselves as individuals and recognized the uniqueness of others. Sailors, the uninfected, always wanted to understand their opponents. In discussions and negotiations, Sailors continuously put themselves in the shoes of their opponents. Sailors were clear about where her right mind should have accepted as true the lie that goons were victims. On the contrary, they were sociopaths and were supposed to be incarcerated. They chose to be brutal toward the innocent. They were active participants in the craziness and did not have any mitigating circumstances. They were guilty, and they had not yet been brought to justice.

Professor Kryvoruchko emphasized that the land was the headquarters for guerillas and thugs just as a poisoned apple was a place for toxins. The disease gave goons and the vulgar herd a scientific basis to show their origin. Goons used the opportunity to boast of their ignorance and barbarism. Plebes widely used the phraseology provided by doctrine. They displayed unimaginable audacity. They declared that selfless intellectuals needed to be ashamed of being intelligent and science-oriented. Intellectuals and the uninfected were humiliated. Despite the fact that they spent their lives working toward advancement in the sciences, they were destroyed. Contrary to their victims, the leaders felt great. They smelled like pickled vegetables and dressed like baboons. They had only a few gyros in the brain and sounded pathologically stupid. They were afraid of any revisions to their doctrine. They croaked. They were shortsighted and maintained outdated concepts. They recited doctrine like parrots. It was a crime to doubt doctrine or attempt to change anything. An inconsistency happened when the Founder, who'd written the doctrine, did not want to follow the foolishness anymore. He inexplicably died.

The goons were infected by lies. The courage needed to resist them and become a Sailor was an internal decision available to anyone. Not many remained uninfected, and the opposition was small. It was shameful that many

The goons were criminals and liars. They epitomized nothing. They devised, fabricated, and exaggerated events. They blamed everything and everyone. As faithful servants of collective thinking, they fabricated their past and struggles of being harassed by the aristocracy. They certainly did not have horrible living accommodations like those in the communal setting. They made up their stories. Before being infected by toxins of distraction, the population had comfortable accommodations, nutritious food, and the opportunity to get an education and practice their spirituality.

Those infected by the disease of lunatics declared themselves distinct because they were born as children of the working class. Many insignificant habitants wanted to become significant by using lies, pretension, and daydreams. Plebes displayed their importance by fancying their own significance. The easiest way to show their importance was to declare that they were inherently special by birth. To appear special, they showed devotion to the doctrines. To keep fidelity to the doctrine, they made up sob stories about the troubles they'd endured. They claimed the nobility oppressed them. They carried the sickness and infection through their lies and placed the sickness in the minds of others.

The goons were bacillus carriers who presented themselves as revolutionaries of collective thinking and praised thefts by bandits as revolutionary achievements. Thugs were invited as willing participants. Goon ideology was mob mentality. The lies polluted minds. The truth was that goons were incarcerated for drinking in public, disturbing the peace, and theft. Those convicts did not have any excuse to present themselves as revolutionaries. Eventually, only the naive believed them. No one in his or

# A Sailor's Psyche

*A* Sailor was an individual with many unified fragments, which consisted of the copies in his memory of characters he met, books he read, movies he saw, and more. Those fragments constituted a Sailor's psyche. A Sailor identified his fragments. He knew their characteristics. He also knew that any individual could be a goon. Every fragment in a Sailor's psyche was important. A Sailor operated through dialogues, which meant understanding each of his fragments. He solidified his psyche as a whole. Sailors' psychology showed an efficient way to solidify the psyche through dialogue. Sailors unified and healed their psyches. The goals of Sailors' psychology were individuality and reconstruction of the psyche by using dialogues. Every Sailor was responsible only for his own psyche and did not participate in collective craziness.

Both the celestial and terrestrial groups were infected by obscenity. They did not resist. They were complicit in butchery. They snitched and reported on victims. Any participants in the carnage had to be condemned. They had not been forgiven. Their crime was not justifiable. The snitches had a few brain cells intact and knew the difference between right and wrong. They chose to become goons, which was the main reason they needed to be condemned. They needed to have their Nuremberg trial or at least a Hague court. Such accountability would help to get rid of the perdition. The victims were not forgotten. Sailors felt the goons should not get away with the carnage. It should not have happened, but it did happen. Because of firm resistance to contamination, many dissidents shared nameless mass graves.

trick to feed the naive with delusions. The uninfected were presented as duped and seemed stupid.

The collective made everything smell rotten. Infected by profanity, the surroundings were like a stinking pit. Everything was decayed, putrid, corrupt, and unsound. The leaders were sociopaths and enjoyed gambling. They knew they were immune from paying debts and did not care about losing. They played using human lives. They were insolent and gluttonous. They were unconcerned with the suffering of others. They were brainwashed to believe the collective was never wrong. Sociopaths used the notion of collective thinking as a way to avoid responsibility. The reality was bizarre. Pathological liars did not talk about the continuous misery. Fake celestials spoke only of doctrine. They quoted it as if it were the Bible. They claimed suffering was a necessary sacrifice for future welfare and prosperity. The sociopaths in charge of collective thinking were verminous bumpkins, brutes, and beasts.

Professor Kryvoruchko stated that to resist the goons' influence, one needed to be an individual. Sailors analyzed the revulsions of collective thinking and the misery of a communal setting. A Sailor was a breath of fresh air. With psychological analysis, Sailors found that problems were more complex and discovered that the expletives of collective thinking always had existed and caused the psychological abnormalities of those inclined toward violence. Collective thinking and a mob mentality were patronizing and imposing atrocities. Sailors' psychology brought notions of individuality, negotiation, and dialogue. The goal of Sailors' psychology was to build strong uniqueness and unification. It involved healing psyches damaged by the plague.

jackets. They also wore leather caps, but they were not capable of resolving any problems. In the past, before infection by perdition, the land had been prosperous and promising. The problem was that the czar was feeble. Opportunists saw a moment of weakness and grabbed power away from him. They destroyed the system of the past but did not have a new one prepared. Building a new system required professionalism, responsibility, and experience. In every person who lived in the time of damnation was trauma. Goons who'd thought that ruling the village would be easy became helpless in the face of mounting problems. The field fell into the abyss. The Founder of the collective saw the scary gulf. He quickly rejected the idea that imbeciles were smart enough to rule the colony. He came up with another slogan: "Study, study, and study."

It was too late; it was impossible to remove all the barriers. After the Founder's death, the era of perdition unraveled into an inescapable horror. The collective's thinking was fiction and not built on facts or evidence. Their whole idea was stupid—a nightmarish hypothesis. Ironically, the collective called it the real project of the colony. The insanity went so far that the word *abstraction* was forbidden. Many were arrested for using the word *abstraction*. In the meantime, fake celestials told lies about a future in which everyone would be rich and prosperous. They called their fraudulent speech "reality talk." In the meantime, the Aboriginians in the communal setting lived in inhumane conditions. Pseudoterrestrials—the Aboriginians—could not get rich; it did not matter how much they worked. In an environment dirtied by obscenity, delusions replaced reality. Any fake celestials involved in the falsification of facts were lying. The doctrine was a

The Mafia and the goons had organizations with a similar structure. The Mafia never were enemies of the communalists. In fact, they were socially close. Relations between the communalists and the Mafia were tricky. The Mafia was apolitical. It existed in a different universe. Mafiosi held on to many years of unchangeable habits. Most importantly, the communalists trusted them. The Mafiosi in the prisons were in privileged positions and actually controlled all internal interactions. Most of the time, the guards did not deal with the regular prisoners; they talked to the kingpins in charge instead. The Mafia kept their independence. When the communalists decided to use the Mafia as a tool, the relationship between the Mafia and the communalists turned sour. The Mafia did not bend.

Commissars were unable to establish normal lives for anyone. The children of arrested parents were placed in orphanages, which were places of horror. Children were abused by staff as well as other children. An orphanage held the same horror as a prison. The staff were antisocial and took advantage of the kids. The older children took clothes and food from younger children. One group of orphans would gang up together in a pack and fight with other gangs. One who was not a member of a gang was left unprotected and was abused just for the sake of entertainment. Life in the orphanages clearly showed that the commissars were shortsighted. They did not understand that putting on tough-looking leather jackets was not enough. They would not solve problems by horseback riding and wearing their breeches tucked into calf boots. They needed a quickness of the mind that they lacked.

Professor Kryvoruchko stated that the goons did not have any skills. Commissars paraded around in leather showed their superiors that others were less significant. The Golden Horde was also a communalist state in which horsemen considered themselves to be superior to others. As communalists, they united by capturing territory. They did not allow their cavalrymen to have any uniqueness or dissent. They were an entity wherein all Aboriginians had a desire to work together, and for a while, they did.

The Nazis had a collective structure. They had a genetics-oriented society. Their main goal was to prove they were of superior genetic material. They were adulterated by the poison of meanness. They destroyed uniqueness. Without any guilt, they ferociously killed the uninfected. They were capable of infecting the entire world. They wanted to cleanse it of many questionable genetic combinations. To gain promotions, they bragged about their genetic superiority. It was a colony of doctrine with paradigms of collective thinking.

Life in the collective and communal states resembled the time of invasion by barbarians. All the constructs of collective thinking were primitive. Many around the globe did not seriously understand the danger of doctrine. No one could have imagined what happened in that land. For outsiders, it all seemed absurd, but that was the wrong time for laughter. In reality, the communalists' lives were a big tragedy and pure buffoonery at the same time. Commissars wore clothes of a special style that brought to mind the clothes of Mongolian and Hun warriors in medieval times. The village of goons attracted the antisocial. Profanity united many sociopaths. They felt entitled, and without any guilt, they took the possessions of others, raped them, and killed them. They were surrounded by many orphaned children whose parents had been executed or were imprisoned in Kolyma.

the courage to change the old ways. His ruling was called a time of stagnation.

In that time of stagnation, there were a couple more intermediate leaders. They were buffoons and did not do anything worthy of mentioning. The stagnation continued until there came a reformer and revisionist. He was an honest player. The land was not used to having a truthful leader. It was dangerous to be a visionary. The habitants dismissed him and took him out of his position. The doctrine cracked. All of a sudden, a decent thing happened: the old territory of goons infected by disease fell apart. It was a promising time.

Sailors realized that something honest could happen to the infected populace. Unfortunately, the place was bewitched, and nothing came of the opportunity for change. In the postcommunal time, things did not change much. The nation was still a collective. The postcommunalist leader was an opportunist and a drunk. He only wanted power. His game was erratic. After him, a leader followed who was cunning and shrewd. He was a heartless hunter and acted as if he were a spider. He smiled as he waited for a fly to get stuck in his net. Sometimes his game took a while, but he always prevailed. Often, he got his plans through.

From 1240 to 1502, the Golden Horde was a collective of the Middle Ages. It was a militarized entity with the goal of conquering the world. It did not allow any distinctiveness. It was well organized. Without any guilt, it savagely killed all opposition. Nevertheless, its Aboriginian habitants were able to express their constructive ideas on how to create a better military and achieve advances in territory. For the sake of promotions, they often got in quarrels and bragged about their importance. They

Professor Kryvoruchko stated that after the death of the Founder, the new leader, who had little education and was afraid of innovations, stopped all changes. He was a scoundrel. He returned to the old policies of primitivism. He stated again that a housekeeper could manage a factory. The followers of the new leader had low intelligence and little education, but they already had developed diverse mannerisms and ambitions. The old ways of domination were comfortable for imbeciles. They did not want anything new. They were gambling. They had many things to lose. They chose to support Superior Leader, who was a dirty and scary player. It was a big mistake. The new leader did not spare anyone. He wiped out the perceived resistance that had not existed. He did not trust anyone, and his supporters had the same fate as others. He used the secret police as a tool. He saw his surroundings as treacherous. Eventually, he killed many of his cohorts. Being a fool, he became a tyrant. To scare any who were uninfected by the plague of silliness and push them to obedience, he gave a lot of power to the secret police, who monitored everyone. If any uninfected individuals had the audacity to resist his command, he tortured and killed them. As a tyrant, he expected them to work for free and give up their lives for him.

Professor Kryvoruchko stated that eventually, the tyrant died. His death occurred under murky circumstances. The next leader acted as a drunken merchant. He was a stupid player. He laundered money and made reckless bets. He became a liability to his cronies, and they impeached him. He died in isolation. His replacement was more reasonable and played carefully. He was not vicious and was not stubbornly stuck to doctrine, but he did not have and become great, all of them were characters. Sailors focused on endeavors and thoughts of enhancement versus entitlement and primitivism. The solid Sailor's psyche resisted the influence of psychological bugs. If many Sailors were around, the shadow of the disease could not cover the world again. Sailors would discontinue the habit of focusing on monstrous doctrine. They also knew the difference between manipulation and negotiation. Sailors used dialogue instead of manipulation and confrontation to support a healthy psyche and encourage distinctiveness and diverse talents. As individuals, Sailors explored their own psyches and used the greatness of individuality and creativity. They were uninfected by ruination. They had whole psyches. They could make their own lives blossom and thrive. As a result, they could be proud of themselves. Sailors did not allow the past to return and take over. Contrarily, morons infected by disease overvalued dreams of power and domination. They felt entitled to take from others.

The Founder of the collective, filthy with toxins of foolishness, was a vigilante who wanted to please his mother. He wanted vengeance against many in the colony for the death of his brother, who was executed by the czar. By settling scores, the Founder took on a high risk. He bluffed a lot and pretended he knew all the truths of equality. He did not know anything. He won by chance, despite the fact that his doctrine was atrocious and had no validity. Providentially, the colony trusted him. When he won, he did not bluff anymore. He understood that to achieve revenge, he'd gone too far, and he realized the nonsense should stop. He reversed his attitude. He wanted to end doltishness. He gained a new vision for the future. He saw reality as a tangle of worms. As soon as he had a new vision, for some unknown reason, he suddenly died.

The celestials lived a lifestyle different from that of the terrestrials. Their lives had a high quality, and they were comfortable. They lived in special colonies separated from Aboriginians. In the eyes of Aboriginians, the celestials were a distinct type who were supposed to be admired. The main function of the terrestrials was to produce a stock of beautiful females for the pleasure of celestials. Many terrestrials accepted that setting and were happy. Their daughters had celestial lovers. Day and night, the drivers of celestial comrades crossed the streets of their birthplace to find beautiful girls from Aboriginian tribes. Those girls would satisfy the sexual demands of celestials. Both groups were dogs. The difference between them was in their economic status.

The collective had a lot of inconsistencies. Pseudoterrestrials, or Aboriginians, were the workers in the colony. They were poor. In the meantime, false celestials enjoyed luxury. They also strongly guarded their society against Aboriginians. Marie-Henri Beyle (1783–1842), better known by his pen name, Stendhal, was a nineteenth-century French writer. He performed an acute analysis of his characters and the society surrounding their psyches. He was one of the earliest and foremost known practitioners of social psychology. Stendhal analyzed the possibility of crossing from low socioeconomic classes to higher ones, but his analysis was not encouraging. Such crossing of the road was almost impossible. The terrestrials sacrificed comfort and lives of pleasure, while celestials were on top of the world.

Professor Kryvoruchko's relatives were business-oriented. Sailors reframed their psyches to face reality. They did not allow devious dreams to take over their psyches. They were aware that disease was taking away the initiative and spirit of exceptionality. To achieve change in the psyche be able to lead the people to new inspirations. The postcollective region required a leader with an original vision. He would be able to move forward and would not be afraid that a few would feel the opposite. In time, he would attract many followers. The question was still open concerning what substitute would replace the national idea of military superiority. When the answer to that question was found, the transition would be more feasible. Presently, the future was murky, and the new leaders were playing the nationalism card. Germany changed its national idea of military hegemony in exchange for financial fineness. Contrarily, the postcommunal structure again supported leaders with strong military orientation.

According to Professor Kryvoruchko, the communal state was a mockery of the futuristic visions of many utopists. Their ideas were based on dissociation between the concrete and the fictitious, between reality and utopia. Everything in the killing field was built on distorted dreams and a utopia transformed by delusion. The trend of thinking maintained that delusions were real and that deceptive perceptions did not exist. Pseudocommunalists, infected by sickness, were eager to accept that flimsy structure. They insisted the configuration was entirely a product of environment and was real. Even the word *abstract* was taboo. They replaced reality with untested ideas. As a result, all scientific law gave way to political correctness. Obscurantism was the ultimate ruler of science, art, technology, and human relations.

The habitants were roughly divided into two types: false celestials and terrestrials. The first type spoke only doctrine and appeared to be advanced. They quoted ideological doctrine to justify all of their decisions. Contrary to them, the terrestrials were not as advanced.

## The Communalist Army

*T*he pseudocollective was frequently victorious on the battlefield but lost the fight for a bright future. It was clear that attempts to capture more territory merely displayed the grabbing instinct of primitive man. A change of national identity would have been painful. The nation loved the kingpins, who followed the animalistic instincts of the crowd. The leaders did not want to change the old ways of life. In their primitive view, possession of more territories brought more superiority. Applicable to the situation was the following proverb: "Winning one battle sometimes leads to the loss of the war."

The postcollective state was an intermediate before the new leader came. He would not lead them back to the embryonic tradition of primitivism. He would lead forward. He would open the mind to the vastness and joy of abstraction. He also would admit that the old national idea was obsolete and not needed anymore. He would appoint a justice to uncover all the criminality of the communal past. He would truly lead the domain. He would find concrete, progressive ways to modify their national idea. Everything about the old national ideas was cloudy, and all past proposals were primitive.

Sailors' fresh ideas included a nation with a new leader who was business-oriented. Of course, the new ideas would create a huge number of enemies. Most of their adversaries would be delusional. In the killing field, anyone could be a foe. Leaders exploited the old mores. They reigned on the incapacity of generating innovative ideas. Uniqueness was dead. The most important thing for the postcommunal setting was eventually to find an individual who would stolen into slavery to sexually satisfy Japanese soldiers, the young girls were brainwashed by communalists to act voluntarily. Being politically correct, the young girls in the killing field properly executed their duty. They provided sex. As a result, the collective had many derelict children.

A Nuremberg trial for communalists was a dream that probably never would become real. It was an uplifting dream. The trauma of the past certainly affected modern life. It was important to recognize what damage the disease had done to their psyches. Eventually, when communal ideology had its time in court, the world would see the statistics behind all the inhumane offenses of communal rule. The court would get pathfinders to identify the mass graves and would put up monuments for the victims of the ruthless, inhumane regime. The goal was to understand how the shocking past impacted the present. Also, it was important not to make the same mistakes and to prevent the ugliness from happening again in the future. The trick was to uncover the roots of the mockery and find a way to heal. If the postcommunal population would have let go of their main goal to expand territory and threaten the rest of the world, the human race would not have perceived them negatively. Unfortunately, the postcommunal regime had a lot of sentimentality for the past, a time when the collective was a strong military power. It forced the world to quake in fear in front of it.

they declared that children were required to have an allegiance to the communalist ideology and report to police on others who might be against it, including their relatives, neighbors, and educators. By following the instructions of their leaders, the children became informers from an early age. In contrast to Boy Scouts, pioneers were skillful snitches and would continue to be stool pigeons in later life. Without those skills, children were not suitable for the killing field of morons.

Abandoned and orphaned children were everywhere because commissars were antisocial and abandoned their pregnant mistresses. They did not want to accept any responsibility. Before becoming the party leaders, they'd been afraid of being fired from their jobs. Now it was different. The new ideology transformed them. They tricked others into thinking they had wisdom, compassion, and inspiration and gained the power of rulers as a result. One thing they mastered was the ability to brainwash the innocent.

The commissars used illusion and deception. Not one of them knew what direction to take. The commissars boldly rephrased the old catchphrases. They covered their tracks with slogans and stereotypical posturing. They called young girls comrades and proposed that they fight adversaries from rancorous classes. They declared that all workers were the rulers and that young comrades must support them. They presented themselves as more experienced workers. They emphasized that they were too busy to build a new reality and did not have time to get sexually involved. The girls who were close to them, as young Aboriginians, had the duty to satisfy their sexual urges. It seemed that more experienced comrades needed cheap sex. In contrast to the Korean comfort girls who were including inspiration, adoration, and worship, had ended. In the new reality, a woman was a comrade with whom to fight hostile enemies. Commissars told citizens that the old feelings of love for women had simply been a way to leave them out of revolutionary battles. They said that women, when subjects of veneration, could not be equal fighters. In other words, when admired, a woman could not be a fellow fighter. Commissars' wives changed their status and became party helpmates. The marriage certificate became outdated and obsolete. By declaring love free from limitation, the antisocial commissars took the opportunity to have sex with many young lovers. In the past, they'd gone out to work to support their wives and children, but now they simply sucked up to receive positions of power. They used it for self-gratification. The best way to quickly achieve their goal was to praise and immortalize their kingpin. With his name, goons were leaving and dying. It was a cult of personality. Superior Leader had the status of a god.

## Infection of Degeneration

The crippling infection of degeneration made parents dimwitted, relieving them from their responsibility to raise children. Pseudocommunalists promised to take care of all children but did not know how to do it. Disease marked the infected territory with a red color; red banners were everywhere. The pseudocommunalists placed on the shoulders of children pieces of red material, marking them as special. They called them pioneers. After that, of a kingpin and, under the leader, soldiers whom he could trust. Others were replaceable trash and did not have any value. More advanced structures required the presence of human standards. The mafia soldiers, like wolves, showed fidelity only to their kingpins. They did not accept any different doctrines. Contrarily, communalists were the breakers of the old system and did not have any indication of what to do next. They did not want anything complicated and embraced the criminal structure as a result. They were not unique. Simplicity always was attractive; before them had been many losers who were attracted to simple populist solutions. Unfortunately for the old guard, primitivism won over simplicity. To cover their criminal base, the communalists were vigilant. They deceitfully denied any reality. The members of the old guard were in prison.

The communalists brought an end to old-fashioned love. The rhetoric of love lost its attractiveness. The old love became humiliating, disreputable, disgraceful, ignominious, and shameful. The leaders of the communal setting were antisocial. They made a variety of adjustments to the system to satisfy themselves. It was impossible to imagine what the communalists were ready to declare to please the crowd. They did not care about morals. They condemned traditional morality. Hypocrisy was everywhere. Contrary to the public's brainwashing, their corruption was a way of life. If someone came to his or her boss without a gift, that was perceived as disrespect. Human relations became primitive. Subdued sex became a standard. Cover-ups for on-duty sexual interactions were present everywhere. Aboriginians of the communal structure called them social meetings. Ménages à trois and other sexual practices became normal. Commissars declared that sophisticated feelings toward a woman, than others. They used the doctrine to their advantage. The antisocial habitants in the media secretly laughed at the doctrine. They were aware that the bombardment of images they provided was a lie. They knew they were luring the inexperienced into risky and shady transactions. They were supposed to present the notion that it was easy. They used inflammable but empty slogans. The populace forgot that free cheese was only in a mousetrap, and they were cheated. The whole idea, promoted by the antisocial of the land, was to trick naive sheep and rob them of all uniqueness. Leaders were criminals. They knew well their scam. They took over and used power to magnify themselves.

The communal setting secretly accepted the criminal structure as a base of stability. Only after their time passed did it become clear to everyone that the communalists had a criminal base. They covered the natives with flammable slogans. The leaders had antisocial tendencies. They were capable of making up any nonsense. One of the slogans of the collective polluted by perdition was that those in the working class were naturally smart. They could perform any miracle without business skills. They could make the killing field prosperous. The criminal structure had doubts about the trustworthiness of the media. They did not believe in the jingles of the doctrine. They used it for their own needs. The mafia did not care about primitivism. They kept their troops simple but not primitive. The hardcore criminals had a steady set of notions. They did not believe in empty promises or slogans. For them, only the head of their clan and his soldiers existed.

The criminal concept always was clear, and the criminal structure was unshakable. It had existed for many centuries and was based on animal instincts and the structure of wolf packs. The criminal structure consisted for the military and space explorers. Their ambition was to expand from one ocean to another. They also used excessive brutality to keep order in their gained territories.

The pseudocollective wanted to be the rulers of the world. The killing field resembled the initial elevation and then subsequent decay of other promising but failed empires. In a variety of communal settings, it was agreed that murder was a necessity. The description was clear. One murderer's intention was correctly understood by other murderers.

A loss of exceptionality and originality was a consequence of communal settings. The area was surrounded by barracks filled with plank beds, dusty and dirty pallets, snaky informers, and abusive guards. There was no law. Lawlessness was everywhere, and the great power was doctrine, which was not allowed any revisions. The biggest achievement of the communal setting was an ugly series of slave camps, wherein every commissar had unlimited power to impose his own severe rules.

Professor Kryvoruchko stated that communalists were oriented toward increasing territorial influence and brainwashing others. They captured psychological territory in naive minds through their fraudulent indoctrination and ideology. The collective promised to bring a new structure to human relations but were stuck in a medieval configuration. They were imposters who were lost. They did not know where to go. They promised to lead forward but instead regressed backward. The pseudocollective brought the killing field back to medieval times.

The pseudocollective was run by morons filthy with plague. The nation was in complete disarray. The antisocial had an unbreakable structure and resisted psychological bane. The few with antisocial tendencies adjusted better military-type uniforms. Under the effects of the ruination, instead of being oriented to the West, leaders blamed the West for their moral turpitude. They accused the West of poisoning food, sending disease-causing bacteria to the cities' waterfronts, and messing up everything that was important to the killing field.

Sailors acknowledged that the communalists had regressed and brought back the barbarian age. Their clothes were monotone. The odor from the inhabitants was terrible. They did not use any perfume. They promoted austerity. Naturally, they did not have camisoles or chiffons. The disease-producing commissars in dirty clothes looked like ancient savages. They wore leather pants and leather jackets and did not shave their faces. They did not take showers. They were a strong, militarized entity.

Professor Kryvoruchko stated that those infected by martyrdom had problems designing underwear, shoes, and dresses. The lack of toilets and toilet paper contributed to the bodies' smells. The rare bathroom did not have toilet stalls and was always dirty. The area did not have enough hot water to allow the population to have everyday showers. If an apartment had bathtubs, people did not use them as intended but instead used them for watering sour cabbage and pickled cucumbers. Superior Leader and the rest of the collective washed themselves once a week. The collective had many public baths with shallow two-handled metal washbowls for multiple uses. The bathhouses had extended hot-water norms. Like the rest of communal life, the one action that included the use of hot water was predictable. On Friday night, the lines to public baths were a mile long.

The collective persecuted any individuality or originality. They used the same slogans. Their clothes were primitive uniforms. They created coveralls—clothes new to be proud of and indefinitely repeated the doctrine that a large territory made a colony of populism great. On the contrary, territories with many inhabitants required a great deal of care and created a lot of expenses. Instead of staging military interventions, countries should have traded their best products. The quality of merchandise should have created national pride and increased money flow to the treasury. The public had to know that an iron fist created only slavery. The few books in existence about the slave camp did not completely reveal the horror, and the public deserved a complete investigation with all the facts exposed. The practice of slavery came from many generations back, when barbarians, ancient fighters, were infected by different psychological germs. They rejected human values.

Sailors recognized that communalists presented the West as a monster. The West looked like a disgusting scarecrow to those habitants. That attitude had changed over time. Peter the Great wanted a connection with the West. Emperors Peter the Great and Catherine the Great did not approve of a negative attitude toward the West. In their rulings, the new currents from the West were respected. Czar Peter I was remembered as a man from the West. He got away from the brutal bear stereotype. His armed forces did not present themselves anymore as the savage aggressors from the Golden Horde. Peter the Great and Catherine the Great made soldiers looked refined. They were clean shaven, wore fancy clothes, and danced a pretty quadrille. Nevertheless, the national attitude never changed. There was huge territorial growth. Inhabitants called their terrain great because of its size and capacity to swell. In the meantime, the fancy attire did not stay long. The collective changed their flamboyant dresses to simple incompetence was a way of life. To compensate for their uselessness, they used rudeness in their ruling.

## Primitive Vulgarisms

*P*rofessor Kryvoruchko stated that the chubby leaders of the collective displayed primitive vulgarisms. The Aboriginians of the collective acted like parrots repeating doctrine. Because of their bickering, even dogs and cats were abused. Children were victims. The neglected women lacked appropriate attire and elegance. They worked in construction, dressed in coveralls and rubber boots, and did not have any products for feminine hygiene. Women in localities adulterated by distress lost their feminine tenderness, using foul language and drinking alcohol. Primitivism was a way of life. All abstractions were forbidden, and everyone was paranoid about American spies. To please fake celestials, ideologists were afraid of innovations. They were not capable of understanding much anyway. They displayed negligence to everything important.

It would have been desirable for the postcollective to turn away from the idea of accumulating more territory. Unfortunately, they did not. They remained one of the dangers of modern times. To clean up all the filth and grime, communalists would have to have a new Nuremberg trial. Everything they presented was a misrepresentation of reality. The great killing field, with its traditions of nobility, dignity, and splendor, was influenced by idiotic doctrine. The homeland degraded. It did not find anything accomplishments included enthusiastically informing on their neighbors. They restated many senseless ordinances. They silently implemented every silly decree demanded by their foolishness. They were deplorable and needed a kingpin and a roof over their heads. They required a protector in the higher echelons of the hierarchy to whom they could kiss up. It was also undeniable that they had a passion for food. They used their positions as footmen to keep their passion running. They all were overeaters. Fake celestials and their offspring were plump and sluggish and involved in the consumption of delicious food. They wanted to impress others. The delicatessen on the table was a sign of success in life. It included many types of food that were not available in regular stores. Only special places had certain luxuries, including caviar, boiled sturgeon, hard smoked sausage, and aged wine. For the best condition of reproduction, fake celestials consumed everything through government distributors.

The goons were severely dimwitted and had a profound lack of skills. They knew well how to steal and take from others by force. Otherwise, when they had nothing to steal, they felt useless. They did not adore diamonds or masterpieces of art, but they worshipped food. As false celestials, they came from the bottom of the socioeconomic hierarchy and did not have any subtlety to understand the beauty of diamonds. In the past, they'd used to eat leftovers from the seigneurial table. They now used the domain's wealth to buy food. They had distributors available only for celestials. The food symbolized their pride and created a feeling that life was not being wasted. They did not care about fairness because their well-fed bellies were most important. For a village of morons tainted by poison, themselves to the end and acted the same as the Huns. In the killing field, the influences of ancient times still existed. Morons still focused on the expansion of territory. It was hard to imagine the old lifestyle attracting many collaborators, but unfortunately, their escalation continued and threatened the world. For many, the danger of invasion became unbearable and could not continue. The postcollective somehow changed its old image but had the same national idea and never changed its populist perspectives. The postcollective and collective had many similarities; only hygienic rules and the dress code became different. The old ways would continue until the masses were willing to challenge the collective's lies. The communal setting had to be defeated not from the outside but from the inside. The Golden Horde cracked because they focused only on increasing their territorial influence. The same tendency toward decay was observable in the killing field of the new Huns.

It was a mystery how the ideologists, polluted by the sickness of scoundrels, brought goons to power. The fake celestials were only capable of filling up their stuffed bellies. The revolt that brought fake celestials to power was absurd. A bunch of guzzlers killed many and destroyed a civilization refined by Peter the Great and Catherine the Great. Rednecks became rulers. In exchange for food, they sold to the West priceless masterpieces, including antiques, art, gold, crystal, porcelain, and artisan works. It became clear that fake celestials, unclean with toxins of swindle, were merely uneducated working-class habitants. In their origin, they were skillful ass kissers. In the management of the killing field, they did many idiotic things, but they were forgiven because they enthusiastically repeated citations from doctrine. Their with them. Germany became a center of art, sophistication, and ideas of love and acceptance. For Germans, economic horizons were more important than territorial theft.

As a result of its inability to change past habits, the postcollective was not able to endorse the new attitude. Adulteration by many curses existed even prior to the czarist's time. The collectivists were barbarians. They were part of the Golden Horde. They slept and ate with horses, which shared their daily activities. They dressed in dirty clothes and had a bad odor about them. The ancient communalist fighters were the best equestrians and brave combatants.

Sailors looked at the genetic makeup of the land ruled by present communalists and at the history of the land, looking even before the time when it was ruled by czars. Many families in that locality filthy by ruination were descendants of various tribes in the Golden Horde. Their ancestors proved to be excellent warriors but were savages who did not follow any rules of hygiene. They continued the seizure of territory from other countries but did not manage the land well. Their primitive lifestyle was without any pretense, but their bravery was not without its attractiveness. That lifestyle continued into the present. They grabbed the biggest territory in the world. Unfortunately, despite being excellent thieves, they were not good factory managers.

The symptoms of barbaric behavior followed Aborigin into the present. Even though thievery happened less and less, there were, unfortunately, those who stole territory. The old ways lost their magnetism for the ordinary but not for the few in power. Even though unlimited cyberspace existed, barbarians still wanted to be great and conquer others for their territory. Pseudocommunalists and their Founder had tried a different approach and abandoned the populist doctrine but failed. Barbarians were true to included more sanctions and, eventually, partial exclusion from the internet. The world community would not tolerate land grabbers. The biggest losses came from an embargo on interactions with others and from forced social isolation. The nation had to change their primitive idea of what it meant to be different and more sophisticated. They needed to consider how to enrich their homeland. When they brought the population to a higher socioeconomic level, more sophisticated ideas would appear, and they wouldn't need a primitive land-grabbing attitude.

In a continuation of the past, postcollective thinking focused on persistently using the military to steal territory from others and hammer neighbors. They sang the same old tune instead of promoting free choice and a new destiny. Their approach would never become special because it was primitive. For many centuries, the Golden Horde's attitude worked for them and kept the land together, but it was not a visionary solution. Theft worked in a paradoxical way. As a result of the ongoing practices of grabbing and enlarging, nationals lost more territory than they gained. The postcommunalists used the silliest and most primitive solutions imaginable. Their thinking was confused and focused on Aboriginian cheating. They were the scarecrow of the world. They were not happy with themselves and not accepted by others. Until they stopped the big monster in their psyche, it would not leave them. Their primitive nationalist thinking never served anyone. Nevertheless, as a punishment for resistance, they assassinated nonconformity. For them, it was easy to do so because they disregarded fatalities. Contrary to Aborigin, post-Nazi Germany was a tolerant nation. The Germans did not try to fight the whole world and were friendly with all of God's creatures. They brought prosperity to their neighbors, who were happy to work asked for clemency. The citizens of democratic Germany accepted the new national idea of being part of a united Europe. The Valhalla was no longer on their minds. They did not want to grab further territory. They no longer believed themselves to be superhuman.

There were crucial differences between the communalists and the Nazis. After the loss of the Cold War, communalists blamed the whole world and denied any atrocities. After the fall of the collective, the postcommunal leaders did not accept any responsibility for the extermination of tens of millions. The postcommunal system did not have a Nuremberg trial. For them, the dead were just dead, not the victims of inhumane actions. Because they were not a part of the atrocity, they did not feel responsible. The new postcommunal leaders never knelt in front of mass graves or shed even one tear for those unjustifiably eradicated. The new postcommunal leaders wanted to avoid responsibility for almost a century of enslavement and torture. They did not express any guilt for the misery of millions. Their excuse was that because they were born later, they'd had nothing to do with those atrocities. They refused to take responsibility for stupid brainwashing slogans, decaying shared dwellings, stinking boardinghouses, and merciless penal complexes.

The collective was a ghastly creature in human history. Nevertheless, in the time of the internet and unlimited cyberspace, the postcommunalists continued to sniff out more territory. They grabbed pieces of land from their neighbors. The postcommunal state kept the same national idea. They acted as if the world owed something to them and should not judge them for robbery. They continued following a great mission to enlarge their territory. Their business orientation was in their pens. The consequences that, they designed a new means of extermination: gas poisoning.

Because they were infected by the illness of scoundrels, one could not hate all the disease-ridden. There was evidence that some of them resisted deadly perdition. Even in the time of the Nazis, many Germans disclosed that they hated the Nazis. They did not yell it stridently enough, but they existed and even tried to assassinate their führer. Regardless, their protest was not loud enough. The killing machine quickly consumed them. The question was still open: Who was a traitor, and who really committed treachery? One could not question the fact that many were afraid to resist infection and even took advantage of the status quo. It was undeniable that the collective wanted to work with the Nazis. However, the Nazis presented communalists as a brain-dead flock of freebooters. They equated communalists to savages descended from the Golden Horde. To have an excuse for stultification, Nazi propaganda always pointed a finger at communalists. Deep in their hearts, the communalists admired the Nazis, whose mentality was close to theirs. They were with the Nazis at the beginning of the war.

Professor Kryvoruchko stated that after the Second World War, Germany did not look for excuses and admitted their past. They had guts, changing their national idea of being superhuman. After the war and the collapse of the Nazi regime, Germans did not pass the blame onto someone else. They took responsibility. The leaders of democratic Germany came to the Nazi death camps and asked for forgiveness. The new leaders did not have any connections to the Nazis, but when they became influential, they took responsibility for the Nazis' deeds. They knelt in front of burial grounds full of exterminated men and women and

Contrarily, the collective and communal structures had not had their time in such trials yet.

The collective created villains not seen before in the history of mankind. Sailors wanted to help everyone be aware of the role of the disease in uninfected lives. Trials had not happened yet for many of the monsters who deliberately spread the epidemic. The communalists, who intentionally soiled many innocents with poison, were guilty of atrocities. People could not trust that they would administer self-punishment. In fact, they falsified the evidence of their crimes and insisted the mayhem was a necessity of the time, done for the benefit of Prolet-Aryans. Whatever the court's name, the Sailors believed the future would punish the communalists. To prevent a recurrence of the past, the villains had to have their day in court so the world would know the truth.

Professor Kryvoruchko stated that the goal of the slave camp was extermination. The place was in the North, far away from the public eye. Guards kept prisoners in inhumane conditions. The collective deprived them of basic nutrition. Looking back, one could not say who were worse: the Nazis or the collectivists. Sailors claimed they were no different. The ugliest mass murders started before the Nazis, in a communal setting. The Nazis had not come to prominence yet. They copied the idea of concentration camps from their older comrade, the collective state. The communalists invented extermination centers but called them slave camps. The Nazis saw that the world was silent in the face of those atrocities and took advantage. Using the older mentor's rhetoric, they called the extermination camps correctional camps. The Nazis' methods also involved starvation and inhumane conditions. On top of soiled by toxins of malice, was against human affability. The ugly incompetence brought death.

The collective deized women. The women, instead of being an inspiration, became comrades in arms. It had been different during the reign of Peter the Great and Catherine the Great. During and after their rule, a lot of poetry and novels had been dedicated to women. European influence had been everywhere. The men had performed duels to defeat rivals in love. The women had been seen as tender, fragile, ethereal, and delicate. Their dresses had been works of art. Many men would have given their lives to protect the honor of the ones they adored. After the revolution, everything changed. All of a sudden, women became strong, dependable comrades and partners. Love was an anachronism. Just like men, women wore leather pants and jackets. They did not wear perfume or other cosmetics. The women lost their special status and became equal. They drank alcohol and used profanity. They looked no different from men. Worst off were noblewomen. They did not have the elusive protection of the workers' class. They were subject to discrimination and could be beaten, raped, and robbed. Contrary to the men, the women did not deteriorate back to the mind-set of the Golden Horde, but they eventually transformed into a new ugly form.

Sailors underlined the horrible role of infection in the culture. The worst psychological damnation in history affected the habitants. The affected became the Nazi and collective states. They were worse than ogres. Historians were not in a position to compare the degree of the viciousness. People knew about the atrocities and carnage of the Nazis because of credible evidence. Nazi crimes resulted in the Nuremberg trials, which identified responsible parties and established their punishment.

and deceiving. Naturally, they lacked nobility, honesty, and decency. Nevertheless, because of their brutality, they accomplished the communalists' old idea to grab territory. Opposite the Red Army were a few nobles from czarist surroundings called the White Army. They were not as brutal. They were honorable, brave, and dependable. They disappeared because they kept the soldiers' honor. They lost to savagery and brutality. The collective captured their territory and covered it with darkness.

The collectivists killed all who crossed them. Their steps were marked by struggles and killings. Those infected by the black germs, the Nazis, created a bloodbath in the middle of Europe. Everyone smelled it. Contrarily, communalists did their killings in the North, where no one could see them. Because the frost did the job of killing for them, they didn't need bullets or poisonous gas. The communalists were terrible. Commissars were violent and fought among themselves to hold power. The battle for power continued for seventy-five years. Infected communalist men submitted themselves to populist slogans. They were forced to be obedient and submissively fulfilled nationalist doctrine. They corroborated with obscenities, atrocities, and humiliations. They were forced to believe that the collective was great because it had the biggest territory, but they overlooked the fact that communalists had corrupt police who persecuted the innocent, incompetent business planners, and monsters as politicians. They always bragged that they had the best ballet; the best symphonies; and a few good theaters, writers, and poets. They did not know the wisdom that exceptions proved the rule. Some flowers could grow on stones and sand, but people could not harvest enough millet from them to feed everyone. It became clear that the doctrine was a big scam. Everything, basements, land near train tracks, and water hatches. They were dirty and dressed in rags. They were the horrors of the cities. They were worse than rats. The collective killed their parents and left no one to take care of them. Some of them were dumped onto the streets by their caretakers. They were infected with lice and infectious diseases. They fed themselves by stealing and attacking the weak and elderly. They did not have mercy on anyone. They kicked, bit, and stole from others.

The collective had no remorse for doing evil. The homeland was full of psychopaths. They somehow re-created the time of the Golden Horde. They were free to kill, ransack cities, drink alcohol, use drugs, chase women, and take justice into their own hands. They called that group of hooligans the Red Army. Their supremacy allowed men to easily relieve their urges. They could do practically anything without experiencing guilt. Their infected leaders told them that whatever bad they did was valid. The meanness of their actions was justifiable. They needed to be tough because their demeanor frightened their class enemies. The infected leaders said the goal was to destroy their predecessors' attitudes toward the working class by showing their strength. According to the infected, the minorities had been oppressed by the previous regime and were habitants hungry for power who took advantage of the moment. Because of those misconceptions, Jews and other minorities became scapegoats. The guilty blamed them for confusing innocent communalist men. In reality, minorities simply carried out the will of the infected.

The attitude of the Mongols was to take as much territory as possible. The Red Army continued that trend. The collective became the biggest evil empire imaginable. They were able to reach their goal by killing, torturing,

## Pseudocollective Chaos

In that region, dogs and cats abandoned by owners added to the horrors of communal living. They ransacked the trash, attacked those who carried food, and defecated everywhere. Infected with rabies, they salivated and bit others. When they were in packs, they attacked everyone. They would not let anyone go until they'd finished with him or her.

To defend themselves in case of animal attacks, the Aboriginians usually carried big sticks. Images of the collective were similar to those of lands after military battles. The collective brought a prosperous land back to the time of the Mongolians' and Huns' conquests, but in reality, their destruction was much greater. The communal settings brought something never seen before. Their existence was pure obliteration. The ruling slogan was that the precommunal structure must be demolished. Nevertheless, everyone considered survival first because the future was not clear. The richness and fruitfulness of their culture were destroyed. Settlements in a colony of doctrine were built like big prisons. The name of the prison was the collective, or the communal state, where many were insensitive like animals. The innocent victims of the psychological plague were dogs and cats.

The distress of the pseudocollective was deadly and killed many children. The weakest were the biggest victims of the devastation brought to the barren land. Millions of homeless children crossed the terrain repeatedly and did not have any chance to find food or lodging. They got food from garbage cans and slept in places deemed unacceptable for normal humans, such as evicted houses, the military were able to develop their ideas in practical ways, but many others were exterminated.

Sailors put everything in order. The powerbrokers of the collective proposed primitive solutions to complex problems. They did not permit their unproven, untested, and fraudulent political constructs to be reformed. Reform was not even a possibility. They insisted their concepts were real. They pushed their unverified ideas on the naive and did not understand the weakness of their unproven political hypothesis, refusing to negotiate or compromise. They engaged in brainwashing. They used confrontations and manipulation to put sick ideas into innocent minds. They were afraid their doctrine could be discredited and labeled as a falsehood. They created rules and regulations that prevented the truth from getting out. They enrolled the naive to be paid informers or volunteer collaborators. They used ordinary citizens as propaganda messengers. They infected the collective with stool pigeons. Falsehoods and lies were weapons in their hands. The Founder was more realistic. Eventually, he brought to light the region's madness and wanted to stop it. Nobody knew what happened to him, but shortly after his change of heart, the Founder died. His comrades in arms did not recognize his new quest. The communalists did not want any changes. Because of the low educational level of the leaders, complex ideas were not popular.

The collective was a primitive structure. It did not value and was afraid of the uninfected who brought innovation to change life for the better. Because of that nonsense, many honest and uninfected were ultimately executed and replaced by criminal minds who did not care on what basis the criminal structure was built. They were not sophisticated. They used a primitive approach: deception given the name of the collective and communal state. The criminal structure was strong on its barren surface but became a big and ugly edifice. To prove their validity, they built their system using primitive labor and created slavery under the guise of labor camps. The system attracted the naive and antisocial, who became huge supporters of primitivism and enforced their criminal concept. The same type of habitants who supported primeval structures carried on into present times. The population of cockroach lovers who admired meek resolutions remained quite large. The number of simpletons was always large. It would take a long time for them to understand that they were wrong and that primitive solutions did not work.

The Aboriginians were speculators who repeated like parrots that the system did not require reform and could work as it was. In exchange for being foolish, they were rewarded with a lot of medals and given prestige as dedicated party leaders. Because they were afraid of reform, communalists missed a number of opportunities. A few brilliant managers proposed changes that would allow the country to grow. They did not succeed. The communalists did not grant any mercy to the reformers. Sadly, innocents lost their identities and became part of a herd. In the meantime, the military machine was relatively free to use innovations. Several scientists affiliated with

Sailors set out to help habitants who were infected and sickened by psychological germs. A conditioned person would regain his flexibility if he were quickly isolated from the generators of indoctrination. The one way to be saved from political persuasion was to counter the programming and distance oneself from indoctrination. Sailor psychologists and anthropologists were interested in the pathology associated with the communal setting. In the past, many futurists had entertained themselves with thoughts of replacing everything private and individual with collective property and possessions. The idea was attractive. Unfortunately, like many fictional ideas, it was only a fantasy. Being infected, the leaders ruled in inappropriate ways and destroyed fantasy. The crowd were just insects to them. To keep power over the cockroaches, the leaders transformed them into zombies.

In the meantime, a few imposters presented themselves as gods, and the starving crowd accepted them and followed them like robots. The masses did not see that in reality, their leaders were primitive power grabbers without any administrative skills. The market skills of the self-imposed guardians of the collective were poor. They presented themselves as martyrs and did not want to acquire new abilities.

Communalist positions in the system were not based on straightforward wages for productive work but attached to political loyalty. The role model for working Prolet-Aryans was a manual worker with a hammer and sickle. The media glorified primitivism in all areas of life. The biggest fraud was the substitution of the complex and sophisticated with the primitive and dumb. The collective called it the biggest achievement of the new regime. Complex ideas were called plots to enslave the workers.

grab power and capture the world by force. They created fictitious enemies who wanted to destroy them.

## The Pseudocollective as Pathology

The pseudocollective was not able to find remedies to starvation and poverty. Contrastingly, the collectivists created slavery and starvation. They decided to use any simpletons who were stupid enough to cooperate with them. Because the regime was not sure how long their time would last, the leaders looked for a fast solution. Eventually, they failed.

The Founder permitted others more sophisticated to establish a new economic policy and allowed the business-oriented to own small private properties and petite businesses. Nevertheless, the collectivists did not allow those active in business to have any associations or political representation. They did not respect the private space, private thoughts, and private capital of others. That respite did not last long. After a short time, those active in business sat in prisons. The word *private* was taboo, and the words *collective* and *communal* were privileged. The ideologists exterminated national cleverness, leaving behind only primitive jackasses. Only a few complex and erudite individuals were still around because they were irreplaceable. As an exception, in a few places, the sophistication and taste of elegance coexisted with barbarian savagery and inhuman cruelty. By some small chance, gallantry survived even in the hell. For many, the collective was worse than hell.

not display anger or a desire to steal anything, created the opposite. The collective work of Buddhist monks was called mandala. The monks made collective graphics formed with colored pieces of sand. After finishing the picture, the monks swiped away the old picture and started a new one. The process gave the monks great pleasure. Mandala was a spiritual and ritual symbol in Buddhist religions, representing the universe. In common use, *mandala* became a generic term for any diagram, chart, or geometric pattern. It represented the cosmos metaphysically and symbolically. It was used as a microcosm of the universe. The creation of a mandala provided the needed exacerbation of energy to be united. Contrarily, the collective only created misery.

The collective simplified the appearance of competence in science, the economy, and the knowledge of industries. Because of their unwillingness to have a deeper understanding of complex issues, the collectivists lived by medieval rules. The incompetent collectivists simplified the responsibility of taking charge of a situation by exerting force. The ignoramus leaders created a structure that was confusing. From outside, the collectivists appeared normal and uninfected, associated with modern Europeans values, but that impression was wrong. The supreme leaders brought to the collective cruelty, harshness, and a totalitarian structure. They preached violence. They took capital by force from the affluent. For naive folks, they used primitive but heart-moving patriotic and sentimental slogans of equality to cover the cruel and sadistic nature of their intentions. Any complexities and abstractions were not in favor. Even more, they perceived them as a danger. The wealthy, business-oriented, educated, and uninfected were seen as threats to the primitive nature of the collective. Behind all their slogans was a clear desire to by marasmus the poorly educated opportunists. Bugs of marasmus inserted into them the primitive idea of achieving equality by stealing wealth from the uninfected population.

History showed that primitivism was not an answer for societal inequality. The temptation to take from others never was an answer for inequality. Dealing with social pollutions and commotion was not an easy task and certainly not a primitive task. The solution to social problems required the creation of think tanks composed of economists, social workers, and sociologists who understood how to solve issues and avoid accepting temporary solutions. As history showed, a primitive solution, such as taking wealth from the rich and distributing it among the unfortunate, was a mistake. Those were not approaches even of the Golden Horde. Those were not appropriate methods for any arrangement claiming to be advanced and sophisticated.

The idea of taking from the wealthy did not have the anticipated result and, in the long term, had an opposite effect. Robbery from the wealthy created a criminal structure with kingpins in charge. The structure was labeled a collective. The situation became grave. The criminal entity, like communalists, took wealth from the affluent but did not invest it in the business world. They cut the needed bough for future investments. They took money from the middle and upper class but did not have the brains to capitalize on it.

The process of building an elusive image of the future was done by glorifying torture and suffering. Communalists labeled hardworking, business-oriented habitants as enemies. The collective took everything from them, including their lives. Collectivists acted like the barbarians of the Golden Horde. Buddhist monks, who did communal existence. That split was seen across the whole system. It was not a surprise that outsiders observed something incongruous there. Many analysts mentioned that they noticed the split between brilliance and primitive savagery.

Those infected with cretinism did not act sophisticated but performed as empty-headed people. They used primitive solutions as a way out. They spouted answers to complex problems that attracted many naive habitants. In many countries, there was inequality as well as poverty, illiteracy, alcohol and drugs, slander, and many other maladies and troubles. In those societies, the intellectuals thought about those problems. The communalists had a different way of thinking. Instead of creating a middle class, the collective promoted education mainly for illiterate habitants with low IQs. They destroyed the competitiveness of brilliant minds. They duped the shortsighted by refocusing them on future equality. They created outlandish displays in the form of military parades and national celebrations. At the same time, they destroyed the intelligent and educated, who threatened the status quo of imbeciles.

Under the influence of the collective infected by stupidity, people had no shame in taking from others by force. It was a criminal attempt to blame the successful and fortunate for the unfairness of creation. Those infected by entitlement felt that being left out justified atrocities. Collectivists lost the feelings of guilt and shame. They stole from others, misrepresented the past, and denied the nature of their actions. Infected by illness, they portrayed the worst habitants on the fringes of society as oppressed and misfortunate. In reality, misery was not a result of oppression. The revolt did not start because of the unfortunate. The fact was that the germs infected

Terrestrials received handouts in the form of slogans and cheap watches that temporarily made them happy. They enthusiastically licked the hands of the authorities. In the homeland, snitching was present at every level and a fact of life. From childhood, squealing was an obligation of the infected by false claims of commitment. The collective skillfully brainwashed people to believe it was their duty to believe in equality. The poison of doctrine's encouragement to be a snitch took away from terrestrials any guilt. They even informed on their friends.

The pseudocollective offered them many stories about snitching and presented it as a patriotic act. Everything was geared toward protecting the status quo. The terrestrials even felt proud of being informers, as if snitching were an act of patriotic duty. It was impossible to grasp the level of cretinism in their heads. The leaders kept those infected by cretinism in poverty. In general, they were tenants in communal apartments with one restroom and kitchen. Nevertheless, they put a lot of effort into workplace competitions and informed on others in order to receive cheap rewards.

All the power of the land was in the hands of the murderous Superior Leader. His butcher and villain, Felix Dzerzhinsky, kept everyone terrorized in the sinking colony of doctrine. It was bewildering that a civilized location could be duped so easily. Later, the elite, infected by stupidity, gave power to several disgraceful jokers. At the same time, in the same area lived talented uninfected persons, such as composers Dmitri Shostakovich and Aram Khachaturian; genius Joseph Mandelstam, a poet who died in prison; and Joseph Brodsky, a poet who died in exile after receiving the Nobel Prize. The colony of doctrine declared that a miserable life reflected a fantastic

The collective dangled carrots on sticks to create a tightly controlled society. Leaders had brainwashed workers. Eventually, they developed a system of promotion for the Aboriginians who advanced in competitions in the workplace. Workers received few monetary rewards; they received political ones instead. In every factory was a red banner with a local hall of fame. The ideologists placed on it photos of those who won competitions. The terrestrials were busy. They put a lot of effort into winning those competitions. They also had an enormous determination to spy on their neighbors and write denunciations of their fellow citizens and coworkers. They were encouraged to inform and become stool pigeons. Most of the prized workers were also finks. The slogan of power in the working class encouraged everyone to be a snitch. The collective was cheerful when workers rushed to report on everyone around them. The ideologists were happy because a number of snitches showed how well they had performed their brainwashing. The collective controlled every breath of their wards. It was a big jail for terrestrials and was governed brutally.

False celestials in the collective had feelings of entitlement. The elite of the collective enjoyed high-quality lives, much better than those of the rich European merchants. They had big houses and private chauffeurs in beautiful cars. They had many ways to fool Aboriginians and made them insignificant. The secret police were vigilant in order to keep celestials safe. To prevent any discomfort for the ruling elite, they collected information of any kind. The informers received few rewards, and the collective did not care whom they took advantage of. In a structure like the collective, only the idea of a bright future was sacred; the present well-being of individuals was not important.

The fastest factory workers with the most stamina who came in first in factory races won trophies. They received inexpensive watches with inscriptions of the community symbol or paper charters that had an emblem glorifying the collective. In reality, the terrestrials did not have any rights. The same divisiveness was seen during apartheid in South Africa. The party leaders, polluted by toxins of lunacy, did the same things to the terrestrials that were done to black residents in South Africa. The only difference was that in South Africa, the black population was informed from birth that they were not equal, but there, the herd were brainwashed to believe they were equal. The Aboriginians willingly exchanged gold for cheap frippery. Buyers from European countries received gold in exchange for trifles, including tinsels, trumpery, brightly painted glass, and wooden beads.

The collective cheated in the same way the slave owners in South Africa did. The collective was devious. They did not care that it was wrong not to pay fair wages and to deceive others with fairy tales about heavenly life on earth. Celestials brainwashed terrestrials to believe they were competing to have a bright future. Competitiveness forced Aboriginians to work longer hours. Duped terrestrials were encouraged to participate in socialist competitions. The winners extracted more coal than other coal miners did. Everywhere, champs produced more than other workers, but it did not result in fair wages. The celestials provided comfortable lives for themselves, but terrestrials received the same salaries for higher-quality work. The herdsmen did not care about the feelings of the herd. The collective created a system of pacifying rebels. It dreamed up many projects requiring slaves, and everyone involved could be sent to a concentration camp.

impurity of the red pest. The false celestials' cattlemen kept their positions by using brute force and exploiting official media. Leaders who sounded stupid and looked just as imbecilic were introduced to the masses as wise, thoughtful, honorable, and elevated. The masses needed herdsmen to lead the sheep and cows. Without them, the herd would be lost. Celestials misled the terrestrials' minds with fables about equality, which was the biggest lie.

## False Celestials and Terrestrials

*P*rimitive Prolet-Aryans and Aryans were not equal to the talented and business-oriented. They were imbecilic, genetically damaged by germs of pretension, and need psychological help. They entered the world the same way others did, but after birth, equality ceased. Newborns had different IQs and a variety of talents. One important talent that differentiated the uninfected was business orientation. False celestials were not talented and did not have business orientation. For them, it was not important what abilities habitants had. They were crooks who were capable of selling their nonexistent talents, and they became important regardless of the fact they were just empty place. Their family ties were important too. In a colony of doctrine, it was most important to merely relate to celestials. They misled terrestrials to work on the promise of future equality. In reality, they would never allow terrestrials across the line into celestial clans. For terrestrials, equality was a dream.

In the collective were competitions for terrestrials.

toward any minorities. In the killing field unclean from the scourge, there was real apartheid. The Jews and Armenians were limited in their admission to universities and positions in industry. They did not have any law to protect their dignity. Brainwashing by false celestials about the protection of doctrine led to discrimination against minorities. Superior Leader promoted a policy of more opportunities for the older brother, Aborigin, which was also a scam.

Professor Kryvoruchko tied up his inquiry by declaring that in all the stages of the collective's development, unfairness and disparities always existed. The possibility for Aboriginians to cross from terrestrial to celestial was zero. The hypocrisy of the collective was that they preached equality. They emphasized that inequality in the collective was impossible and never existed. After the death of Superior Leader, the cult of personality was revealed. The goal of the cult of personality was to please terrestrials. They quickly reestablished a new cult. The collective could not exist without a cult. The collective quickly reanimated the cult of celestials. After revealing the cult of Superior Leader, celestials hypocritically bragged that no one could avoid the punishing sword of the collective. By bringing to light the crimes of Superior Leader, the party leaders saved themselves. As soon as the cult was exposed, a clique of celestials began a fight to take a ruling position in government.

In the homeland, the dead king was a criminal, but the new one was not much better. As they said, "The king is dead; long live the king." To take the throne, celestials used lies, deceptions, and assassinations. They fought like spiders in a jar. The unfair competition was an everyday reality of their environment, which suffered from the them to fight for the victory of doctrine. Similarly, the Nazis placated Germans with a special mission to fight for the Third Reich. Superior Leader praised the communalists, calling them smart. He hid his face behind collectivist doctrine. The doctrine was the mind of Superior Leader and the dilemma of the Founder's life.

In the communalists' state, the power of doctrine was absolute. The collective was led by many and hypothetically was wiser than any individual. The collective was supposed to be prudent and strong. After the demise of the Founder, idiots believed again that doctrine made sense. They were wrong because the doctrine brought only starvation, death, and deprivation. The infected were hypnotized by their special mission. In front of them, they perceived glory and superiority. They were simply brainwashed. Superior Leader was miserable and mistrustful. He confused habitants but formed a collective state. He created a confusing construct under the name of a collective, which split the land into many worthless districts. He tricked with alphabets, languages, and the names of national districts printed on maps. It worked because habitants felt that being part of collectivist thinking made them bigger than their small regions.

In summary, Superior Leader was a manipulator and used different ethnicities in his swindle. He joined the revolution as an opportunist to satisfy his desire for control. He was against the theory of melting pots. He placated communalists with a special mission. To reach his goal, he gambled with lives.

Superior Leader's mother was a cleaning lady for Armenian and Jewish families. Thus, Superior Leader secretly disliked Armenians and Jews. It was his hypocrisy. In the collective, he was not supposed to have prejudice uniqueness, claiming the collective was more advanced. In the meantime, he was able to unite a bunch of sociopaths and failures. In the English dictionary, *sociopath* was a synonym for *psychopath* and referred to someone with a psychopathic personality whose behavior was antisocial and often criminal. A sociopath lacked a sense of intolerance, moral responsibility, or social conscience. Superior Leader gained all of his power not because he was smart but because others were stupid. Nevertheless, he also had his own challenges. To consolidate his power, he was intolerant of anyone who could question his cult of personality.

Superior Leader did everything the opposite of how the Founder had. As a result, he reversed the Founder's policies and split the collective state into many republics. Inside of the big republics, he created smaller autonomic republics. He split them further into autonomic and national districts. He abandoned the idea of a big melting pot and promoted the idea of big brothers, the Aboriginians, who were supposed to be superior to all other ethnicities. The big brothers' language was the main language. Different ethnicities, in their territories, would read and write in their own languages, but their alphabet was Cyrillic.

For some reason, he made an exception for the celestial and Armenian alphabets. He likely saved them to humiliate; those alphabets was the turned around Hebrew letters. To show his greatness, he created languages from dialects and proclaimed himself to be an expert in languages. He called himself a defender of doctrine. He did not hesitate to arrest and kill the supporters of the Founder. He performed a palace coup. The sociopaths around him kept quiet.

Superior Leader placated the communalist population by declaring that they had special qualities that allowed association with any clans and appeared to be an outsider. He associated with habitants of different ethnicities. As a child, he lived in a confused environment and was abused. Nevertheless, that did not justify his viciousness and staunchness to enslave others with doctrine and force them to perform physical labor. He revived medieval notions of fighting for vague causes. Eventually, his monuments were destroyed, as well as his doctrine. His portraits, as symbols of his vileness, were for sale in small antique shops. Many wanted to forget his name, with the exception of a few leftover believers of his doctrine.

The Founder and Superior Leader had different constructs of doctrine. Most importantly, there were distinguishing qualities in the way the leaders interpreted collective thinking. In approaching doctrine, the Founder of the collective had an attitude a pole apart from that of Superior Leader. In the beginning of his reign, the Founder appeared to be a maniac. He was a staunch defender of doctrine and psychologically split. Later, he understood his misconceptions. He saw the poverty and bloodshed his doctrine had brought to his colonies, and as a result, he became a unifier. The Founder wanted to dissolve everybody's laments in a melting pot and forget about ethnicities, religions, and languages. He wanted the whole territory to be collectivist and implement one language similar to Esperanto. He became disillusioned with doctrine and stopped its ridiculousness. Without second thoughts, by his authority, he put a stop to the old policies. However, conveniently for his opponents, he died soon afterward.

Superior Leader became a leader of the collective and defender of doctrine. He was more indoctrinated than the Founder initially was. He spit minds apart from

Besides unusual cruelty, he did not achieve much in terms of historical significance. His projects were built on human bones and left uncompleted. They were abandoned once assessed to be financially unviable. Critics contested his role in the war with the Nazis, and many things about the war were kept as state secrets for a long time.

Superior Leader was a beast and created a lot of confusion in his life. He came from a toxic environment. His childhood was traumatic. Everyone around him understood only strong fists to the face. He had a lot of fear in his life and learned how to impose fear on others. The damage he received as a child he inflicted upon the world. He was a simple man and was not trained in various human subtleties. He did not understand the beauty of diamonds and other luxuries. On first look, he fit the description of different characters. He was static; in all his roles, he did not show any dynamics. He was stationary, displaying some sadness, and made the naive feel guilty. Contrary to his idol, Adolf Hitler, who was plastic and dynamic, Superior Leader was rigid and looked monumental. He was prison material, roughly mannered and sad. He used foul language and drank heavily. He was never pictured exercising, eating, or dancing.

The biggest secret of Superior Leader was that his roots from his father's side came from North Terrestrial. According to legend, his mother too was of a mixed celestial and Turkish background. He was born in the Caucasus Mountains, where many were proud of their roots. Celestials knew much about lineages and roots. They excluded from their surroundings anyone who did not have celestial ancestors. The population there belonged to different clans. The elderly kept a strong association with celestials in their clan. Superior Leader did not have much a man who sacrificed pleasure in the service of doctrine. His life concept was alien to a woman's view of a man's courting. In his life, a wife's place was as his servant, and children were supposed to be his stooges. He denied to a woman any voice in his surroundings. His wife married him when she was a teenager. She did not have any life experience. Later on, she understood that something was wrong with her husband. She started to criticize him. She could not stand to be around him. Then she mysteriously died.

The constant suppression of his urges and sinful temptations was evident in his numbness to the suffering of others. He avoided any display of feelings. As a result, he did not develop a strong attachment to his family— not to his wife, parents, children, or friends. All his life, he manipulated everyone and protected his secrets. It was an act of deceiving himself about his urges. He was angry at everyone and justified the killing of millions by promoting himself as a protector of doctrine. As a sacrifice for doctrine, he placed himself above everyone. He became even higher than doctrine. He called himself the father of all nations, but in reality, he was the biggest villain in modern history.

Superior Leader was also an admirer of the führer. The last project of his life was the extermination of all Jews. It was a final contribution to Hitler's cause. The führer lost the war; nevertheless, Superior Leader admired him and looked to him as his role model. Hitler was not known as being a great family man, and Superior Leader was not famous as a family man himself. His wife was not happy. He refused to save his older son, who died as a prisoner of war. His daughter hated him because he jailed her lover. Ultimately, his younger son, who looked like him and followed his behavior, became an alcoholic.

him. He was aware that he had many shameful weaknesses and was afraid of being exposed.

Superior Leader had big secrets. Nevertheless, it did not matter how much he covered them; he was still a tyrant. The problem was in his denial, resentment of himself, and channeling of his urges into violence. He surrounded himself with submissive men. He resisted his various urges by abusing alcohol. He was a heavy drinker. He had an intimate male friend who, like him, was a recidivist. During his incarcerations, that man was his cellmate. He was afraid his mate would reveal his secrets and put out an order to kill his best friend. The rumor was that he got upset that his friend did not show him the expected loyalty. He projected himself as a strong person but was weak in the face of challenges. The humiliation of the man was a way to suppress his own urges. It was a way to deceive himself about his real intentions. In covering his temptations, he was secretive and vigilant. The fact that he promoted drinking as a sign of masculinity might have contributed to his instability. In his gatherings, he ordered his cronies to drink alcohol. Everyone around him was a heavy drinker. In his opinion, tolerance for alcohol was considered a sign of great strength. He always mentioned that Peter the Great had used alcohol as a screening tool of working abilities. He quickly humiliated someone who did not meet his standards. He was cruel to anyone who easily got drunk and even urinated on someone who appeared to be as drunk as a zombie. During his time as a leader, alcohol was cheap and widely available for consumption.

Superior Leader's vision promoted brutality and domination. God forbid anyone crossed him. He had little desire to define himself in the eyes of women. He did not display much attraction for females. He positioned himself as rich, but right away, he broke basic colonial law by killing many rich habitants. The colonial law stated that when someone wanted to drink water, he or she should drink it but should not splash water onto the faces of others. By following the colonial law, he could help the poor get richer and enjoy wealth by creating opportunities for them to make money. Instead of learning from the rich, he killed them and deprived the killing field of its most productive segment. He created a doctrine full of regressions. He lived by ancient tribal law, according to which outsiders were to be killed or enslaved. He declared that before individuals were captured by outsiders, they were supposed to kill themselves. He also displayed a reptilian instinct by capturing and destroying many lives. No one stopped him. If he had not been restrained by something, namely his own death, he would have taken additional lives. It was a fortunate death. The enormous monster perished. During his life, Superior Leader united many sociopaths around him. Deep down, he was a stingy recidivist. He was in jail for many criminal offenses. He ended up being a criminal kingpin and often changed criminal rules to his liking. He showed his creativity by bringing back from medieval times slavery and torture.

Superior Leader's psyche was fragmented. He demonstrated a big split in his psyche and had amazing transformations. He knew his instability and surrounded himself with stooges. Because his psyche was split, he did not have any dialogues in his life. Instead, he always had confrontations and manipulations. In his internal interactions, he felt as if he were the victim of a plot. He always tried to defend himself. He did not accept himself as equal to others. He never admitted if he did something wrong and always felt that something bad had been done to many Armenians. He did not show any sympathy to them. Nevertheless, he gave them leadership positions in his government and army. It seemed he had better feelings toward celestials, but he killed many of them too. During his rule, he was bigger than any emperor was. He also butchered more habitants than any other ruler. He was a bloody dictator whose goal was to create his own empire by any means, and he achieved his goal. Many felt his name should be revered. At least some of his ideas contributed to the creation of the multicultural approach that later became popular.

Superior Leader was consistent in putting down Armenians. He kept enclaves of Armenians in different ethnic areas. He did not want enclaves united with the main population of the National Armenian Republic. That condition led to many military collisions and the massacre of Armenians. During his reign, he did not show any sympathy to Jews either. He did not allow the teaching of Hebrew. He also organized the Jewish national district in the Far East, where Jews had not lived before. Jewish organizations begged him to give Paradise Island to the Jews, but he refused. Later on, he suspected the Jews were not happy with his decision and wanted revenge. He distrusted them and felt they were plotting against his rule. He disbanded all Jewish organizations and killed their leaders. At the end of his life, to stop Jews from claiming Paradise, he decided to forcefully send all Jews to the border with China and exterminate them.

Superior Leader was a monster. He was from gorgeous Celestin, where many great habitants were born. He broke all colonial laws. He was a beast. As a personality and a leader, he presented many controversies. His doctrine had a financial basis. He stated that he wanted his wards to be dialect. He created the collective state, which had many fraudulent autonomic republics. In the future, he called himself the father of all nations, which he himself had artificially created. His ideas came from childhood, when he had not known who his father was or to what ethnicity he belonged. The Jews received an autonomic region on the border of China instead of the proposed Paradise. Armenians gained the Armenian Republic, albeit a small version of it. A big part of territory with an Armenian population was distributed to various autonomic republics. He gave North Terrestrial the status of autonomic republic, which later led to wars between Celestin and the North Terrestrial Republic.

The collective had several leaders, but Superior Leader always was king. He was able to bring the naive from different ethnicities together. If he felt challenged, he easily exterminated the challengers. He did the same with Jews, Armenians, and communalists of all ethnicities. His behavior resulted in many controversies. He refused to give Jews the right to create the Jewish Autonomic Republic of Paradise, where there was ancient Jewish culture. Organized Jewish communities had existed there even before the destruction of the first temple in Jerusalem. Instead, he gave to Jews a piece of land on the border of China in the Far East. The place had a difficult-to-pronounce name but was harder to live in. It had vicious and dangerous insects and savage animals. Superior Leader did much to destroy Jewish culture. Nevertheless, he was outwardly helping to organize Israel. He wanted to show the West that he was not anti-Semitic. At the same time, he planned the destruction of all Jews.

Superior Leader's role in history involved many controversies. He hated many habitants. He exterminated ideas were the opposite of the ideas of the Founder, who'd wanted to create a realm that was a melting pot of various ethnicities. The Founder and his followers wanted to build the nation-state by the example of the United States. They wanted the new kingdom looked upon as a loving place for all nationalities. They claimed that all workers were brothers, and there should not be any ethnic or religious differences. The Founder and his followers even proposed a new language, Esperanto, to replace all the different languages. They called for followers to forget about their national differences.

Superior Leader had his own ideas of national policy. He implemented his ideas after the death of the worshipped founding father of the collective. He wanted a multiethnic approach. He controlled the masses with an iron fist. He bragged that he was a great leader because he assigned a piece of territory to every ethnicity. He understood that it was easier to govern a divided population. Polluted by psychological illness, he wanted only power. He divided all the territories of the collective and assigned to each ethnicity a piece of land.

## The Triumph of the Superior

Superior Leader's proposal prevailed. To placate the main population, he proposed to have the Aboriginian language become a communalist language, and it became the main language of the collective. He created many artificial languages and phony self-governments. Many little groups had their own language, even if it was just a revolutionary activities, he skillfully endorsed himself as being unjustifiably persecuted. He was recognized for his sacrifices. He was placed in prison many times. He met many angry habitants who blamed the government for their problems. Most of those habitants had their own issues.

Superior Leader was always able to get money for his dubious activities. He distributed them to several unprincipled cronies. He knew how to use innocent idealists. He was able to control the naive and did not care if they were ethnic minorities, misfits, bisexual, homosexual, or psychologically distorted. He gained recognition as an expert in relationships with different nationalities. After the communalists' revolution, he participated in the buildup of the collective as a communal state. He always repeated that collectivist thoughts were loftier and that individuals needed to obey the collective.

Superior Leader developed many ludicrous ideas. In the new regime, he was assigned to the department of relations among different nationalities. He was strongly against any melting-pot theories, which were the creation of the Founder. He gained supporters. He proposed the idea of the national collective, wherein every nation had its own autonomy, and he would assign a national setting to each of them. He knew that to control territories and habitants, he needed to divide them.

In the past, Superior Leader had gotten a lot of recognition for his activities. He was a hunter for money from venal creatures. After the death of the Founder, he became leader of the whole native land. He attracted followers with his ideas. Acting like imbeciles, followers were ready to die for their leader, and many of them indeed ended up dead. They died by the hand of their hero. His priest in the Orthodox Church. He did not need to pay for anything because his Armenian family supported him. He chilled his relationship with his Jewish family after he decided to be a priest, but his motivation did not last long. Because he did not love his parents, it was difficult for him to love God. He did not last long in school either. He was soon expelled, and his relationship with his Armenian family cooled.

After leaving seminary, Superior Leader faced hardship. He blamed Jews for dissuading his conversion to Judaism and Armenians for encouraging him to become a priest. It was clear that religion was not his cup of tea. During childhood, he had smallpox. He hated his face, which was damaged by the illness. His portraits did not show the deficiency because his big mustache covered his face. He did not complete Orthodox school. He did not become an ordained priest; instead, he was a laborer. He found work as a general laborer, but conditions at work were poor. He was injured and did not get fair compensation. He was angry at the ownership. When he heard the dogmatic ideology, he liked the idea that any imbecile with a working-class background was smart enough to be in charge of the government. He joined the revolutionaries.

Sailors continued to identify the fragments of Superior Leader's psyche. He had many fragments in his psyche. He blamed Armenians and Jews for his struggle, but he had many friends among them. Like him, they were dissatisfied and hated restrictive government policies. He used everyone and everything to reach his goals. He concentrated on opportunities and was a clever speculator. He dedicated his life to revolution. Without any basis, he wanted credit for being a great leader. During his the implied collective. Not without reason was it said that insanity could be close to geniality.

Being a tyrant, Superior Leader continued to be a mystery to many. His mood was paranoid, and the whole world felt it. His behavior was derived from his childhood. Love was important for him, but as a child, he did not have it. His obsession with control came from his childhood. As a child, he did not have control of his life. He never received any love from his father. His mother was often upset and poured out her frustration on her son. He was abused as a child. He was afraid of his mother and blamed her for his suffering. It seemed he did not forgive his mother until she died. He never had close ties with either of his parents. His mother worked as a housekeeper in two houses; one was Armenian, and another was Jewish. As a child, he was welcome in both houses, possibly because of the hospitality of the Caucasus region. One of the legends surrounding him claimed that his mother was probably in intimate relationships with the heads of both families. When she got pregnant, she informed both family heads and her husband that she would have a child. She made them all believe they were fathers. According to the same legend, she was not sure who the father was.

As a young boy accepted by Armenian and Jewish families, Superior Leader learned some Yiddish and Armenian. At one point, he wanted to become a Jew, but the head of the family talked him out of it because in the Jewish faith, the religion followed the mother, and his mother was a Christian. Because his mother was not Jewish, he would have a hard time converting to Judaism. He got closer to his Armenian family, who were religious. With the help of the head of his Armenian family, he went to an Orthodox Church school and decided to become a

Superior Leader's murky birth. He decided Superior Leader could not work with him in the coalition and could not be honored as equal to Aryans. He also had serious doubts about the cleanliness of celestial heredity.

Hitler rejected Superior Leader as an equal. Superior Leader's first name sounded Jewish, and he was not tall. Hitler changed Superior Leader's first name to Jew and called him Little Jew. Hitler's goal was to liberate the implied collective from presumed Jewish influence and, in the future, make it a real Aryan ground with lots of space for his allegedly superior race. In contrast, Superior Leader used the means of self-exaltation to manipulate others. He was a gambler. Much like Hitler, he was a maniac, but he also was antisocial and paranoid. To please the empty-headed, he did not care to execute Police that followed his orders. He did not have a conscience.

Superior Leader was a great deceiver. When the Nazis attacked the implied collective, he immediately changed his approach toward the Jews and became their friend. He proclaimed himself to be the savior of the Jews. During wartime, he had a lot of Jews around him, and many of his cronies married Jewish women. When there were official receptions, he was surrounded by Jewish women. He looked like a leader without any prejudices. In reality, he was very prejudiced, mainly against Armenians and Jews. He cunningly fooled his allies in the coalition. After the war, he changed his attitude again. He was astute. He used the mystery surrounding his birth to his advantage and was able to relate to different ethnicities. His nationalistic theory attracted many fools who were uneducated but had a lot of pretensions. He was able to create the largest tyranny in world history and became the ultimate ruler of which he believed would bring about a new world order. His nationalistic ideas remained alive in modern times.

Superior Leader was a frightening figure with a big, bowl-shaped mustache. Without any formal education and with little information about culture, he was devious enough to promote himself as an expert on culture. He declared that if simple workers could not understand products of art, then art did not have the right to exist. His slogan was that art should be the servant of primitive folks. His populist slogans gained a lot of support from primitive Aboriginians, who acted as imbeciles with feelings of entitlement.

Superior Leader's work on nationalistic subjects was published in Nazi Germany. He insisted that celestials were Aryans. Every crazy man was crazy in his own way. One crazy could like or dislike another. Hitler, struck by delusions of grandeur, applauded Superior Leader's ideas about the role of the older brother to other ethnicities. Hitler had a schizoid personality. He designed different costumes and rituals for his followers. His cohorts displayed bizarre mannerisms. Hitler created his own hierarchy of different ethnicities. He called it a new order of the universe, wherein the most important ethnicity was German. He also welcomed the prospective collective state to join the coalition of nationalist states.

Superior Leader joined Hitler in occupying lands possessed by those not Aryan. The difference between Superior Leader and Hitler was that Hitler really believed in his ravings about the special mission of Aryans. In his delusions, Hitler wanted all Germans to be great. He believed Aryans were leaders of the different cliques and were at the top of social hierarchy. He had doubts that celestials were real Aryans. Somehow, he found out about languages from tales. It was his biggest venture, and it helped him become a king of the region. In all his national policies, he was shrewd. He declared that Aboriginians were the big brothers of all other ethnicities. Under his rule, everyone was supposed to have his or her ethnicity listed on identification documents. He implemented quotas for different ethnicities admitted to educational institutions, job allocation, and media exposure.

Under Superior Leader, the motto of the implied collective was that a housekeeper could rule the government. He, in his stewardship, made many political moves to promote himself as faithful to communalist culture. He promoted himself as an expert linguist as well, even though he hadn't completed high school. His ambitions regarding languages were based on the fact that he'd worked for a year in a printing house. His educational background included a few years in a religious school. Based on his experience working in a printing shop, he created ordinances. On his order, officials substituted Cyrillic, the communalist alphabet, for many other ethnic alphabets. He made Azerbaijan, which had a Turkish population, write Turkish words in Cyrillic. Moldova's Latin population was to write Romanian words in Cyrillic, and so on. He implied that ethnicities that were part of the prospective collective became different from their original ethnicities. He promised that during his rule, the Aboriginians would become celestials. He could manipulate anything. For reasons known only to him, he allowed the Celestin and Armenian alphabets to keep their original letters. Otherwise, he skillfully used the communalist nationalistic feelings as hooks and climbed to the top of the hierarchy. He excessively wrote on nationalistic issues. He wrote about the special mission of the prospective collective, defiant, perhaps because of the adverse fragments in his personality. He somehow justified the behavior of his so-called father, who'd left his mother. He believed that in a similar situation, he would have acted the same way. His wife reportedly committed suicide, but many sources doubted that. It was possible Superior Leader accidentally killed the unruly woman, who was not accepting of his controlling power. It was another secret that he took to his grave. He had many secrets surrounding him. He was a powerful kingpin or even a king. He was able to do whatever he pleased. One of his intentions was to keep the secrets of his life sealed.

As a king, Superior Leader encouraged nationalistic pride in living in the biggest territory of the world. Because of their huge territory and strong military, Aboriginians were brainwashed to believe they lived in the greatest living situation as well. Superior Leader called himself the father of all constituencies because his rule created many ethnic regions. They took the form of national republics, national autonomic republics, and national districts. It was an ambitious project, but in a time of globalization, it looked ridiculous. Superior Leader created a system with the Aboriginians placed on the top. When all ethnicities involved were not equal, all multicultural projects became manipulative. Unfortunately, the pseudocollective did not have democratic leaders. Superior Leader was a scoundrel.

Sailors wanted to understand how Superior Leader's psyche had become tainted with insanity. Many ethnicities in the would-be collective were dirtied by psychological toxins of pomposity, and Superior Leader attached to them some pieces of territory. Many of those ethnicities did not even have alphabets. They spoke different dialects. Superior Leader created some organization that formed or their contributions to celestial life. They seemingly did not accept that terrestrials lived in Celestin.

Marriage to terrestrials was a shameful thing. The two cultures, including their music and dance, were close, but celestials perceived terrestrials as savages and low class. Many terrestrials, to avoid having a stigma attached to them, changed their last names to sound more like celestial names. Superior Leader knew the truth that his father, who had a celestial last name, was a terrestrial. The situation was confusing. He did not accept and always covered up the truth. For celestials, the terrestrials' ethnicity was shameful. He kept the secret that he was part terrestrial. It seemed that after many years of uncertainty, he somehow accepted that he was the son of the man whose name was on his birth certificate. He never mentioned to anyone that he had terrestrial roots. When someone found out about his secret, he purged that person. Superior Leader never revealed his secret to anyone.

The leaders were generous if they wanted to be. They gave away as presents big regions, such as North Terrestrial and Paradise Island. As a ruler of the prospective collective, Superior Leader gave away North Terrestrial, where his assumed father's family was—a special privilege. The gesture seemed like an acceptance of his father. On his decree, North Terrestrial gained the status of a republic. He even incorporated part of the neighboring territory into North Terrestrial and deported to Siberia the indigenous population of those territories. He presented himself to the world as a real celestial. He did everything he could to prevent others from discovering his roots, to the point that he killed presumed whisperers. His secret made him even more miserable and untrusting.

As a child, Superior Leader was mistrustful and

Legend stated that the mysteries started from Superior Leader's birth. He came from violence, which was persistent during his childhood. He had the name of his presumed father on his birth certificate. The controversy started with the question of who his real father was. The man on his birth certificate never felt he was the boy's father. He never showed any attachment to his presumed son. In childhood, Superior Leader did not look like his father, but in his later life, he gained some resemblance to his papa. He was uncertain until the end of his life who his real father was. He was mad that his mother put him through that mystery and refused to clarify it. He deliberately did not attend his mother's funeral. He learned from early childhood that the world was tricky, and he could not trust anyone. He could not figure out where the roots of his mistrust came from. However, he did not know the situation with his mother was not questionable altogether. Because of more than few sexual partners, she honestly did not know who his father was.

When Superior Leader was a child, his drunken father called him insulting names, such as mongrel and crossbreed. In front of his son, he accused his wife of being a whore and having their son from someone else. He was often upset, and in alcoholic rages, he beat his wife and called her a slut. He also beat the young child in his custody, whom he called a bastard. Superior Leader was a miserable child. His father later abandoned his wife and child and lived in the capital of Celestin. His daddy got fully involved with alcohol. He also had a secret that confused his son. Some researchers believed he never was the celestial he claimed. He was a terrestrial man with a celestial last name. The celestials never accepted terrestrials as equal. They did not acknowledge the terrestrials' talents was a manipulator and cheater. He did not believe in choice. He did not play card games because he played games with lives. His bets were dirty with germs and affected millions. Most of the time, he was bluffing. Until he died, he got away with his con. He created a biosphere of informers, and all localities were like prisons. He talked about the creation of a new mystical order of celestials. He was empowered and felt entitled to play dirty. When he won, he made a big deal out of it. Again, compared to the losses, the wins were not big gains.

His biggest win was in the Second World War. During the war, he played fair with his allies and got the biggest gain of his life. All of his existence was at stake, and he was forced to play by the rules of civilized society. He showed consideration for the feelings of allies. During that time, he did not swindle. As a result, he was remembered as one of the few leaders able to resist the Nazis. In all other games, he played with loaded dice. He was against everyone, created his own rules, and did not care about anything. In his deeds, he did not care about others. He was remembered as one of the bloodiest tyrants in world history. If he had not existed, the world would have been a better place.

Superior Leader was from a gorgeous, mountainous community called Celestin; it was a great place with great habitants. Unfortunately, even that place had exceptions. Superior Leader was known as a game man, but he had one exception: he played dirty games in different places. Because of his games, he changed the psyche of the whole world. He was a good chess player but was best known for the intricate deceits he played on the naive. He remained a mystery, and there were many who either worshipped or hated him.

primitive. The Jews would have experienced a different fate if Paradise had been given to them. They would have lived happily in Paradise. The land would have flourished because they were business-oriented. They built fountains and irrigation and distributed spring water. Catherine the Great wanted to grant Paradise to the Jews and increase the flow of money to the treasury. The grant did not get through because many were biased. In the same way, Superior Leader grabbed territory and held on to it as part of the nationalistic ideology. As a result, Paradise was a jewel used by the infected. It did not matter who was right or wrong. It ended up in the hands of monstrous habitants and had an uncertain future.

Superior Leader's primitive impulses were working. A nationalistic plan to expand by any means necessary was the most primitive, animalistic impulse. It was a vicious rule that put cruel suffering upon the uninfected. The world needed to remember their deeds and avoid disease-ridden minds that killed their neighbors, took their possessions, and destroyed many lives. Tensions would exist for many years ahead, and a curse would impose influence on many, even some who looked healthy. Paradise was an example of a place of confrontation. The place was sick and deranged. It would never stop poisoning innocent minds.

## The Bets and Games

On impulse, players made bets. They won or lost. With different attitudes, the same game could involve honest negotiation or heartless manipulation. Superior Leader geographer, activist, philologist, zoologist, evolutionary theorist, philosopher, writer, and prominent anarchist. As an economist, Kropotkin advocated a communist society free from central government and based on voluntary associations between workers. He wrote many books, pamphlets, and articles. The most prominent were *The Conquest of Bread* and *Fields, Factories, and Workshops*, and his principal scientific offering was *Mutual Aid: A Factor of Evolution*. He also contributed an article on anarchism to *Encyclopedia Britannica*'s eleventh edition. Scholars and intellectuals died in jail, and uneducated tyrants occupied positions of influence.

Sailors were able, through many examples, to show the inhumane origin of Superior Leader's ruling. Superior Leader was a manipulator and sadist. He tricked everyone into submission. He boasted about himself by patronizing others who had naive dreams of being important and doing something significant with their lives. Mainly, he used a nationalistic scam. Superior Leader presented himself as a skillful shepherd who could lead the herd. Compared to the losses, the benefits of his game were marginal. When he lost, he blamed others and used intimidation to inflict fear.

As many times as needed, Superior Leader used Jewish dignitaries. In return, he did not show any kindness and did not give Paradise Island to the Jews. He did not believe in deviation from or revision of doctrine, which threatened the rigidity of primitive doctrine. He did not give anyone else a chance to flourish.

Such persecution was the goal of a sucker. Superior Leader was a primitive manipulator—primitive, not simple. Primitivism was an enemy of simplicity. In negotiations, people made simple decisions. To give a friend something was simple and wise. Paradise was not offered to the Jews who had lived there for thousands of years. It was

It was painful to abandon the old traditions. The Western part of the psyche was destroyed. The trend eventually ended up with fidelity to one clan leader. The Eastern roots grew, and the nation became a clan. It was a cult. The leader became a symbol of communalist nationalism. Superior Leader was a kingpin. Throughout history, he was known as a tyrant. Using nationalistic doctrine, he led his land to complete isolation. His kingdom suffered from many humiliations but had a strong military. He held the whole world hostage with threats of military invasions.

The paranoia and manic tendencies of their leader brought repression and atrocities to the population. The supposed collective represented a festering wound protected by a nuclear shield. It was temporarily constructed, because it existed in a tight form only while the leader was alive. The führer of the implied collective died, and the construct bulged. The tight structure was a temporary construct. When loosened, it turned into chaos.

## Prince Kropotkin versus Superior Leader

History would have been different if Aborigin had had another leader who was an intellectual. The antipode to suppositional collective life was suggested by a great scholar named Prince Kropotkin, who proposed a system that could make all the population of the estimated collective equal and free individuals. According to *Encyclopedia Britannica*, Prince Pyotr Alexeyevich Kropotkin lived from December 9, 1842, to February 8, 1921. Prince Kropotkin was a confrontations. Eventually, the predators swallowed purity. The infected Aboriginians repeated the lies about their greatness. The nationalist goal of the presumed collective was expansion into different areas and by any means. The pseudocollective committed many murders, violated neighboring territories, and brought terror into the lives of many nationals. They occupied many countries, brought down their governments, incarcerated and destroyed citizens, and still proclaimed themselves as a great provision. Naturally, every location wanted to feel great. They were living in the world's biggest con. The pseudocollective that terrorized its neighbors, creating horror and putting fear into habitants' lives, could not call itself great. It was hard to imagine how a confrontational and manipulative state could be great. That behavior was not a stipulation for a great future.

The implied collective was abnormal and killed their own soldiers with stupidity. In the beginning of World War II, the soldiers of the Red Army did not have any warm outfits, clear commands, ammunition, or great desire to die for doctrine. To stay alive, many soldiers defected to the Nazis. The putative collective was a manipulative construct. When the economic infusion from the West started, it brought food, clothes, and weapons. Ideologists, instead of doctrine, spoke about fidelity to their leader. They even allowed the clergy to get involved on one condition: they had to praise the leader. They felt stronger and sent secret police to be barrage detachments who shot on soldiers who left their positions on the front line.

In prior history, Aboriginians had sought to be close to the West and shown disrespect for Eastern tradition. Originally, the psyche in the would-be collective was built on fidelity to doctrine that had some Western traits. During the war, the psyche changed to Eastern fidelity to the authorities.

might not succeed. The outcome of a negotiation was a contract. If it was not a fair contract, the parties would not follow through on it. Negotiators had to be sure there were enough benefits for both sides to motivate the execution of a contract. The side that started negotiations needed to know what benefit they were looking for.

One of the most important aspects of negotiation was the atmosphere. When negotiators were nervous about other things outside of negotiation, they probably were not good negotiators. Usually, when both sides were motivated to get issues resolved, negotiation was successful. It was important for both sides to know what the other side wanted; otherwise, the lack of understanding foreshadowed trouble.

The pseudocollective, like a savage animal, wanted hegemony and new territory to expand. It was a terminally ill construct that affected many minds. The animalistic fragment wanted to confront and manipulate. The sickness was a plague that infected fragments. The people needed diagnosis and procedures to deal with sick fragments. The humans' fragments wanted to negotiate and make their lives more comfortable. They needed to distinguish which fragments could be leaders in their psyches and which ones were followers. They needed to take care of the sick fragments. It was possible that animalistic fragments could take over, and they did not value the feelings of others. In that situation, people did not have compassion or softness. They displayed the heartless and unreasonable anger of primitive creatures. The animalistic part was on display during the pseudocollective's heyday. The killing of many uninfected habitants was an everyday fact.

The pseudocollective was a killing machine. Innocence was replaced by a life full of animalistic manipulations and

Negotiation was mainly a human quality, but it required the knowledge of negotiation techniques. Otherwise, confrontation and manipulation took place. To antagonize and alienate others, one did not require any human qualities. Humans acted as animals. Foxes and wolves were the best manipulators, and tigers were the best confronters. There were many foxes, wolves, and tigers among men.

## Negotiation as a Part of a Sailor's Psychology

*A*boriginians were bad negotiators. Only benefits could motivate others to have successful negotiations. The negotiator also could have benefits beyond what was being negotiated. The movie *Schindler's List* showed that Jews negotiated more than just money and labor; it was their lives that mattered. The benefits of those negotiations were money for the Nazis and, for the Jews, their own lives. It worked. The Nazis got their money. The Jews stayed alive. It was important in negotiation for the negotiators to clearly understand what reasonable benefits they could negotiate. One had to find out what motivated the other side. It was another level of being.

The pseudocollective did not know what it wanted. Many times, manipulation was the animalistic desire to make a statement. It was a display of empty phraseology. It was the start of bigger manipulation. One of the ways to manipulate was by confronting.

If a negotiator did not understand his counterpart, he did not know what he really could achieve, and the negotiations pride of being a nation of culture. Aboriginians forgot their Khazarian and Golden Horde roots. Even Aboriginians called themselves communalists. They should have remembered their past. They forgot it. Instead, they were obsessed. They wanted to be remembered as the rulers of Malantia. The Khazarians practiced Judaism, and they were the rulers of Malantia and collected taxes. Aboriginians were the tax collectors for Khazarians and the Golden Horde.

Dreams always were pleasant, but even they vanished. If the collectivists would have been nice to Jews, everything would have been different. They should have let Jews be citizens of the Republic of Paradise. In return, the Jews would have renovated Paradisan irrigation, wells, and spring water and gotten along with Paradisan Tatars. Together they could have rebuilt vocational resorts and agriculture. Most importantly, they could have brought innovation to Paradise. They would have made life pleasant, as in Israel, but without the danger of radical Islamist attacks. When dreams came through, they were not dreams anymore but more like predictions. The dream for peaceful coexistence would probably take a long time to come through.

The pseudocollective was primitive, inflexible, and rigid. Leaders resented negotiations and were proud of their manipulations and cheating. However, many important things in life, including the art of negotiation, required sophistication and knowledge. Otherwise, negotiations would not succeed. Mutual benefits were not easy to find. Compromise required flexibility and the understanding that without benefits, there was no reason to negotiate. To find appropriate benefits for negotiation, at least one side had to put themselves in the position of their counterpart.

in Paradise even before the Byzantine Empire. They had been living in Paradise since ancient times. They were largely divided into two communities: Krymchaks, who followed rabbinical Judaism, and the Karaims. In Paradise's history, many Jews from neighboring countries had lived there. Paradise was heaven for Jews, and they exercised great influence on it. When the Khazars took over Paradise, many of them embraced Judaism, which helped the Paradise Jews to become the de facto rulers of the ground and continued until 1016, when the Khazars were dispossessed. After Catherine the Great conquered the region from the Ottoman Empire in 1783, she opened it up to Jewish settlements, hoping the Jews would serve as a bulwark against the Turks.

Although Jews were barred from living in the major cities, the peninsula promised open spaces and freedom to adventurous Jews. They sought new frontiers and were willing to take up spades. Jews in Paradise always had a promising future. Paradise was a fertile place where many were happy and gave happiness to others. Jews built irrigation and constructed vocational resorts that were the jewels of the world. When the collectivists took over Paradise, the land started declining and eventually became a sorry sight. They faced landslides, interruptions in electricity, and problems with irrigation and water supplies.

Jews were slaves of the pseudocollective. They knew how to be productive in duress. As in Egypt, the Jews helped the pseudocollective to have a multiethnic and international appearance. It was a poor move on their part. They were willing to forget their own history and religion and become part of the pseudocollective. Actually, they gave the pseudocollective everything, including the not shot but were instead killed by crowbars and axes. The Malantians got away with many murders. Because the Malantians would not ask for forgiveness for their crimes, not even symbolically, they were marked as manslayers. Sailors believed they had to straighten out their actions and, even symbolically, punish murderers who probably had died long ago. Otherwise, the confusion would continue. They would always blame someone else. They would not receive respect from the West.

## Paradise Island

Malantians faced facts that history stole from them. They blamed a minority who had done nothing wrong. The discrimination against Jews had to cease. Because some imbeciles could not stop, the poison spread. Bullies did not have an excuse to kill the innocent. It did not make any sense and did not help anyone. Murder required condemnation. People needed to look upon themselves to find and punish the guilty. There was no doubt Malantia should also regain credit. They did well in their history. They insisted they were the main builders of Malantia. Aboriginians bullied Malantians into submission and insisted they were more important. Malantians, in turn, mocked the Jews. Dissension between Malantians and Aboriginians went on for a long time, and the confrontation seemed as if it might never end.

There were few places where Jews were happy. Jews in Paradise were happy. The great historical role of Tatars in Paradise was undeniable, but Jews had lived in Malantia were comprised of a number of different groups, including Ashkenazi Jews, Mountain Jews, Bukharans, Krymchak Jews, Paradise Karaites, and Celestin Jews. Malantians were jealous of the Jews, who had their own strong cultural identity. The Jews remembered all of their saints (zaddikim), who were important to their history and were their nobility. They had enough history of their own and did not want anything from others. Because of their independence, they experienced hatred from other groups. Presently, not many Jews lived in Malantia. Many of them had been killed, and the survivors had migrated to Israel and the West.

Ironically, instead of accusing Aboriginians, Malantians accused the Jews of many fictitious crimes. They blamed Jews for interfering with their history. It was craziness. Malantians hated the collective state but were not able to express their resentment directly. Nothing made sense. During quarrels and instability, they killed Jewish women, children, and the elderly as well as men. They were merciless. At the end of World War II, the Germans were blamed for all the atrocities, but they were not the only killers; many Malantian Nazis killed their neighbors as well. Often, Germans were not around, but Malantians were. It was a mishmash. The Jews were an easy target to stir up anger. Malantians were terrible tormentors and had to admit their role in the atrocities.

The guilty ones needed punishment. The henchmen should have paid for their atrocities. As a result of the atrocities, many were killed, including Rivka; her daughter, Lizochka, who was a baby; and old Hershel. The Malantian bullies did not use bullets because the Aryans did not give them guns. They killed with crowbars and pickaxes.

Professor Kryvoruchko stated that his relatives were

was still an intermediate nation. Many European countries hated the collective and saw them as ideological tax collectors. Many countries wanted to get away from indoctrinators' nagging. Some did so. The subordinates of the pseudocollective in the West hated their lord. Contrary to the West, in relations with Eastern countries, the collective was more successful. Asia was more willing to relate to them. The pseudocollective was not happy to be together with the East. It insisted on its bond with the West. Undeniably, the collective wanted to be closer to Europe. They complained that Europe had rejected them.

## Denial of Collective Association

Professor Kryvorucko stated that unfortunately, Malantians did not treat Jews well. Jews were close to Malantia, which wanted to embrace Judaism. In the world, everything changed. No one accepted Jews. Many Europeans became hostile to Jews, who did not feel appreciated and were not comfortable. That was the main reason they helped the pseudocollective to achieve an international self-concept. Jews provided assistance to communalists in capturing the collective identity. They wanted to have the benefits of being accepted, but the collective did not give them any credit. When people used to say "the collective," they assumed that meant Aboriginians.

Many Malantians hated the Jews. During the Nazis' heyday, neighbors killed many Jews. Before World War II, Jews made up a little less than one-third of Malantia's urban population. They were the largest national minority. Jews concept. In reality, communalists did not value their ethnicity. They had duality in their self-concept. They did not accept that Aborigin was an intermediate nation. In the past, the elite had called themselves Aboriginians and been cautious not to offend anyone. Communalists looted their brothers. No doubt they looked up to the Western ethnicities. During the Golden Horde's halcyon era, nobilities had two names: Slavic, the Western influence, and Tatars, the Eastern influence. In later times, Aboriginians separated themselves from Tatars. Nevertheless, Tatars' books described Aboriginians as excellent tax collectors. They were brutal to malicious tax evaders.

According to the Tatars' sources, the capital of Aborigin became important because it facilitated the collection of taxes for the Golden Horde. Aboriginians were brave, enthusiastic, and militarily strong. They brutally collected taxes by beating, burning houses, and killing. They were brave soldiers and proud to relate to the Golden Horde. Presently, they wanted to distance themselves from the Tatars and presented themselves as the rulers of Malantia. Malantians resisted them. After the end of the great Mongol horde, Aboriginians never had a strong Western identity. The world did not understand Aborigin. Napoleon overestimated their Western influences and lost his war. The Nazis did not count on their strong Christian roots. During the Patriotic War, Superior Leader revived Christianity, and the Nazis lost. Nevertheless, Aborigin was a mystery.

The pseudocollective structure always had totalitarian power. They re-created the Golden Horde. It could not function as a democratic state. If the Golden Horde had come back, people would have seen that the collective had an important position. For the time being, the collective were related to the Mongols. They claimed that actually, Aboriginians had stolen their identity from Malantians and were part of the Golden Horde. In their opinion, Aboriginians mixed too much with the Golden Horde. In their view, only Malantians were real. Malantians said the Aboriginians' epos was plagiarized from Malantia.

In contrast, Aborigin always denied the influence of Mongols and emphasized closeness to Malantians. That interpretation of history was confusing because the facts were flawless and sometimes stated otherwise. Aboriginians denied Eastern influences. Their alphabet was a mixture of Greek and Latin. Their genetic code revealed a mixture of different genes. The presence of the Slavic inheritance was clearly dominant. Aboriginians denied that Aborigin was an intermediate state between the Mongols and Western society.

Aborigin was located between the West and the East. The collective promised to give communalists a strong Western identity, but it moved back to the East. Undeniably, the collective made an attempt to move forward to the West, but in reality, it ended up dipping on the Eastern side. In the collective, the Golden Horde came back and brought back the old ways. Damnation blinded the leaders. In the name of their new Prolet-Aryan identity, the collective viciously killed the uninfected with a virus of grandiosity. They took women by force. They replaced the rules of the Bible with rules of demagogy. They incorporated an influence from the East based on modesty, a Spartan lifestyle, and sacrifice. The primitive concepts of the pseudocollective's ideology were important to plebes. The opportunity to rob and kill as retaliation for presumed suffering was important to them. Second, becoming leaders of the world was also an attractive typically built on experiences, but the pseudocollective did not have a stable base. It was in a state of madness.

In the past, Malantia had been a loose federation of several tribes who were inspired by the collective. Malantians had an ordinary structure that resembled the existing Eastern states of Khazars and Tatars. The rulers were not Aboriginian. Their origin was not significant. Most important were the population they ruled and the structure of their states. Modern citizens of Aborigin claimed the Malantians as their cultural ancestors because they needed a Western orientation of cultural heritage. They wanted a connection to the West. The region, in the middle of the eleventh century, stretched from the Baltic Sea in the north to the Black Sea. Malantia was under Khazar Khanate and paid tribute and taxes to the Khazars. It wanted to have the Khazars' religion, Judaism, but the kingdom rejected their request. They suspected Malantia of a lack of sincerity. They felt the Malantians had made up their dedication to Judaism to avoid paying taxes.

Aborigin became autonomic from the Khazars and got close to the Byzantines. When Aborigin had commercial ties with Byzantium, it became semi-independent. It moved away from Malantia. Unfortunately, because of harsh economic factors, ties with the Byzantines did not stay strong. It weakened the native land, resulting in their economic collapse. The state of Aboriginians became part of the Golden Horde, which ruled the Aboriginians for two hundred years. An intermediate state, Aborigin did everything to accommodate the Golden Horde. It was split between West and East. According to Malantian sources, Aboriginians were less associated with Malantia and more so part of the Mongol horde. Nationalistic Malantians insisted that the ethnic Aboriginians, genetically speaking, possible recovery. Creativity was the last fragment to give up. Despite the fact that the killing field was a garbage pit, the ballet was remarkable. The movements were precise and militarized. The stage resembled the battlefield. The ballet showed the fictitious lives of historical characters who were warriors. There were many marches, fights with swords, and confrontational dances between two male groups. Onstage, strong males protected the petite ballerinas who jumped around. Cultural activities, including ballet, were an instrument used to mislead outsiders. Ballet was a group activity with only a few individual performances. Huge symphonic orchestras and dance companies promoted the supposed collective lifestyle.

The fraudulent collective covered its real nature. It was a monster that took pride in capturing and torturing. The stench abounded. The sycophants showed loyalty to leaders and competed for the approval of authorities. The sycophants were not secure and, in a moment, could fall into disgrace. The whole collective was all about slavery and lawlessness. The hamlet, made vicious by ruination, did not value democratic ways and looked for change. As in the Mongolians' and Huns' eruptions, the population was a herd in need of a shepherd. Habitants displayed fidelity to authorities but condescension toward neighbors. The big village was a mixture of different ethnicities and did not have national traditions. Only the strong military was a source of national pride. The longest national idea involved enlargement of the territory through the capture of neighboring lands. The population displayed a lot of cringing, obsequiousness, groveling, sycophancy, and adulation. The curse spread quickly. The fraudulent collective went in the direction of nationalistic hysteria. The indoctrinated favorites changed rapidly. A psyche was got their nutrition from the black market. It was a danger to cook something better than what others had. As a result of that fear, many habitants were afraid to cook in the communal kitchen. They prepared meals in their rooms. The hellhound's forces could arrive at the doorstep at any minute. There was no place to hide. When the police came to arrest one of the neighbors, everyone, including informers, would wait to be the next to be taken away. The women would cry and pack their little purses with warm socks and hard crackers. In jail, some arrested neighbors tried to clarify among each other who'd informed on whom and then disclosed that they suspected each other of being stool pigeons only to find that the informer was someone else. Their fears paralyzed all common sense. The communal setting was a den of snakes. Constant fear covered the region.

## Nowhere to Go from the Source of Primitivism and Aboriginian Existence

*I*n the meantime, individuals uninfected by the virus of splitting continued to do ordinary things. They drank tea, played poker, and walked their dogs. Under the sword of Damocles, in Aborigin, few wrote music, poetry, or ballet. The moves and jumps in the ballet were perfect, but it seemed as if all the dances were performed at gunpoint. The psyche kept some fragments of creativity alive in the hope that the system would change. When the body stopped functioning, the last organ to go would be the heart. The body, till the last breath, left the chance of informants, who were everywhere. Anyone could be an informer. It was hard to believe how many stooges were in every communal setting. The defrauding ideologists called them patriots and conscious citizens. In the killing field, no one could refuse an offer from the police to be an informer. Neighbors silently guessed who was one and suspected everyone, even their own children. Among the habitants working on the black market were many informers. The authorities kept the black market going to prevent unrest and make habitants feel guilty for using it. Their goal of using finks was to check for private political statements against the ruling party and its leaders. Even informers were not safe to work without paying them for protection. A businessman on the black market would employ a roof, a police official who usually received part of the profits from all his transactions. In return, the official would provide the businessman with protection. If one active in business did not have protection, he was right away caught with something illegal and imprisoned.

Professor Kryvoruchko established that because habitants did not know their rights and everything was forbidden, everyone was afraid of something. Neighbors were reasonably afraid they were surrounded by informers. The informers had a duty to inform. It was easier for snitches when more people lived together. The infected created many communal apartments. In Greben, the capital of Malantia, there were too many of them. They had a chokingly human scent inside and many hateful habitants. The habitants were terrified of not reporting right away because somebody else might report before them. When habitants were arrested, they usually never came back. They could be arrested on suspicion that they were spending more money than they were earning and

They denied genetic selection. They did not accept the realities of phenotype selection, the environment's selection of traits, genotypes that came from mutation, or the alteration of DNA sequences. The infected ideologists fed on the population's naïveté and indoctrinated them with the concept of equality as a substitution for truth. Falsifying that concept, doctrine insisted that habitants were born equal and therefore should live together in a communal setting. The communal setting was handy for snitches because it made their job easier. The pseudocollective was a clearly primitive substitute for anything sophisticated and created the possibility of brainwashing.

Professor Kryvoruchko underlined that in reality, equality ended after habitants were born. It was correct that all habitants were born in the same way and supposed to have an equal number of opportunities to succeed. Habitants had differences in appearance, health, and, most importantly, IQ, as well as other dissimilar ethnic characteristics. Ideologists were justifying equality. They covered up the fact that misfits ruled their vicinity with ignorance. Dogmatic germs created the biggest manipulators in human history. The blunt, misfits, and shortsighted were the rulers of the land. In the meantime, Malantians did not want to be similar or equal; they wanted to be significant. They fought for their distinction and self-determination. They insisted that habitants were not born equal and that equality was a lie.

Professor Kryvoruchko learned that being a fink did not prevent someone from receiving the attention of the special economic police, the OBHSS. Being a fink helped in some instances but not always. Snitches, like others, had to pay protection money. Nevertheless, the position was desirous for many, and the police continued to enroll and con artists. They closed the religious institutions and declared that religion was an opiate for the masses. They put priests, mullahs, and rabbis in slave camps. They talked a lot about ethnic equality and believed the collective mind was perfect. Contrarily, sane habitants said that every life counted.

Aaron got the basis of the brainwashing: habitants were born equal, but some, by stealing and fooling, got rich. Agitators yelled that opulent habitants were enemies of the collective. The middle and upper classes were labeled as usurpers and exploiters. Despite his theory of equality, Superior Leader clearly placated the Aboriginians as the smartest. He imposed projects to immortalize his place in history and exalt himself. Supreme Leader wanted to cleanse the world of habitants who disagreed with him.

Radicals magnified dogma. Millions died from hunger and inhumane conditions while working on the projects. The constructions did not have any standards or correct calculations. They were inspired by propaganda and did not function correctly. The radicals used the citizens as slave labor. The lives of millions were wasted for nothing. Crocked ideologists used fabrications to pull in more slaves. The secret police became the biggest power, and snitches supporting the police were everywhere. To acquit their atrocities, they declared that the deaths were necessary to glorify crocked dogma. Primitivism ruled everywhere. It was no coincidence that the infected denied genetics. Dishonest dogma did not recognize genetics as a science because it was an obstacle to the notion of equality. Because genetics denied the nonsense that habitants were born equal, radicals stipulated that genetics was the creation of a bunch of charlatans. The infected ideologists slandered genetics. Their ideas were wrong and primitive.

Aaron mentioned that the idea of becoming rich and being somehow unique was certainly more pleasurable than the idea of being equally poor. In Western countries, the majority of habitants were interested in making money. They had the opportunity to make money and get wealthy. Though the society promoted equality and an opportunity to become rich, it didn't work for everyone. Unfortunately, not everyone achieved that goal. It was not easy. It required resilience and persistence. Many infected habitants did not want to take a risk and put in extra effort.

## THE TABOO OF WEALTH

Aaron realized that in Aborigin, business orientation was anathema. The persecution of the rich was like the persecution of Jews by the Nazis. In the killing field, being rich was taboo. Leaders denied that a businessman had a talent in the same way an artist or technician did. Red and black bugs caused the same hatred and harm, pointing to a mad ideology that could only have come from vulgar and shortsighted losers. It was a shameless manipulation of the word *equality*. For example, the statement that any of the land's janitors could be the head of a corporation was propaganda that had nothing to do with equality.

In the new hierarchy, Aboriginians became the older brothers in society. They built more labor camps and packed them with habitants who doubted the general doctrine. The infected gained new ambitions and enacted more persecutions on the population. Corrupt leaders of the region, unclean with toxins of insanity, were swindlers mixture of radical attitude and utopian philosophy. The philosophical part sounded complex, and ideologists did not use it because it required knowledge. They used a radical attitude. The explanation was simple: just like the criminal code, it was based on fidelity and punishment for betrayal. Failure was not accepted. It maintained that habitants should be suspicious of class foes. Every neighbor should be fearful of betrayal by other neighbors, who could be class enemies. Thus, the habitants were in constant trepidation. Many doubted they would even come home the next evening. They lived in constant dismay.

That trend continued for many years. The secret police terrorized the whole populace. They aimed fear at the whole world. Ideologists were quick to create fictitious adversaries who wanted to destroy their precious doctrine. It seemed the whole world was against them. All their cases were fabrications created to instill fear in the population. They were busy purging because accomplices of foreign hate against them were everywhere.

Aaron stated that every ethnicity was special, and habitants wanted to be proud of their ethnicities. The fraudulent dogma misleadingly said that all ethnicities were equal, but in reality, no one embraced equality. It might have been true that habitants were equal in front of God, but radical dogma denied religion. Some ethnicities did not want to be equal. There was nothing glorious about being poor among the poor. When the Malantians saw on TV or in newspapers a famous Malantian, they were proud. They liked that there were habitants of their ethnicity who'd made it big. They wanted to be individuals; they did not want to be a colorless part of a land soiled by hate. In Malantia, the crazy policy and behaviors of commissars generated a great famine.

traveler's family back in Aborigin to use as hostages. The government decree stipulated that in case of a defection, all the remaining members of the traitor's family would be arrested and sent to Kolyma.

## GREBEN, MALANTIA

*M*alantia was part of Aborigin and later became independent. As part of the collective, because of the dogmatic epidemic, it was poor. Malantians were considered the same ethnicity as Aboriginians but seen as much less advanced. Malantians hated to be on the periphery, which was the way the Aboriginians saw them. They did not want to be part of Aborigin. Pseudodoctrine did not allow any deviation and prevented Malantians from having an original ethnicity. As a result, many showed their displeasure with the politics of the collective.

Aaron realized that the essence of the stupid doctrine was pure terror. The ideologists used little philosophy and a lot of propaganda. The infected used a drastic doctrine that did not tolerate any different ideology. Otherwise, it would not have been an infection. It mainly used a straightforward, radical attitude. It was limited in deviation and had implacability. Everything was simple and had abrupt findings. The main goal was producing fear. An ideology of suspiciousness flourished in Aborigin. The doctrine and corresponding ideology were completely senseless. The radical ideology was just a fantasy of college dropouts and imbecilic minds.

Some parts of the pseudodoctrine displayed a

Aaron became friendly with a magician who was also a member of the group, and they played cards and shared different tricks. There was a lot of patriotic phraseology from other performers. Aaron was in the war. There was a high probability he could be shot by a brainless bullet. Many soldiers fought with old rifles and ripped clothes, and as they lay on the ground dying, other soldiers would step on them. Aaron understood that there was not much meaning in dying by following stupid commands. He did not allow himself to be cannon fodder. He saved his life. After the war, if he'd wanted to, he could have continued dancing in the Azerbaijani dance ensemble, but Aaron left dancing and returned to business.

Aaron was born into a family of businesspeople and had business orientation. In the killing field, all business was moved underground, and businesspeople were considered thieves. Aaron wanted to have an honest business, so he went to the West. He did not want to have anything to do with criminals. He left the collective to become a multimillionaire. He did it in an honest way. He eventually retired from his business and lived in Miami, Florida.

The business-oriented habitants were locked in Aborigin like in a jail and were considered thieves. When the borders were closed, people were not able to do business in an honest way. They were not able to leave. The talented stayed in the suffocating atmosphere of primitive indoctrination. Life in the killing field was deadly. The borders were closed. There were strict regulations on anyone going in or out of the land. Superior Leader announced that anyone attempting to flee abroad would be executed. Habitants even needed permission to travel from one city to another. When a celestial visited Europe or the United States, officials invariably kept members of the youngsters were on the streets, joining rogue gangs. Other signs of degradation were everywhere. People bought food on the black market, and instead of in a kitchen, they kept their food in their sleeping quarters. Neighbors were scared and did not trust each other. Women were angry and drank. Their children were unruly. Many single mothers appeared to be sexually deprived. They brought sexual partners home. They sent their children to the streets while they had a pleasurable time. On the streets, the youngsters quickly got smart and rough. The boys would meet with horny females and lose their virginity. Private dwellings were a sign of wealth. Contrary to the poor, the rich youngsters spent a lot of time at home, in warm places.

Aaron was not a frightening boy anymore. He copied Rudi and wanted to live well. In the killing field, every business was taboo. Nevertheless, Aaron took the risk to start one. He endangered himself frequently, but he enjoyed all his endeavors. He worked on the black market. Sofia played a terrible role in his life. She became jealous of Sashko, who was Aaron's partner. Because of her report, Aaron and his partner ended up being jailed and sent to prison. Sofia did not report Aaron specifically, but after his friend was arrested, he was arrested too. Only with the help of his father did Aaron become free again.

Aaron, after a miracle accomplished by his father, was released from prison and started dancing with a folk group. At the time, fast folk dances from the Caucasus Mountains were popular. Aaron was accepted into an Azerbaijani dance group. He became a valuable member of the group. During the Second World War, he danced at different military bases and factories, as well as on the front lines. His group had performers with a variety of specialties.

filled the communal kitchen and adjacent rooms. In that environment, the new man could not be born for a long time.

## Pseudodogma Promised Fast Changes

Aaron was overcoming many challenges. He was shy and wanted to figure out how to survive. Aaron learned that the ideologists promised quick changes in habitants' lives, but their promises were not fulfilled. There were many angry habitants. Vileness could not succeed, and inequality was everywhere. The ignobility did not accept deviations from the doctrine of equality, which stated that all habitants were born equal and should be equal. The doctrine was a bunch of fabrications. The state was supposed to provide habitants with equality, but it did not. As a result, the only reality was that no one was safe. In the killing field, equality did not exist. To prove their pseudoscientific theory, the followers of pseudodoctrine implied that for the government, robbing, killing, abusing, and invading the privacy of others were acceptable. Snitches were everywhere. Pseudodoctrine brought frightening innovations in the form of communal apartments and empty shelves in food stores. Habitants had only one way to soothe their souls: by drinking vodka. Soldiers sold themselves and were willing to have sex for a bottle of vodka.

Aaron already knew that double standards existed in personal relationships. In the killing field, a lonely woman could buy a soldier as a sexual slave for a bottle of vodka. Meanwhile, as mothers played with soldiers, their by dirty trickery, students acted as rogues and harassed the newcomer. Aaron faced many pranksters. More than a few acted like bullies. The unruly children reacted to him like bulls to the color red. Aaron was powerless. His sister-in-law dressed him like a character in movies about royalty. The rogue children harassed Aaron. Even though they did not have fresh clothes or nutritious meals, they felt supremacy in being Prolet-Aryans. Some boneheads would collect semen in little paper pockets and, without any embarrassment, toss it onto the heads of students. The die-hard ideologists continued to talk about the new man. Even they knew that nothing would change. To prove the pseudodoctrine, the liars from the ruling elite probably would have justified the actions of the semen throwers. They would have found something to prove the action of the rogues. It would have been a joke to say so, but they probably would have said that masturbation was a progressive means of fertilization for the new man. The truth was that there was no new man, but there were plenty bullies, sociopaths, and snitches.

In summary, the manipulative rogue children hurt poor Aaron. He looked for a way to adjust in school and prevent getting harmed. Eventually, he found a way. It was not the best but allowed him to survive. In the future, he would be able to save people. He became a Sailor.

Aaron chose the only available way for him to survive. No one wanted to help him. He became manipulative. Aaron decided to befriend a bully and pay him for protection. He made a move that neutralized his tormentors. The new bodyguard and bully became his mentor. Aaron's new associate was a product of communal life. In overcrowded communal apartments, there was one toilet for many families. There was no shower or bath, so bad smells for her problems, she blamed her partner, Aaron. She complained to her mother that her partner was not on her level and slowed her down, and as a result, he could not properly lead her. She was under the influence of her mother, who saw her as perfect.

Rudi also displayed double standards. He would never become a Sailor. He never defended his brother but enjoyed playing cards with him. It was a family tradition that came from their father. Rudi was older and was an excellent player. In the meantime, Aaron was a lonely teenager. Rudi took pleasure in being in the company of his brother and taught him different card tricks. They both came from one nest, a little village in Byelogoria. It was a burden to be provincial. Aaron's niece always made fun of his accent. His brother did not say much. They understood each other without talking. Rudi did not care about the stories his daughter and wife made up about his brother, but he kept silent. Aaron suffered from low self-worth. He did not tell Rudi that all the accusations were fabrications. He knew Rudi did not care. The brothers did not talk much. They enjoyed cards together instead. Nevertheless, the mother and daughter told lies. They needed a scapegoat. For Aaron, being a newcomer was not an easy existence. He decided not to react to women who wanted to put him down. In the future, his brother would betray him too.

In school, Aaron faced the double standards of the educational system. Lies were everywhere. The collective created double standards in attempts to change the nature of man. The doctrine spoke about the birth of a new, refined man and declared rogues as socially friendly. As a result, communalists produced a huge number of rogues with a criminal understanding of bravery. They even masturbated during their school lessons. Infected books of Leo Tolstoy and Fyodor Dostoyevsky resided. He was amazed at how fast the place changed after it was taken over by scoundrels. Many inhabitants were sent to Kolyma. Aristocrats, businessmen, teachers, industrialists, artisans, tradesmen, mechanics, and servicemen once had lived in the city. Now the living space was empty. The beautiful apartments were transferred to communal settings and packed full of habitants from the heartland who had sacks of potatoes and firewood in their rooms. It was vile that the creation of Peter the Great had become a big hostel. It was beyond comprehension that a city with many castles located on 101 islands could be given to lumberjacks dwelling in the wilderness.

In the city captured by rough habitants, all relationships became lowland relationships. The familial associations changed. Even in polluted systems, family connections meant something. Aaron was a dancer because his family was wealthy, and he was immediately introduced to something elegant and attractive: ballroom dancing, a serious activity. He learned the fantastic moves of the waltz, foxtrot, rumba, and more. His partner was his niece, who at one point was a chubby, awkward girl but later became a prominent actor and acclaimed Argentinian tango dancer. At first, Aaron stayed away from his niece as much as he could, knowing in advance what a terrible role she could play in his future. Eventually, she reported him and her future husband, Sashko, to the secret police.

Sofia had double standards for everything. Her life was typical for a celestial girl and was a copy of others' relationships in Aborigin. She was selfish and manipulative. She felt that only distorted reverberations were effective. First of all, as a chubby dancer, she could not admit that she could not move quickly. Instead of taking responsibility like a savage animal who'd come to a civilian setting. When he learned that Sofia's father was a lawyer, everything became clear. In his understanding as someone from the village, every lawyer had that kind of life. He matched Sofia with her setting and understood that she was of a different class. He was flattered by her attention. It appeared both of them were attracted to each other. Sofia's mission was to go to the simple habitants and make them happy. Many girls from rich families became involved with bums. Under their influence, the bums became classier. Soon Aaron suspected Sashko and Sofia had made love.

For Sashko, love was a strong stimulant and took him away from the street. Accepted into new trappings, Sashko suddenly asked Aaron to help him in his academics. They did homework together. To his surprise, Aaron discovered that Sashko was not stupid and could learn. Sashko spent a lot of time with Aaron and Sofia. Sofia's younger sister, Clara, was not with them. She was busy with books and school assignments. She also was much younger than Aaron and Sashko. Sofia's mother was alone too and did not bother them. She was in her daydreams and stayed in her room a lot. She daydreamed about being an aristocrat and was happy with her fantasies.

When the youngsters did not study, they played different games, such as cards. Aaron tried to memorize the sequence of cards in the deck. He was able to do it well and always won. All three had a good time, and their friendship became stronger. The collective was quick to eliminate the upper and middle classes. It removed the motivation to climb socially. Instead of making the middle class bigger, the collective destroyed it. The leftover habitants from the middle class mixed with Prolet-Aryans.

Aaron loved a special city where characters from the

the new kingpins were for separation. It was the biggest swindle in world history.

Sashko was a terrestrial who pretended to be a celestial. In the killing field, dancing activities were left to the rich and uninfected. Once, when Aaron was dancing, Sashko waited for him. Sofia saw Sashko and became interested as she observed him. Sashko was a big, muscular adolescent and not at all homely. He was a wildcat, but Sofia did not live in reality. She was naive and driven by hormones. She wanted Aaron to introduce her to Sashko. Sofia lived in an apartment of five rooms for one family and did not know how other habitants lived. She had two bathrooms for her family, a bath, a shower, and a big kitchen with a window. The apartment also had a big balcony. Every week, a woman from the village would come to wash her family's clothes and bring them firewood from the basement. Her father would hire someone to chop their wood for them. Sofia and Sashko were from different planets. Sofia was a celestial.

At the same time, Sofia, brainwashed by the indoctrinated leaders' phraseology about equality and goodwill, was stubborn. She refused to recognize how her lifestyle was dissimilar from terrestrials'. She did not see how different from her the habitants on the other side were. She dreamed about saving the poor boy and making him happy. She also felt guilt from the brainwashing about the oppressed habitants of society. She asked Aaron if he'd introduce her to Sashko. She did not know what kind of sludge she had stepped into. Sofia insisted Aaron invite Sashko to their place.

When Sashko came to their apartment, he was shocked that habitants could live in such luxury. He saw the classy furniture, porcelain, wooden floors, and high ceilings with chandeliers. He did not know anything like that. He was for Rudi but were suitable for Aaron. As a result, the next day, Sashko's date did not show up, but Aaron got lucky.

Aaron was an attractive, clean, and well-dressed young man. The time came for the youngster to lose his virginity. The woman from Siberia was attracted to him and hungry for intimacy. The next day, they walked to her house, and she said that if Aaron wanted to, he could come inside for a cup of tea. He wanted to and went inside. Lara rented a small room in a communal setting. She offered Aaron a little wine. After drinking the wine, Aaron became more aggressive and pushed Lara onto the bed. Lara did not resist and only begged him to be quiet. She was afraid the neighbors would hear something and report her to the room's owner. Lara quickly undressed, and then Aaron did the same. Once naked, he kept his genitals covered with both hands. Lara opened his hands, saw his circumcised penis, and liked it.

When Aaron left Lara's house, Sashko was waiting for him. He'd followed Aaron and Lara, walking behind them, so he'd known where Aaron was. He had many questions. Aaron mentioned that he would visit Lara again in a few days. After a short silence, a blushing Sashko confessed that he had never been inside of a woman. He was a virgin. Sashko was a simpleton who fooled around with his bullshit stories. He was a true son of his homeland. The collective was filling the whole world with nonsense that they crafted with pathos and phraseology. In reality, all their promises were empty. The population did not know where to go or what to do. One thing was clear: the infected pretended to be leaders of the world. The real kings and rulers, such as Peter the Great and Catherine the Great, wished for integration of their nation with other countries. Contrarily, in front of Prolet-Aryans during their breaks. Sofia was his niece, but they were not close.

Aaron and Sashko often walked the streets of the gorgeous city. In the collective, interactions between the sexes started on the street. Time passed, and something important happened to Aaron: he lost his virginity. One day, as usual, he and Sashko were walking on the streets, when the new development took place. The situation did not look like anything unusual; a young man simply started talking to a woman on the street. On that day, Sashko chased after one young woman who passed by on the city's main promenade. He got her to talk, and then they walked together. At that time, there were no bars in which to talk to passersby. It was common to start a conversation with a woman on the street, in a store, or anywhere else. After talking to the young woman, Sashko came back to Aaron, and by his jubilant appearance, Aaron understood that Sashko had gotten a date.

After Sashko's successful interaction on the street, Aaron felt tempted to do the same. He also chose a young woman and went after her. He approached a young woman nicely dressed in a fur coat and started to talk to her. The woman looked at him and laughed but continued to talk with him. He walked with her a little longer, and the woman told him she was a student in a culinary school. Her name was Lara, and she came from Siberia. Aaron introduced himself as an industrial college student instead of a high school boy, and he added a few years to his age. Aaron did not have much confidence in himself, but he was handsome, with red cheeks, brown eyes, and black hair. His clothes were not bad because his sister-in-law dressed him in fashionable suits that had become too small

## Low Morale in the Killing Field

Sashko was a bastard. In the communal setting, sexual interactions were based not on love but on lust. Sashko was the son of a single mother who had come to the big city from a village. He was a product of the communal setting and did not know how to culturally relate to others. He grew up in poor lodging where he had fifteen neighbors. His mother worked in a leather factory and was exposed to terrible odors. After work, she simply wanted to drink and have sex. She gave some money to her son, sent him onto the street, and told him not to come home until late at night. Before that, she bought vodka. With the bottle of vodka in her hand, she went to the next street, where the military base was. She would ensnare a soldier hungry for sex, who jumped the fence. She brought him to her place. The soldier, who'd given an oath to listen to his commanders and defend his homeland, forgot about the oath and his duty when he saw a woman with a bottle of vodka in her hand. The soldier who jumped the fence would walk behind the woman like a prisoner of war.

In the meantime, Aaron's life changed. He lost his Byelogorian accent, and he could have become a professional dancer, but he wanted to be independent. He had business orientation in his blood, and he loved money. To please her husband and follow the royal traditions, Sofia's mother was not cheap and bought clothes for Aaron, such as good suits, shirts, and ties. He looked nice. Sofia was not a match for him with her attitude toward life. He needed to create something. He did not want to dance as much as Sofia did. He did not want to perform in factories were also used as laundry rooms, where big boilers to heat water were located. They washed their clothes by hand. There was no hygiene to speak of. The wood and clothes were kept together in the same place. In other settings, the wood was kept outside on the patio, where children's places were. Instead of a playground for children, the patio was used as storage for the wood, so children had to play on the street.

Like the other tenants, Sashko usually washed his face in a communal sink that did not have any disinfectant. On Saturday night, the population of the town would go to have a swab. Sashko went to the city's communal bathhouses once a week. In bathhouses, the lines were a mile long. Inside the place, habitants would go to the steam room, where they whipped themselves with the branches of young birch trees. In a communal setting, the bathhouses were one of the few pleasures of a Saturday night. In the killing field, everything was forbidden. Lines were everywhere. Habitants stood in lines for simple commodities. Days passed by quickly. A day mainly consisted of standing in lines for diverse goods. A single store had many lines for different items. It took a long time to make even a simple shopping trip. Keeping habitants busy in big lines was probably part of the conspiracy. To avoid unrest, the authorities would push habitants to be busy all the time and think only of survival and buying necessities. Habitants were preoccupied with getting basic nutrition, clothes, and everything else. They also avoided lines and broke rules. In the end, habitants were so tired that when they came home, they only wanted to have a little rest.

neighbors who bought food on the black market and at the back entries of stores were scared. The prices on the black market were significantly higher, and habitants were afraid of being questioned about where they got their money. When tenants in communal apartments bought better food or had nice furniture, one of the informers among the neighbors would report them to the secret police. Right away, an investigator from a special police unit that was supposed to fight against plunderers and speculators would come. The accused would bribe the police investigator with a bottle of vodka. The investigator was happy. The informer who'd flagged the situation would receive some money from the police.

Sashko was right to describe his mockeries. Everyone was supposed to bribe and be bribed. Being bribed was a form of respect. The police did not offer carte blanche for snitching. The informers were investigated and needed to pay bribes just as others did. There were so many of them that police did not consider them valuable. Many neighbors were informers, but other stool pigeons could easily report on them too. The occupants who received food from the shadow economy were scared. The shelves in stores were empty, and they purchased food on the black market. They did not want to be reported to the authorities.

Because anyone could be an informer, tenants did not want the neighbors to see what they were cooking. In every room was a portable kerosene stove. The tenants would cook food they'd bought on the black market. Every room also had a wood stove to heat up the room. In the summer, tenants would buy and cut wood for the winter. Some tenants kept wood downstairs in the vault. In the winter, they carried wood from the basement into their rooms. In many houses, the basements where habitants kept wood

## Animal Instinct Took Over

The kitchen in a communal setting had only one stove for all residents. Many tables to prepare food were assigned to each room. For every room, there was one personal lightbulb in the kitchen, and in the hallway was a personal switch for each lightbulb. There were also many bells on the entry door, one for each room. In the hallway hung many electric energy counters, one for every room. In all common areas, the tenants used their own switches for lightbulbs. There was one toilet for everyone. The tenants were always fighting in line to prepare food and use the toilet. In the kitchen, there was no place for food safeguarding. The tenants did not trust others and did not keep their food together. They retained food in their rooms, and the food smelled rotten. There was no refrigeration. The atmosphere was terrible, and the rooms had pests, vermin, and a lot of bacteria. In those apartments, there were no showers. The habitants went once a week to public baths to wash themselves. They had to wait in big lines, and hot water was not always available. The neighbors were angry and had constant fights about many things, mainly communal duties. Tenants were irritated by the line to use the toilet, the unwashed bodies, and the line to use the stove to cook food. They suffered from a bad smell that came from the rooms.

Habitants were losing their human qualities. They became insensitive to the suffering of others. They were annoyed with the living conditions and attacked each other. The meanness infected them. It was a time of deficit. When habitants wanted to have something more than what was available in stores, they went to the black market. The in villages and in big cities, people had had food, work, and appropriate dwellings. They'd received fair wages that allowed them to have necessities. The new revolutionary regime took the old income from villages. The members of collective farms were starving. It was unbelievable how fast life deteriorated in the formerly prosperous region. To keep helpless villagers on collective farms, the leaders took away their identification cards. Without papers, they could not move from the collective farms. The villagers, according to idiotic doctrine, were less enlightened and needed guidance. They were destined to be the worker bees because they were not able to comprehend the deepness of foolish edifice.

The villagers succumbed to hunger and dumped the dead in the forest. They were without food and work in their rural communities. As a result, hungry and without papers, they moved to the big cities. They took mostly horrible jobs. For them, the city was like a fairy tale. In the metropolises, they saw big buildings, cars, and theaters. They did not mind that they had to live in a communal setting. The city was packed with newcomers tied together with laces, cockroaches, and rats that multiplied daily. The collective did not have methods to fight parasites. The animals spread infectious diseases, and the habitants became sick with typhus, dysentery, and more. The hospitals were overcrowded, and sick habitants were everywhere. They lay in the hallways and corridors. There were not enough beds, so sick habitants were required to lie on the hospital floor.

Sashko was proud and boasted about his actions. He felt like a hero of Aborigin. Like the majority of inhabitants in the workers' paradise, Sashko, who came from the village, had lived in a communal setting for most of his life. Apartments that previously had belonged to different wealthy habitants had been reconfigured to accommodate the many habitants who moved to the city from villages. The new lodging had few places to sleep and a common kitchen for several families, with one sink for drinking water and preparing food. There was one toilet for many rooms. They did not have any hot water. In the restroom was one sink that everyone used as a washbasin for his or her hands, face, and clothes. In the communal apartments were up to fifteen rooms, and in every room was a family of at least two or more habitants.

The setting was a place for much naughtiness. Sashko bragged to other children about his mischief, which actually looked like a mockery. He would play pranks involving the restroom. When he was out of the restroom, he hammered nails from outside, but the door appeared to be locked from the inside, so the neighbors thought someone occupied the restroom. They stood in line and knocked on the door, but no one answered. With the door locked, they could not get inside. They ran to their rooms and defecated into pots. They had only one room, and their other family members saw them do their business and smelled the stench from their defecation. Because the toilet was locked, they could not dispose of the fecal matter. Villainy was one of the symptoms. The communal setting was a terrible sickness.

Dogma was irresponsible and did not care about habitants. The headless neighbors did not care about each other. The happiest creatures in the communal setting were insects, bugs, and cockroaches. During the czar's regime, by chance did criminals use knives and hammers to attack habitants. Aaron saw how a tough guy would turn around with a hammer in hand and indiscriminately hit habitants on the head. Now he was one of them, but the difference was that those tough guys grew up in unheated apartments and were always famished. The boys were like Sashko. When they saw girls, they exhibited the street strategy of bullshitting, which included elements of acting.

Sashko was prepared and felt good in a classroom filled with beautiful girls. He talked a lot and always lied. He also knew a few girls from his communal apartment and told Aaron they were easy. Aaron would get red-faced in front of the girls, and his speech became inaudible. Seeing that Aaron lost confidence in front of girls, Sashko pushed him to talk to them or touch them. He demonstrated to Aaron a move that he called "attack on the bust." He yelled, "Crazy is attacking!" and touched the girl's breasts. He knew already who would smile and giggle and allow him to do it. Sashko told Aaron he waited for girls on the street and followed them into the halls of their apartment buildings. They would allow him to touch their breasts and put his hands between their legs. Sashko was a rogue, but he did not overstep criminal rule. When a girl rejected his advances, he backed away. According to criminal rules, a man could buy girls but never force himself on them. He knew that with his poor clothes, lack of money, and rough manners, he would not likely get consent to go all the way. He pretended a lot and bragged to Aaron about his intimate interactions with girls, but in reality, he did not have any. The lovestruck youngsters would write notes and poetry to the girls about their feelings. They accompanied the girls, the objects of their admiration, home and carried their schoolbags.

showed that he could fight brainwashing in his own way. He promised himself he would never live in communal apartments. He dedicated his life to the prosperity of his family. With all his good qualities, Rudi did not become a Sailor, but for a long time, Aaron copied his brother.

Aaron progressed with a street education. His Byelogorian accent became less intrusive, and he was not as naive. He was not afraid of bullies anymore and drank beer with other adolescents. Aaron was not prepared to deal with girls. Scoundrels, with their bravado, made interactions with the opposite sex confusing. In school, exciting news came that their all-male school would be mixed with the nearby girls' school. They would have girls in their classes. The integration eventually happened, and into the class stepped beautiful redheads, blondes, and brunettes. Sashko knew a little bit more about the opposite sex. He followed the street logic that a man could talk girls into anything. Most importantly, he should not stop the drivel running out of his mouth. The opinion on the street was that to gain a girl's attention, the prerequisite was the ability to lie as much as possible without being caught. The intention was to entertain girls. The girl somehow knew the boy was lying but simply did not care. The charade was based on the simple logic that girls lived in a fantasy land, and fabrications kept the girls' dreams alive. It sounded as if a man who did not lie to a girl was naive. The criminal code was against violence toward girls. The girls' attention should be bought. In school, the girls had power. Some of them had criminal boyfriends who were good with knives and appeared violent. The girls did not care and were proud to have them.

Aaron knew the pseudocollective was represented by a symbol: the sickle and hammer. A sickle was a knife. Not

His younger niece, Clara, daydreamed a lot and did not participate in the family's harassment of her uncle. Aaron helped her. Their next-door neighbor, an intellectually challenged boy, always pulled Clara's hair. She was afraid to leave the house alone because of him. Aaron intervened and talked to the boy's brother. Using his new authority, Aaron told him to keep the boy on a figurative leash. The brother of the boy knew about Aaron's relationship with tough guys and promised the attacks would stop. Later, Aaron asked Clara how the boy was behaving. She confirmed that the hair pulling had stopped. Her life was back to being ordinary. In her later years, she married a naval officer, had children, and lived by the ocean in the Far East.

Aaron developed a different approach to family discord: he silently listened to his sister-in-law's stories and showed compassion in his face. He appeared attentive to her stories. She told him that when Rudi had been a student, she, having noble blood, had not minded living in a communal apartment. She remembered that when she'd bought an old wardrobe from an old, starving aristocrat, her neighbor had reported her to the local police. She'd been investigated for possibly being attached to the old regime. She'd been scared the police would find out about her relationship with the king. Of course, her relation to the king was a fabrication and a result of her illness. Her husband, Rudi, had resolved the issue easily by bribing the policemen with a bottle of vodka. The police had stopped the investigation. That was a typical demonstration of the actions of members of the party enlightened by idiotic dogma. They would disregard information about a class enemy for a mere bottle of vodka. Rudi displayed his resistance to collectivism by bribing officials. He supposed to have only one ambition: helping the regime to survive. He was a guardian of the system and destroyed all obstacles to the smooth implementation of callous regulations.

The new man did not have ambitions and, as a zombie, looked only for the best of the doctrine. He was supposed to spread his beliefs and could convert disbelievers to accept his truth. The name of the new man was *moron*. The man was supposed to radicalize those around him with nutcase doctrines. Sashko was one who showed that the dogma duped habitants with the idea that doctrine was capable of creating a selfless man who would be just a cog in the machine. The imprudent guidelines accounted for many things, including stultification of habitants' individuality and organizations. The doctrine was fooling other countries.

## Learning to Survive

*E*motionally, Aaron came to a crossroads. He decided he should not talk much to his sister-in-law and other members of his family. To his amusement, his relations with them improved. When Aaron kept silent, he was no different from a dog or a cat and seemed to lack individuality. His sister-in-law did not have any issues to dwell on. She continued dreaming of being of noble blood, and Aaron, with his heavy accent and the manners of a villager, did not irritate her as much. Sofia always copied her mother's attitude, and she stopped her accusations that Aaron caused her discomfort when they danced together.

Interestingly, Sashko, contrary to Aaron, had a mother. By the doctrine's regulations, as the son of a single mother, he could not be expelled from school. His mother received some money from the government, and she did not care how long Sashko was in school. In some way, she benefited from Sashko. According to regulations, she was paid as long as her son stayed in school. He was the oldest child in the class, and he was a typical bully. His hormones also ran high. He sometimes masturbated during class. He ejaculated into a small paper container and threw it onto smaller children. He had fun and laughed when doing so. He learned from a young age that to be in charge, he had to be nasty.

Dogma proclaimed that the new economic conditions would create a new kind of man. It seemed that economic changes were not enough for the new man to be born. The semen of Sashko landed on the heads and faces of the younger students, who did not protest but instead scrubbed away Sashko's semen from their clothes with their bare hands. Their hands became sticky and tacky, and their clothes were stained. The teacher, who was motivated to bring education to the working class, did not understand what was going on and was confused. He did not know that the one member of the ruling class, infected by psychological germs, was spreading his semen over the heads of the children, who in time were supposed to become rulers of the land. Sashko fertilized with his semen the young descendants of the ruling class in the workers' paradise. The students were afraid of him and never complained to the teacher. It did not matter anyway because Sashko could not be expelled. There was no expulsion policy in educational institutions, and on top of that, he was the child of a single mother. Sashko was not hurt anyone. Sashko ordered that Aaron fight with the children who attacked him. He would join Aaron in beating the crap out of those children. Aaron became powerful and saw fear in the eyes of others when he was around. When children beat him up, they were merciless. In contrast, he was not cruel and never was brutal. Sashko taught him that to survive and gain respect, he must be aggressive and hurt children. Aaron found a different solution. He learned that he could, with his gestures, give the impression he was hurting kids. Only to follow Sashko's lead, Aaron acted as if he was aggressive. He was a good actor. He waved his hands around and made different grimaces with his face. He believed that being with Sashko was the only way to survive. He wanted to please Sashko by being sure others were fearful of him. In his acting, he exercised restraint and did not overstep a believable threshold. He did not follow his rage to the point of being overly aggressive. With Sashko's lead, he lost the feeling of being a victim.

Sashko Belay exhibited delinquent behavior. He had a mother but did not have a father. In his life, he only wanted to break rules and play cards. He did not have money. He and Aaron agreed that the loser would receive a snap on the nose with a deck of cards. Aaron was a good card player. The card games gave him a lot of power over Sashko. He could have won all the time, but he did not; he often purposely lost. To keep his grip on Sashko, he would not show him his mistakes, which Sashko repeated all the time. Aaron often snapped Sashko's nose with a deck of cards. He did not enjoy manipulating others and did it no more than was necessary to be safe. Sashko was his weapon, a bad boy who was much older than the other kids. Sashko did not care about learning and repeated every grade several times.

emotions. Rudi put his brother in the custody of a mentally ill woman. Habitants in the world often talked about adults abusing children. That was indeed an unfortunate aspect of life. Children should have been safe from the violence of adults. However, there was another aspect of children's lives ignored by the infected dogmatic: no one talked about bullying. That topic was taboo, but everywhere, children were being abused by bullying children. The boys and girls were united in small groups and gangs. They attacked, kicked, punched, and harassed other children or fought with other groups for influence. Bullies were everywhere. Aaron was in trouble. His predicament was such that he was exposed to everyone as a designated victim.

## The Life of Sashko Belay

Unruly children were unruly everywhere in the world. In Aaron's class was a big guy who was older than the other students in the class. His name was Sashko Belay. He was poorly dressed and always asked for a couple bites from other students' meals. Aaron asked Sashko for protection, and in return, he offered Sashko his lunches. Aaron succeeded in hiring a security guard. Sashko Belay accepted his proposal. Later in life, he became Aaron's best friend. In exchange, Sashko Belay also requested that Aaron follow all his orders, including the order that Aaron had to drink beer and smoke. They picked up from the streets half-smoked cigarettes. They were Sashko's favorite brand, Belaymore. Beer was sold on the street in kiosks, and they would share a big mug. In the past, Aaron had

Aaron's sister-in-law had seen those clothes in movies, on handsome movie stars. The picturesque habitants in movies were from the mountains of Tyrol and appeared to be aristocratic. She was quick to dress Aaron in that out-of-the-way attire. When he came to school, he appeared humorous. In a city full of communal apartments, Tyrol clothing was a representation of the bourgeois lifestyle. Aaron displayed a socially alien character and became a scapegoat for students.

The children saw him as a foreigner. One day Aaron sat behind the school table, and his briefcase lay on the shelf under the table. The other children put containers full of ink on top of his briefcase. He could not see them because they were covered by the table. When he took his briefcase out from the shelf, the containers of ink fell onto his clothing and stained it. At home, his sister-in-law yelled at him and accused him of not being careful enough. He complained that some children hit him and called him Orangutan, a twist on his name, Aaron. They also used other nicknames, such as Abram and Zelman, to emphasize his Jewish ethnicity. His sister-in-law responded that it was he who was bothering the other children. That was why they picked on him. She insinuated that children did not attack him without reason.

With his problems, Aaron was alone, and no one cared about him. His sister-in-law and niece emotionally abused him. Other children in school physically abused him. He did not know what to do. His mother was dead, and his father was in prison.

Rudi did not want any responsibility for his brother. Besides providing material goods for his family, Rudi did not want to be involved in anything. He was withdrawn from his children too. Rudi did not care much about

The instructors saw him as talented but criticized Sofia. They did not see any talent in her. She looked thick and clubfooted. Her mother bought a lot of gifts to change the instructors' opinions. She also paid for individual instruction. To Sofia's credit, she had an industrious mind and truly wanted to be a dancer. At that time, not all the ballroom dances were popular. Sofia put her sights on the Argentinian tango, which was more of a picturesque dance and did not have as many strict rules as other dances. As soon as her presentation improved, Sofia grew shapelier. She already had made up her mind not to be a dancer and wanted to be an actor. She was attractive and was determined to achieve her goal. Her Argentinian tango became pleasant. Eventually, Sofia found another partner, and Aaron was free of her. Aaron's genetics pushed him in a different direction. He became active in business and made money.

## Abusive Children

At school, the children saw Aaron as different. His sister-in-law took custody of him. She got him clothes. She dressed him like a German tourist from Tyrol. A mountainous region, Tyrol had frequently changing weather and carried a large selection of winter and summer costumes. It had clothing and footwear for all ages. The clothes were designed for mountaineers and had a distinctive style. The clothes matched that astonishing vicinity but were not appropriate for the city. The attire included long underwear, socks, parkas, pants, and hats.

to avoid any confrontations and did not suspect he was being manipulated. He ended up on his wife's side. He felt he was committed to his family. At that time, he was unaware of his wife's mental illness. He did not expect to have a delusional person as his wife. He did not have a clue that something of that nature could happen to him. He denied that something was wrong with his wife. He did not protect his brother from his wife's delusions.

Aaron was a new person in a big city and was an easy target to become a scapegoat. He did not know what his sister-in-law wanted from him and blamed himself for his perceived shortcomings. He did not understand that a mentally impaired woman was putting him down to compensate for her own imperfection. He tried to be good. He did not have a clue about mental illness and how to recognize the symptoms of delusion. He was confused, lacked self-confidence, and was frightened. The mentally ill woman drained his self-worth. He was overly compliant and did not have the tools to resist bullies.

Aaron was a dancer. In the killing field, dance was one of the few activities not forbidden. It required a lot of time to learn. Habitants mainly danced the Charleston and Argentinian tango. Other dances, such as the waltz, rumba, and bolero, were less popular. Aaron danced all of them. The parents of dancing children needed to spend quite a bit of money. The activity was unavailable for habitants in communal apartments. It was another life for those who could afford it.

Sofia's mother enrolled her daughter in different dance competitions. She spent a lot of money on dresses and shoes for the events. The results were bleak. Sofia continued to blame her partner. However, Aaron was able to memorize the dance moves and led Sofia to better performances.

to cheat at cards. Sometimes Rudi entertained himself by imagining how his life would have been different if he'd become a professional card player. He dreamed that his brother would pick up his skills and become a card connoisseur. He wanted to live his dreams through his brother's life. He did not have a son, but his younger brother was an appreciative student.

Only to please his wife, Rudi would get parental with Aaron. He would explicitly state that he was disappointed in him. He would not listen to what Aaron had to say in response. He would state that he was not interested in any of his excuses. He emphasized that he wanted Aaron to be more serious and focus more on dance. The lectures were all a gimmick because he actually did not care how good or bad of a dancer his brother was. He was focused on a different area. He knew that Aaron was a quick card learner and was good in chess. That was important. His parental notations and advice were a game. In reality, he was glad he had someone to play with.

Aaron did not mind playing games and loved spending time with his brother. Aaron loved his brother. He was happy learning a lot about different games. Rudi enjoyed playing games because they helped him to release his stress. Rudi also was happy because he could talk to his brother in Yiddish, the language of villagers. His wife and daughter felt that Yiddish was a language for peasants and never used it. They made faces and grimaced when they heard the brothers speaking in Yiddish. Aaron had learned Yiddish in his small village in Byelogoria. The brothers' relationship was strong, but the night cuckoo could manipulate anyone.

Rudi had to choose between confrontations with his wife and a relationship with his brother. Rudi wanted and out of the back doors of stores for much higher prices than in retail.

In Rudi's house, there were always guests. His wife pretended to be an aristocratic woman and played the piano. She invited important habitants. Rudi was an excellent card player and kept his guests busy playing cards. He also showed his guests tricks with cards. He could play for money, but he did not. He was in a different business and never mixed it with cards. He was content with what he was doing. He was not a big talker. He could have made a lot of money by playing games, but he did not. He liked card games only for relaxation. He enjoyed playing not only cards but any game. He played chess, checkers, and Bahamas. His wife and daughter were not fans of games. He dreamed about having a son in his family, but his wife did not want another child. He was happy that his brother had come to his house from Byelogoria. Aaron was much younger. Rudi could practice his parenting skills on him. He played with Aaron, who liked card games as well as many others. They were from the same nest, where their father, Isaac, was a master of different games.

Rudi showed Aaron the cards tricks with which he entertained his guests. Rudi knew a lot of tricks. He adored cards and loved to shovel them. When he played with his brother, he never won from him. He always pointed out the mistakes his brother made. He allowed him to make another bet or redo his incorrect moves. With his skills, Rudi could beat anyone, but he did not try. He had his own business as a lawyer. He made a good living. He was not a croupier. In his work, he was secure. He placed high bets and won. He was superstitious and did not want any interference to spoil the games. In work, he was strict, but in his family, he was soft. Rudi showed his brother how power over him. His sister-in-law and niece talked behind his back. Sofia's mother was jealous of the relationship between her husband and his brother. She told Rudi that his brother was not a good dancer and was not making an effort to improve. She continued to nag him about how unappreciative his brother was and said that Aaron did not understand how lucky he was to have Sofia as a dance partner.

Life after the communal revolution was confusing. The policies in big cities sounded stupid, but no one challenged them. To justify an economy of slavery, the officials chattered about a clean society in which all business-oriented individuals stopped their exploitation of the masses. It was gibberish because the economy got weak without business competition, inadvertent discoveries, and unforeseen innovations. The officials talked about an economy that was calculated in advance. They rejected a budget based on demands and consumption. They provided goods not according to the habitants' needs but by their own choice. They declared that the government could regulate demands of goods. It was much easier to say than to do. The economy had its own rules and did not follow stupid political doctrines. The result of the new economic reality was dark. The economy for slaves did not do well. Aborigin had the most corruption. Showing up to an official without a bribe was a sign of disrespect. The old tradition of bribing continued. The habitants' demands moved to the black market and started a big shadow economy. The shelves in government stores were empty. The black market satisfied millions of customers. Bazaars were part of the shadow economy. It was a time of deficit. Goods were sold on the black market, in bazaars, about big cities. As a villager in a big city, Aaron also was an easy target to be patronized, but Aaron was strong and flexible. Despite his young age, in his life were many dangerous situations. Because he loved dancing, he was able to overcome the different challenges in front of him. He thought many times that his life would have been bleak if he had not had dancing as a means of escaping stress. For Aaron, dance was his stimulant. Contrarily, many infected habitants found in liquor the joy of life. They saw it as a way to let out their emotions.

Aaron was different. He did not have difficulty letting out his emotions in dancing. Sofia, to cover her own weaknesses, gave Aaron insulting feedback about his dancing ability. Even though she had no clue what it meant to dance properly, she always lectured Aaron about how to dance properly. She insinuated that she made mistakes because Aaron did not lead her properly and did not move her in the right direction.

Other girls in the group, waspish city scum, saw that he did not correct Sofia, even though she was wrong. They too started to blame him for their mistakes. He became a scapegoat for the group. In the group, some girls wanted him to hold them tightly, but others wanted a gentler grasp. He tried to accommodate everyone. When he did make a mistake, he apologized many times. Because of his submissive behavior, the girls were more empowered. The girls made up fictitious stories about health hazards caused by his mistakes. They tied bandages around their wrists and elbows. They told him they were limping because of him. They made him feel miserable and then laughed behind his back. He was not protected. His mother was dead, and his father was in prison; he was powerless, and the girls did not know how to be generous with their relation to the dead czar and wanted her daughter to grow up like a fine lady, as royalty was supposed to be. Sofia was an overweight, nasty girl, and no one wanted to be her partner. Aaron was a godsend. When he danced, his life was different, and he felt as if he were flying. He did not care with whom he danced. As a villager, he was not welcome in the big city.

Rudi's wife and older daughter talked negatively about Aaron's manners and his Byelogorian dialect. They implied that Aaron was a peasant. Nevertheless, Sofia understood that she would never have a partner more talented than Aaron. Because she was not a good dancer and was aggressive and negative, she did not have a partner in dance for a while. At her dance academy, no one wanted to dance with her.

Contrary to Sofia and her mother, Aaron's young niece Clara was romantic and sensitive. She did not show any animosity toward her uncle. She was an enthusiastic reader and was not involved in her mother's insinuations.

Aaron's sister-in-law took him to the Red Palace to dance. He was a natural dancer. He'd grown up in a village where folk dances were popular. His father had hired a dance teacher for him. Aaron was well built and had good coordination. In the city, he wanted to impress others with his good manners and was timid. Nevertheless, his sister-in-law and niece always made up nasty stories about him and said that in dance, he was rough and a bumpkin. They accused him of twisting Sofia's hand or stepping on her foot. Aaron felt terrible. He did not believe he was a good dancer. The mother and daughter tried to brainwash him to believe he was lucky to be Sofia's partner. He was lucky their bitterness did not make him a hater of the big city, as many villagers were. They had negative feelings partner, and Aaron was no exception. She was a Jewish princess. He was different from the others because he kept his mouth shut. The palace was beautiful, but in front of it was a big portrait of Supreme Leader. It was a display of pomposity. Next was a big motto that spoke of happy habitants. It appeared as a declaration that everything was great because of the wise leadership of Supreme Leader. The palace, in the past, had been the residence of an important person. The owner had a reputation as a gracious host. He threw dance parties with a sophisticated dance floor with layers of rubber and other protective materials under the wood. Villainous underlings used the palace to advertise the achievements of the regime under the guidance of Supreme Leader.

As a little boy, Aaron had spent time in a village jail with his parents, but he was not jail material. In his soul, he was a dancer. When villagers danced, they released oxytocin and adrenaline into their blood, and he loved the feeling. He'd started dancing as a young boy in his village. There in the gorgeous city, he danced with his niece Sofia. She put him down all the time. He did not care. He did not think too highly of himself. First of all, being from Byelogoria, he had a heavy accent, and his manners were different. He came from a village and did not know any of the big city's customs.

Sofia, who was looking for a partner with whom to dance, grabbed him right away but made his life glum. She complained to her mother that Aaron stepped on her feet, squeezed her hands, and even pushed her. To please her mother, she fabricated problems to show that she hated her partner but kept him because she was dedicated to dance. Her mother experienced delusions, and in her dreams, she was a dancer. She talked loudly about her from books, he saw communal apartments with an odor of dirty clothes and fermented vegetables. The consequences of the psychological infection were a tragedy for the whole population. Only a few habitants lived in reality. Compared to other discomforts, the reveries of Rudi's wife were not a big deal. Aaron did not care. He was a survivor.

His brother, Rudi, lived a good life because of his connections: on one side was the police, and on the other side was the criminal world. He had many friends in different precincts. He could get valuable papers signed by authorities by bribing them. He was a meek, typical go-between man. He was helpful in many stressful situations but not without requiring a percentage for his help. His charges were reasonable, and he had many customers. Being busy himself, he did not care that his wife was acting strangely. She dreamed about being an aristocrat and even being related to nobility. She refused to accept as true that she came from a little town and was the daughter of a shoemaker. She entertained herself with stories that she was an illegitimate daughter of one of the cousins of the czar, a count. Because Aaron was a boy from a small town, he reminded her of her real roots. She hated him, but she did not mind using him. Aaron's sister-in-law was a follower of aristocratic traditions and taught her daughters ballroom dances. They were taught in the Red Palace for Youth Pioneers. Because of Rudi's connections, his daughters were assigned to the best instructor. The lessons were free, like many things in the workers' paradise.

Rudi's daughter Sofia was heavily influenced by her mother. She was negative toward her dancing partners. Because of her chubbiness, boys refused to dance with her. Only one boy was left, her uncle Aaron, who was a little older but was thin and slender. Sofia put down every it was found that she had a mental illness and suffered from intrusive delusions. One of her false impressions was that Aaron would sexually hurt her daughters. She always spoke badly about Aaron.

Meanwhile, his accommodations were good. He lived in his brother's luxury quarters. He had his own room in a big five-bedroom apartment bought partly with his father's money. In his hometown, he'd gone to school and been a good student. He understood that he did not have a future in the academic world. His father was in prison as an enemy of the state. He also had a hobby: he liked dancing. He knew the dance of the Cossacks and how to dance with a sword. He knew that as a son of an enemy of the state, he would not be able to get into college or a dance academy. He was lucky to not be living in a communal apartment with a strong stench from a communal toilet and one kitchen for all tenants with no refrigerated food. All nutrients were kept in different rooms and smelled. Everything had its price, and Aaron was not an exception. Aaron tolerated the paranoia of his sister-in-law. He was a healthy adolescent. He'd come to the gorgeous city from a village. He needed to survive.

## The Past of the Gorgeous City

Professor Kryvoruchko visited the gorgeous city. He read the books of Leo Tolstoy and saw homes where, a long time ago, there had been ballroom dancing, beautiful dresses, and nurtured habitants. He could not find in the homeland any references to the past. Instead of characters

Isaac could find a few places in prison where he could work away from the pit, but the mine was the only place that suited his plans. That deposit of gems was the one place where he could get them. He loved gems and loved to keep them in his hands. He loved their forms and colors. He also could find more gems than anyone else. As time went by, an escape plan started to form in his mind. He had someone he cared about, so his risk was justified. He had Glasha, and he wanted to have freedom. His ideas were dangerous and unthinkable to implement, but Isaac was a gambler.

## Gorgeous City in Aborigin

*A*aron was in the new city. After living in his village, he found the city gorgeous, but life in the big cities was stressful. Rudi, Isaac's older son, lived in the gorgeous city. He was able to complete university and became a lawyer and public notary. He did not go to court for different cases and did not work for any big company, but he still had a comfortable life. Rudi was able to make money. He lived downtown in a beautiful city, close to the famous Winter Palace, the past residence of the czar's family. He was married and had two daughters, Sofia and Clara. He was a good provider. His wife did not work but bought fashionable clothes and had lunch in fancy café houses on Remarkable Boulevard, the main esplanade. His brother Aaron lived with him. Their father was in prison, and the boy did not have blood relatives nearby who would take him in.

In Rudi's family, Aaron had a problem. He could not get along with his sister-in-law, Rudi's wife. Later, disclosed that she had a daughter named Galena who lived in an orphanage in Byelogoria.

Glasha was smart and honest. Isaac learned to trust her. He did not want her to be endangered by the smuggling of diamonds. He did not want her to be at any risk. He was sure he could get away with many things and did not need anyone to help. Eventually, he shared with Glasha the secret place where he hid his gems. He wanted her to have them if something happened to him. He had Glasha exclusively, but he did not know how long he could protect her. In prison, things changed quickly.

Isaac understood the prison's essence and core. He knew that in prison, without bribes and gifts, he would not last. To survive in a prison camp, he had to rat, steal, and bribe. He was not surprised when the colonel, for whom he repaired watches, asked him to be his snitch. Isaac took the offer but only as a means of survival. He knew he was an informer only formally. He was not a rat. The colonel would wait a long time for information from him. Nevertheless, the position of informer helped him gain the trust of the colonel, who offered him herring, potatoes, and vodka. Isaac knew the colonel wanted something from him. Eventually, the colonel, after drinking a few shots of vodka, asked if Isaac could, in exchange for a variety of privileges, secretly smuggle a few gems for him. The colonel would instruct the criminals in charge not to pressure Isaac too much. Isaac received the same proposal from a thief who was a foreman of his block. The foreman also asked Isaac to smuggle diamonds for him to put in a mutual fund of thieves. The prison was the same as everywhere else: muddy with abhorrence.

Isaac was a survivor. He was not a thief or political prisoner but just a kern, one who was supposed to work.

talked with someone from a village in the middle of the Byelogorian Forest. There, it was a different story, and she was lucky to meet him. Women did not have any conditions for needed hygiene. They suffered a lot and were often in bad shape. The aristocrat woman was skinny and appeared to be starving. Isaac told her that he would provide her with food but that she must stay away from prostitution because he wanted exclusivity. Isaac learned how prison operated and what he should do to protect his woman. He brought a gift to a nasty old woman, a thief, who was in charge of the women's block. She knew him because sometimes Isaac was invited to play cards with thieves who were higher than she in the criminal hierarchy. The agreement was that she would not send the aristocrat woman to pleasure the guards.

Isaac had been an entrepreneur and gambler all his life. He knew that to get things done, he must pay. As a business-oriented man, he knew that if he pleaded for pity and begged, he could get something for free, but that was not for him because he was not a beggar and never was pitiful. He understood that when he asked for a favor, he had to give something in return. In prison, women were oppressed more than men were. Isaac paid with alcohol, food, or whatever was needed in order to ease the burden on his woman. All his favors were rewarded with bribes, gifts, or counterfavors. He knew that otherwise, no one would have mercy on his woman. To survive in prison, a woman needed a protector. Isaac promised to provide protection to his woman, and he did. He bribed everyone in the working area where the woman was assigned. The aristocrat woman was named Gloria, or Glasha for short. When Isaac told her that he was from Byelogoria, she metal nets. In prison, there were different coalitions of women. The majority stuck to their own groups, but a few joined different groups. Among the women were the wives of political prisoners, thieves, and killers. The political prisoners were mainly aristocrats and intellectuals who never had learned how to survive. They were half alive from the hard conditions and could not take care of themselves. The criminals took advantage of them. Women provided sexual pleasure for a cigarette, one potato, or whatever was marketable. The criminals used them as concubines, and the women would blow them for a bowl of soup or a piece of bread.

Isaac saw one woman who reminded him of his late wife. They talked. Isaac found out that the woman was an aristocrat who was around a group of monarchists. Mainly, the political prisoners stayed in their own groups. Nevertheless, besides the fact that the woman had a good education and manners, she was a survivor. She did not have any powerful protector and was happy to sell herself for a piece of bread or anything valuable. Only male prisoners in power were able to keep women on a regular basis. Women often went through many patrons. Few men, despite the harsh conditions, fell in love. The men met in a common area with their women, their objects of romantic love. In prison, there was not a place for privacy. Because prisoners were everywhere, the relations were platonic. The women were regularly used by the guards, who could have them behind the common area. Some women even looked to guards to have sex. They wanted to get pregnant because they believed that after their death, their children would live on in their stead.

Isaac was able to have the aristocrat woman. Outside of the prison, the aristocrat woman would not even have

Hebrew. In the little library in the camp was an old Jewish Bible, and a few Jewish habitants prayed together. Isaac prayed with them. During his visits to the medical ward, Isaac looked for a place to hide his future treasure. He saw that one of the wooden planks in the floor behind the medication shelf was loose. He lifted the plank, and under the board, he found a place to hide his future treasure. He knew that the most significant job in his life was to transfer the treasure from the dirt of the Kolyma River to the hidden place in the medical building.

In the medical ward, he repaired watches and delicate appliances. He knew the job could keep him alive. From the Kolyma River to his hiding place, he took only the best and cleanest diamonds. Meanwhile, he was friendly with the doctors. They were called to the village when villagers got sick. They could be needed in the future. He also found books on geography in the library. He wanted to figure out where he was. Also important was that he was able to get a little alcohol through the doctors. Doctors were famous because of their control of alcohol, which was valuable in the camp. Isaac did not use the alcohol for himself, but alcohol as a bribe helped Isaac to have the protection of important criminals. He also was not tortured during work by the slave drivers. In the meantime, he increased the size of his treasure trove. He repaired watches and played cards to survive, but the diamonds were for something else. He did not yet have a clear plan for them.

In the prison, the women were forced to sell themselves. They were not treated better than the men. The work was hard for men, but women did it as well. The women in the labor camp worked with the men in the mines, looking for gems. They wore prisoners' clothes. They looked for diamonds by shoveling sand and dirt and washing it in in charge of distributing food, work assignments, and work schedules. They were seen as important. They were allowed to have luxuries, such as tobacco, better food, means for playing cards, and paramours from the female block. The kingpins were the other privileged group. They were assigned to watch to make sure the actions of criminals complied with the criminal code. They were at the top level of the hierarchy of thieves. Several other prisoners in the camp also had more food than others, including individuals with calligraphic skills, who helped to write letters and applications for clemency; doctors; tailors; and shoemakers. Isaac was only an ordinary survivor, and his winnings in cards brought him a little food and some clothes. Most important was having respect and being around the most important prisoners. He was afraid to win too much. If a man could not pay, to keep his honor, the loser would kill the winner. It was one of the rules of honor in a slave labor camp. If Isaac had been killed over cards, no one would have cared.

In prison, many died from sicknesses, hunger, and heavy work, and one more death was unheeded. In prison, many things could save one's life. The most important were physical strength, an elevated position in the criminal hierarchy, and marketable skills. Isaac not only could play cards but also had another marketable skill: he knew how to repair watches.

The prisoners did not have watches, but the officers and guards had them. A few important prisoners in the barracks, such as the heads of blocks, doctors, cooks, and a few more, had watches as well. The doctors in the medical barrack called Isaac to repair their watches. Some doctors were Jewish, and Isaac played cards with them. Isaac had gone to Jewish school and knew how to read holy books in stolen from him anyway. He lived among thieves. The gems were a cause of fights between prisoners that occasionally resulted in death. He would not risk his life. He knew that his life there did not have any value to others, so he was cautious.

The adults engaged in some childhood activities, such as playing games. The thieves played cards for stolen stones, which they hid from the guards. Political prisoners did the same but played chess instead. As a child, Isaac had learned to play both games. In his village, cards and chess had been popular. Isaac's father was famous for his hospitality, and in his house, he and his friends always played cards, chess, checkers, dominoes, and Bahamas. He taught his children how to recognize cheating in cards. The parents taught their children how to spot chicanery. Isaac saw that in prison, many thieves broke the criminal law and played with marked cards. He did not care. He was able to memorize any deck and did not need any marks. His father had taught him the first rule: if a card player did not know how to play and knew the cards of his partners, then that information was useless for him. Most important was the knowledge of how to play. Isaac memorized the deck. He did not care about marks. He played not to win but to survive. He always was hungry and cold. He played for little things, such as pieces of bread or leftovers from a bowl of soup. His biggest win was a pair of socks.

## Prison Informers

Isaac reckoned that the snitches lost any fear. All the important jobs were held by criminals who cooperated with the guards and ratted on other prisoners. They were

were obedient to their kingpins. With the permission of the guards, the kingpins ruled the prison.

There were women in the prison too. They were victims. They suffered from cold and hunger even more than the men did. They worked in mines. The way for women to avoid victimization was to become the mistresses of kingpins. Many who could not keep powerful men became prostitutes. They provided sexual services for a bread ration or for a little tobacco, which could be exchanged for bread. The structure of the prison was a little model of the society adulterated by infection. The guards were the ultimate authority, but the prison was actually run by criminal authorities. In the harsh environment of prison was a man who was not a rough thief but able to protect his woman. He was not a kingpin. His name was Isaac Kaufman.

Isaac reported that Kolyma was worse than any other prison. Kolyma River was a big cemetery. Many habitants found death there. One could end up in prison for criticizing life in the killing field. All year round, the prisoners searched for diamonds in Kolyma River. It was impossible to escape from the tundra. Sometimes prisoners were allowed to go to a nearby village for supplies, coal, or feed for the horses. Naturally, the guards were concerned with the safety of the gems and watched to make sure prisoners did not take them to the village. Prisoners who took gems out of the camp to the village were usually executed.

In his life, Isaac saw many remarkable gems. He spent all day in the cold water, digging and washing the dirt to find one beauty. It was difficult. Nevertheless, he enjoyed gems. He adored their size, shape, and color. He knew all the gradations of gems, which was knowledge the other prisoners did not have. When he found gems, he would not hide them. He did not have a place to keep them. He knew that gems would be

Diamonds and gold were found in Kolyma in the far north. In that area, it was very cold, and only a small population resided there. Prisoners were not the towns' habitants and villagers. Kolyma River was a big depot where many were sent just for being rich. The prisoners did not have appropriate clothes, nutritious food, or even a warm place to sleep. They were sent there to die. No one cared. The place was the biggest area in the country and could accommodate many prisoners. Among the prisoners were informers who reported to the guards, but their tattling did not help much.

Being an informer in Aborigin was not a shield from being arrested. After reporting on habitants, informers were arrested too. That was one reason Kolyma was called the heart of the planet. It was unavoidable. Every member of collectivist thinking could end up there. The prison sentences were impossible to predict. No one was immune to the horror of being sent to Kolyma. Every member of collectivist thinking knew that Kolyma was large and had enough space for everyone. Journeys on the Kolyma River seemed long. The work was too difficult for the hungry, who were also dressed too lightly for the cold weather.

Nonetheless, prisoners believed in miracles. Desperate prisoners played cards to win loaves of bread or warm clothes. They gave up the last thing in their possession for a shot at more. Kolyma's prisoners could not have survived without fairy tales. They told stories that were impossible to believe. They talked about lucky winnings. Cheating at cards in criminal society was not acceptable. It was like taking from prisoners their belief in marvels. Honesty in the game was safeguarded by criminal law. In a prison's hierarchy, the prisoners were distinguished by their social makeup. The goners and kerns did most of the work. The so-called servants, known by the number six,

In Kolyma, there were a lot of political prisoners, along with burglars, pickpockets, bandits, and thieves. The political prisoners had their own groups. The criminals had more privileges than political prisoners because the commissars perceived the criminals to be socially desirable. They said that because of the inequality of the past, bandits were victims of an unfair distribution of wealth. Thus, they had been forcefully pushed into criminal activities. The criminals, not the guards, ran the camp. Isaac was strong and tried to survive. He'd lived in the village all his life and had done different types of jobs. He was also a good chess and card player. He used his skills to play chess with political prisoners, who, by their status, did not play cards. He played cards with thieves who amused themselves by playing cards during their free time. Prisoners had little food, but Isaac was able to win a little bit of food from criminals. The guards secured the perimeter of the camp. They allowed the criminal groups to control food and work assignments. Some criminals had a lot of power, and they could decide who lived and who died. In general, they were fair. The criminal code was more lenient than indoctrinated rules. The commissars believed in slavery. Some jittery prisoners were able to avoid death because the guards were not completely in charge. Otherwise, everyone would have died in no time.

## Isaac and the Dangers of Kolyma

*M*any times, Isaac recalled the horror of Kolyma River. He wanted to understand how, despite those misfortunes, he'd been able to get the woman of his dreams and diamonds.

joke that asked why a member of the killing field did not inform the police of his own daily activities. The answer was that he forgot. The punch line of the joke was that the other members did not expect that kind of behavior. Everyone was surprised. They did not comprehend how that kind of unordinary conduct took place. Eventually, they found out what happened and why the member tainted by infection forgot to inform. It happened because the member knocked back a couple drinks and lost his vigilance. He was punished because his drinking companions reported. The answer to the joke was simple and realistically displayed the situation. The conclusion was that the member did not have any excuse for not informing and must not forget to inform even if he had a few drinks. The member was reprimanded and sent to Kolyma River. The point was that everyone should be sure he or she was the first to inform. Strangely, after that joke spread, no one was laughing.

In the north of Siberia, prisoners were exterminated on a colossal scale. Kolyma was a region in the far northeast of the communal society. It shared a boundary with the Arctic. The climate there was the most severe in the world. It was believed that Kolyma was a death sentence for prisoners. There it was cold, but prisoners did not have warm clothes and had little food. They did not have protection against blackflies, midges, and mosquitoes. In the camps, prisoners got sick and died every day. Isaac was lucky to be alive. The prisoners lived in barracks and slept on wooden benches with six prisoners in a row to keep warm. All six criminals were the servants of a major thief and were known by the number six, which was the lowest position in the prison's hierarchy. More important prisoners had fewer than six prisoners sleeping together. Only a few had beds with bedsheets, pillowcases, mattresses, and blankets.

north by ship. The majority of passengers with him on the ship were prisoners who had been arrested for so-called counterrevolutionary activities. Isaac's life was handled by the slave camp's administration, primarily the main directorate of corrective labor camps. In the slave camps, millions were wiped out by harsh conditions. Isaac ended up in the labor slave camp on the Kolyma River with a ten-year sentence that was equivalent to death in prison. It was impossible to get out of prison because there were no cities around, only tundra as far as the eye could see for hundreds of miles. The camp had all the attributes of a servile habitation, including millions of goners as slaves. It was an administration of slave drivers. Brainwashed habitants did not feel any compassion toward the slaves of the communalist society.

Stool pigeons were part of the system. The ugliest display of the sick relations in the land unclean with perdition was in the enormous amount of freelance finks. They reported on every step of their neighbors. To continuously increase the number of slaves, the infected had the help of stool pigeons. The psychological germs led to symptoms that activated many hideous traditions, including betrayal, manipulation, and vile behavior toward others. Most informers did not bother to sign their denunciations and just identified themselves as "well-wishers." They did not snitch for money. Many were empowered by their hatred. It was an easy way to get rid of someone undesirable or someone they perceived as annoying. Many informed because of a fear that someone else could be faster to report, and they would be charged as accomplices. Interestingly, being finks did not protect them. If a stool pigeon was reported on by someone else, he got in trouble just as his victims did. In a communal setting, being an informer did not offer much protection. However, it gave a sense of power and a feeling of superiority. There was a

The opposite of beauty was ugliness. Their malicious, dreadful social structure was presented as the glory of collectivist thinking. It took away freedom. Slavery was everywhere in the communalist society: in factories, on farms, in prisons, and more. The majority of slaves were in prison. They lived in cities and the countryside. They were provided with all the basic expediencies. They lived in their communal apartments and had worker uniforms and some food. On the farms, slaves were put to work for free. They did not have the right to travel or any other freedoms.

Aaron pondered that far-fetched dogma was a master of fooling. The whole population was enslaved by it. The slaves of collectivist thinking lived in rotten conditions. They lived in places enclosed by barbed wire, with guards and dogs watching them and preventing their escape. They were deprived of appropriate housing, protective clothing, and nutritious food. Many were detained in purification or slave camps designed to exterminate them. Slavery emphasized the idea of complete ownership and control by a master. It was a state of subjugation that involved captivity, burdensome and degrading labor, and bondage to a cruel master. Individual slaves could be transferred to prisons if they denied the doctrine and declared that killing and robbing innocents was unfair.

## Slavery at the Kolyma River

Isaac reported that the infection easily turned the whole of Aborigin into a slave state. The police sent some slaves to Kolyma to fulfill the quota. Isaac was transferred to the to the wonder of the world. Many uninfected habitants were subdued by the beauty of gems and became involved in the diamond trade. Most importantly, diamond lovers knew and respected each other. They talked about their purchases and warned others about scammers, swindlers, and police informers. The radicals in leather jackets, with their stupid rhetoric, could not purge diamond devotees of their passion.

Even though it was dangerous to possess gems, the rich were united in their love of something stunning and dazzling. Many poor habitants also dreamed of having diamonds. The corrupt police waited for any pretext to confiscate diamonds. The thieves were after diamonds too. Only the brave habitants who had known each other for a long time were able to trust and cooperate with others. They trusted each other with their lives. The gemstones represented true beauty and were not for half-wits but only for the advanced. The trend continued, even though it was as if diamond lovers were underneath the sword of Damocles.

Psychological germs had influenced and inflamed the primitive mob, who acted as savages. The half-wits were destroying the lovers of diamonds. *Classical Myth and Legend* said that Dionysus, a tyrant of Syracuse, would force a habitant to sit with a sword over his or her head, suspended by a hair, to demonstrate fidelity to the king. Life in Aborigin was tense, but the diamond lovers believed that something should remain stable in a time of confusion and chaos. The role of stability was assigned to diamonds, which always were a symbol of beauty and an antipode to cruelty. Diamond connoisseurs were united to worship perfection that was contrary to contrived doctrine. Gems were not tangential and could be seen and measured.

The most hidden evil of the collectivist thinking was slavery. The collective forced habitants to live in captivity.

Fidelity to diamonds was a form of resistance to demons. Diamonds were an opposition to deceitful doctrine in the same way that honesty and sophistication were to ugliness and primitive behaviors. Unfortunately, there were men everywhere who lied about their selflessness, ideologically correct behavior, incorruptibility, crystal-clear honesty, and devotion to the party line. They were commissars.

Contrary to the infectious phraseology, diamonds were symbols of love, family values, and loveliness. Diamonds could not deceive because the differences between diamonds were not hidden and were easy to recognize. Females around the world dreamed of having gems. A real man, to please his sweetheart, brought her diamonds as an expression of his love. Even habitants in dark areas of the world knew about diamonds. The gems were judged by size, color, and clarity. The shape of a diamond could influence its color and create liveliness and sparks. Different cuts created reflections of different angles and lighting around the gem. The diamonds were crafted into geometrically precise forms. Jewelers were druids of the stones. Jews had discovered the miracle beauties of diamonds and were the best jewelers. They were druids of gems. The untrained eye could not understand the small differences between gems. Experts in diamonds knew their every color and shape. Exceptional stones were photographed and depicted in paintings. Yellow diamonds, or canary diamonds, were less popular. That attitude was reflected in human relations. In many cultures, if habitants wanted to degrade others, they called them yellow. Taste in diamonds sometimes changed. Habitants enjoyed black diamonds, but white and other colors were still desirable.

Jewelers as well as anyone who had handled diamonds and had a deep knowledge of gems were not easy targets to brainwash because they were not simpletons and were close for building materials. The deceptive, primitive doctrine became more important than the Bible, which enlightened the world with humanity, law, and wisdom. Meanwhile, the collective proclaimed to the world that their military was the most sophisticated of all. They bragged about the possibility of taking over the whole world.

In Aaron's thoughts, the rulers of the territory, fouled by infection, resembled the feudal lords of the East. There was no difference in reality. The rulers captured a lot of territories. They kept their territories with an iron fist. In the killing fields, the worst parts of medieval times came back. The new sovereigns brought back the horrors of primitive times. Their existence resembled the times of the Mongol invasion, when the land was split into principalities. In medieval times, the lords of principalities were always ready to grab more from others. They fought each other for power, land, and influence. They killed habitants, took their land and possessions, and enslaved men and women. They were quick to trick, poison, humiliate, and torture. The commissars did the same and even more. The only difference was that in medieval times, the feudal lords were chosen by their special blood connections. In the killing field, rulers were chosen differently. To keep their positions, commissars continuously restated distorted doctrine and praised Supreme Leader.

In the killing field, honesty stopped. The dishonest tricksters were opposed by small acts of decency. There existed only one beauty that was not easy to destroy. It was unquestionable that the beauty of gems stood in opposition to the ugliness. For many years, gems had been a symbol of elegance, taste, and style. In contrast to the wicked social structure, they were splendid. In the subsoil of the terrain were many marvelous treasures. Jewels were the beauty of the earth. Many minds enjoyed the majesty of gemstones.

## The Chastised Farmers

*M*illions of prosperous farmers were accused of being enemies of the state and, without any court procedures, were ultimately convicted and imprisoned. In that region, right away, there was a shortage of food and other necessities. The propagandists told lies. They blamed the shortage on the fact that there were traitors everywhere. The doctrine was a vermin that harmed the national economy. They were transforming normal habitants into zombies. They would not accept that they were vermin and infected habitants. As a result of the illness, the masses acted like imbeciles, because only the foolish could have believed in the sickening propaganda. The infected destroyed the fruitful fields that in the past had had great agronomy and exported food products around the world. It was remarkable how quickly the best agriculture was destroyed. In the famine, tens of millions died in Malantia and other areas.

To keep obedience in the region, the pseudocommunal regime created slave prisons specifically for miserable farmers. The propagandists had the difficult job of proving that the system worked. They did not try to find out the reason for inequality in farming. They did not find a method of enriching barren terrain. By using killing and lies, they succeeded in brainwashing. With help from the secret police, they silenced the whole population. The habitants were scared. Many waited to be arrested. They were anxious to prove their fidelity to the communal regime and enthusiastically informed on their neighbors. Priests, ministers, mullahs, and rabbis were in prison. Churches, temples, and mosques were converted to storage

Leo Tolstoy wrote about habitants with high moral standards. They were spirited aristocrats with nobility, honor, and pride. They gave their lives to defend their morality.

The collective ruined literature. The pseudocelestials laughed at complexity and promoted primitivism. They interpreted the sophisticated feelings of the heroes in Tolstoy's and Dostoevsky's books in a primitive way. Further, schoolteachers condemned them as outdated. Their biggest con was a fable about the unfairness of wealth distribution being the cause of all evil. As a matter of fact, the pseudocelestials did not share equally in the distribution of their newly acquired fortunes. They took for themselves everything they could. Their role model was the Thief of Baghdad, a petty bazaar thief. There was no morality in Aborigin.

The people infected by sickness did not like stability. Leaders did not want to deliver any of their promises. The Prolet-Aryan salamanders gave themselves permission to destroy lives and break apart families, leaving children without parents. Pervasive suggestions were everywhere. The pseudocelestials promised that a perfect world would come soon. They brainwashed the naive and created unrealistic expectations. They were not able to provide people with anything. They also were the biggest accusers in the world. They blamed everyone and everything. The general was a victim of brainwashing as well as a target of primitive abuse. The little bit of leftover conscience was the reason the Founder of the collective was disappointed and reversed the process of his habitants' stultification. He had a splash of common sense, but soon after, his heart unexpectedly stopped. He was an example of the imprudence of having any conscience in the killing field.

assigned different IQs that were impossible to change. Their intelligence was a hereditary quality in the same way that beauty and ugliness were genetic.

For some habitants, unfairness began at birth and without any unfair distribution of wealth. Morons always would be morons. Some habitants were born with low intelligence, a lack of business skills, and ugliness in appearance. The White Army general did not consider himself highly intelligent. He did not value his exceptional ability to learn strategy, tactics, and military maneuvers. He denied the fact that inequality was part of existence. He repudiated the fact that his intellectual capacity was not equal to that of one with a low IQ. Only shortly before the morons in power executed him did he realize their stupidity. He finally understood the realities of life, but it was too late. The general was wrong to join the bandits and terrorists of the Red Army, who took habitants' wealth by force. He was killed because he was too smart. He was not equal to cretins and imbeciles, and they understood that.

## Leo Tolstoy and Fyodor Dostoevsky

*F*yodor Dostoevsky wrote about the struggle of being antisocial and the nature of ethically skewed minds. In his books, the characters were fragments of one psyche, illustrating the complexity of thought. He wrote about struggles of the human psyche and different forces that split the psyche into different fragments. His work also declared that the consensus of the less corrupt and uninfected proved that pseudodoctrine was a joke.

## Trade Unions

*U*nlike the approach of indoctrination in the killing field, trade unions provided protection for the disadvantaged. In civilized countries, they were more honest than corrupt pseudocelestials. With unions, instead of killing and torture, the underprivileged had social protection. They were aware and knew their rights in the distribution of wealth. According to *Wikipedia*, one of a trade union's main aims was defending and advancing the interests of its members in the workplace. Trade unions worked independently from any employers. If a worker needed protection, he or she joined a trade union. The infected field was not educated in employee relationships and did not believe in trade unions.

In an unjust and savage world, the profanity damaged habitants' thought processes. The population, infected by toxins of frenzy, had many antisocial and sociopathic men. They did not experience guilt or shame when they took from others. Further, they were proud of duping someone who trusted them. As thieves, they felt entitled to everything that was not theirs. The false Prolet-Aryans had false trade unions. They were part of false dogma. Ruination had broken different fates and enrolled bamboozled assholes as orators. Even the White Army's general became a Red Army officer. The general was a smart man, but he was brainwashed with ideas of social equality and fair distribution of wealth. He overlooked the fact that it was unfair to take someone else's fortune by force. He felt that life should be fair to everyone. He did not accept that life was fundamentally unfair. The biggest instance of unfairness happened during birth, when newborns were

## Byelogorians Were Special

*I*saac declared that Byelogorians were different from Aboriginians, who were frequently mixed with the Golden Horde. In the past, Byelogorians had not mixed much with the Golden Horde. They had better Slavic genes and were not easily infected by psychological disease. They were culturally close to Lithuanians and Poles. Aboriginians treated them differently from Malantians. They did not claim they shared the same history or were the same habitants. They allowed Byelogorians to have their own place in history. In Byelogoria, many ethnicities coexisted peacefully, including Malantians, Jews, and Aboriginians. Jews, as in everywhere else in Europe, were assimilated. As with other ethnicities, they had suffered from affliction and been deprived of law and justice.

Isaac spelled out that the goal of pseudocelestials was indoctrination of idiots. The killing field, infected by dangerous bugs, created a fake police force. The police were without any control. They declared that they did not require any new knowledge or schooling. They felt they were especially smart and knew how to protect the killing field. A bunch of uneducated fools replaced criminologists. Because they did not know any books of law, the police were worse than any criminals were. The only way to please them was by bribing them. Women traded sex for their security. Rednecks were lustful pigs and enjoyed the opportunity to use their position to abuse women and find slaves for pseudocelestials.

in frigid Siberia. Their neighbors became their victims. The whole world resented the vile habitants. Most saw their behavior as damaging and deranged. They were an insult to the human race. They killed Czar Nicolas, the head of a dynasty that for many centuries had given them food, warm dwellings, and the possibility to succeed in their endeavors. They killed the czar's entire family and ransacked his house. The Prolet-Aryans isolated themselves from any moral values. They spread an epidemic around the globe. They did not have much in the way of brains and wanted others to be similar. They infected a lot of habitants, who acted like stooges. Eventually, the rich and prosperous terrain ended up poor and isolated. The mamzer wanted to be legitimate.

## Way to Freedom, Part 6

Prolet-Aryans created the Iron Curtain around Aborigin. They put themselves against the Aryans and won. Eventually, the butchers and silly maniacs, the monsters of the Holocaust, were put to sleep. The war ended. The villain's body burned. The occupied and destroyed Aryan region was forced to pay retribution to the victorious winner. Infected conquerors sent the defeated scientists and soldiers to work and used them as slaves. By using their work, they were able to extend their miserable existence. With the help of captured experts, Prolet-Aryans acquired modern technology. They used any opportunity to enslave scientists and threaten their neighbors. As a result of their menace, the world was always on guard.

mainly as an ant heap. He did not care how destructive his paranoia was or how many died. Superior Leader did not care that an odor of dirt, dust, and dishonesty was around his name. In his paranoia, he acted filthily and violently. Being a gangster, he did not know a more appropriate response. He was a page of horror in communal history. He reversed the new processes and pulled out the old working-class hegemony.

Professor Kryvoruchko stated that in the opinion of many spectators, paranoid Superior Leader was probably one of the players who'd arranged the killing of the Founder. Psychological infection again took over the big cities and little villages. The situation was out of hand and reached a dramatic scale. Manipulation was everywhere. Many habitants lost their human status. They became Prolet-Aryans and pretended to be from redneck families. They mocked fairness, and they were vigilante watchdogs for righteousness. They justified their passion for kleptomania. They felt that behavior was necessary for better social groups. They believed in the doctrine that claimed the prosperous habitants of a higher socioeconomic level were robbing the poor. In their opinion, they themselves were not robbers but claimants. They were taking back what they thought was theirs. They wanted to take the space occupied by their enemies and build a new reality. Prolet-Aryans wanted to show their skills and prove their superiority. They introduced the red terror, and their hands were drenched in blood. Instead of learning how to have prosperity, they were attackers and rapists.

Professor Kryvoruchko recognized that while using slogans of fairness, the perdition did horrible things. The red terror justified confiscating, robbing, torturing, breaking in, and killing. Collectivists sent habitants to die to be rich. Thus, he could not accept the dusty and smelly atmosphere of communal habitation. As soon as he saw the results of the butchery he'd created, he became disillusioned. He changed his attitude. He decided to move from fictitious and unreachable dreams to reality. As a result, he scratched most of the idiotic postulates of his theory.

Under fresh directives, things changed. Previously, in his dealings as a university dropout, he'd received a higher standing by bashing educated habitants. He shared his revolutionary delusions with the masses. First of all, he wrote a book about how a small group of terrorists could take over a big state and install a communal regime. He achieved what he preached. He was the number-one terrorist home-wrecker. Apparently, at the end of his life, he decided he did not like what he had done. In the past, he'd given his heart only to the working class. According to his new attitude, different backgrounds could be useful. Commerce invited habitants from various classes to produce. It stopped the onslaught of political correctness and everyone who was not suitable to his doctrine. The new proposal shook the postulate of the hegemony of working-class habitants. Without that postulate, future supreme leaders had difficulty in brainwashing their subjects. Not many leaders liked it.

## The Founder's Burial

When the renovated Founder died, immediately, the killing field's new economic reality reversed. The new superior leader was paranoid. He saw the infected locality mobs. He promoted a realm infected by ruination as the most progressive state, more advanced than the states of Europeans and Americans. Normally, nations learned from history, but he claimed Aboriginians must learn from doctrine. He believed the collective regime could spread around the whole world. It was a fantasy. The world would not buy it.

The killing field's past was enlightened by Peter the Great and Catherine the Great. They acted as agents of a European lifestyle. Peter the Great opened the homeland and its primitive lifestyle to the influence of sophisticated European customs. Peter the Great encouraged his subjects to shave their beards, drink coffee, and wear fashionable garments. Catherine the Great persuaded her lieges to follow elegant European etiquette and loved bijouterie, fancy dresses, and handsome attire for men. She danced ballroom dances. In her time, habitants socialized as ladies and gentlemen. The crackpot Founder acted no differently from other kings. He suffered from grandiosity. He wanted Europeans to learn from Aboriginians. After the Founder's innovations, the next antisocial leaders arrived. The Founder's reforms were forgotten.

## Founding Father, the Lunatic

Professor Kryvoruchko explained that Founding Father, who created the infected doctrine, was a lunatic who grew up in a rich family. He had a prosperous home and was nicknamed Redhead. His mother loved social balls, the theater, and fashionable clothes. He knew what it meant that the idea was nonsense and decided to stop the circle of lies. With his new ordinance, he ended the junket of the beast. All of a sudden, he brought to collective thinking more realistic ideas. The unrealistic thoughts were not valid anymore. The regime no longer used the slogan that every working-class villager had inherited business orientation and organizational talents. By his new decree, the business-oriented habitants from different social groups were moved to higher scale. They no longer were called class enemies and instead were labeled tolerable entities. According to a new regulation supported by the Founder, friendly, business-oriented habitants could be from diverse classes. He called on villagers to learn business and protect what was theirs. The renewed Founder opened up business opportunities for every class. His motivation for going against his own teachings was unknown.

The many pseudocelestials did not like those changes. Soon a sudden sickness befouled the Founder. The sudden demise of all his newborn ideas followed. Pseudocelestials appreciated his unexpected passing. Even though he'd been an unpredictable oaf, his life had triggered the gratitude of forgiving terrestrials. After his death, his corpse was placed in the box called the Mausoleum in Red Square, next to the Kremlin. His new deeds were shattered. Business orientation once again became anathema. After him, the locality had many supreme leaders who acted as morons. As the designer of doctrine, the dead Founder remained on display in Red Square.

The innovative Founder of doctrine had made a sudden move that looked more refined. Even after his reform was stopped, people worshipped him as a king. He was a populist who knew how to lure hungry habitants. He was a shrewd and antisocial politician. He placated uneducated superhuman and were successful managers. They aggrandized one who did not have business skills but had an Aryan ethnicity. The brainwashed simpletons used that crap as an argument. In Aborigin, imbeciles wanted to be smart. They bragged about their Prolet-Aryan origin. They were goons who cited the postulates of false doctrine. The goons felt entitled and were ready to use nonsense and filthiness to keep power in the wasteland. They destroyed any bright gleams of talent in others just to prove they could do it.

Professor Kryvoruchko figured out the reason so many Jews became followers of Founding Father, who promised equality: resistance to prejudice. Many villages were against Jews who did not work on the land. They believed that many ethnicities lived in their territory and brought the fruits of their labor in one sack. They had land to work, but Jews and Gypsies in particular were not attached to any area and seemed to have everything in an easy way. Many farmers thought Jews were living on the land of other ethnicities and benefited from others' territory. The Jews were called parasites by the prejudiced.

## The Founder Father

*T*he new oppression came from the doctrine of the Founder, who, on top of being sick in his body, was sick in his head. Nevertheless, he had a moment when a flash of reality occurred. For some unknown reason, he was able to see that slogans about housekeepers being managers of large factories did not work. Eventually, he understood followed by counterprogramming. Some interventions of counterprogramming were equal to a vaccine. The lucky population left the dangerous place. Only when removed from the disease-ridden land were habitants able to assert who they really were. They realized they were not puppets but individuals with solid psyches. The infected were not totally lost; their salvation was possible.

Aaron knew that the many miserable did not have any place to go. They were deluded by the psychological sickness. Therefore, slavery was possible. The Founder, the creator of doctrine and a complete lunatic, made untested assertions that hardworking industrial workers could easily replace business-oriented habitants. The notion was nonsense. Even a little child could have understood that the workers, even those who were honest and had the best imaginable work ethic, did not know how to manage a business. Miraculously, some of them were able to learn new skills, but it took them a long time. Aboriginians' inability to achieve any targetable results stemmed from mismanagement and a big layer of bureaucracy. In the end, they were not able to accomplish anything. Their work was unproductive and became expensive. In their plans, instead of saving money, the simpletons lost it. The new design required some knowledge of how to manage and how to calculate the reliability and validity of a project. It was also necessary to acquire some academic knowledge about the subject of interest. The killing field placed unjustifiable expectations on the uneducated, who were not able to produce results, and then they punished someone else for their failures.

Indoctrination was used to successfully deceive habitants with the same nonsense. The Nazis declared that habitants who were of Aryan descent were basically disagreed. The mystery of European Jews continued. Whether European Jews ever were in Israel or had the same ancestors as other Jewish groups were questions that carried on.

The *New York Times* questioned the origin of the Ashkenazi. An article titled "Are They 'Jews' or Are They Really Khazars?" stated,

By reconstructing the Yiddish mother tongue, linguists hope to plot the migration of the Jews and their language with a precision never possible before. It had even been suggested by a few researchers, on the basis of linguistic evidence, that the Jews of Eastern Europe were not predominantly part of the Diasporas from the Middle East, but were members of another ethnic group that adopted Judaism.

Everything became more complicated, and it was unclear when educated habitants analyzed those different elements. A good instance of such analysis appeared in Paul Kriwaczek's book *Yiddish Civilization: The Rise and Fall of a Forgotten Nation*. The book contained detailed, convincing documentation that Yiddish-speaking Jews were descendants of the Diaspora. In contrast, for the simpletons, everything was usually not easy and not clear.

## An Efficient Way to Save the Brain

*B*y studying brainwashing and indoctrination, Professor Kryvoruchko comprehended that the most efficient way to save one's brain from inflammable, idiotic persuasions was isolation from the harmful source,

Malantians, but the resemblance to Aboriginians was more distant. In their relations with Malantians, Aboriginians claimed Malantian history as their own. The big brothers did not climb into Byelogorian history. They left them alone, and Byelogorians were independent. Aboriginians did not claim the Byelogorians were not independent. Byelogorians shared part of their history only with Lithuanians. They had never been part of the Golden Horde. The Byelogorians had their own history. They were independent from everyone.

## Ashkenazi Jews

Many scholars also talked about the Ashkenazi, European Jews who had distinguished characteristics that stood apart from those of other Jewish groups. Kevin Alan Brook once wrote, "East European Jews descended both from Khazarian Jews and from Israelite Jews, although few subsequent genetic tests found the little trace of Khazarian ancestry in any modern Jewish population." Different writers had arguments for and against that proposition. Many of the writers made naive simplifications. Eastern European Jewish ancestry was "more complex than previously envisioned." Some said it had roots in European countries. Many concepts stood the same test of time as other arguments. Other writers implied they had genetic evidence of Armenian, Greek, Italian, French, Berber, Slavic, and Chinese introgressions into the Eastern European Jewish gene pool. A few argued that a Khazarian core element was missing, but some about language barriers or relations with customers and suppliers. He felt confident and knew what to do. Many habitants called themselves business-oriented but were not. They were in businesses inherited from relatives or were business associates with talented partners and became successful by sheer luck. In Italy, Aaron unexpectedly entered the business world. He occasionally supplied merchandise to demanding customers. Aaron received many chances, and he was able to focus on the winning ones. The Italian market was new for him, but he did not become stunned or confused. He felt energetic and happy because of his freedom. Later, in Canada, he made a fortune and provided a good life for his family. He contributed to many charities.

## About Byelogorians

Byelogorians were different from Aboriginians. Genetically, Byelogorians had close similarities to Poles. They belonged to the same group. A study of the Y chromosome in East Slavic groups showed there was no significant variation in the Y chromosome between Byelogorians and Malantians. That fact and their vast similarities thus revealed an overwhelmingly shared patrilineal ancestry. The genetic pattern of Byelogorians most closely resembled that of Malantians.

Byelogorians were known to their neighbors as Litviks. In the other words, Byelogorians had associations with Lithuanians but genetically were closer to Poles and Malantians. There was more similarity in lifestyle to the compliance. Most important of all, everyone who knew him was informed of what had happened. No one dared to challenge the criminal rules once criminal justice had been done to the wrongdoer. The criminals were serious about enforcing their rules and were not affected by feelings of mercy or compassion. The criminal code emphasized many unethical offenses, and cheating at cards was one of the worst. The punishment for that offense equated to collaboration with the police.

Aaron always felt the theory that communal life, a primitive lifestyle, was superior to sophistication was a deception. That point of view was primitive and saw only black and white. Life was a scary game, and survival required a lot of skill. Aaron's past imprisonments had been steps in the game of his life. Outside of the killing field, he was free and enjoyed his independence. He'd left behind an area of killing doctrine, where everything was fraudulent, and relationships were faked. Simplicity was a fake, and primitivism was a glorified sham. The investigation of politics and the killing of businesses were a mockery. Investigators used fake evidence and crooked logic. In the past, Aaron had sold a lot of fake items. Habitants did not have enough money for genuine diamonds, and Aaron sold them fake diamonds they could afford. The notion of having a good life was an unreachable fantasy, and the business-oriented habitants made money on fantasy. The false diamonds themselves were fantasy.

Aaron was a smuggler of his independent spirit and brought it out of collectivist thinking. Aaron smuggled out of the killing fields his Sailor's soul, which was untouched by society. His life force had a high value as great as a real diamond's. Because of his business orientation, Aaron discovered and implemented opportunities. He did not care

## The IQ Test of Cards

$\mathcal{A}$aron knew a lot about customs in the killing field. Cards provided an IQ test, proof of suitability, and career prospects. Habitants received promotions during card games with their superiors that they could not have received through hard work. Cards were played on different levels. Proficiency in a card game could be a ticket to higher levels of society. Card games were everywhere. Workers in factories played during breaks, homemakers played, and men at scientific institutes played, as did celestials and terrestrials. Card playing involved every level of society. Cards were an escape, pleasure, and means of winning. The lives of card players were full of excitement. Many immigrants wanted to try their luck and possibly become rich. Card houses were all around, with kingpins guaranteeing honest games. Cheating at cards, by the thieves' code, required severe punishment. The most common type of punishment was a group of criminals having the cheater in the ass.

The criminal code was stricter than any civic law and had different means of punishment. One form of punishment did not kill but instead transferred the cheater to a low life. In the eyes of others, the person was not clean, and everyone despised him. In jail, because he was filthy, he could not eat at the same table with others, and a dirty phrase, such as "Suck the dick," was scratched into his metal plate. Some penalties for breaking criminal concepts were worse than death because many unattached, free, and desirous women were in the killing field, and the stigma of a man being sexually used by other men was humiliating. The offender could be drugged and afterward beaten into cleanse the world of presumably inferior races. The führer had declared that all his associates were superhuman. His supremacy had become vicious. Without any regret, he'd butchered his own habitants and the citizens of other countries by throwing them into gas chambers. Then the commissars had purged the rich and noble.

Rich immigrants in Italy knew each other. They stayed connected after reaching the countries of their destination. Some became partners in business, and others simply stayed in the same social network. For immigrants from the killing field, Italy looked like a big Americano bazaar. It was their first experience with the spirit of the free market. It was a fantastic journey, but they wanted to settle permanently. Aaron's family chose Canada. In the future, Aaron opened a meat factory and then invested in butchery. He got rich and enjoyed his wealth.

Later in life, Aaron bought a house in Miami and took pleasure in being around his successful neighbors. During his life in the West, he did not lose contact with other immigrants. Florida was a state populated by prosperous compatriots from the killing field. In Miami, he bought a house close to his friends. Whenever Aaron heard Canadian or American hymns, he would cry and think about his late father, Isaac; his father's friends; and his relatives around the world. He spent summers in Montreal, an international city, where he had another house. In the winter, he moved to Miami. He often visited Jewish districts of both cities, where he would eat fresh bagels, pastrami, and matzo ball soup.

primitivism won, while fairness lost. Aaron was immune to the illness.

In communal thinking, habitants played a variety of games underground. Most of the games were products of the shadow economy of the black market. It was impossible to kill a game because life itself was a game. Humans were alive when they calculated different probabilities and chose the best possible conditions. Aaron resented any possibilities that involved criminal activities. He wanted to immigrate to a nation that was quiet. An honest game could be anywhere, but he did not want a spotlight placed on him in connection to his old friends. He was not comfortable having his past exposed. In the USA, there were too many compatriots, and he did not like revelations and commotion. He also was troubled when around habitants who cheated in their enterprises and used a criminal attitude in business. He was not a prison type and had been incarcerated only because the killing field did not allow room for entrepreneurship. He wanted to play an honest game and do business the right way because in his opinion, only pathetic players cheated. Aaron and his family wanted to go to Canada. His son, Sam, convinced him that in Canada, he could play an honest game. Aaron did not know that Sam had been given an assignment to go to Canada.

Nevertheless, in the West, Aaron had a different life. In his past, Aaron had found it impossible to trust a nation with an epidemic. Everything in Aborigin was a lie. Aaron felt he'd wasted a big part of his life. He remembered his life in the communal setting as if it were a movie. He thought that maybe everything was unstable because of the solar activity. As a result, there'd been the Patriotic War. The Nazis had talked about a special mission to had coached him on what to say. He asked to exchange a doll for a place on the market to sell Aaron's merchandise. Later, Luigio was always around to help Aaron.

Another Italian, Luke, was not connected with the collective. Luka had been in Odessa during the Second World War and helped many Jews. He continued to have many Jewish friends in the killing field and continued to conduct business with them. He was delighted to work with Jews because he knew the generosity and kindness of his friends. Because of business connections and sentiments about mystical Aborigin, Luka was always ready to help. He also had connections to the Italian Mafia, which made him useful. He could fix everything from legal problems to financial contraband. He was trusted and smuggled currency, transferring rubles to dollars.

Habitants in the pseudocommunal setting would give Luka's friend Russian rubles, and their relatives around the world would receive dollars in return. Luka did opposite transfers; when people gave him dollars, he would deliver rubles to their poor relatives in the killing field. In his life, many things, on first glance, looked simple but, given a second look, were not so. Luka did not help Aaron without receiving benefits of his own. He knew that Aaron, whom his friend had referred, was business-oriented and could help him in business. He knew where to place his bets. Aaron was a skillful gambler. Around him, nothing was simple. As a result, the immigrants looked for his help and were driven to him. Many immigrants consulted him, and he was glad to help. He made up winning games for them. Because they were fed up with simplicity, they asked for something more sophisticated. Infection by psychological germs destroyed complicity. Diseased dogma always declared that fairness triumphed. In reality, only

Aaron might not have been a perfect person, but he was not a drifter. He was a Sailor. He was an individual outside of collectivist thinking. In Italy, he was not confused and used every minute to enjoy his freedom. His life was good. In a communal setting, he was like a worm who lived in a deep hole. He avoided the bright light. In Italy, he did not want any lights focused on him or his family. In his life, dark forces did not want to leave him alone. He defended himself by using skills that had helped him survive in the killing field.

## Aaron's Freedom

*I*n Italy, Aaron was a free man and kept away from criminals. He was happy, but not everyone could get away from the collective. One Italian somehow became his friend. Luigio emerged in Aaron's life not by chance. He had an agenda. During the Second World War, he'd been taken captive as a war prisoner of the collectivists. To survive in prison, he'd signed an agreement to cooperate with the secret police. He'd become a stool pigeon and informed on other prisoners. He thought the past was gone, but it came back. After many years of silence, he received an order to help Aaron. In the beginning, Luigio thought Aaron was an agent of the secret police as well, but later, he had orders to report to Sam. He was also instructed that he should not talk to Aaron about his business with Sam. Luigio was a small-time businessman at the flea market. He met Aaron in the Americano. It looked like a coincidence. He made Aaron a proposition he could not refuse. In reality, Sam punishments. Givi agreed to everything and complied with all the conditions. Aaron's family kept the secret. Nevertheless, the incident somehow got out. Perhaps because of that incident or any number of others, Spider was killed in a skirmish.

Looking back, Aaron wanted to understand what about his behavior had brought him such conflict. It seemed he'd done everything right to avoid confrontation. He had wished to evade it, but instead, the opposite had taken place. In Italy, the liberty was overwhelming, but Aaron was modest and avoided stupid bravado. He did not create clashes. He just followed his family's traditions. For recreation, he enjoyed himself with card games. He played not for money but only for relaxation, and his hobby had gotten him in trouble. Accidentally, he'd come into the view of rogues. Among the immigrants were criminally oriented characters. One of his guests had been a loquacious person who brought his name to the attention of rogues. However, as a result, he'd overcome his challenges and made the lives of fellow immigrants much safer.

Because of the dregs, life in Rome was tense. The toughs took over the immigrant community. They advertised their kingpin and a place of gambling where immigrants could safely play cards. They discouraged expatriates from gambling in other places. They promised protection, but in reality, they were card sharks and dastardly villains. They cheated at cards. They did not want the immigrants to be out of their view. Among immigrants, playing cards and billiards was a common activity. The criminal kingpin, Givi, had a gambling house where immigrants were robbed of their money, even though the kingpin vouched that the place was safe. When Aaron stopped the lawlessness, everything was clear.

what had happened because Givi's substitution of a spurious card had been done so quickly. He asked himself if he might have been wrong. He also did not have any idea where Spider kept the original card. He took a big risk, but he was ready to take any risk necessary. He grew less anxious when he saw the big cuffs on Spider's shirt.

If something unforeseen were to happen, the card club had maneuvers and strategies to resolve the issue. Spider's thugs moved on Aaron to hurt him. Luigio took out his revolver and said, "Get back, bastards, or I'll shoot your heads off." The thugs complied. Uncle Cat took out his own false gun and pointed the false revolver at Givi. Sam and Vlad came closer to the card table. Aaron told Givi to open the cuffs on his shirt.

Because Givi had switched cards quickly, Aaron was simply guessing, but Givi did not have any other places to hide the switched card. Aaron understood that Givi was good with his hands. He'd spent his whole life swindling and cheating. Under a threat to his life, Givi complied. When Givi opened the cuffs, the original card dropped from his hand. Uncle Cat introduced himself and said he'd seen and recorded that violation of the thieves' code. He said it was a severe offense. He mentioned that he could kill Givi right then because Uncle Cat represented the thieves' gathering and would be reinforcing the thieves' code.

Because Givi's belief that he was special had been crushed, he was speechless. Eventually, he negotiated. He asked what condition would be required to end the situation peacefully. Aaron said they were not in prison and did not want the thieves' concepts continued in Italy. Nevertheless, he had his conditions. He proposed that Spider stop pimping girls, harassing their relatives, looting baggage, and threatening immigrants with bestial and best-looking man and did not have a girlfriend because no girl was a match for him. In reality, he was a narcissistic and conniving son of a gun.

Givi was manipulative, and Aaron used it against him. In the beginning, Vlad asked Spider for a rematch and said his father-in-law had an original old Breguet watch that had an archive registration in Switzerland and in Paris. The archives had sustained registration of Breguet watchmaking for more than two centuries. Abraham-Louis Breguet had had an incomparable career. Because his principal criterion had been preventing oxidation and corrosion, contemporary habitants could enjoy his wonderful creations.

Sam, Aaron's son, knew that Luigio had a pistol and wanted him to bring it to the card club. Finally, there was Uncle Cat, who had authority equivalent to that of a kingpin. He was supposed to watch Spider and make a signal with his hand when something was fishy. When all of them came to the card club, Vlad showed Spider the Brequet watch. He also mentioned that instead of him, Spider would play his father-in-law. Spider already knew something about Aaron. He remembered that an ordinary player had been able to beat Aaron. Givi took the offer and started to stir and shovel the cards from the new deck. Aaron understood that in the beginning, Spider would not do anything until his opponent got tired and inattentive. He was right, because the game continued for an hour, and Spider did not make a move. Uncle Cat sent signals with his hands several times, but they were false alarms, and nothing extraordinary happened. After one hour, Uncle Cat made a signal with his hands, and Aaron saw a different card.

Aaron stopped the game. He did not know for sure

He was careful not to create temptations for scammers, but if worse came to worst, he was ready. He was tough. He did not have any desire to be in the spotlight, but he could be deadly to offenders. In the past, everyone who'd wanted to get him had come to a bad end. The disgraceful kingpin did not know what kind of predicament he'd gotten himself into. As a result, Givi was later sorry he'd started his sting. He was not careful and overestimated his strength because he used the temptations of an enticing new land to make immigrants vulnerable to his manipulation.

## Misled Immigrants

*I*n Italy, many immigrants were tricked and later victimized. Givi and his collaborators designed games to patronize the naive and steal everything from them. He felt as if he owned the world. That feeling continued until he started swindling a gamer of a higher standard. Every game had a strategy that showed the character of a player. Aaron understood the personalities of players by analyzing their tactics. He was able to find the weak areas in bullies and put an end to harassment and manipulation.

The immigrants became victims of sadistic criminals. Girls were forced to do favors. Givi was heartless. He wanted only to dominate the powerless and confused. He was sadistic. Like an offended child, he got back at everyone who was around. His behavior had nothing to do with his sexual orientation. He was attracted to but never openly expressed his desires to have sex with men. He was close to his mother, who thought her son was the smartest

Givi had played him. When the debt became significant, Givi's bodyguards started to threaten him. They promised they would have Vlad's back—or, in less savory parlance, fuck him in the ass—if he did not pay. They scared him. Only then did he understand that he'd been lured like a little mouse into a trap. A long time ago, Aaron had told him that if he had problems, Aaron could help him. Now, at the most stressful time in his life, he would tell Aaron everything. After Vlad shared with his father-in-law his problem, Aaron decided to share it with Sam as well. The family stood up for Vlad.

The family got together, and the three of them designed a plan. Their plan also involved Luigio, Luka, and Uncle Cat. The plan was simple: Vlad would propose playing with Givi on Aaron's expensive Swiss Breguet watch, which his father, Isaac, had given him. Instead of his son-in-law, Aaron would get in the game. He found out that Spider liked watches and would do anything to win. If their plan did not work, Aaron had another plan that would involve his business partners, Luigio and Luka, as well as Luka's Mafia connections. Aaron covered all the different possible outcomes. He understood that the second plan required some investment because Mafia attendance was not free. Aaron was ready for any expense to help his son-in-law. He knew he, not Vlad, was the real target.

Givi played in an enclosed area, but Aaron knew everything he needed to know. If he failed with the first plan, his second plan was to accuse Spider of breaking the criminal code by forcing girls into prostitution. He knew that in life, anything could happen, and he could be a target of aggression and get seriously injured or killed. He did not remember that he ever had been eager to be in upstart places. He did not care to be higher up or in front of others.

was an ordinary player but felt he was above ordinary. He was flattered to play with Givi, the godfather of his locality. Vlad was naive and did not understand that Spider was creating a net to drag him into. He was immensely flattered to receive attention from the kingpin. Givi picked up the false diamonds and, with the false diamonds in tow, he and Vlad went to the card club near Fiumicino Airport.

Givi made a big show during the card game. He was losing and praised Vlad for a good game. Vlad was an ordinary player who simply hoped luck would be on his side. It did not work on Givi. Givi had played cards all his life and came from a family of card players. Perhaps among his coworkers at the textile factory Vlad was good, but there he was among high-level players. He was out of his league. Nevertheless, Vlad wanted to be an equal. Only much later he did realize his position in life. He was a disciple. As a follower, he became a successful man. As soon as he realized who he was, his position in the world changed. He became wealthy and had a hospitable house, an attractive wife, and three beautiful daughters.

## Vlad's Naïveté

*V*lad was green. He did not know that the naive were victimized by Givi, who skillfully placed immigrants in his cobweb. Vlad knew that Aaron did not value the false diamonds. He'd brought from home more than a few false diamonds, and he bet with them. Soon Vlad lost all his bets. He wanted to sustain his position in the game. He continued believing in his luck and did not understand that how to cheat with cards. He crafted a couple deceits on his own. He often cheated and was never caught. He was able to get every last penny from losers. Naturally, being a hypocrite, he would severely punish someone who was caught cheating. He savored his superiority over ordinary immigrants, such as Aaron, whom he underestimated.

Givi wanted to be famous and powerful. He rubbed his hands together in anticipation of an easy con. He was the biggest contributor to the common criminal fund used to bribe judges, help escapees, and pay many other expenses. He knew that as a kingpin, he had some dark spots in his inauguration. He believed he balanced them with his contributions to the thieves' fund. He was on a mission. For him, immigrants were mosquitoes who existed only to help him overcome the dark spots and make him great. Outside of his mother, Givi did not care about anyone. He shared with her his plans for fresh trickeries. He was always ready to design new swindles.

He started working on Aaron, who appeared to be easy prey. He right away connected the name to the man who'd protected the troublemaker and source of false diamonds. He wondered how much audacity someone must have to protect a troublemaker. He started to create his web. Spider's bodyguards approached Vlad and invited him to see Givi. Among immigrants, there were some who did not have many opportunities. Vlad was one of them. He wanted to be important and show his new family he was capable of accomplishing things. He was not business-oriented and did not have many skills. He was pleased to see a kingpin. Spider made him feel important. Vlad saw that Spider was playing with diamonds lying openly in drawers. He knew the diamonds were false and did not have much value. Givi asked him if he wanted to play. Vlad shortage of money. Their dwelling was in a communal setting. They lived in one small room in a big communal setting with a common kitchen and toilet. Vlad did not have any business skills but wanted to have a good life. He was a typical Aboriginian: out to please celestials. He was good looking, tall, and muscular. He possessed the heart of Golda, who had a butchered nose job and was self-conscious about her shortcoming. Vlad did not care about her small deficiency. For him, it was important that her family lived in a separate large apartment. Most importantly, she had a father who was a moneymaking machine. Vlad wanted to prove he could be an important person as well. He was an easy target for Spider, who was creating a net around Aaron. Being naive, Vlad was proud of the attention and befriended the kingpin. He moved directly into the trap. Spider used Vlad in his plan to ransack Aaron's wealth.

## The Children of Talented Parents

*T*he children of talented criminals were not always as smart as their parents. Spider was slyer than his father. Spider did not value habitants who were bad card players. Those habitants simply brought all their possessions to him. He knew how to juggle with cards, and no one was able to catch him. Spider's father was a great card player and gained the position of godfather because of his excellent playing skills. He did not use his skills to cheat, but he had knowledge of distorted cards and taught Givi a few tricks. Spider was a good student and knew well from Odessa and been slightly disappointed to find that the diamond was not real but was a cubic zirconia.

Spider's bodyguards visited the young fellow and found out that the young man did not know anything about the diamond. He told them he'd won the diamond in a card game from a man named Aaron. The bodyguards beat the man, but the young fellow didn't tell them much because he did not know anything. He told them where they could find Aaron. He said he did not know if the diamonds were real or false, and he'd never had any diamonds before. Spider intuitively felt he could make a jackpot. He sensed that someone who had false diamonds had real ones too. Before he started designing the con, he gathered information and analyzed it.

First, he checked Aaron's surroundings. He gained information about all the members in Aaron's family. He right away dismissed Sam Kaufman as a figure without interest. For him, Sam was merely a student and a nerd. He studied medicine and wanted to reduce suffering. Spider could not have imagined that Sam was spying for the communal empire. He also did not picture Sam as a patriot of collectivist thinking who was proud to be an informer. He did not know how Sam felt about the rich, such as his family, who'd gained their wealth through the shadow economy. For Sam, it was not fair. He believed they should give their possessions back to habitants. Unlike Sam, Spider wanted all the possessions for himself.

Givi found out that Golda, Aaron's daughter, was a bookworm and involved in excessive reading. His special interest was her husband. Vlad became an object of interest because he was someone of many ambitions. Through informers, Givi knew everything about him. Vlad came from a single-parent home where there was always a friendly. They agreed to help each other. They agreed that taking possessions from emigrants was pure lawlessness. Uncle Cat said it did not matter that kingpins paid into a common criminal fund. He was against pushing girls into forceful prostitution, which was against the criminal code, and the heads of the criminal hierarchy would not want it.

Givi was counting money when his bodyguards came. They said the husband of one of the working girls had threatened to go to the immigration authorities and tell them everything. The upset husband knew that before rushing to the hotel to be a prostitute, his wife gave their little children sleeping pills. The bodyguards told Givi they'd beaten up the man and broken his nose, but now he was hiding in the apartment of an immigrant named Aaron. For Givi, the rudeness of ripping off immigrants was a matter of pride. He shared the profits of his swindling only with his mother. With feelings of greatness in his guts, Givi called himself a master of the con. He was a designer, planner, and analyst of sophisticated schemes. Givi knew the weakness immigrants experienced in front of enticements. He lured immigrants into his cons by using temptations. He was good at ploys and worked his designs carefully. He worked out the small details. He concocted many different ways of duping gullible simpletons.

Givi did not expect any resistance from those who did not have any rights, as any wrong move could jeopardize their immigration. They felt helpless in the face of evil. Spider remembered Aaron's name because he'd played cards with a young fellow who'd presented a false diamond as collateral. They'd played a couple times, and Spider easily had won the diamond from the young man. After the game, he'd checked the diamond with an old jeweler